Madge Swindells was born and educated in England. As a teenager she emigrated to South Africa where she studied archaeology and anthropology at Cape Town University. Later, in England, she was a Fleet Street journalist and the manager of her own publishing company. Her previous novels, including *Summer Harvest*, were international bestsellers and have been translated into eight languages.

Winners and Losers

MADGE SWINDELLS

WARNER BOOKS

A *Warner* Book

First published in Great Britain in 1999
by Little, Brown and Company

This edition published by Warner Books in 2000

Copyright © Madge Swindells 1999

The moral right of the author has been asserted.

A CIP catalogue record for this book
is available from the British Library.

ISBN 0 7515 2906 0

Typeset by Palimpsest Book Production Limited
Polmont, Stirlingshire
Printed and bound in Great Britain by
Clays Ltd, St Ives plc

Warner Books
A Division of
Little, Brown and Company (UK)
Brettenham House
Lancaster Place
London WC2E 7EN

Acknowledgements to my daughter, Jenni Swindells, for her valuable editorial input; Cliff Warren, Ashley Joyce, and Cathy and Derek Chivers for their research; to Jeffrey Sharpe for his moral support; to Iain R. Loe, research manager of CAMRA, for his patience and information on the brewing industry; to Viva! for their input; and to all my friends who helped me in one way or another.

Prologue

Coventry, 4-6-1057

Godiva, by my troth, thou shal not go,
To titilate the hoipolloi. God, no!
Bare-arsed rebellion shal not change my mind
I'll have you whipped and scourged. I've been too kind.
You'll cool your boldness standing in the stocks
And there you'll stay until you catch the pox.

The Earl raved on. Godiva didn't care,
She would the morrow ride all in the bare.
Till Leofric vowed to tax the poor no more
She would reveal herself like any whore.
But suddenly cold fear assailed her heart,
And sent her to the scribe, that smelly fart,
To order every commoner and lout,
To close their curtains and their eyes, about
The time when she would pass by on her mare,
In case the wind should ruffle up her hair.

How slowly passed the night until the dawn,
Our knyght lay sleepless, fearful of the morn.
The world would laugh for centuries to come,
At how his wyf revealed her dimpled bum,
Because his greed had left the peasants broke,
They couldn't even buy themselves a coke.
But later came the thought: she'd never dare!
He'd call her bluff, such courage was so rare.
No one would know his wyf had sworn an oath
To bring down taxes and disgrace them both.

1

Chapter 1

So they had lost. How was that possible when she and the rest of the creative staff of Ogden's had slogged all hours, far beyond the call of duty? Sam couldn't remember when she'd last had a free evening, let alone a day off. Nowadays she even dreamed slogans, waking with a start to grope for the light switch and her notepad, which was always handy. Ideas surfaced at the oddest times, even in her sleep.

She tried to ignore the pain in her guts and the hammering in her temples as she chewed her thumb and gazed sadly at Walter, her boss and her lover, who was standing behind his desk looking gloomy as he spelled out their position. His total capital was tied up in this small agency, which was why she had worked so hard.

'Are you listening, Sam?' Walter snarled.

'Is there any point?'

'For God's sake, shut up!' It was Fiona who'd snarled and that hurt. Sam looked round at Ogden's tired, talented but underpaid creative staff, who were crowded into Walter's small office. For once no one was cracking jokes. Walter was wearing a charcoal mohair suit, white shirt and dark tie. Dressed for a funeral? How fitting. Here and now they were burying Ogden's.

'The battle was well fought.'

She stirred uncomfortably. Walter wasn't usually banal. And why did he look so guilty? She gave him a long, hard stare.

'The bank pulled the rug from under my feet. After

an all-night session, I sold out to Mug and Mug at noon exactly. The good news is that I sold all of us too, every last man jack of our creative staff. We all have a twelve-month contract and Samantha's is longer. She can negotiate whatever terms she wants, within reason.'

Sam grimaced. 'Mug and Mug' was their name for Meredith and Munrowe, and both they and Ogden's had been rivals for BMI, one of the largest computer programmers in the world. It had been a real David and Goliath battle as Ogden's had pitched their talent against the established giant. Presentations had been made last month and they should have won.

'So we didn't get it?'

'Get what?

'The fucking moon and stars, of course.'

'Cool it, Sam! Some of us need to eat.'

'At what price? Joining the enemy after an unconditional surrender?'

Walter choked back his irritation. Sam was so damned naïve. But she, more than any of them, had kept his under-capitalised venture teetering along with her sheer innovative talent. The cheque he'd just banked was partly due to her brilliant ideas. However, she was not used to the business jungle: she cherished idealism and honour. Guilt surged as Walter remembered that she cherished him as well. He'd used her. He dredged up a smile.

'Sam, there was nothing unconditional about the surrender. Quite the reverse. Look at the contracts. You'll all be much better off.'

Something felt wrong, though. A terrible suspicion took root in Sam. Was that why he'd wanted the BMI account? So that the enemy would have to buy him out? Was that why she'd slogged every weekend and just about every night for months? She'd wanted to save the agency for all of them.

'Why would they want a team of losers? Explain that if you can.' She saw Walter flinch.

There was a long silence while he fiddled with his tie. His face reddened, his Adam's apple wobbled and she could see moisture gathering on his brow.

'Because we won,' he said. 'We won the contract. What else? Your slogans, Sam. You'll be heading their new creative team.

'Quiet! Quiet!' He had to shout above the roar of incredulous anger. 'Hear me out. I'm retiring, but you lot will handle the contract you fought so hard for. What difference does it make where your offices are? You'll have security, better pay packets and bonuses. You'll have to sign two-year restraint-of-trade clauses, but that's all. Meantime we have a good deal of reorganisation ahead. Take a long weekend. See you all Tuesday. You, too, Samantha.' He paused by the door as everyone shouted at once.

'That's what you were after, wasn't it, Walter?'

'The big payoff.'

'So we weren't bankrupt at all.'

'Expect my expense chits, Walter.'

'I never told anyone but I ran a credit check on us. We weren't in the red.' Rupert, the art director, seldom spoke in public. He took off his glasses and polished them with his handkerchief.

'It's us who've been sold, not the business,' Sam tried to explain. 'And Walter pockets the cash. They couldn't afford to lose BMI, could they, Walter? And you knew that.'

'That's not what I said, Sam.'

'But you're a fucking liar, Walter.'

4

As the clamour of voices merged to a noisy blur, Walter fled, slamming the door behind him.

The phone rang. Someone picked it up. 'It's for you, Sam.' The voice from the switchboard said, 'Sorry, love. I was told no calls, but this one's urgent It's John Carvossah.'

'Hi, John. Is Gramps okay?'

There was a faint tremor in John's deep voice. Sam listened, frowning slightly as her grandfather's plant manager invited her to lunch. 'Sure. See you at one. But just so I don't worry till then, what's wrong?'

'Nothing! Well, nothing immediate. I want you to know what's going on. Trevor's fiddling while Rome burns. It's your heritage, too.'

'That doesn't sound like nothing,' she said worriedly.

'I'll explain over lunch. See you then.'

Sam glanced at her watch and frowned. She'd have to hurry. She grabbed her bag and went to the cloakroom. Fiona hurried after her.

'Don't take it so hard, Sam. You'll do well there. Longer holidays, better pay. They even have a tennis court.'

'Fuck the lot of them! I'm not signing restraint-of-trade. Besides, I need to get a very bad smell out of my nostrils. I may go home for a while.'

Fiona's large blue eyes glowed with compassion. She adjusted her Prada skirt, shook her blonde mane over her shoulders and tightened her belt. 'Where's home?'

'In the sticks. The ultimate backwood. Better known as one of the last unspoiled patches of ancient England where nothing penetrates the local yokel's equanimity except the rising price of beer. My grandfather has a small brewery.'

'Walter'll miss you.'

'Not for long. There was nothing serious in it for

either of us.' Not now, anyway. Sam knew she could never forgive him.

'I've always fancied him.'

'Feel free.'

Sam watched Fiona appraise herself in the mirror.

'I could never see what you two had in common, Sam,' she said.

'Ask him!'

'Actually, I did.' Fiona's face was hostile. 'He said you dazzle him with your talent and give him a permanent hard-on. Plus he's occupied full-time trying to hold his own in the brain stakes.'

'He said that? I'm amazed.'

And a lot more, Fiona remembered, but she wasn't going to say so. Not wishing Sam to see the envy in her eyes she turned back to the mirror and reapplied her lipstick. Some girls had everything and it was so unfair. Sam had a smooth, olive skin, sensual lips, thick eyebrows over dark velvety eyes and her hair was an untidy mop of near-black curls. Yet it hadn't been her looks that Walter had raved about, but her impulsive, warm nature.

'Sam, d'you *really* think that Walter and I . . .' She looked round, but Sam had left.

Chapter 2

John was waiting outside the Good Earth restaurant. He beamed his potent, sexy glow her way, the full works: candid lust, admiration, a conspiring grin, and a slight perplexity that read, Why are we still apart? It was 100 per cent contrived: she had watched him turn it on dozens of times in varying degrees of intensity, depending on whom he was trying to charm.

'God, it's good to see you, Sam. You're looking marvellous. I've missed you.'

There was nothing significant about John's features: large baby-blue eyes set in a squarish face, blunt, even features, topped with sun-streaked light brown hair. He was a typical regular guy, a champion long-distance swimmer, a sailor, ex-college rugby. A man's man, yet every woman fell for him – except the woman he loved.

Sam had been in high school when John had joined Woodlands and she'd fallen for him with all the passion and agony of teenage love. She still went hot all over when she remembered how, on her seventeenth birthday, she'd proposed.

'If you want to marry me when you're old enough, I'll say yes,' he'd promised. He liked to tease her about it when she was cross with him, but now on her part there was nothing between them but sibling love. His arm, though, lingered around her shoulder. She fended him off, parried his small-talk and hung on to her patience as they were shown to a table in the corner.

'Okay, John. Just give it to me straight,' she said.

'Someone's got to talk some sense into your grand-father.'

'Go on.'

'We're in trouble, but he won't look the facts in the face. Brewing beer isn't what it used to be. Traditional British beer is on its deathbed in any event, but in Kent its demise is being hastened by illegal imports that undercut local beer. The tax is outrageous. Beer drinkers are buying their booze in France and bringing it back as and when they feel like it.'

'Not everyone can nip across the Channel for the odd pint.'

'True, but every Tom, Dick and Harry is operating out of cheap rooms in Dover, sending unemployed youths shuttling backwards and forwards on the ferry and the hovercraft.'

'Don't they get picked up by Customs?'

'With twenty-one million travellers flowing through Dover?'

'You're all gloom and doom today, John.'

'There's worse. What's bugging Trevor is a criminal gang smuggling in beer and liquor from stolen consign-ments. He's taken it upon himself to find out who they are. He's got some idea that they're specifically trying to weaken our position so we'll sell out. That's crazy because we're small-timers. We don't count.'

'Trevor must have his reasons for thinking that.'

'Listen to me, Sam. I'll be blunt. The old man's getting on – you have to accept that. Thinks he's back in the SAS. Silly old bugger!'

Sam was getting annoyed with John's criticism of her grandfather. 'What right have you to say—'

John's hand closed across hers. 'Okay! I'm sorry. You

know how I feel about Trevor – he saved my life once, after all. But we have to do something. He's chasing smugglers when he should be concentrating on the brewery. We're badly overdrawn, Sam. The bank have been pressurising him to sell out now that he's had a good offer.'

'*What?*' A few heads turned their way. 'No one told me about an offer,' she said. Suddenly she felt angry. Everyone seemed bent on selling the ground from under her feet. First Walter, now Gramps. And why hadn't either of them told her?

'Don't sound so bitter, Sam. An old-established Czech brewery called Balaton's have been bidding for Woodlands for some time. Trevor's turned down every approach so far, but they've fixed on a generous price and the bank's putting pressure on him to accept.'

'How would they do that?'

'By reducing his overdraft ceiling. He doesn't have the cash to buy his hops or pay wages.'

That was a shock. Sam's cheeks burned. 'What do you think, John? D'you think Gramps should sell out?'

'Let's just say that I have the best interests of the family at heart. I don't believe Trevor's capable of handling the brewery. I'm sorry to say this, but he seems to have gone senile . . .'

At this monstrous insult to her grandfather, Sam's blood boiled. After John had gone bust with his own business Trevor had taken him in, given him shares and a job for life. She'd never known why. And this was how John had chosen to repay him. Sam kept her face impassive as she hit back. 'I had a letter from Shireen,' she said. 'She's getting married. She may come back to England to buy her trousseau and say goodbye.'

Easy to see that she'd scored a bullseye. She'd never seen him quite so thrown. She stood up. 'Hope you won't think me rude but I have to get back to the office. I'll talk to Gramps. Thanks for lunch.'

At the door John caught up with her and grabbed her arm. 'You haven't changed, have you? Hit and run! That's your style.'

'Let go of my arm. I'm not listening to insults about Trevor. When he's senile, if that ever happens, he'll be twice as bright as you'll ever be.'

She wrenched away her arm and stalked out.

John paid the bill and walked the few blocks to the car park. Then he dialled the office for messages. Mona, the plant's typist, whom he liked to describe as his secretary, answered his private line.

'Mr Carvossah's out today,' she gabbled and hung up.

'Damn the stupid bitch!' He dialled again. 'Mona, listen! It's me, John.'

'Oh! It's you!' She giggled. 'I thought I'd seen the back of you for the day.'

'Any messages?'

She reeled off the two he'd been expecting. 'Hang on! There's another. A Mr Kupi! Here's his number.'

The name threw John into panic. He hardly noticed when Mona cut him off with a brief 'Bye.' He was already plunged into recollections of the day he'd met Hans Kupi, a good eight months ago.

It had been just a day like any other, blue-black clouds resting on chimney-pots, gulls circling and screaming fit to bust your ear drums, surf thundering on the pebbled beach so you could hear it half a mile away. John had had half a mind to skip the Smugglers' Arms, but as he hovered indecisively outside the door, rain began to splatter around him and he flung open the swing doors.

The pub was dark and dingy. Rob, the barman, who was

also the manager, seemed to be nursing a hangover. One glance at his grey eyes, glittering behind gold spectacles, told John that sales were falling and gloom rising. John dredged up a grin. 'How's it, mate? Heard the one about the sailor and the mermaid?'

'You told me that one last time. You're slipping, John. Business that bad?' For a big man, Rob had a surprisingly high-pitched voice.

'Don't be daft, we're making profits hand over fist.'

'You said that last time, too, and I didn't believe you then, neither. What'll it be? The usual? I told you what the problem is, but no one your end did anything about it. We get the youngsters here and we need some of these new fancy beer blends. Only the oldies like the real ale. You're a good listener, John, but do you ever pass on the facts I give you?'

'Course I do.'

Rob was off on his favourite sermon. A glass of apple juice slid towards John. He took it – he'd rather have had a beer, but he had a liver problem, although he was only twenty-eight.

A crowd of Belgian tourists came in and John made his escape. He carried his juice to a seat near the window to write a report. Next minute the table wobbled as someone sat opposite him. A quick glance assured John that the pub was half empty, so there was no shortage of chairs. When he turned to the intruder, though, something about the man's eyes stifled John's complaint.

'The name's Hans Kupi. I know you by sight. John Carvossah, yes? He was dressed smartly in a tailored grey suit and hand-made silk tie, but for all that he looked like an ex-con, with his cropped grey hair, strong eyes and a steel tooth.

'How d'you know my name?' John asked.

'I made it my business to find out. You and I need to get together, John.'

'I can't place your accent.' John frowned and wondered how to extricate himself.

'Czech. I'm a brewer from Pilsen, but I'm intending to expand very soon. I've been looking at Woodlands and chatting around the company's pubs. I've heard great things about you, John. You've been trying to push the company into the twentieth century before we reach the twenty-first, but you're not having much luck, are you? The old man likes to run things his way.'

'He's a great guy,' John said defensively. 'Bit conservative, that's all.'

'You're loyal. I like that, John, but carry on like this much longer and you'll all be out of work. That's why I want to step in.'

Kupi stopped talking and sipped his beer, gazing round at the old oak beams, the gleaming floor and the empty tables.

'How d'you mean, step in?' John asked, as his curiosity got the better of him.

'Well, I've had a couple of guys scouting around for a company for the past year and Woodlands seems to fit the bill. Old Rosslyn's getting past it and there's only the two granddaughters to inherit the company, which is heavily overdrawn.'

'Why are you telling me this?' John couldn't make up his mind whether to be interested or downright insulted.

'I'd like to have you on my side, John. I'm looking for a good MD to run Woodlands and I pride myself on being a good judge of men. I'm making a bid for the company soon. Don't oppose it. That's all I'm asking.'

John felt baffled and cornered. He ran his hands through his hair. He wasn't designed for business and he knew it.

'You've done your homework, Kupi, I'll give you that, but you don't know me from a bar of soap. Cut the bull and tell me what you're after.'

Kupi shrugged. 'How come you haven't investigated exporting your beer?'

'Same reason we haven't tarted up the pubs or introduced beer blends, I guess.' The moment he'd spoken John wished he hadn't. He flushed and Kupi noticed.

'Difficult to know where your main loyalty lies, isn't it? To the company, to your pals working there who need their jobs, or to the chairman, Trevor Rosslyn. Talk to him. There's a huge growth market for strong beer in Russia and I know the Russian market like I know the back of my hand. Try and talk him into producing some strong dark ale or stout.' He fell silent for a few moments. Then he placed a briefcase on the table. 'John,' he said, 'I want you to think of this as a down payment on future bonuses because I'll be taking over the company for sure. Right now, though, I need a plentiful supply of good strong ale and I'm looking for a source. I can't satisfy market demands in the East. Produce the right beer and there's a fortune to be made.'

'We tried exporting to Russia, but organised crime controls the railways. We couldn't get a look-in.'

'Don't worry about that. I pay my way.'

John gazed speculatively at him.

'Life's passing you by, John. Where are you going? Woodlands will be bust within a year and you'll be out of work.'

Kupi was right. John knew he'd settled into a groove of third best. His car, his home, his clothes and his girlfriends, or lack of, labelled him Mr Average. When he read about self-made wealth he wanted to throw up. The media never got tired of rubbing your nose in other people's success. He knew he was poised on the cliff-edge of giving up. He had a small salary and a high commission rate – but you can't sell if you're peddling the wrong brew.

But what was Kupi saying? An electric shock zipped through John. Ten thousand pounds in cash in the brief-case he was pushing under the table?

'Work with me towards a takeover and you'll do well,' Kupi said. 'Let me know what's going on there. Talk Rosslyn into launching a new stout so we can get into exports fast.'

John felt dazed as Kupi shook hands and left. No harm done, he thought. I haven't signed on the dotted line. I'm not committed to do a damn thing for that bastard. Besides, what's the harm in exporting beer to Russia?

Cautiously he shuffled his feet around until they encountered the briefcase. He pushed it towards his seat and glanced round to see if anyone was looking. No one was. 'Be seeing you, Rob,' he called, as he left.

Outside the door he opened the briefcase a chink and saw the neat stacks of notes. He glanced at his beaten-up Ford Sierra. Collector's piece, he often told himself, but suddenly it looked what it was: battered. 'You've seen better days, old girl.' He patted the bonnet.

Perhaps he could dump the briefcase or, better still, hand it to the police. But that might prove messy, and possibly dangerous. He could hand it back next time Kupi contacted him. Yes, that was his best bet. But ten thousand quid? And tax-free, too.

Looking back now John thought of how fate could rub your nose in the shit when she had a mind to do so. The following day his engine burned out so he used the cash as down-payment on a new car. That's funny, he thought. I walked into that pub a free man and I sold myself for ten thousand quid. A surge of bile rose into his mouth.

Chapter 3

Sam spent the afternoon clearing out her office. Half of the staff were maudlin drunk and Walter kept hovering around explaining what a wonderful deal she was getting. 'You can't just walk out on me, Sam. I can sue. You're on contract and you have to give notice. Or had that small point escaped you?'

'Get real, Walter. My contract's up in three weeks. You going to sue for that?'

He stalked off, leaving her to lug two heavy cartons to her car. She arrived home feeling depressed.

Usually Sam had only to walk into her Hampstead apartment and close the door to feel at peace with the world. Admittedly it was in a basement and dark on dull days, but it led directly on to the Heath and the windows looked out on to a slope of flowers she had planted in the spring. Today she put on Handel's *Messiah*, made some tea and admired her wild-life paintings. But she still ached with tension. Pure, fresh air was what she needed most. She rifled a cupboard for her trainers and set off. Jock, the caretaker's collie, came barking after her and soon the two of them were racing around one of the ponds. Returning at seven, she flung herself into housework, a chore that was sadly overdue. She was packing her office gear into a cupboard when she heard a knock at the door.

It was Walter.

'You're not welcome, Walter. Go away.'

'Sometimes you're such a child.' He pushed past her

into the hall, went into the sitting room and sprawled on the couch. 'What you're doing, Sam, is called cutting off your nose to spite your face. At twenty-four, you'd be the youngest creative head in London. You'll never get another chance like this. How can you even consider ruining your career just to get back at me? You're upset because I didn't tell you, but honestly, Sam, I didn't know. How could I have known?'

'You've lost me, Walter. How am I hitting back at you? What difference could it possibly make to you whether I move or not?'

'Don't you know? Can't you guess?'

'No and no.'

'The BMI contract specifies retaining the same team who thought up the campaign. That means you. No you, no contract! Mug and Mug's offer specifies both the BMI contract and the team involved in winning it.'

'So you really were selling me.'

'You'd only have to stick it out for a year.'

'After signing restraint-of-trade for two years where would I go if I left? Stop kidding me, Walter.'

'I can reduce that to a year, and I'll give you a cut. Ten per cent. What d'you say?'

'You've got a nerve. Bastard! You used me.'

'Don't be so hasty, Sam. Creative head of one of the most important agencies in London is quite a coup at twenty-four.'

'You're repeating yourself.'

'What'll I do if I don't sell out? At my age, jobs are hard to come by.'

Why had she never noticed the loose folds of skin under his chin, or the bags under his eyes? What had deluded her into thinking he was dynamic and fascinating? Right now he looked defeated.

17

'You're a has-been, Walter. A middle-aged has-been who never was.'

'Do it for friendship. We had some good times.'

'Did we? I only remember sitting up late while you coaxed me into producing bigger and better ideas, slogans, images, finally the entire campaign. You paid me next to nothing. We're through, Walter. Please leave.' But he would not. Only later, when she threatened to call the police, did he reluctantly amble to the door.

'Must I beg you, Sam? Is that what you want? Or perhaps you're hoping I'll marry you.'

He dodged the missile and slammed the door, leaving Sam to sweep up the pieces of an antique vase bequeathed to her by her battiest aunt.

After he'd gone, Sam sat down to have things out with herself. She'd been had and it hurt, but she'd learned a valuable lesson and it wouldn't happen again. Walter's ethics were his affair, not hers. As for the job, maybe she'd take it after all – but only after she'd been home for a holiday. Right now a long, lazy summer didn't seem such a bad idea. Perhaps Trevor needed company.

Sam glanced at her watch. Ten p.m. Not too late to call him – he never went to bed before midnight. She dialled and listened to the ring for a long time. Why was no one answering? She felt uneasy, but that was absurd: he could be having a dinner with friends, playing bridge, or having a game of chess with the vicar.

And nothing ever happened in Bourne-on-Sea. The tiny village dated from medieval times, and still had rows of Tudor cottages, several oasthouses, four old pubs, narrow cobbled lanes and an old stone church surrounded by an ancient yew hedge. Nearby on a hill overlooking the sea was a half-ruined stone castle and tower, which had been in Sam's family for generations and which overlooked a beautiful village green, one of the finest in Kent, surrounded with chestnuts. Nearby was the old barn that Rosemary, Trevor's secretary, had renovated for her amateur dramatics.

Thinking about the village and her grandfather made her homesick. Suddenly Sam realised there was nothing she wanted more than a quiet summer at home.

Chapter 4

Trevor climbed out of the 4x4 and remembered a long-ago night like this: a faint white scythe of a moon, ground mist rising, faintly luminescent. It was cold for May, but of course, they hadn't felt the cold in those days. He and his squad, George, Robin, Vim and Michel, had been squatting in the trees. George had been breathing down his neck, as he was now, and Michel, always too impatient, had been longing to get into action.

But why was his mind meandering back to the war? And why to that night?

'Let's get on with it, for fuck's sake.' Michel, of course. Some things never change.

'Remember to wait until the boats are unloaded, mate.'

Michel winked and cocked his thumb. 'Good luck!'

Leaving Michel in the 4x4 parked on the cliff-top overlooking the cove, he and George shrugged on their backpacks and set off. Their route lay over the cliffs and down to a pebbled cove near a deserted road, a mile from St Margaret's Bay. Infrared binoculars, a camera with a telescopic lens, a crossbow and a half-bottle of Talisker whisky to keep the damp out of their old bones completed their kit. No such luxuries in those days.

God, he remembered that night as if it were months ago instead of fifty-five years: they had carried only their rifles and three big charges, each a long, perfect cube of explosive, with the neat white primers nestling inside and a tail of detonating cord. They had come past the lake and kept to the trees and undergrowth along the Mze river, skirting Nyrany until they struck the suburbs of Pilsen. There they had waited.

Trevor could feel the same dampness of mist on his face, but this time he was warm and comfortable inside his Vortex windbreaker. He could have done with something like that in those days. Then perhaps he wouldn't be so plagued with rheumatism now.

'You okay, George?'

George nodded.

Gazing at his friend he felt a sense of camaraderie that he hadn't felt since they fought in the Czech underground. Friendship and his problems had brought the three of them together again.

'Just like old times, eh?'

'My knees don't feel the same.' But George was okay.

Half jogging, half walking, they made the beach in half an hour, but by this time Trevor's breath was loud and rasping. As for his back, the pain was terrible.

'D'you think they'll use the same place again, Trevor? What if they dodge around a bit?'

'Then we'll start again.'

It had taken Trevor weeks of nightly observation to find out where they landed the contraband liquor. Squatting uncomfortably on shingle, behind a clump of rocks, the minutes passed slowly. That's what his war had been about mainly, waiting.

He remembered how he had crouched behind a pile of sleepers for two hours after they split. At last, dogged with a feeling of unease, he had crept down to the Pilsen signal depot to place his charge before belting back across the yard, flesh crawling, to the tracks. He could see the dark depot, dim lights glowing from the cabs, the smell of oil and coal smoke all about him. The next ten minutes felt like ten hours. Then he let off his charges. Moments later he was racing back up to the trees, his footsteps muffled by the blast, followed by shouts and shots and running feet.

Why hadn't their three charges gone off in unison? He'd glanced at the luminous face of his SAS watch. Thirty seconds . . . then a minute. What had gone wrong? He'd pictured George and Michel being dragged off unconscious to the Gestapo cells. Two minutes . . . forty-five seconds . . . Three minutes . . . Then he'd heard the second explosion, which echoed around the yard.

'Now the next. Come on, then. Let it off.' Fifteen minutes later came the third, muffled, fainter. It seemed to come from further away than it should have.

George and Michel had returned at dawn to their meeting-place, on the other side of the Mze, their hair plastered across their red sweaty foreheads, their feet blistered. George had lit a cigarette, leaned against the tree and frowned at Trevor.

'It worked, but not as well as it should've. They'll be able to repair most of the damage, Trevor. We need more explosives.'

Robin was next to arrive. 'Why was there so long between the second and third charge exploding?' he asked. 'I don't like it. Let's get moving.'

Plagued by memories, Trevor stirred uncomfortably. The headlights of the truck rumbling down the track towards the beach brought him back to the present. He grabbed his binoculars and climbed on to a rock, staring out to sea. Far off, he saw three brief stabs into the darkness, and from the truck came an answering flash.

'Don't underestimate the enemy. They're still as ruthless. Stop at nothing, the bastards. They'll be here in minutes Watch out, George, they're bound to be armed.'

Trevor stepped backwards, but missed his footing.

Twisting off-balance he felt a sharp wrench in his back as he fell on to the shingle.

'Shit!' For a confused moment he thought he was floundering on some Czech riverbed. Scrambling up, he set his mind against the agonising pain and pulled himself together. His limbs seemed to have seized up on him and he had never felt so cold. Of all the disasters he'd faced in life nothing compared with old age. He glanced at George crouched beside him, his swollen face twisted to an expression of pure agony. 'You all right, George?'

'Bit short of breath, that's all,' he gasped.

Their plan was simple enough. The moment the boats were beached, Michel would summon the police by cellphone, giving their location. He would wait for the crates to be unloaded before switching on the powerful hunting searchlight mounted on their 4x4. While the smugglers were blinded and confused, George would fire at the truck's tyres with his crossbow. Trevor would take photographs of the truck driver and his accomplice. Then the three of them would make their escape under cover of darkness, leaving the police to take over.

As the truck revved up and reversed down the beach, six motor launches roared through the surf. 'Action stations,' Trevor muttered, watching the smugglers racing to unload.

The minutes lasted hours. Then Michel went into action and the cove lit up with surrealistic light. For a split second no one moved. Then Trevor clicked his camera, and George fired his crossbow, bursting the front right tyre. The smugglers scattered. George fired again. Another bullseye! The truck was tipping dangerously.

'Good! Let's get the hell out of here.' Trevor turned to run towards the cliff path but found he could hardly move his legs.

The driver raced from the truck, swung up a rifle, aimed for the searchlight and fired several shots in rapid succession. A sudden scream echoed around the cliffs while the cove was plunged into darkness.

The zigzag path up the cliff face was just ahead, and Trevor had almost made it when he heard a noise behind him. He froze as a tall figure, wearing a balaclava, swung a cosh towards his face. He fended it off, grabbed at the cosh, and dredged up long-forgotten skills in unarmed combat, but his limbs wouldn't obey his commands. Christ! He should have kept fit. How had he got like this? He felt himself falling. There was a sudden movement, a blinding flash in his eyes and a searing pain in his head. Someone was kicking him. The pain was intense, but his fears for Michel and George were worse. He wanted to stand up and fight, but he couldn't move. He heard police sirens in the distance. Then there was nothing.

Chapter 5

The sign read: 'You are in the heart of Woodlands country.' There would be twelve more before she reached the turn-off to their home, and another four to Bourne-on-Sea. Sam was only vaguely aware of half-grown lambs chasing each other over the fields, and crimson poppies in the hedgerows, as she raced towards the hospital. Her mind was on her grandfather. Who would want to beat up an old man of seventy-seven? She'd been in turmoil ever since John had called her with the news. She longed to kill whoever had hurt Trevor. She would if she could. Bastards! She loved him, and she owed him. The very essence of her childhood happiness stemmed from him.

It had been a dismal March morning when she and Julie, her five-year-old sister, had been delivered into his care. She'd been eleven, and sadder than any child should be for they had left behind all that they loved. Both girls were scared half to death. After a long, sleepless night on the plane, travelling with their former neighbour, now widowed and depressed, they'd walked out into a cold, terrifying place where the wind howled, the sky was low enough to suffocate you and the damp sneaked right into your bones. She'd tried hard to remember Grandpa, who'd visited them in Zimbabwe two years before, but his face eluded her.

As a trafficker in slogans and images, Sam could only guess at how much care Trevor had put into choosing his opening gambit. He'd been waiting at the gate when the woman had formally handed his grandchildren into his keeping.

'I'll be with you soon, madam,' he said. 'You must be cold and tired. There are tea and crumpets in the sitting room and the housekeeper will see to your things.'

Holding their hands, he had pulled the two girls across the courtyard towards the stables.

'Well, now,' he said, 'come and have a look round. You see those Shetland ponies there? They were sired by your father's pony. It belonged to him, so naturally they're yours.'

'What's this one's name?' Julie had asked.

'Shaka. You can ride him later, if you like. And how d'you like our carthorses? The finest in Britain. Our family is famous for breeding them. This one was your father's – he was thinking of taking it to Zimbabwe.' He paused. 'Take a look over here.'

They'd peered into a basket at a black dog with velvety eyes, nursing eight black puppies.

'May I touch one?' Sam was entranced by the fat, wriggling bodies and pink noses.

'Of course.'

She knelt down to fondle them and stroke their mother.

'She looks like Caesar, but he was killed in the raid,' said Julie.

'That's because she's Caesar's sister. You see, Julie, your father's favourite Labrador, Brutus, sired a long line of champions and Sarah here is one of them. She's very proud of her puppies. Of course they're yours, too, since they were your dad's.'

Sam remembered how she'd briefly forgotten about sadness in the joy of discovering that not every beloved thing had been lost.

'Your father planned to come back here one day to take over the brewery. Perhaps you two will want to take his place. Think of me as the caretaker of all that was your father's, and all that will be yours. We shall be close friends, I know.'

Sam thought now of how she had crept into the stable bewildered, lost and acutely aware of her orphaned state. Half an hour later she'd emerged as a landowner with a grandpa who loved her and a puppy of her own. She would call him Brutus, she decided, and she'd claim him just as soon as he could leave his mother. Julie had let go of her hand. She was talking excitedly about joining the local riding school.

Nothing could ever replace Sam's beloved parents, but she was loved and she belonged here. She had roots. Suddenly the cold was not quite so scary. Since that day, Trevor had always been there when they needed him and they'd been brought up with freedom and love.

And now this awful thing. First John, then Rosemary, Gramps's secretary, had spoken to her at five a.m. to tell her that Trevor had been mugged. Rosemary was tearful as she explained that the police had taken him to Casualty, but he'd been moved to another ward. His femur was broken, Rosemary said. She'd be calling a Harley Street specialist first thing in the morning.

Sam had packed an overnight bag and left at once. Now she parked and hurried to the hospital reception desk. She gave her name and was shown into an adjoining room where a man stood up and held out his hand. He was tall and thin with a long, bony face, black bushy eyebrows and eyes the colour of pewter. He was saved from ugliness by his expression, which was warm and amused. Instinctively she liked him.

'Samantha Rosslyn? I've been waiting for you. I'm Inspector Neville Joyce. Please sit down.'

'Oh, God!'

'He's recovering, Miss Rosslyn. Please relax.'

Sam struggled to handle her relief without breaking down. 'Surely you remember me,' she said, steadying her voice. 'You're Uncle George's nephew. When did I become Miss Rosslyn?'

'Top marks for memory. It's a good ten years since we last met. I won't keep you long. I want to talk to you about your grandfather. He and I go back a long way. I've always admired him, but this time he's stretching my tolerance. I want you to persuade him to leave the sleuthing to us.'

'What sleuthing? You'll have to fill me in.'

'Last night Trevor and my uncle, plus another old friend, waylaid a foreign gang smuggling in a large consignment of stolen beer. Your grandfather took photographs, but the thugs destroyed the camera. I know he thinks we're dragging our feet on the beer-smuggling. Problem is, it comes under Customs and Excise. We can't get a look-in. Believe me, I've tried, but this business finally brings it into my territory.

'Trevor was badly beaten, resulting in concussion and a broken femur. Michel Cesari, a Corsican, was shot. He's in intensive care, but recovering. George had a minor heart-attack.'

'These three old men tried to hold up the gang while they called the police, but they can't turn back the clock, much as they'd like to. Did you know that during the war George, Michel and your grandfather were together in the Czech underground? Did Trevor ever show you his medals? One of them's the VC.'

Sam's eyes stung. 'I had no idea . . .' She took a deep

breath. 'He never told Julie and me much about his war work, Neville. He may have thought we'd had enough of fighting and he was right.'

'Well, very briefly, the three of them ran a huge Czech outfit. Managed to pull the various groups together without in-fighting.'

'I wish I'd known.'

'Well, it's a long time ago, but he was famous for a while. So was your grandmother. She was decorated by the King, too. I admire your grandfather, Sam.'

She tried to smile, but she had to bite her lip to hold back her tears. 'A lot of people do,' she whispered. 'I'm one of them.'

'Then please try to stop him interfering in criminal matters that other people are paid to look after.'

Sam was determined to stay cool. 'Love and control are not the same at all, Neville, but I doubt he'll give you much trouble with a broken femur.'

'You sound just like him.'

'Have you heard how the others are getting along?'

'Better than they deserve. Silly old codgers!'

What a cute word. She made a mental note to use it next time she had to create slogans for the elderly.

'I'm glad to hear that. If I have any news for you, I'll call you. Have they broken any laws?'

'George carried a crossbow. It's lethal and absolutely illegal. He used it to shred the truck's tyres.'

'A crossbow! This affair gets more ludicrous by the minute. Will he be charged?'

'Probably not.'

Sam stood up to leave, but Neville clamped a heavy hand on her shoulder. 'I think your grandfather's right, Sam. There's a widespread network of organised crime behind the liquor smuggling. I'm telling you this so you can see that it's not something he can tackle on his own. He wouldn't stand a chance. I can't emphasise this strongly enough. He mustn't get involved.'

Chapter 6

Trevor was asleep, his nose hidden under plaster, his eyes swollen and bruised. God knows what the rest of him looked like. Sam reached forward and clasped his left hand gently in both of hers.

How peaceful he looked. She'd never seen him so still before: he was always moving, changing expressions, gesticulating with his hands, like a foreigner. He told her once he'd adopted this characteristic for his intelligence cover during the war and he'd never lost it. His hair was white and wiry, cut short and ragged. His eyebrows were thick and black without a trace of grey and this, together with his hawk nose and high cheekbones, gave him a Romany look.

Trevor's hand squeezed hers. She gazed down into his black eyes and tried to look stern. 'Ah! You're awake at last. How do you feel?'

'I'm all right. A bit sore, I suppose. What are you doing here?'

'Rosemary phoned me. You had no right to be endangering your life. You should think about your family. We're not at war.'

'I wouldn't be too sure of that, Sam.' He tried to move and gasped with pain. 'It's a new kind of war. The innocent against organised crime and its corrosive network of influence, which is bent on sweeping away all decent standards.'

'Wow! That's quite a statement for a man with

concussion. But, Gramps, wouldn't you be better off trying to save Woodlands from the takeover bid?'

'John told you?'

'Yes. Why didn't you?'

He squeezed her hand again. 'Perhaps because everything seemed to happen at once. A few months ago, we were getting along fine. We weren't making profits, but I had all sorts of plans to change that.' He grimaced and reached for his water. Sam passed it to him.

'Everything's changing in the liquor industry. We had to come up to date fast, so to finance this I pledged my personal shares to the bank. I've used some of the cash to renovate a few pubs.

'A month ago, Balaton's made an offer for Woodlands. At the same time, the bank lowered our overdraft ceiling saying our shares had gone down in value. Then they told me they'd had a good offer from Balaton's to buy them at market-related prices, which is far below the true value. And you know why. I've always valued the land according to its potential for growing hops. In terms of real estate it's worth far more.'

'They can't buy our shares. We're a private company.'

'Yes, they can, if they give us sufficient notice to raise the cash to buy the shares ourselves. And we can't. I've made a few mistakes, Sam. We have too much cash tied up in stocks of stout. I predicted . . . Well, never mind that. If we don't sell out or come right within six months the bank are threatening to put us into liquidation.'

'That's criminal!'

'That's business. Not our way of doing things but legal all the same. Help me up, Sam, I'm so damned weak.'

She put her arms under his shoulders and tried awkwardly to hoist him to a sitting position. 'You weigh a ton.'

As he struggled to help her his pyjama top fell open revealing his bruises. There was hardly a place that wasn't purplish-black and swollen.

'Oh, God! Gramps, you must be in agony. They worked you over good and proper. What was it? A baton?'

'Hobnailed boots. I'm sure he'd had some practice. But I'll mend.' Trevor leaned back and closed his eyes. Then he said: 'Sam, if I could prove that organised crime from the Eastern bloc is trying to get a foothold in the British liquor industry, the bank would be morally prevented from selling out to them – think of the bad publicity. But as things stand now with me in hospital, we'll have to accept their offer. An old cripple and a girl cannot pit themselves against organised crime. Ten million pounds is too low a price, but it could be worse. I want you to handle the sale. If Balaton's learn that I'm in hospital they may be tempted to reduce their offer.'

Sam couldn't get to grips with the situation. How could they sell Woodlands? It had been in the family for generations.

'What if we don't sell?'

'In six months' time, as I said, we might find ourselves in liquidation. Or if the bank sells them the shares, they'd have the controlling interest. Then they'd screw us. Either way we'd land up with nothing. Rosemary was here earlier with our lawyer, Michael Johnson. You've met him a couple of times. I've signed power-of-attorney in your favour.' He smiled, and she could see what an effort it cost him to try to look cheerful. 'How's Michel?' he muttered.

'Neville Joyce says he's fighting back but still in intensive care.'

'Find out how they are, please, Sam. I'll never forgive myself.'

33

'You shouldn't have gone after the smugglers. Neville's right, you're not young any more. Besides, what can you do? You weren't even armed.'

Trevor flinched, then sighed. 'What a mess! They tell me I'm to have an artificial hip. That'll put me back a few weeks. Can you take a holiday from the agency?'

'No need. Walter sold us down-river to the enemy.'

'And you didn't see this coming?'

'I never thought.'

'You won't get caught twice that way. I guess it hurts.'

'Yes, but not for long.'

At that moment the nurse came in to say that the specialist had arrived. Half an hour later he came looking for her and beckoned Sam from the doorway. 'I'll have to pin the femur right away. He'll be in hospital for two weeks and after that he'll have to take it easy. Within a month he'll be walking around with a crutch. Meantime I want to move him to a private hospital nearby. He tells me he has medical insurance.'

'Yes, of course, thank you. I'll go back and tell him.'

Trevor took the news stoically. 'You should go now,' he said. 'You have to take over. Cheer up. We'll start again. Give or take a month, I'll be as good as new.'

Sam left, unconsoled and unconvinced.

Trevor closed his eyes and sank back on the pillows. He listened to Sam's footsteps fading down the corridor. She closely resembled her grandmother, who had been resourceful and loyal, but maybe a bit headstrong, just as Sam was. He knew she would cope admirably.

Today, when he had awakened to see her perched on his bed, her black hair tumbling forward over her face, her brown eyes shining with compassion, she'd looked exactly as Anna had looked the morning he'd regained consciousness expecting to find himself in a Gestapo cell. Instead he was in Countess Anna Stepinac's barn. He smiled as he remembered moments snatched in ditches, woods and caves. After a few months, he'd begun to dread the end of the war, imagining that it would mean their separation. Instead she'd married him. The war had been the best and worst of days.

Chapter 7

Why should they lose Woodlands? Woodlands was Trevor's birthright. Hers and Julie's too. How could she lose out twice in a lifetime?

Sam remembered her last image of their other Woodlands, in Zimbabwe. She and Julie had been staying with neighbours for the night after a birthday party. They'd gone home to find grim-faced soldiers standing among smoking ruins and slaughtered animals. No one had wanted to explain about the absence of their parents, until . . . She brought her mind back to the present with a jolt. Such memories were taboo.

Their home now was one of the finest old farmhouses in Kent. Their grandfather ran the brewery with John, and for the past five years Tom Bowles had run the farm.

The sight of the house brought calm to Sam as she swung up the driveway. She longed to go inside and soak up the peace and reassurance, but she drove on.

Brutus, her Labrador, who knew the sound of her car's engine, raced out to meet her. She pulled up and made a fuss of him. He was getting on now and it showed, but he jumped in and she drove on, bypassing the house, to the new office block where she parked. From here she could catch the familiar sour smell wafting from the brewery, sited behind a copse of fir trees on the other side of the paddock.

The office block was a simple, double-storey building with a canteen, reception area and boardroom on the ground floor, and six offices above. Sam hurried up to Trevor's office, which would be hers for a while.

Rosemary was staring out of the window. She wheeled round and Sam was shocked at her haggard expression. Rosemary resembled a river reed, tall and thin, stooped as if battered by hazardous winds but youthful blue eyes animated her once lovely face.

Sam couldn't help remembering that it had taken Trevor weeks to get Rosemary to accept a desk-top computer and learn how to use it. 'Rosemary has learned to resist change because for her change has always been unkind and mainly for the worst,' Trevor had explained. 'Understanding beats criticising.'

'Are they operating, Sam?' Rosemary asked now. 'I've been so worried. Thank goodness you're here.'

'He's very determined and obstinate. That should see him through this.'

'I'm glad you got here at any rate. Michael Johnson, is waiting in the boardroom. You've met him, haven't you? You have to sign some papers before the meeting this afternoon at three o'clock. A team of lawyers and accountants from Balaton's.'

'My God, Rosemary, why didn't anyone tell me?'

'I suppose it's my fault. It's not like me to forget, but with all this drama and worry . . . I would have cancelled except that they've flown over from Prague.'

'Don't worry. I'll play for time.'

'The bank won't give you much and Matthew Dearlove insists on being present.'

Sam squared her shoulders. 'Okay, Rosemary, I need our latest figures – bank statements, balance sheets . . .'

'Give me five minutes. Would you like some coffee?'

'Mm, thanks.'

Rosemary got busy on the intercom and shortly afterwards Mona came in carrying a pile of files.

'Hi, Mona, thanks. Just put them here,' Sam murmured. Mona's clothes were more outrageous each time Sam came home: the shortest, tightest black skirt she could squeeze into, a near-transparent, white blouse over a black bra, and five-inch platform shoes. Her long, Titian hair tumbled down her back in a pony-tail. Lately she had acquired a walk that looked as if she were dancing the rhumba, or perhaps it had something to do with the weight she had put on.

Sam got stuck into the accounts. Moments later she said to Rosemary, 'These figures can't be right. We can't be this much in the red. Why don't we sell more beer? What's our capacity?' She rifled through the figures until she found the production reports. 'It says here that we have the capacity to produce forty thousand barrels a year, but it's more than a decade since we ran at full capacity. We're selling less than half what we used to. Yet we own forty pubs and they should sell at least two hundred and fifty barrels each a year, which would amount to a quarter of our production. We used to sell the rest to hypermarkets, wholesalers, exports and other pubs.'

Rosemary gave an indulgent laugh. 'We're losing out in all our markets. Partly the sin tax, but also because beer's for wrinklies, according to the youngsters in the pubs around these parts. They're into beer and redcurrant juice, that sort of thing.'

'Why aren't we producing blends?'

'Mr Rosslyn thinks it's wrong to turn the nation's youth into alcoholics.' Sam knew that some of those drinks had an alcohol content of up to 6.5 per cent.

'Why should he worry? Under eighteens aren't allowed to buy booze.'

'Have you seen the labels? Look around, Sam. Decide for yourself if the messages are for eighteen-plus.'

'The nation's youth is the responsibility of its parents,' Sam said firmly. 'Ours, on the other hand, is to keep out of the red. Where's John, by the way?'

'He's been waiting to see you.'

John breezed in exuding confidence and good humour. 'Hey there, Sam, cheer up.'

'Why?'

'I came to offer you my moral support at this afternoon's meeting.'

'I don't need moral support. I need ideas. What would you do if you were in my shoes?'

There was a long pause. 'Have you been through the figures?' he asked.

'Yes.'

'You need a massive revamp of just about everything, blends, labels, advertising, pub décor, the works. All this will need cash. Personally I'd sell out.'

Johnson looked worried as he presented her with a copy of the power-of-attorney. 'This is a heavy responsibility, Sam. Try not to say anything. Be guided by me. I have your best interests at heart and I think you'll have to accept Balaton's offer. It's your only option. A very generous offer, I might add. I doubt Woodlands is worth ten million in its present loss status.' He left abruptly.

But how could you value a home? Sam wondered sadly, as she gazed out of the window. How could you buy or sell the trees, the otters in the lake, the castle or the river where the trout swam and the ducks lived? Could you set a figure on centuries of history told in old leatherbound books in the library? Woodlands was more than the brewery, it was a way of life, something they guarded and had fought for. She was part of Woodlands and Woodlands was part of her.

Rosemary bustled in, clearly trying not to show how worried she was. 'Shouldn't you get out of your jeans before the meeting? How about your black suit?'

'For a funeral? We haven't killed Woodlands yet. I'll wait a bit.'

For as long as Sam could remember Rosemary had been worrying about what was and wasn't appropriate. In her tailored grey silk suit, pink blouse and pearls, she looked almost as if she were playing a role. Rosemary had been Trevor's secretary and bookkeeper for over twenty years. She came early and left late. Sam knew she ran the local amateur dramatic society, but she had never seen her act.

'Rosemary, what did you do before you joined Woodlands?'

The question took Rosemary by surprise. She blushed. 'A bit of acting and dancing. Once I was a Bluebell dancer. We were famous in our time. We had to be tall and have long legs. We toured Europe and the Middle East for years. A sheikh once put a ruby in my navel. I wear it on a chain sometimes.' And with that she closed the door and Sam heard her heels clicking down the corridor. She glanced at her watch. Almost two o'clock. Damn! The butterflies were having a regular free-for-all in her stomach, her palms were damp and slippery and it was hard to breathe. In a few hours, though, it would all be over. She'd play for time and eventually give in. Then Gramps would enjoy his retirement with enough cash to live wherever he liked. Worse things could happen.

Like losing your birthright to a bunch of thugs?

Chapter 8

Sam felt like a minnow lost in a shoal of piranhas. The opposing team had come in force: Zoltan Hemzo, lawyer and nominee of the Balaton family, a grim-faced, sinewy man with shaved, iron-grey stubble for hair; his tough-looking, blonde secretary, who was not introduced; Hans Kupi, a fiftyish accountant who looked as if he'd spent a lifetime doing hard labour, and two men of indeterminate age who were described as advisers. Everyone wore grey suits and white shirts, including the secretary, and there was something not quite kosher about all of them, although Sam couldn't put her finger on it. The home team comprised Matthew Dearlove, their bank manager, Johnson, their lawyer, John, Rosemary and herself.

Hemzo, sitting opposite Sam, folded his hands on the table, fixed his pale eyes on her and forced his mouth into a grimace. 'Greetings from the Balaton family. Whatever you want to know, my dear, you have only to ask. You must realise that ten million pounds is a most generous offer. Your banker and your lawyer are agreed on that.'

The home team looked as eager as trained dogs. John was almost salivating. No doubt they were imagining some of those millions coming their way.

'My client has chosen Woodlands because you make an excellent beer and you have an old-established and renowned reputation,' Hemzo went on. 'They are anxious to acquire the same kind of firm. We have a ready-made market but we are unable to meet all the demands, hence

41

our search for new sources of beer. So let's put our cards on the table.'

Despite her hostility, Sam had to concede that Hemzo was convincing. Her doubts began to fade as her regrets strengthened. She realised he was winding up: 'I presume you are in agreement that the sale should go through now.'

'Subject to certain guarantees.' Sam opened her notebook. 'Shall we go through them?'

'Whatever.'

'We should like to retain the house.'

Her banker laughed. More guffaws all round. They seemed to have reached an understanding that young women should be seen, heard and tolerated, but never taken seriously.

'That's out of the question.' Kupi spoke for the first time. 'The house will become a management training centre. We intend to make extensive alterations and additions.'

Sam tried to hide her shock at the thought of them crawling all over their beloved home. She seemed to hear its shrieks wafting in the wind as she leafed through the papers again.

'Your offer is pathetic for the brewery, the pubs, our homestead and the farm. There's another thing. Most of the village depends on Woodlands, so I have to consider the staff's job security. First and foremost a year's employment contract for every permanent member of our staff. Of course, that's a minimum, some must get longer than a year.' This point was not up for debate: Sam remembered how relieved Ogden's creative staff had been when they knew their jobs were safe.

Hemzo's eyes gleamed with amusement. Sam felt like a mouse in the paws of a playful cat.

'Sorry, no contracts,' he said dismissively.

Sam was puzzled. 'You're bringing in Czech staff?'

'Maybe. A few.'

'What about our blender . . .' Sam stopped short. 'You're not going to brew here, are you? You're bringing in Czech beer and putting our labels on it.' Gripping the table, she leaned forward and glared at all of them in turn.

'Miss Rosslyn, how our client runs this company will be his affair once you've sold out,' Hemzo said pompously, 'but let's get one thing straight. Your grandfather asked you to handle the sale of Woodlands and, as his nominee, presumably you will carry out his wishes. I believe he was satisfied with our price.'

'He asked me to negotiate. That's not the same as consent. That's why I want these contracts now, before I sign.'

There was a long, icy silence.

At last Sam broke it. 'I don't think you understand. Our village depends upon Woodlands. We only employ forty villagers, but there's supply companies, a sports club, several pubs, a grocer, a butcher. Need I go on? Woodlands keeps the village going.'

'Change happens. You can't hold back.' Kupi smiled, flashing his steel tooth.

Sam felt inadequate to cope with this new development. She stood up and paced the space behind her chair.

'I don't like it at all. My grandfather said nothing about closing the brewery. He'd never agree to putting so many people out of work.' She glanced at Rosemary, who seemed frozen into immobility. Perhaps she was wondering where she would go next. John had flushed a deep red and she could see the sweat gathering on his forehead.

The bank manager fired a broadside at her. 'What choice do you have, Sam? You've been over the top for months.

It's out of my hands now. You won't be able to pay wages or harvest the hops so everyone'll lose their jobs anyway. Who'll run the place with Trevor incapacitated? You can't mix business and sentiment, Sam.'

'Only my friends call me Sam.' She turned to Hemzo. 'Why make an offer to a company losing money hand over fist? Let's face it, our market is shrinking daily and we operate in a country where anyone foolish enough still to be brewing beer is taxed out of existence. So why us? Why are you swamping the market with cheap beer bearing labels similar to ours?'

There was murder in Hemzo's eyes.

Michael put his hand on Sam's arm. He squeezed hard enough to hurt. 'Miss Rosslyn is overwrought by her grandfather's accident. Of course she doesn't mean that quite as it sounds. We've had a great deal of competition from cheaper foreign beer and this has played havoc with Woodlands' marketing. We are aware that it has nothing to do with your company.'

'Are we?'

Sam shook off her lawyer's arm and leaned over the table. Hemzo's eyes had clouded. 'Unless I receive guarantees for our staff's job security, I can't negotiate,' she said.

There was a long silence. Then Kupi spoke. 'No contracts. That's final. Our offer stands for twenty-four hours. We want your decision by this time tomorrow or the deal's off.'

'But I don't need twenty-four minutes, Mr Kupi. As things stand now, my answer is *no*.'

Rosemary's voice rang out shrilly. 'Would anyone like some more coffee? Let's have a short break before we start again, shall we?'

There was no response as the enemy team left in

strict pecking order, John trailing disconsolately after them.

As soon as she reached her office, Rosemary in attendance, Sam picked up the phone and dialled the hospital. 'Hello. Put me through to Ward C6, please.' She gripped the receiver with slippery hands.

When the sister assured her that Trevor was fine but still asleep, Sam almost burst into tears. She collected herself quickly. 'The operation was successful. We're not so fine. We need money fast, Rosemary, and plenty of it.'

'We could rob a bank.'

'I have some savings,' Sam said.

'Don't! You might as well pour your cash down the drain.'

'I have no choice. We have to plug the holes before we can start reorganising. Why didn't Trevor?'

'It all came upon him so suddenly. One minute we were limping along and then we were losing out badly. He made an error of judgement. He guessed that tastes would change so he laid up stocks of stout. On John's advice. Trevor probably won't mention that.'

Sam watched her thoughtfully. 'So where did John get that information?'

'His reports, he said. He does a spot of market research every month. Actually it's a just a case of traipsing round the pubs listening to their gripes.'

Sam sighed heavily. 'And instead they want sweet beer blends. How could he be such an idiot?' She pulled herself together fast. 'Well, we can do that. We need professional market research on modern taste. Perhaps Walter . . .'

Rosemary watched her curiously. Sam was pacing the office, hands clasped behind her back, staring accusingly at the wall. Suddenly she flicked her fingers and turned to Rosemary, eyes blazing with excitement. 'We'll start at once. Phone Walter. Tell him to get here with the team tomorrow. Call John. Tell him to get some blends ready in time for a marketing meeting. Oh, and, Rosemary, advertise – well, maybe you should ask around the trade for a brewery manager. John's on the road, I'll be on admin and marketing, we need a production manager. That was what Gramps did, wasn't it?'

'More or less.'

Sam sat down. 'Rosemary, I want weekly figures of all sales, to wholesalers, retailers, pubs, and exports.'

'Fine.' Rosemary sighed with relief. 'Where's Julie, by the way?' she asked.

'On tour with an animal rights group somewhere in Siberia. Evidently there's rumours of dancing bears, trapping sables and suchlike.'

'Good God! I hope she comes home in one piece.'

'Oh, she will. There's a whole bunch of them.'

'If it's all right with you I'll go home. Thought I'd drop in at the hospital.'

'Give Gramps my love. He'll be only half conscious, Rosemary. Best not to worry him with all this bad news.'

'I wouldn't dream of talking business.'

'Tell him I'll be along later. See you in the morning.'

As Rosemary's footsteps faded she felt a pang of loneliness. Then the telephone rang. 'Mona told me you were back, Sam, but when you didn't phone . . .'

Her silence was worse than a reprimand.

'I'm so sorry, Helen, it's been an awful day. I've just called the hospital. Trevor's fine.'

'Naturally. He's a fighter. Mona said you'd be here for supper. Is that right?'

'Just leave a snack in the fridge. A sandwich – anything. I've no idea when I'll get back.'

'I've aired your bed and your room's ready for you.'

'Thank you, Helen.'

'I hear you're running the old place for a while. It doesn't seem five minutes ago when you were a wee lass in pigtails . . .'

She went on at length, while Sam wallowed in guilt. How *could* she have refused the Czech offer without asking Trevor?

As soon as she rang off, she grabbed the accounts and pored through them again, but it didn't get any better. Eventually she buried her face in her hands. 'Talk about tilting at windmills. What *have* I done?'

If Woodlands went under because of her, Trevor would be out of pocket to the tune of ten million. Somehow she'd have to get it on its feet – and fast. The solution lay in new blends and new labels, revamped pubs, a positive export drive, plus top-rate marketing and advertising. Well, at least she knew enough about the last to realise that she needed a lot of cash. Sam had exactly £89,000 invested in unit trusts. She had saved some and inherited the rest from an aunt. She decided to transfer it to the business account first thing in the morning. It should last long enough to produce a new beer blend and market it, she persuaded herself. She wanted a new name, too.

As always, her need for inspiration led Sam to the library, a long narrow room along the west side of the house, facing on to the paddock. It was a comforting room, with a sense of energy and continuity. One wall was reserved for family history: earls and admirals, whores, crooks and clergymen had all played a role in the Rosslyns' ancestral past. Even Lady Godiva, and her ride naked through Coventry, was recorded, for there was a direct link with her in Trevor's maternal line.

Sam thumbed through the volumes. They belonged on

home territory beside the castle where, in 1040, the first Lord of the Manor of Bourne-on-Sea had been appointed and given a field with the castle for services rendered to the Crown. It was all recorded in the Domesday Book.

Nowadays the title 'Lord of the Manor' was more or less obsolete. Its main interest was to American tourists who bought their mugs and tankards, decorated with a picture of the half-ruined castle and the family crest. Sam sat and doodled, discarding one futile idea after the next. There seemed to be no way to capitalise on this ancient white elephant. Could she sell the castle? It was half in ruins, would cost the earth to restore. Besides, it was part of a package: castle, title, two fields, fishing rights and some ancient documents lost hundreds of years ago.

So why not sell the title?

The thought hit her like an electric shock, leaving her tingling. She burst out laughing. Of course. That was the answer. Why had it taken her so long to think of it? She'd heard that American millionaires were paying handsomely for castles and titles. She'd use the cash to establish their new beer lines. How much could she ask? Half a million dollars? Trevor wouldn't mind, and even if he did, they had no choice. She would contact the Manorial Society first thing in the morning and put the title on the market.

Chapter 9

She was late. She'd forgotten the time while she was holding her solitary think-tank in the library. John was leaning over the railings gazing fondly at the lake with a loaf of bread and a pint of lager beside him. Woodlands' best, Sam assumed. He was tugging bits off the loaf and distributing it to twelve greedy ducks and two black swans.

The scene was idyllic: the old Tudor pub had been tarted up, newly varnished beams shone black against freshly whitewashed walls, leaded panes sparkled, window-boxes were bright with geraniums, and new shocking-pink canvas awnings added a continental touch. The Castle Arms was their oldest pub and the one she loved best. It stood in the shadows of the ruined castle, had been in the family since the seventeenth century. Since then, mainly in the last century, the family had acquired another thirty-nine pubs. In other words, Sam reminded herself, forty loss-situations to pull round.

John saw her and his face lit up. 'Hi, Sam. How long have you been standing there?'

'Just arrived. I'm sorry I'm late.'

'No problem. How's it going?'

She shrugged. 'Things could be better. Well, actually they could hardly be worse.'

'Yes, well, I guess I knew that. And how's Trevor doing?'

'The operation was successful, thank God. Rosemary's there now.'

'She's crazy about him. Did you know that?'

She tucked her arm through his and leaned over the rail beside him. 'I think I'd suspected it. John, we have to talk business. Can we sit down?'

'First I'll buy you a drink. What'll it be?'

'What d'you think? Woodlands, of course.' She laughed and leaned back, taking in the scene. For the first time in her life, she realised, she felt slightly ill-at-ease with John. This was a new role for her, his boss instead of his friend, and she had to bully him, but they'd always got on well.

John was returning with two pints of Woodlands' best. 'We're badly in the red, John,' she said as he sat down.

'I know that – everyone knows it. And you've landed yourself with the job of pulling a rabbit out of the hat. Okay, come and sit down here where it's nice and quiet and I'll cry on your shoulder.'

Sam listened quietly while John spelled out his soul-destroying task of trying to sell Woodlands' beer to hyper-markets and off-licences. 'It's hard for me not to be angry, Sam. I love the old man, but I've been nagging him to get up to date for a couple of years. Every time I get my nil bonus statement I want to puke. It could have been so different.'

And every time I think of Kupi I want to puke even more, he agonised. 'Listen,' he went on. 'I've samples of what's selling in the car. They've been there for days. I was going to have another attempt to make your grandfather see sense. Won't be long.'

Sam sipped her drink. She always drank Woodlands' beer as a matter of loyalty. In the London pubs where she met her friends, Woodlands wasn't often available so she drank Scotch instead. It struck her that she didn't like beer much, which was not a good start.

John staggered back with a large carton he dropped on a bench beside them. It was full of drinks and paper mugs. 'Look at these. Anyone can see they're designed for kids. They shriek: "Hold me, buy me, drink me." Tasting time, Sam.' He took out six mugs and placed them in a straight row on the table before pouring a little from each bottle into one. 'Keep the mugs in the same place so we know which is which.'

Sam sipped one. It tasted good so she drained the mug and took another. Five minutes later she leaned back. 'This one first,' she said, pointing at a mug. 'Then that one, then that.'

What was it she had taught her clients? There's no such thing as problems, merely opportunities for correction. After three more samples success seemed just round the corner.

John stood up. 'I'm going for a pee.'

Sam shrank behind the tree just as Tom Bowles, their farm manager, passed her table. They'd never liked each other. He was a cold man with a handful of farming degrees, obsessed with orderliness and profits. They'd had many long battles over his desire to cut down trees, grub up hedges and plough pastureland. To him pigs were pork and domestic pets a sign of idiocy. Fortunately Trevor always took her side.

When John returned, she said, 'What d'you think of the idea of selling our title of Lord of the Manor?'

'That's something you should be asking Trevor.'

'And I will, tomorrow, but meantime d'you think anyone would want it?'

'Not worth much, is it?'

'Not really, but the fields might be.'

But even if she sold it, it would take a while to get the cash. She needed money now.

John felt wretched. He could see her anxiety and longed to help. He would have done anything to save the brewery and the villagers' jobs, but he'd spent the cash Kupi had paid him and he was trapped. Kupi had told him to find out the brewery's precise financial expectations and indebtedness, and John felt a heel to be spying on the Rosslyns. He tossed back his beer and wondered what he was going to do.

Sam spoke first. 'Everything looks so normal. Hard to believe we're making such a loss *here*.'

'We have the old regulars, but we're losing out on the younger generation. We *can* woo them back but we need good blends. Beer and cider, beer and apple juice, beer and redcurrant juice. How about beer and mead? Then we need better names and better marketing. We need new ideas. What about a pop concert? Get a song written round the name and some sexy young pop singer dressed in next to nothing screaming her lungs out. We could hold it in the ruins. It'd look macabre in the moonlight and the audience would park themselves in the fields and woods around and quaff our drinks.'

Sam took over. 'What about a beer festival?'

'Or what about combining them both?'

'D'you think it would work?' Sam asked.

'Don't see why not. Can you borrow more cash?' John asked.

'Maybe. Honestly, John, I've pulled enough clients out of the shit, but it's so much easier when it isn't your money, or your overdraft, or your neck the bankers are breathing down. I'm scared. I don't want to make things worse for Trevor.'

An hour later, the table was littered with half-empty bottles and glasses and Sam knew all there was to know about blending beer. Suddenly she realised how dizzy she was. 'Oops! I'm sloshed.'

'You need feeding. Let's go inside and I'll treat you to a lasagne.' He staggered in, carrying the box of samples, with Sam behind him. The mellow light reflected on oak beams and panelling, rows of bottles and barrels. There was a strong smell of liquor, tobacco and polish. It could have been any pub, anywhere. There was a small but vibrant crowd – she knew them all. When they caught sight of her someone started clapping. There was a cheer, rather cracked and wavery. Then someone called, 'Three cheers for Sam.'

'It's not my birthday,' Sam shouted.

'No, it's ours,' Mona called out. 'We still have jobs, thanks to you.'

John went to the bar and Sam sat down at a table and watched Greg Selo come across to her. 'Is this a private party, or can anyone join in?'

'It's a beer-tasting ceremony,' she said dreamily. 'Come and help us. I can't taste anything any more.'

Greg looked like a Cossack with his high cheekbones and thatch of black hair that grew in all directions, but rumour had it that he was Czech. Sometimes he reminded her of a beautiful, untrainable horse, with his flared nostrils, dark eyes and the wilfulness that showed in the set of his lips. He always seemed larger than life, and for reasons she didn't understand sent her libido soaring. He'd arrived in their village a year ago and bought a big old house. Since then he'd lived a quiet life except for frequent trips abroad. Not a breath of scandal touched him. Yet to Sam his modest behaviour contrasted strangely with his wild, extravagant beauty and his incredible masculinity. So what's he trying to prove? she wondered. And why am I so damned aloof? Who am I scared of? Him or me?

His lopsided grin was so appealing, yet his eyes remained impenetrable. He's a hell of a tough guy pretending to be a softie, she thought. She found herself wondering what he'd be like in bed.

He took her hand in his and stroked it gently. 'I've missed you, Samantha.' Sam nodded nervously, feeling scorched by their closeness. 'Sam,' she murmured.

'Sam's too boyish for you. You're the sexiest woman I've ever seen.'

John returned with two plates of food and more beer. 'Eat up,' he said. 'And fuck off, Greg, this is a business meeting. We don't have time to listen to your nonsense.'

Greg grinned, pulled out a chair and sat down.

He ran an import–export business in London and he seemed wealthy, but he was liked locally for his sense of fun. He sang at the pub, he danced at every opportunity and he'd overtaken John in the local heartthrob stakes. He flirted with everyone, but he never had a regular girlfriend.

By now they were surrounded. Everyone wanted to shake Sam's hand and congratulate her.

'How did the word get round so fast?' Sam frowned in annoyance.

Mona tripped towards them, ringlets bobbing, breasts bouncing, eyes sparkling, bright red lips curling into a smile.

'Ask her,' Greg whispered.

'Have you ever heard of a *confidential* secretary, Mona?'

'Sure I have, and I know what they earn. I'm just the only girl left in the typing pool. But don't worry, Sam. If anything had been to your disadvantage I wouldn't have said anything. I've certainly heard of friendship and loyalty.'

'Well, that's a huge relief.' Sam decided to have a word with her in the morning.

'Your problem, young lady, is hard cash.' Paul, the nurseryman, placed a heavy hand on Sam's shoulder and pulled out a chair next to her. He was a dark, thickset man, with coarse features and small brown eyes set under heavy black brows.

Sam smiled at him as she pondered on the mystery of sex appeal. Paul had it. Greg had it. Agatha, their local dressage champion who resembled her mounts, was fighting off her queue of admirers. But Mona, so pretty and voluptuous, couldn't get a man.

'I had the idea of selling the title,' Sam said, testing the water. 'What do you all think of that?'

'Title?' Paul queried.

His daughter, Maria, thin, dark and exquisitely tiny, leaned over his shoulders. 'You know, Dad, it's on your tea mug Mum bought down the pub. Lord of the Manor of Bourne-on-Sea, with those silly cats pawing the air.' Her down-to-earth Cockney accent clashed with her exotic looks.

'Lions,' Sam corrected her. 'The title goes with the castle and a couple of fields.'

'Jesus! Someone's going to love that title,' Agatha called out. She shrieked Establishment from her accent to her Dior scarf thrown over her shoulders. 'Maybe enough to part with half a million. Only recently Lady Jean Fforde sold the title of Earl of Arran, plus a ruined castle like yours, and she got four hundred and twenty-five thousand at auction.'

'It's not the same at all. Lord of the Manor of Bourne-on-Sea doesn't really mean anything,' Sam argued.

'Lord Bourne sounds okay to me,' Rosemary teased from the doorway.

'Oh, hi, Rosemary! When did you get back?'

'Just this minute. Trevor's fine. He sends his love.'

'You see the title's not . . .' Sam felt at a loss for words.

'Mere details, my dear.' Greg put his hand casually round her back, but his fingers were prodding the nape of her neck.

She tried to pull herself together. 'To pretend it's in any way a ticket to the Establishment would be immoral and maybe illegal.'

'Come on, Sam,' Agatha shrieked. 'It's all archaic. A title's a title to a foreigner. Grab the money and run. That's what my dad says.' Her father was a famous Harley Street surgeon, but her parents were divorced. It was rumoured that her mother, who kept stables, was having an affair with the blacksmith.

Rosemary returned holding a glass of Woodlands' apple juice. 'Sam, Trevor says don't come tonight. He wants to sleep. Tomorrow will be fine.'

'Oh. All right.' She felt disappointed.

Jim, the publican, hovered behind Rosemary looking anxious. 'Aim high, Sam. You've nothing to lose.'

'Just the family title.'

'What a snob you are,' Mona said.

'Shut up, Mona,' John cut in. 'Sell it leasehold and ask for half a million.'

'Pounds?'

John looked at her doubtfully. 'Okay, make it dollars.'

'I'm going home.' Sam stood up. 'It's good to see you all again. We had fun tonight, John.'

'Plenty more where that came from.'

Her head was buzzing with drink and ideas. 'Night, everyone.'

'I'll run you home.'

'Thanks, John, but I need the walk. See you.'

It took another ten minutes to get out of the pub.

Everyone wanted to shake her hand – the doctor, the vet, the vicar, Jeff Brink, who ran the bird park opposite, all good friends and regulars. It would be a pity to change it, Sam thought.

Chapter 10

It was only ten p.m., but Sam planned an early start the next day. To clear her head she leaned over the fence listening to the ducks settling down for the night along the mud-flats. Twilight lingered and purple-dark mists were drifting over the calm water. Frogs croaked under willow fronds and everything was as it should be and always had been. How could business losses and marketing ploys affect the ducks and the trees and the rushing river? It all seemed so apart from the world of profit and loss. Yet who knew what might happen here if Balaton's had their way?

She was crossing the car park when she heard a voice calling in a hushed stage-whisper: 'Sam! Over here, Sam.'

She saw a tall, thin figure standing beside a white Mercedes. 'My God! Shireen? Oh, how wonderful to see you!'

Sadness forgotten, Sam ran towards the girl who had been her best friend since early childhood and hugged her. 'Wow! You look so . . .' She searched for the right word. 'Beautiful' was uppermost in her mind. But Shireen also looked tragic, and a vital spark seemed to have been extinguished. She had lost her special glow, and there seemed to be a barrier between them: Shireen's large brown eyes, once so candid, were veiled.

'You look sophisticated and so lovely.' Sam hugged her again.

'We've both had to grow up fast. I hear you'll be running Woodlands.'

'Who told you?'

'My father.'

Strange that Shireen should know, since she'd only found out herself when she'd refused Balaton's offer a few hours ago.

'Where can we talk, Shireen? Let's go back to the pub. We've such a lot of catching up to do. Are you happy? I heard that you're engaged. Who is he?'

'So many questions. So impulsive. You haven't changed a bit, Sam.'

To Sam this was strangely hurtful. After primary school, she and Shireen had spent six years together at a local public school and although Shireen was half Indian, they had always been taken for sisters. They'd been there for each other through the bad times, and one really harrowing patch when Shireen's mother had left home. They'd gone on their first dates together, comforted each other through first love, shared their fun, their pocket money, even their boyfriends.

'I've missed you, Shireen. I sent you so many letters at first. Have you any idea how much I missed you?'

Shireen reached out and held her friend's wrist as if to steady herself. 'I'm not the person you took me for,' she said. 'That's why I didn't write. It took me three years on the Indian plains listening to my grandmother's daily lectures before I realised I knew nothing at all about myself. I was nothing more than a bundle of hot desires and crazy ideas. All we ever thought about was how to get more joy out of life.'

'And we did all right, didn't we? Specially Friday nights.'

Traditionally, Friday and Saturday nights had been disco nights. Wearing tracksuits over disco wear, they left at midnight by way of their sixth-floor window and took a well-known circuitous route, from ledges to drainpipes to roofs and more ledges, to the ground. They jogged to the nightclub, left their tracksuits in the cloakroom and danced until four a.m. when it closed. Then they had three hours to kill before they could jog back to school and join the enthusiastic athletes who had just completed their early-morning run around the playing-fields.

'Hey, Shireen,' Sam was whispering, 'remember the six-inch rule and Blotch?'

'How could I forget? She actually had a ruler.'

'And she kept it in her pocket.'

'And shoved it between us when we were talking.' Now they were both laughing uproariously.

'Looking back, I can see we made her life hell,' Sam said. 'You used to be such a daredevil.'

A wave of nostalgia burst over Sam and suddenly she was back in the spring of 1992. She was eighteen, Shireen was seventeen and they were longing for fun. The school, originally a famous boys' school, had introduced the six-inch rule with the admission of girls. Students of the opposite sex had to maintain a six-inch space between them and Shireen had been caught by Blotch getting off with a cute sixth-former.

Blotch, their housemistress, so-named because of a birthmark on her cheek, had gated Shireen over an exeat weekend and was writing to her father to explain why his daughter would not be coming home as planned. Sam had decided to stay with her, which aroused Blotch's suspicions.

'I'll never forget the time she kept watch with her binoculars. Remember? I can still hear her yelling, "What's going on?" as I wobbled along the parapet. And you pretended you were going to commit suicide.'

'Don't come any closer. I'll jump,' Shireen ad-libbed. 'Don't try to stop me.'

'That's *exactly* what you said!'

'I dropped on my hands and knees and began to crawl towards you. I remember I said, "I'd rather die than face my father after this."'

'And Blotch started to cry,' they said as one, convulsed in helpless laughter.

'Come back. I won't write to your father.' Shireen mimicked the housemistress's Glasgow accent. 'Honest to God!' Now they were laughing louder, unable to stop.

'She gave us cake and hot chocolate and cried about the unbearable strain of trying to cope with a hundred randy boys and forty nubile virgins.'

'Forty *virgins*!' They fell about laughing.

'Four, maybe,' Sam said. 'We were so ashamed because we were two of them.'

Shireen stopped laughing and frowned, remembering how she had lost her virginity. And all for nothing. 'Are you still . . .' she asked Sam.

'I had an affair with Walter, my boss, but he turned out to be a creep.'

'We still made the nightclub that night.'

'Yes,' Sam said. 'It was our best night.'

'We worked hard. We passed our exams. Why shouldn't we have fun, too?'

They sat in silence.

Sam felt her friend's sadness and tried to make it better. 'Okay, so I forgive you. You never liked writing. It was one of our few differences.'

When Shireen turned her head, Sam saw tears in her eyes.

'Sam! I'm here to buy my trousseau.'

'I've seen happier brides. Are you in love?'

'I've never even met my future husband. I've seen pictures of him. He's old. Well, maybe fifty plus. And he's wealthy. A widower with two grown-up sons.'

'How can your father do this to you, Shireen? You've been brought up English. You have your rights as a British subject.' Sam flung her arm around her friend's shoulders and hugged her hard.

Shireen's mouth was quivering. 'Father changed after Mother left home. He turned against the West. He's going to retire in India and he wants the family back there. He's returned to the old ways. I can't do what Mother did. He'd be destroyed.'

'That doesn't give him the right to run your life for you. You're twenty-three years old, Shireen. You can do whatever you damn well like. Stand up for your rights. Remember your mother, Shireen – she stood up for hers.'

'That's the problem. Look at the damage she did and the hurt she caused. I don't want to be like her. There's more to life than self-indulgence.' She sighed. 'I'd better go, Sam. Forgive me, but I had to see you. I wanted to say how sorry I am about your grandfather. If I had my way, we wouldn't have a warehouse stocked full of cheap beer. It would be Woodlands' only. I'll try to see you again. It's best you don't contact me.'

The sight of Shireen standing in the car park with Sam had been a shock to John. He'd waved, but she'd turned away and got into the car, yet he was sure she'd seen him. Best not to intrude, he'd thought, watching the girls talking in the car. Then she'd driven away. He hadn't even managed to see if she wore a wedding ring.

As he returned to the pub John felt lightheaded with joy. Shireen was back and he loved her. Anything was possible.

Rosemary, who was talking to Greg nearby, watched John's face light up. She hadn't seen him so happy for a long time. She frowned and lost the drift of the conversation.

Greg was expecting an answer. 'Sorry. What did you say?' She tried to pay attention, but he was unusually talkative. The Castle Arms was Rosemary's second home, although she never drank more than two shandies.

Jeff Brink was a little tipsy, she saw. He'd pulled off a coup, he'd told her earlier. Strange-looking man: his whole face seemed slightly out of symmetry, one eye fractionally larger and higher than the other, his strong straight nose a trifle off-centre. Even his prominent cheekbones didn't match and his hair receded more on one side than the other. He was from Zimbabwe, and he ran a bird park opposite Woodlands. He'd begun ten years ago by collecting exotic birds and breeding them successfully. Now he'd turned his acres into a tropical forest with trees and shrubs and ultraviolet lights. 'Drinks all round,' she heard him call to the barman. 'Talisker for Peter here.' He clapped the frail vicar on the back and the priest's eyes watered.

'Not every day you hatch a clutch of emus,' he boasted. The drinks arrived, and the vicar sat nursing his glass of single malt with a dreamy look in his eyes.

Rosemary managed to lose Greg. She leaned back on the counter and savoured the atmosphere. There was a smell of newly polished wood, the pungent scent of Woodlands' pure ale, tobacco from Jeff Brink's pipe, the scent of sea mist drifing through the open window, the hum of voices, clink of glasses, and the mellow light reflected from dark oak beams. She soaked in the scene – it might have to last her a long time, if Woodlands went bust.

'Hey, Rosemary! What's this we hear about a pop concert and a beer festival?' Dearlove, the banker, called out.

'That's the last thing we want in Bourne-on-Sea. Can't you talk Sam out of it?' Agatha's face was cerise. She was prone to dark moods and surly tempers. 'It'll bring the plebs here and once they find out about our beaches . . .'

'We don't want them trampling round the lake,' Paul grumbled.

'We'll never see the back of them,' Greg added.

Everyone was talking at once.

'There's something I should tell you all,' Mona cut in. She paused for dramatic effect. 'Sam's only selling the family title because the brewery's broke. She needs the pop festival too.'

'And it's up to us to help her.' Rosemary scowled at Mona.

'Not much of a title, is it, really?' Jeff mused. 'You don't even get to be a sir.'

'To an American, a title's a title. I suppose it all depends on how we treat the buyer. We should make him feel important,' Rosemary said.

'Bowing and scraping?'

'Why not? We could call him your lordship.'

'He'll expect to hobnob with the Queen and get into the House of Lords.'

'Nothing's impossible,' Mona put in. 'My mum's cousin works in the kitchens at Buckingham Palace. Once a year they have a staff garden party and get to talk to the Queen. Mum's allowed to take one guest. She could take him. She'd be glad to help out.'

'That's perfect, Mona. He'll think they're all nobs.'

'Bet he'll wear a Stetson.'

'Half a dozen cameras slung round his neck.'

'Ten to one he'll be from Texas,' John said. 'With a mouth as big as his oil well.'

'Don't worry, Rosemary, we'll bow and scrape as much as he wants,' Mona said.

'I knew I could rely on you. I'll see if I can persuade the scout master to send some kids to clean up the river and the lake round the castle. Oh, and for those of you who don't know how to do it, I'll be giving lessons on how to curtsy up at the barn. I must go. I need an early night.'

Greg clicked his heels, clasped Rosemary's hand and bowed low over it.

'Why, that's perfect, Greg. You must join our group.' Rosemary left with a cheery wave.

Chapter 11

As soon as Rosemary left the pub her face creased into lines of anxiety. She hurried along the riverbank, down the steps beside the waterfall to the road that zigzagged up the chalk hill to her cottage. It was only a fifteen-minute walk, but by the time she neared home she was almost running. Would it be standing? Would there be smoke pouring out of the windows, or perhaps a gas explosion? Or what about a burst hot-water cylinder? She could discount all of these possibilities, but she could not erase the image of her cottage reduced to a pile of rubble.

She heard a miaow. Looking down, she saw that Tibby had come to meet her.

'Oh, Tibby. You shouldn't come down to the road. It's not safe.' Picking up the huge, scarred tabby, she hugged him close. He dug his front claws into her shoulder and purred loudly. When she reached the crest of the hill she saw the cottage in the moonlight, safe and sound. She gave a small prayer of thanks and fumbled for her key. Once inside she switched on the lights and the television, opened a tin of cat food and poured a bowl of milk. Then she gazed with satisfaction at the neat stacks of provisions. Enough for a siege. She touched each mug, hanging on its hook, and glanced at the cutlery lying in the correct sections of the beige-lined drawers. All was as it should be. Tibby was home and so was she. Nothing had changed in the past twenty-four hours.

Rosemary went outside and sat on the garden bench.

From here on a clear day you could see right across the Channel. It looked so peaceful, as if nothing could change. But she had seen how change could strike home with the speed of summer lightning.

Rosemary had learned to hate change at an early age. It had begun with her parents' intent concentration on the radio. To this day, Rosemary hated the radio. At six o'clock sharp her parents lost all interest in her as Dad twiddled the knobs on the great walnut box with the brown fabric speaker. After numerous tries and high-pitched whines, a voice could be heard telling them news, which sent Dad scurrying for a beer and brought out criss-crossing furrows on Mum's forehead.

Then little Rosemary would grab the cat and creep off to her small rocking-chair with the Noah's Ark cushion and rock solemnly to and fro. To this day she could remember Chamberlain's doleful words to the nation on the fateful morning of 3 September 1939. She hadn't fully understood what they meant, but she'd sensed approaching doom from Dad's shocked white face and Mum's tears.

Nothing got Mum down for long, though. Early next morning they had rushed to the Co-op to buy blackout material for the windows, but it had sold out. Mum and she had gone home and got out all their spare blankets.

'How do we know if it's dark enough?' Mum asked Grandpa, who had popped round for a cup of tea and a game of cribbage.

'If the light comes in, it'll shine out. Stands to reason, doesn't it?' But however many blankets they nailed over the windows, stabs of light still penetrated the room.

'What will we do for fresh air, then?' Mum demanded, when the fourth blanket was nailed up. For the next week they hammered up blankets each evening and took them down each morning. The wooden window-frames were split and the blankets were shredded round the edges. Then the blackout material arrived and Dad made blinds while Mum lined the curtains.

A month later, Dad went off to war and Mum cried a lot. She started to talk to Rosemary as if she were an adult. The little girl sensed her mother's loneliness and tried hard to be the person she needed, acting like she understood, even if she didn't.

Then came the day when Mum bought a gun from Uncle Leslie and hid it at the back of the larder. 'Never go near that gun, my girl,' she said. 'That's for when the Jerries come. Everyone hereabouts has got a gun. They won't get far. Believe me. We'll fight to the end, every last one of us, even if the government surrenders.'

That afternoon Mum took her along the prom as usual, but now the beach was crowded with bulldozers, trucks of sand and cement, piles of stones. Teams of men were running around shouting at each other, huge concrete blocks were rising along the high-water mark, and roll after roll of barbed wire was being uncoiled.

An old man stepped forward, pointed a pitchfork at them and shouted, 'Halt! Who goes there? Friend or foe?'

'Friend,' Mum said, trying not to laugh.

'Mum,' Rosemary tugged at Mum's hand, 'why doesn't Bert remember us? He brings our milk every morning.'

'Sh!'

'Advance, friend, and be recognised.'

'Should you be walking along here, Mrs Santer? They'll start shelling any time now.'

Bert looked scared, but Rosemary took her cues from her mum, who glanced at the sea. 'They won't start yet. I look at it this way. If it's got my number on it, then it won't make much difference where I am. What's the point of worrying about it?'

They walked on.

'Mum, is Bert going gardening?'

'He's training, practising with the pitchfork. Any day now they'll get their rifles.'

'Why are they spoiling the beach?'

'The blocks'll stop the Jerries' tanks and guns from getting up to the road and their soldiers won't get through the barbed wire in a hurry. They'll never even reach the first houses.'

'Mum, don't they have houses of their own?'

'They want what we've got and they want what everyone else's got, too. That's what war's about. They're greedy buggers!'

'Can I sleep with you, Mum?' she asked, when they got home.

'Course.'

Snuggled up against Mum she'd felt as safe as houses.

Rosemary sighed. Her mum had survived the war but Dad hadn't, and Mum had never really got over that. She was a bit batty now, but they looked after her well enough in the home in Brighton.

Rosemary went inside and locked the door. Tonight she couldn't get her mind off the war. Mum had seemed so strong but when she'd cracked it was for good.

She decided to make a cup of tea and listen to music. That usually calmed her down. That damned office meeting had given her the jitters.

'Time, gentlemen, please.'

Reluctantly John quit the pub and made his way along the short-cut that wound across a field towards his cottage. Uppermost in his mind was the joy that Shireen was back. Once he'd thought she loved him ... why not?

It was summertime. He'd been sprawled in the grass on a Sunday afternoon, sleeping off a pub lunch, and had woken with a jolt to find Shireen kneeling over him, her black hair falling around his face like a curtain, her knees straddling his body, her huge velvety eyes locked with his.

'Make love to me,' she'd whispered.

'No. I love you too much, Shireen, and anyway, you're only eighteen.'

'Idiot!' To his amazement she'd pushed down his shorts and inched herself down on him. Overcome with passion he'd lost control and come too soon.

'Is that it?' She'd looked so disappointed.

'You didn't have to do that.' He'd fumbled for a handkerchief for her. 'You know how I feel about you, Shireen. Marry me – I'll make you happy. I've loved you since I first saw you.'

She'd burst out laughing. 'My father has betrothed me to a man I've never even seen. But perhaps now he won't want me – I'm not a virgin and I'm only half Indian.'

Then she'd sat down and cried and John had realised the futility of his dreams.

After that, they'd met secretly whenever they could. Using Sam as an alibi they had even taken holidays together. By then he understood her better. He'd caught glimpses of the ambition that seemed to be in her genes. Her father, Shun Desai, a tall, distinguished-looking man, with thick black eyebrows and piercing eyes, had arrived in Britain as a penniless youth hardly able to speak English. Now he owned a chain of hypermarkets and a wholesale company that supplied most of Kent with its imported liquor. Desai had been too preoccupied with building his fortune to learn about their romance – if you could call it that. They had got away with it for a year, but then he had found out and acted swiftly. Shireen had been flown out on the next New Delhi flight.

John had called and written to her father constantly, he had even employed a private detective, but he never found Shireen's address.

When John reached his home, a small, whitewashed gem of a place, almost hidden under masses of creepers and shrubs, he half hoped that Shireen would be waiting, but she wasn't.

He poured himself a Scotch, then went out on to the balcony and sat listening to the river and the wind. Shireen was the most beautiful woman he had ever seen, with that curious ivory skin and her huge gazelle eyes. She had every reason to believe that her beauty would provide her with fame and fortune, but working in her father's hypermarket had not been the way to realise her ambitions.

The telephone rang. John made no move to pick up the receiver. He guessed it was Hans Kupi, and he knew why Kupi was ringing. The phone went silent, leaving John shaken and disturbed. He hated himself for taking the ten thousand, but if he played along with Kupi he might end up wealthy enough to win Shireen.

In the middle of the night, Shireen started awake. She'd dreamed she was standing on a raised dais, dressed in her wedding finery, beside a man so old that his teeth had fallen out. He turned and smiled, then said, 'Come, my wife.' She realised the trap had sprung shut and there would never be any escape.

She was still in England, Shireen reassured herself. There was still time to escape. But for the past three years she'd learned to accept fate. She thought about her grandmother, and the house by the river, and her many relatives. In a way she loved them, too.

She remembered the heat of the midday sun that baked the plains and burned your lungs when you breathed. At first she had suffered, missing her father, England, her freedom and Sam, until her grandmother had taught her acceptance.

'Let it flow through you. Become part of it. Let it make you strong.'

Accept life as it comes and conquer desire. That way led to peace and happiness. She could hear her grandmother's voice, like the sound dry leaves made when they were blown across the gravel, as she whispered, 'Die before you are dead.'

Personal ambition was wrong, desire brought only pain. But what about the pain of making love with a man she didn't like night after night for the rest of her life?

Chapter 12

Sam was up at dawn. She intended to visit her grandfather before she went to the office. Helen hadn't arrived yet, so she gulped down a cup of instant coffee and grabbed a roll. Then she fetched her bag and unlocked the front door. It was going to be a lovely day, she decided, as she started the car.

As she swung on to the road she saw a dark shape lying near the verge. Recognition came a split second later. She braked and ran to the dog, calling his name, but his limbs had stiffened and his eyes were glazed.

'Oh, Brutus, what were you doing out here?' She bent down and stroked his head, trying to hold back her tears. She crouched beside him, stroking his black fur. Who had opened the gate and why had Brutus walked out on the road at night? On impulse, she dragged his body to the car and drove to the vet.

Steve was sixty-five and looked twenty years younger. He was a tall, athletic man who kept himself in peak condition.

'It's just too weird, Steve. It's impossible. He couldn't get out. I want a full autopsy.'

She found Trevor eating breakfast and decided not to tell him about Brutus. That would be just another blow for when he came home. She had more than enough bad news for him without that this morning.

She asked him about the hospital, the food and the

nurses, then told him about the previous evening in the pub, Shireen and her trauma.

'Isn't it time you were going? You don't have to stay here all day,' Trevor said eventually.

'Gramps. I have something to tell you. It's best you hear it from me because . . . well, the truth is, I've probably ruined you.' She made a special effort to stare him straight in the eyes. I refused Balaton's offer.'

She searched his face for shock but he looked mildly amused.

'You see, they were going to close down the brewery and use it as a depot. All the jobs would be lost. And our house . . . Well, I have a few ideas to revamp the brewery and pubs and so does John. I'll try to pull us round.'

Trevor caught hold of her hand and squeezed it. 'I was going to do the same if it weren't for the accident. I trust your judgement, Sam. In fact, I have great faith in you. If you need me you know where I am. I'll be back soon. As for Balaton's offer, I don't imagine we've heard the last of them.'

'Right now we need cash badly, mainly for marketing. Gramps, how would you feel about selling the title?'

'Who'd want it?'

'Perhaps a *nouveau riche* immigrant who's looking for ready-made roots.'

'It's not just a title. It's a package and the package includes the castle and the fields around it. Check with the Manorial Society. They'll help you.'

'So what do you think?'

'Give it a go. It might work. I'd forgotten about the title long ago. Sam, listen, for years I have considered myself merely the caretaker of your inheritance – yours and Julie's. Do whatever you feel you must and if you need me I'll help you in any way I can. If it's too much for you, I'll take over again as soon as I can get about. But you seem to know what you're doing.'

The telephone rang beside Trevor's bed. Sam handed him the receiver.

'I'm fine, Rosemary,' he said. 'Feeling great. Now you can stop worrying . . .'

Sam waved and left him. By the time she'd reached the highway, her head was full of slogans and names for new blends.

Rosemary hung up, switched on the coffee machine then opened the back door. The sun had risen and the sky was clear and blue. It had rained in the night and there was a crisp earthy tang all about her. She could smell the grass and the apple mint that grew in clumps around the back door. The sea was sparkling and there was a faint scent of ozone in the soft, morning breeze.

Tibby jumped out of the woodshed and came rubbing round her ankles while she spooned out his breakfast.

Despite the glorious morning, Rosemary was feeling a little jaded – she'd hardly slept. Where was Julie? Last they'd heard was three days ago when a friend called to let them know she was returning overland. Evidently she'd cashed in her return flight, but surely she should have been back by now?

Julie was so vulnerable, a lost child still trying to find herself. She'd always been kind and loving, and she hadn't had her fair share of the love Trevor gave Sam. If anyone told him this, he'd agonise over it, but the truth was, Sam, who was dark, reminded him of his wife and Julie, with her blonde hair, blue eyes and milky skin, didn't.

Rosemary worried about Trevor too. He tried to make light of his pain, but he was suffering. His guilt wasn't helping much either: he'd been foolish and now Sam had to carry Woodlands through a difficult period.

Rosemary hurried to the bathroom and turned on the shower. Five minutes later she emerged pink and steaming. She wrapped herself in her dressing-gown and poured a mug of strong, fresh coffee. Returning to the bathroom, mug in hand, she glanced in the mirror and flinched. The light, catching her sidelong, heightened every line and furrow. She looked more like seventy than sixty-four and even her hair looked colourless, but of course it wasn't. According to the supermarket packet, it was pale shimmering blonde, but right now it looked more like a length of washed-up, sun-bleached rope.

Moments later she was slapping on the Vitamin A cream until her cheeks took on a glow. Drops opened her eyes and made them sparkle, and now she could feel her skin tightening. A smudge of blusher gave her a healthy colour.

Tibby was rubbing himself against her ankles. 'Where's that damned eye-shadow, Tibby? At my age you have to be a cross between Picasso, Jeremy Irons and Einstein just to hold down a job.' The container slipped from her fingers, spilling the powder all over the floor.

Painfully she crouched on her hands and knees and tried to push it into a heap, but it settled into the wood grain. She salvaged enough for today, then gave up. She'd have to buy some more.

She gasped at the pain in her back as she stood up. God, she was stiff. Age was something that had fallen upon Rosemary when she was all unaware. One minute she was pushing thirty and then she was pushing sixty. She was tossed over the humiliating hurdle one sad wet day. Alone and grieving, she'd moved into another decade and drunk herself into a stupor, to wake later looking ninety and feeling a hundred.

She dressed quickly, rinsed her mug and put it back on the rack in its place. She had a passion for hand-painted mugs. They stood in rows on the old Welsh dresser. It gave Rosemary an acute sense of security to have everything in its place.

A last stroke for Tibby, then she locked the front door and hurried along the gravel path to the garage and her beloved Mini. She paused and looked out over the Channel. The sea was calm, the sky still cloudless. It was going to be a lovely day. Below her, the creek sparkled a deep, translucent turquoise. Trevor's boat was rocking gently at its mooring, but where was Julie's? Perhaps a friend had borrowed it. She must ask Sam.

For one last time she gazed at her cottage, the jasmine that was bursting into blossom and the two crimson roses blooming in the flower-bed. She'd planted pansies, lavender, clumps of cosmos and forget-me-nots in the borders. How perfect it all was. What if she were to lose it all? She banished the thought sternly. This was no time for being fearful.

Chapter 13

Trevor heard footsteps and opened his eyes. Rosemary reached out awkwardly and took his hand. 'I popped in on my way to work.' She sounded hoarse. 'I came to see if you need anything. Oh, and should the boat go into the boathouse?'

'No, it's safe until autumn. I'll be fighting fit long before then. How was the meeting?'

Oh, God! Why did he have to ask that? 'Fine, just fine. Things are moving along.'

'That wasn't what I heard from Sam. She was here earlier. She'll need all the help she can get, Rosemary.' He frowned. 'She wants to bring out some new blends. I'm against it, as you know. Perhaps I'm old-fashioned.'

'Or obstinate.'

'Well, I've decided Sam must have a chance to do things her way. It's her heritage, after all. Hers and Julie's.'

As soon as the banks opened that morning Sam transferred her inheritance and savings to the business account. By ten a.m. Rosemary was exhausted and they'd hardly begun. She made some coffee and listened in unashamedly to Sam's conversation. 'Listen, Walter, I need market research urgently, plus new labels and an entire new image. Are you available? ... Yes, of course I expect to pay, Walter ... When can you get down here? Oh, and bring the team ... You didn't get the contract? Hell,

I'm sorry, Walter. I won't say it serves you right. People aren't pawns. No, I can't come back for months, if ever. Trevor's in hospital and I'm trying to keep the wolf from the door . . . Basically it depends on your price, but I need to develop new tastes. That'll take research. I need ideas for revamping the pubs, names for new blends, labels, advertising. I need to know exactly who my market is . . . You will? That's perfect. When can you get here? Fine! See you there.'

That'll take care of Sam's little nest egg, Rosemary thought.

The two women settled down to admin and paying bills.

It was noon before Kupi phoned. Rosemary watched Sam frowning as she answered in monosyllables. Then she hung up.

'Odd conversation,' she remarked. 'He said: "Good morning, my dear. We were all a little hot under the collar last week. Isn't that what you English say?" Then he laughed. His laugh gives me the creeps.'

'Everything about him gives me the creeps.'

'Yes, well, then he said, "Our offer remains unchanged. You can pick up the telephone whenever you like. You have Hemzo's private number." I don't, of course.'

'I do, Sam.'

'I said, "Don't bother. I won't be calling." His reply was rather weird. He said, "But, Miss Rosslyn, you never know. Things happen, sad things, unexpected tragedies, accidents. If or when circumstances change you might want to change your mind. I just want you to know that you can." Then he said goodbye and hung up. Does that sound like a threat to you?'

'Maybe, I don't really know.'

Just after lunch the vet called. Sam listened to him, went

very pale, then flung down the receiver and raced down the passage.

Rosemary could hear her throwing up. When Sam emerged, she said, 'I knew it, but I didn't say until they finished the autopsy. Someone killed Brutus. Steve says he had been heavily tranquillised and that he must have been carried to the road and then . . . Oh, God!'

'I'll call Inspector Joyce.' Rosemary glanced worriedly at her. 'Under these circumstances,' she said, 'Kupi's call was a definite threat.'

Neville Joyce took it seriously, but Rosemary couldn't see that he accomplished much during a two-hour meeting in the library later that afternoon. No new facts came to light and finally they were all cautioned to lock the doors at night, put the burglar alarm on and get a couple of good watchdogs.

A few days later a bunch of oddballs pitched up in the late afternoon and crowded into the brewery for a tasting session. Rosemary went along to keep an eye on them.

'Who the hell are they?'

'Walter's creative team. And Walter, of course.'

'Weirdos, every last one of them,' she said. She went back to the office, picked up the phone and dialled the Manorial Society of Great Britain. 'Just how do I set about selling a title?' she asked.

'Hold on, please.'

Eventually a young man with a Cockney accent came on the line.

'Good morning, ma'am. What is your title?' he asked.

'I don't have one. I'm calling on behalf of my boss.'

'I see. Then give me the details. Earl? Duke?'

'Nothing like that. Lord of the Manor of—'

'Oh, one of those. You've missed this year's spring

auction but don't worry. Plenty of aspiring lords around. Of course, you're duty-bound to point out that it's not a peerage. The title does not allow the buyer to sit in the House of Lords but it has some cachet. You'll probably pick up around five grand.'

'We were expecting two million dollars.'

'Well, what have you got to go with it? Land? A castle?'

'There's five acres of land, more like two large fields, but one of them's got a small wood. There's fishing rights, a ruined castle and a coat of arms.'

'Everyone has a coat of arms. It might pay you to do up the castle.'

'If we had that kind of cash we wouldn't be selling the title, would we?'

'How about documents?'

'I don't know.'

'Hang on, I'll look it up.'

There was a long wait. Rosemary wondered if he'd hung up on her, but eventually he returned. 'There's a number of documents dating back to the tenth century, but it seems they were lost. Pity – they'd be worth a small fortune.'

Rosemary made a note to tell Sam and Trevor.

'Look, you can ask for as much cash as you like for the title. It's getting it that's the problem. I suggest you place advertisements in newspapers like the *New York Times*. *Resident Abroad* might be a good bet. "Come home to a title," that sort of approach.' He gave her a list of ten newspapers. Rosemary added the *Texan Daily* to the list. A nice oil billionaire might do rather well.

The next time the telephone rang, it was Inspector Joyce.

'Sam's in the plant,' Rosemary said. 'Shall I put you through?'

'Just give Sam a message. The entire Czech team left England immediately after your meeting with them. They've remained in the Czech Republic since then. Evidently Kupi called Sam from Prague. Since we have no other suspects, the case is dropped for the time being. How's Trevor?'

'Getting along fine.'

'Give him my regards.'

Rosemary sighed. 'It's not over, Inspector. Far from it. This was a warning. Intimidation. Surely you can see that.'

'Of course, but until they come back into the picture again there isn't much we can do. Keep your eyes open. If you see anyone suspicious hanging around, let me know.'

It was after lunch when Sam popped in, looking exhilarated. 'Listen, Rosemary, Walter's found a pop star for us. She's called Dehlia and evidently she's up and coming. She writes her own songs, but she's a bit odd.'

'She's coming to the right place then.'

'Anyway, we can have a new blend ready in time, as long as we give them enough time to create the right labels. So we need a new name. You and I will have to burn the midnight oil.'

'So what's new?'

Sam looked taken aback. 'It's not as if we do it all the time, Rosemary.'

'Every night so far, but who's counting?'

'You, obviously.'

'Okay, sorry. It was quite fun, but I had to put off my rehearsals.'

'Real life is a little more important that amateur theatricals, don't you think?'

'Sometimes I don't see much difference, Sam.'

Chapter 14

It was a warm evening and the sun was setting as Rosemary took a short-cut across the hills to her cottage. Passing the castle she looked down at the sea and thought she saw a small yacht bobbing towards the cove far below. It looked like Julie's boat, but that was impossible.

She showered, then changed into trousers and a cotton sweater. She had a sandwich for supper as she listened to the news. Then she put her car in the garage and walked up the river towards the ruins. By this time purple veils of dusk were shrouding the countryside, blurring the edges of the trees and making the castle look twice as large as life.

When she neared the bridge she saw a tall, slender figure tying up a boat to the wharf.

'Good God! Julie! *Julie!*' she shouted. 'Welcome home! But what on earth are you doing here?' She ran towards the bridge.

Julie straightened up. 'Rosemary!' Her face was a picture of guilt. Nevertheless, she ran up the bank and gave the older woman a quick hug. Then she was scrambling down again. 'See you later,' she called over her shoulder.

'No, you won't. You'll see me now. What are you up to?'

Rosemary found it hard to be firm with Julie, who had always been her special favourite. She was as blonde as Sam was dark, with masses of silvery tresses falling over her shoulders. Her eyes were large and wide and of a special shade of translucent blue, and she was nearly always laughing. Rosemary noticed that she was wearing the little black opal heart on a fragile gold chain, which she had bought her when she turned eighteen last October. The dark stone emphasised the smooth fairness of her skin. She was a natural beauty who never wore makeup and went around in torn jeans and a T-shirt.

Rosemary knew that Julie hated catwalk modelling. Two years ago she'd begun doing it freelance for pocket money and had been extraordinarily successful. She worked haphazardly, but made a fortune when she wanted to. Now she was on her knees by the hatch, trying to coax something out of the cabin. Whatever it was had no intention of emerging.

'She's been sick,' Julie called.

'Who has?'

'Tasha.'

The boat lurched suddenly and a flash of white shot through the hatch, knocking Julie aside. Rosemary watched the mad gyrations of a dog turned crazy with fear as it tried to free itself from the chain around its neck.

Rosemary slithered down the bank towards the animal.

'You're scaring her,' Julie panted.

Rosemary put her right hand on the dog's collar and her left on its skinny haunches and pressed hard. 'Sit!'

'She doesn't understand English.'

Julie looked a trifle sulky as the dog sat, rolling its eyes, while Rosemary examined its scars and burns, and the raw wound that encircled its neck. It was long and lean, with thin legs and what was left of its hair was silky white with beige and silver streaks. It looked to Rosemary like a wolf.

'Let me guess,' she said. 'You sneaked home without saying hello to anyone, and took your boat back to Calais to collect this creature from wherever you'd hidden it.'

'A friend's garage, actually.'

'You could go to prison and this mangy thing could be shot.'

Julie almost burst into tears. 'Please don't tell anyone.'

'Better come up to the cottage and see what we can find for it to eat. There's raw chicken thighs in the fridge.'

'Rosemary, please, you must understand. I had to buy her.'

'I thought you'd run out of money.'

'I gave them my watch, camera, binoculars and the remainder of my travel allowance.'

No point in asking Julie why, but she did anyway.

'I'm surprised at you, Rosemary.'

'So am I.'

'Because a living creature in pain could never be balanced against a watch or any other possession.'

'Funny how I knew you were going to say that.'

'I'm so worried. I've been having awful trouble getting Tasha to eat. I have to hand feed her a tablespoon at a time. Her stomach has shrunk to next to nothing. She's not usually this scared. The boat upset her. You see, Rosemary, she was beaten by local youths—'

'Hang on to her tightly. I don't want Tibby hurt.' They were walking towards the cottage when the cat shot out through the window and disappeared up a tree. Rosemary opened the door, went into the kitchen and took a packet of raw chicken out of the fridge. She tipped it on to Tibby's plate. The dog gulped it down. 'Take my advice,' Rosemary said, 'and put an ad in the lost-and-found column tomorrow. "Cross Husky Found Starving in London." Or something like that.'

'You're a genius. Thanks!'

'Come on. I'll take you home.'

Tasha got into the car without hesitation.

'Will she chew the seats?'

'No! Well, she didn't when I drove her back to Calais.'

While Rosemary took the long way round to Woodlands, Julie chatted about her trip and how she'd found Tasha. 'They were hoping to sell her to a zoo, but the locals were tormenting her. There's a lot of fear and hatred of wolves, most of it unjustified.'

'Come off it, Julie. A pack of dogs can kill a child, so you can imagine what a pack of wolves can do.'

'Wolves are gentle, sensitive creatures.'

'So's man until he gets a pack mentality.'

'You don't like her, do you?'

'I just think you've taken on a load of trouble.'

'She'll be worth it, I promise you.'

'We'll see. Listen, Julie. Be careful with that beast. Imagine what it would do to local chicken farmers. Lose it and you'll never see it again.'

'It's got a name and it's a she, not an it, Rosemary.'

'It's got genes, too and it's a wolf or maybe a cross-wolf, so remember that, no matter what you tell other people.'

Walter's creative staff were ticking away when Rosemary arrived late at the pub. There were rows of coded plastic mugs full of amber liquid lined up on the counter, and John was playing barman. They were all enthusing over the new blend they'd chosen and for once they'd all picked the same one, which was encouraging.

Rosemary tasted it and frowned. 'I can't understand what you see in it. It tastes like beer with sugar in it to me.'

'Don't worry it's the generation gap.' Fiona simpered.

Sam scowled at her. 'Have a pale ale to take the taste away, Rosemary,' she said.

'The Generation Gap.' That has possibilities.' Walter narrowed his eyes, grabbed his notebook and scribbled in it.

They sat in a circle and tossed out crazy ideas, laughing uproariously. Rosemary wondered if Sam had forgotten she was paying through the nose for this. 'Why don't we try hard to think of a really good name instead of this nonsense?' she asked.

'That's what we're doing, Rosemary,' Sam explained. 'Whatever's in our minds, we fling into the think-tank. Then we stir it and something positive usually emerges. What's uppermost in your mind, Rosemary?'

Rosemary blurted out, 'A grey wolf.'

'What?' Walter wheeled round.

'You said I should say whatever was in my head.'

'But what made you say grey wolf?'

'I just closed my eyes and saw the damned thing.'

'Exactly,' Walter said quietly. 'Pure inspiration! Grey Wolf it is.'

Chapter 15

The advertisement read:

FOR SALE – The Manorial Lordship of Bourne-on-Sea, as quoted in the Domesday Book survey of land and property holdings made in England in the eleventh century (the family line can be traced back to the tenth century and Lady Godiva). Title includes the coat of arms, a castle, mainly ruined, set in five acres of grazing land, with a small wood, fishing rights along the river, and medieval documents, whereabouts unknown.

Offers around two million dollars will be considered. For further information call Rosemary Santer, Secretary, Woodlands, Bourne-on-Sea, Kent, England.

Mendel Mandelbaum, a well-known San Francisco antique-map dealer, read the advertisement quite differently. To him, it went something like, 'Here's your chance to repay your grandson for all he's done for you.'

'I bet Richard hasn't seen this,' Mendel told his ginger cat, Ortelius, named after the sixteenth-century Dutch cartographer. He cut out the advertisement, pasted it on to a sheet of white paper, wrote, 'Thought you might like to see this, Regards, Mendel,' on the bottom and faxed it to Richard's hotel in Chester, England.

He went back to his reclining chair in front of the TV and sat through an entire performance of *The Marriage of Figaro*, without hearing a note. Instead he was ranging back in time and space. He'd married out of the faith but his wife, Juanita, had soon become tired of the dull life he offered and had left him, taking half of all he owned and leaving their two-year-old son, Jonathan, for Mendel to rear.

Jonathan had proved as wild as his mother. Mendel bailed him out of one scrape after the next, but after a run-in with the police after a car theft, he had eloped to Mexico with a half Cuban, half Irish girl of sixteen, where they both died in a car crash three years later as a result of his drunken driving.

Mendel had flown down for the funeral and met the girl's mother, who told him that her daughter had given birth to a son two years before. Mendel returned to San Francisco and persuaded a friend to look after his shop. He flew back and began his search. It took four months to find Richard, who had been placed in a home run by Dominican nuns, and another year plus a small fortune to establish guardianship and take Richard home.

Then he had embarked upon the hazardous business of rearing another young boy alone. He hoped he'd learned from his mistakes. He would be stricter and Richard would spend far more time on organised sport and healthy out-door living. But Richard made his own rules. You couldn't impose discipline on him. And it didn't take Mendel long to realise that he had a genius on his hands.

When Mendel went bankrupt after a fire destroyed his former premises. Richard rescued the business, and the two had been equal partners in this new shop ever since. Whenever Richard bought or sold a rare manuscript, the map shop shared the profits. It wasn't right, but Richard insisted. Not that it made much difference. It would all be his one day, yet it was only a hobby for him: Richard made a fortune in ways that Mendel had never fully understood.

He missed the boy. Richard came home regularly, but not often enough for Mendel's liking. Perhaps this advertisement would bring him back to the States. After all, he'd have to research the market and that would take a while. No doubt he'd find the document he was after and make another small fortune. He'd never known the boy to fail.

Jane Primpton, assistant to the curator of Chester Cathedral, and her unwanted American guest were sitting in the shadowy vaults bent over an old oak refectory table, lit by spotlights on movable frames.

Jane's thoughts were similar to Mendel's. Richard would make her an offer, which would be a fraction of what he'd finally realise, and more of Britain's cultural heritage would fly off to the States. Over her dead body!

Jane's dislike of Richard bordered on a passion. The sight of his curly black hair, his intensely blue eyes and his extravagant good looks provoked her into bouts of irritability and depression. Everything about him was larger than life – even his voice, deep, self-assured and American, reminded her of a Hollywood epic movie.

He was too young to be so sure of himself. Jane wasn't quite sure what it was that she found offensive. Perhaps it was his eyes: a glance from Richard left you feeling naked.

Now he was deep in concentration. He'd become known as the world's leading authority on medieval literature, a position to which she aspired. She had the qualifications, while Richard had only his wits. She watched him paging through the ancient documents as if he were skimming a paperback. No one could read ancient English that fast.

'You don't fool me, Richard,' she snarled, breaking a

long silence. 'Would you care to tell me what you're reading?'

'Why, Jane, I'm sorry. I didn't realise you were interested. It's quite remarkable. Roger of Wendover, thirteenth-century historian, attributes the following viewpoint to Leofric, Earl of Mercia, Lady Godiva's husband. I'll translate as I go: "The ancient Greeks and the coarser Romans viewed the nude human body as one of the highest expressions of the perfection of nature. Leofric, who had a remarkably liberated view for his time, considered that to present a well-formed nude body as an object of great beauty, even art, would be to offer a lesson of inestimable value to the simple peasants of Coventry, whose perceptions had never been enlightened to appreciate such perfection. Therefore he agreed to abolish taxes if Lady Godiva would go forth naked as an example of the perfection of God's work." Incredibly advanced thought considering England was in the grip of narrow, anti-female Church philosophy, don't you think, Jane? What are your views on nudity?'

'Miss Primpton to you,' she snapped.

Richard stood up abruptly, turned away and stretched. His large frame shook.

By the time he turned round Richard had himself under control. 'Miss Primpton, I'd like to make an offer for these documents. I can't give you the exact figure now, but it won't be less than a hundred thousand dollars.'

'Which you'll sell to an American museum for ten times that amount.'

'Could be,' Richard said. 'But I'd like to remind you that you didn't even know you had them.'

He had had the audacity to go over her head to view these documents. For some time he had been insisting that the vaults contained the work of a certain Henry Knighton, a Chester historian who had died in 1396. At his urging, tests had proved that some of the documents in the vault really were fourteenth century.

'I'm sure the curator would like these documents to remain in Britain.'

'Your prerogative.'

Jane tried to control her temper. She was chief assistant to the curator of the vaults, but he was merely an agent. He bought and sold on behalf of American museums and regularly made fortunes he didn't need.

'If that's the case,' he continued, 'I'm afraid I'll have to examine them here. It will take a few days.'

'I can't stop you, since you went over my head, but I'll have to stay here with you to guard them.'

Richard seemed to find her distrust more amusing than insulting.

'Jane – Miss Primpton, relax. If you've got to sit out the day in this dusty old place, I insist that first you come out for a short walk and a cup of coffee.'

She shook her head.

'Come on! It's summertime. There's a sparkle in the air. The sunshine will do you good. You're far too pale and serious. There's more to life than work.'

Jane gasped at his nerve. Moments later he took her arm and pulled her close beside him as they mounted the old stone steps and crossed the marble floor. Jane couldn't imagine why she was allowing herself to be bullied in this way.

Outside the cathedral, the morning sun filled the garden with early summer warmth, and lent a golden glow to the old granite blocks, the cobble stones and ivy.

Richard had discovered a café with a terrace overlooking a river where he took her and ordered coffee and cakes. He began to tell her about his lifelong passion for medieval history and how it had all begun in his grandfather's shop, among the maps, and of the extraordinary feats of would-be forgers who had tried to pull the wool over his grandfather's eyes but never succeeded.

After a while a glimmer of a smile played around Miss Primpton's pallid lips and then she laughed.

Watching her, Richard felt that it had been a worthwhile morning. He'd been proved right about the Knighton documents, which had brought him one step closer to his quest, it was a beautiful day, he'd fallen in love with Chester, and Miss Primpton had actually laughed.

He spent the rest of the day poring over the dusty papers, sorting, filing, notating, and Miss Primpton, who'd finally become Jane, took careful notes and proved an amazingly efficient assistant.

He arrived back at his hotel to find his grandfather's fax waiting for him. It was the most remarkable coincidence, but on second thoughts Richard decided it wasn't a coincidence at all. He'd found that deep concentration brought him that which he sought. Strange but true.

Richard called his grandfather that same evening.

'Unbelievable good fortune, Mendel. Well spotted. I'll be back in the States in a few days' time. Probably Wednesday. I'll stay awhile if that's okay with you.'

'This is your home, Richard. I haven't seen you for a couple of months. Too long, my boy.'

Early the following morning, Richard checked out of his hotel. He had to get moving. This advertisement had opened up all kinds of possibilities. It might be the most amazing piece of luck ever to come his way.

Chapter 16

Someone was inside his cottage. John had just come back from the pub and he hung around outside the front door. Then he walked in.

'Who's there?'

A tall figure unfolded from the armchair. It was Hans Kupi, just as he'd known it would be. Snappy dresser, John thought, noting the Armani shirt, the Dior tie and the expensive shoes. Couldn't do much about his nark's face, though, could he?

'What the fuck are you doing here? How did you get in?'

Kupi shrugged. 'Easy! You're working for me, John. Surely you know that. Or did you think all that cash was a hand-out?'

John began to sweat. 'Never for moment, but that doesn't give you the right to break into my house,' he growled. He'd give back Kupi's money if he could, but he had the impression that wouldn't help. They'd hooked him.

'D'you call this a house? A shack's a better description. Given time, you can have the best, but you must know which side you're on. How come you opposed the takeover bid?' Kupi turned to John's sideboard and poured himself a Scotch. 'What'll you have?' he asked.

'D'you really think you've bought me, body and soul, for a lousy ten grand? I persuaded the old man to stock up with stout, didn't I? That was the deal,' John remonstrated, as he poured himself a drink.

'Perhaps you think Woodlands will last for ever? I've got news for you. It's on the slippery slope. Only I can bail you out. Why didn't you answer the phone last night and the night before and last week? You've been avoiding me.'

'True, I have. They're a great family. I'm fond of them. And they've been good to me.'

'How will they feel when they learn where the deposit came from for your new car? Or how you altered your report sheets about latest tastes in beer?'

'Why, you bastard!' John lurched forward and found himself lying, winded, on the floor. He wasn't sure what had happened. He struggled to his feet, breathing heavily.

'Don't try it again, John. I might have to hurt you.' Kupi sat down in an easy chair. He leaned back, put his hands behind his head and stretched out his legs. 'When you took the money you joined the comrades. Loyalty is all we ask. Once you're in you can never get out, and you, John, are in. You're one of us. I have big plans for you. You own shares in Woodlands, but Woodlands is going to expand. It will be legit. We'll handle all the British exports to Russia and Eastern Europe. Later we'll take in Europe, too. I'll make you a rich man.'

'Who are you? What d'you mean, "the comrades"?'

'Russian-based organised networks. We tried to get into Britain in 'ninety-four, but we were too foreign and that went against us. The bloody British distillers called in Scotland Yard. You, on the other hand, are British born and bred. They'll think you own Woodlands and you will own a part of it. You'll have a respectable base from which to launch a British export drive. Furthermore, they can't deport you.'

'If it's so legit, how come they called in Scotland Yard?'

'Two reasons. An unfortunate bomb explosion in Russia killed one of the guys who tried to sidetrack our service, and then one of them discovered that we control the railways in Russia.'

'But you're Czech.'

'International, my friend. After all, you're British.'

John searched for an escape route, but it seemed there was none.

'So what do you want me to do?'

'How long will that stout last?'

'Six weeks.'

'And I need some figures. Here's a list of what I want. You've got two days.'

'What's it worth?'

'Same as last time.'

A cheap plastic briefcase lay beside his Scotch bottle.

Chapter 17

Rosemary was filled with pride as she watched Sam cope with their problems over the next few weeks. She employed a new plant manager, Ted Holmes, a quiet, self-effacing and efficient man. She stood over John every morning and went through his sales figures. 'This isn't good enough,' Rosemary heard her say quietly. 'We used to sell over three thousand barrels a month. We must meet our target, which is half of that for the time being. The blend's a good one, everyone liked it, so now it's up to you. The pubs must sell more. You have your daily quota of Grey Wolf to move and God help you – and us – if you don't make your target.'

When it was time for Trevor to come home the family converted his study into a bed-sitter.

'Don't think you're coming back to take over,' Sam told him firmly as she pushed his wheelchair towards the car, which Julie had driven up to the door.

'Don't fuss,' was all he said.

By ten she was back in the office. She dictated a few letters and then glanced out of the office window.

'I don't believe it!' she yelled. 'Of all the . . . Just look at him, Rosemary! He's hobbling round the lawn, with a walking-stick. Perhaps you should join him. Just in case he falls or something.'

'Sam, he isn't going to fall and I'm afraid he'd take it as an insult. He doesn't need a nursemaid.'

Rosemary was lonely. Working with Sam was exhilarating, but she missed her chats with Trevor and the friendship they had built up over the years. She hardly ever had time to visit him. She said, 'I've changed my mind. I'll tell him I want to talk about the beer festival.'

Sam gave her a sidelong glance. She could see how much Rosemary wanted to be with him.

She could get on with planning the beer festival and pop concert to launch the Grey Wolf blend. The electricians had been working around the ruin for days laying cables and fixing lights; St John's Ambulance Brigade were setting up a first-aid post, the village shop would put up a kiosk to sell refreshments. She'd organised a lost-child centre, a team of women to sit there, and a lost-dog van. Toilets had been discreetly sited among the trees and there were rubbish bins all over the place. Shireen, dressed as a gypsy, was going to tell fortunes, and there would be an oompah band, a beauty contest and the loan of funfair equipment. She still had to find prizes for winners of the various silly competitions.

Rosemary had found some Robin Hood outfits in a theatrical costume shop and hired them. They fitted so well with Woodlands' image, but Sam knew she didn't look good in hers. Julie had taken one look and shrieked with laughter, flatly refusing even to try hers on. Sam sighed. It didn't matter what she looked like, she decided. It was the overall image that counted.

The puppet show, the pride of the drama group every Christmas, would do the usual Robin Hood play, plus a new skit Rosemary had written.

Later that day, when Sam opened the mail, something fluttered out of an envelope on to the floor. She stooped to pick it up. It was a bank draft for twenty thousand dollars and a letter:

Dear Sir, On behalf of my client, Mendel Mandelbaum,
Rare Maps, Inc., this check for twenty thousand dollars
is tendered to you to purchase an option on your manorial
lordship and accompanying rights, as advertised for sale
in the various media. My client is unable to visit
Britain for a while, but he has tendered this cheque
to show his interest in purchasing the title for the
amount stipulated by yourselves. If you are prepared
to grant him a two-month option on the title for twenty
thousand dollars, kindly advise us directly and our client
will make arrangements to visit you as soon as he can.
Yours sincerely . . .

Below was an indecipherable signature on behalf of
Redgrove, Russel and Rose.

Sam raced into Rosemary's office. 'It worked, it worked,
it worked!' she yelled, throwing herself at Rosemary and
hugging her hard. 'We could have the cash in three
weeks' time.'

'We'll be lucky. He'll probably want to pay in instalments.'

'Be positive, Rosemary. Where's Julie?'

Rosemary frowned. 'Tasha's gone missing and she's out
looking for her.'

'We should have kept the bloody animal in a cage. I
should have insisted.'

The two women stared at each other uneasily.

'Probably be okay,' Rosemary muttered. At that moment
two shots rang out from about a mile up the road followed
by four more in rapid succession.

'Now what the . . . ?' Sam said softly.

They moved to the window and stared out in time to
see a white streak shoot past on the way home.

'I'll go back and lock it in the barn until Julie gets back,'
said Rosemary.

She ran all the way to the house and found Helen bending over Tasha, who was lying prone, panting heavily with a deep red blood stain over her chest. 'Oh, my God. She's been shot,' Rosemary gasped.

'I don't think so,' Helen retorted. 'If I were you, I'd wash that dog fast.' She stalked off, muttering to herself.

Rosemary ran her hands over the thick silky hair but could find no wounds. She dragged the dog to the vegetable patch, tied it up and put the hosepipe on it. Tasha stood still, trembling, until she was washed clean. Embedded in her deep fur were three long crimson feathers.

God, she thought, nagged by guilt, I wonder what parrots are worth? And didn't Jeff have some emus and lories?

Rosemary made a deep hole with a trowel, stabbing the ground to let off steam. It wasn't enough to love every one of this headstrong family. You had to become an accessory to their madness, too. She buried the evidence and led Tasha to the barn.

Chapter 18

It was the day before the concert and festival. After weeks of preparation and advertising, Woodlands and the castle grounds looked chaotic. Men were hammering up a platform for dancing and the makeshift stage. Multi-coloured marquees were springing up like toadstools and the funfair was being assembled.

Everyone was having a good time except Sam and Rosemary: Matthew Dearlove wanted the overdraft reduced immediately, which was impossible.

'Perhaps the festival will bring in enough to cover the shortfall,' Rosemary said hopefully. She was poring through their list of debtors when the telephone rang.

It was Tom Bowles, the farm manager. 'There's a trespasser wearing a bloody great DARE sign taking photographs of the pigs.'

'What's DARE?'

'One of these anti-cruelty organisations run by women who should have something better to do with their time.'

'Why don't you deal with it, Bowles? I'm busy.'

'It's on your property. You sort it.' He rang off.

Sam called Julie. There's a man from some anti-cruelty group photographing the pigs,' she said. 'Can you pop over and find out what's going on?'

Martin Luther Keyes crouched at the side of a pig-sty where a young boar stood immobile in his wooden cage. He could sit and he could stand, but that was all. His energy went into making bacon, not into stretching his limbs or walking. There was a hint of madness in the way he rolled his eyes and bared his teeth. Luther photographed the pig from every angle and moved on. In the next sty, twelve young Landrace piglets were climbing over each other, noisily searching for their mother.

It was then that a feminine voice said just behind him, 'Hello! You're trespassing. Are you lost?'

'No. I'm exactly where I want to be.'

'Who said you could disturb the pigs?'

'They are disturbed. They've lost their mother.'

'Farming's cruel, isn't it? I've been nagging Gramps to give up animals and stick to hops. He's keen to do that, but Tom Bowles, his manager, has a share of the piggery. Tom set the whole thing up, and he's ridiculously proud of his pigs. I hate seeing them kept like this, but I specially hate it when they go to the abattoir.'

Luther didn't bother to turn his head as he said, 'You're a vegetarian, then?'

There was no answer.

He stood up and looked round. Her eyes were a sort of glittering transparent blue, like the colour of hazy summer skies, her skin was pearly, and her hair had a silvery lightness. It framed her pale face and fell over her bare shoulders.

Luther couldn't think of anything to say. He only knew that his blood was pounding round his body leaving him light-headed.

'Naturally I'm a vegetarian,' she said. 'Aren't you?'

'My name is Martin Luther Keyes. I'm here on behalf of DARE, which stands for the Domestic Animal Rescue Effort. We include every working and farm animal in our brief. Your farm manager told me to get lost, but I'm afraid I ignored him.'

'Bowles just called my sister so I came down to see what it's all about. She's busy and Gramps, who owns the farm, has just come out of hospital. I'm Julie.'

'Call me Luther.' He shook her hand.

She pushed back her hair and said, 'Okay, Luther. I'll show you round the pig-sties, if you can bear it. Maybe you'll tell me about yourself and your ideas while we go.'

She set off at a fast pace, past rows of concrete prisons, her hairy white dog loping beside her. Luther followed behind, trying to compose a CV that would impress her. Instead he decided to stick to the bare facts. 'I'm a lawyer, Julie, and I specialise in labour rights. I set up my own practice a year back, and I have free premises in my uncle's building. I'm a consultant to a couple of unions but I could do with more work. A few months ago an animal-rights group contacted me with a proposition. They need a part-time consultant to help publicise their cause and to defend any who are injured in the line of duty – by horses in demos against fox-hunting, that sort of thing. Look at that sow in labour there. She can't move around, she never will. She's suffering from acute depression and hardly anyone cares. Those who do are labelled freaks.

'If the world is to have a new awareness of animal rights, it'll start here in Britain. The caring revolution is already underway. More and more young people *care*. Have you any idea how exciting it is to be a part of this new thought revolution. It must be something like being in Britain when they signed the *Magna Carta*.'

He stared at the dog sloping along beside her on a leash. Was it a dog? It looked like a wolf or a cross-wolf.

'That's a beautiful animal,' he said.

'She's a husky. Her name's Tasha.'

He stretched out his hand towards the creature.

'Oh, no.' She caught his hand and hung on to it. 'She's

so timid, she might bite. I'm taking her around everywhere so that she realises that not everyone wants to hurt her.'

'You two look right together. But she's been hurt often, burned, by the look of things. And look at her neck. Is that what they do to dogs in Siberia?'

Now she looked puzzled, shocked and scared all at the same time. It had been a long shot, Luther thought, and it had hit home. He'd heard about the anti-cruelty team that had toured Siberia and she must have been there.

And you look hurt, too, Julie, he thought.

He wasn't surprised when the dog nuzzled his hand, but she was. Animals liked him, they always had.

'You're the first person Tasha's made friends with. Look at that.' She relaxed visibly.

So you'd trust her judgement before you'd trust your own, Luther thought. He ran his hands over the dog's haunches, feeling the scars, the burns, the sinuous strength of her limbs, and the rough lumps around her neck where she'd been hurt. 'Be careful with her,' he said. 'If she runs off, you might never see her again. She'd kill sheep and sooner or later she'd be shot.'

Her eyes were glittering with dismay.

'I must be going. Nice to meet you. Thanks for all the help. Here's my card.' He shook her hand and left.

Julie watched him striding down the farm track towards his car. His huge oriental eyes had reminded her of the statues in ancient Egyptian tombs. And Tasha had liked him. She'd better go and tell Sam what had happened.

Sam was looking harassed. 'This man, is he going to make trouble for us?'

'Probably. And we deserve it.'

Julie crouched on the floor and flung her arms around Tasha. 'When I saw Tasha in that tiny cage, so small she couldn't move, I thought, what sort of monsters can treat an animal so cruelly? But we're guilty, too. Can't you see that? We're treating the pigs just like they treated Tasha.'

She burst into tears and then, feeling ultra-foolish, she fled.

Chapter 19

Woodlands resembled a battlefield. The car park was jam-packed and still more cars were arriving, plus motor-bikes and coaches full of Dehlia's fans. Music was blaring from half a dozen places at once and the loudspeakers were crackling and whistling.

'Oh what *have* I done?' Sam moaned to herself. Feeling absurd in her forester's outfit, she watched Dehlia's advance guard of technicians in their multi-coloured trucks, bumping over the grassy turf leaving long skid marks. They parked behind the castle and minutes later were swarming over the ruins, with scaffolding and miles of electrical cable.

Dehlia was scheduled to start singing at ten, but mean-time there was plenty of entertainment: the fortune teller – Shireen – roller-blading, a beauty contest, Maypole danc-ing, and traditional sports organised by the Caledonian Society. John was in charge of the beer-tasting, and Steve, the vet, was supervising parking. Greg, Walter and the agency team were going to judge the competitions.

The villagers had turned out in force to run the stalls. They were vying with each other to tempt city youths to try their luck, but the visitors preferred the beer garden, run by Jim from the Castle Arms.

'Just drink!' Sam murmured. 'Drink all our Grey Wolf stocks.'

She looked up and scanned the noon sky. It was too good to be true: not a sign of a wispy cloud, just a vast expanse of azure blue and it was so hot. Thirsty weather. Would it last? It had to.

Rosemary was perched on top of a ladder, hammering the last piece of canvas over the puppets' stage. Jeff Brink was watching her. She called, 'Hi, Sam. Meet Jeff, my co-star. Bet you didn't know he could sing. Don't go away. Stay and watch.'

Eventually someone switched on the music and the strains of *When The Saints Come Marching In* sounded tinny from behind the curtain.

Sam had always loved puppet shows. She watched enthralled, as the curtains drew back and a puppet cowboy strutted on to the small stage, complete with tiny cameras slung around his neck, a stetson thrust on his head and large leather boots with spurs. The second puppet, who scampered on-stage in jeans and T-shirt, wiggling her hips and fluttering her eyelashes, made Sam gasp. She was all tits, with an exaggerated backside, a wasp waist, huge brown eyes, and eyelashes like a horse's tail. Surely not a caricature of her? Without meaning to she pulled her jerkin down hard over her behind. It wasn't that large, was it?

The cowboy turned to the audience and burst into song in time to the music: *'What fun it is to be a lord, It shows how much I can afford, I've a coat of arms and a title, And now I'm looking for a broad.'*

'Quaint, but I don't get the joke,' a deep American voice said, right behind Sam. 'Clearly everyone else does.'

She turned swiftly. It couldn't be— She flushed. No, he wasn't due here for a couple of weeks.

'Name's Richard,' he said. 'I was passing by and I heard the music.'

Sam sighed with relief and grinned. 'Oh, hi. I'm Sam.

Short for Samantha. For a moment I thought— Well, it doesn't matter.'

'Can I invite you for a beer?' he said. 'I hate drinking alone.'

'Why not? As long as you choose the right brand.'

'Which is?'

'Woodlands. That's our beer, but we invited a few competitors along.'

Sam squinted up at him, but he was standing against the sun. He took her arm and set off towards the flags, in long, loping strides, and she saw that he was tall, in his mid- to late-twenties with dark curly hair. There was something very likeable about the way his eyes crinkled up when he smiled.

'The famous British wit. Not subtle but easily recognisable as funny, consequently one laughs. But the joke escaped me. Perhaps you could explain why everyone was laughing.'

They had arrived at the refreshments tent.

'Two please,' Sam called to Jim, as she led the way to a table under the awning. 'We're raising funds to launch several new blends and I hit on the idea of selling our title. Well, it's not much of a title. Once it meant being the local squire, but nowadays it means nothing.'

'You mean you're selling something worthless.'

'Well, that depends,' Sam said. 'We reckoned that a Texan oil billionaire or someone who'd risen up from nothing might want a title. Even this title,' she finished off, feeling foolish. 'Nowadays titles are selling like hot cakes.'

'I see. Well, they can take it or leave it, can't they?'

'Of course. Someone with a poor self-image might pay a fortune for it. That's why it was funny. They've been laying bets down the pub on who exactly will pitch. Hot favourite is the oil billionaire with the stetson hat, cameras and spurs.'

'Ah, now I get it. And the girl?'

Sam flushed heavily. 'I think it was supposed to be me. D'you think I look like that?'

'And is your acute embarrassment because you're the butt of their jokes?'

'Perhaps just because of the butt,' she said.

When he smiled he seemed to become someone altogether different. His blue eyes twinkled, crowsfeet crinkled and his face lit up.

Sam glanced at her watch. It was almost two thirty. Time to go. Suddenly she was very conscious of how absurd she looked in this forester's outfit. Funny how it had seemed okay this morning. She should have worn her customary jeans and T-shirt, not this garish green and gold costume that hardly covered her backside. She stood up. 'I'm so sorry, but I've got to go. Nice meeting you. Perhaps catch you later?' She hurried towards the stage, negotiated the scaffold's open steps and grabbed the microphone. The tall American, she saw, was loitering by the marquee.

A starter's pistol cracked a shot. Homing pigeons and balloons soared up as Sam said, 'I declare the Grey Wolf beer festival well and truly open. Have fun, everyone.'

She moved to her seat: the beauty contest was about to start and she had to help with the judging. Glancing round she saw Greg mounting the steps. Cool, she thought, watching the graceful way he moved. He had the most amazing deep brown eyes and he always looked slightly amused. She couldn't help noticing the way his muscles rippled under his thin, bottle green silk shirt. Pretty good neck too. He sat down beside her and gave her his intimate smile. Fiona, Walter, and Dave from the agency would sit next to him, but where were they?

God it was hot. Her head began pounding. She shouldn't have drunk that beer on such a hot afternoon. Julie could swig down gallons and never get a headache.

She stole a glance down towards the American. He seemed to be having a great time with Julie.

'You're very engrossed, Sam? What's caught your interest?'

Sam turned to Walter. 'I was thinking that we should have used Julie's dog for the labels. It looks like a wolf, don't you think?'

'But surely it is a wolf. I've never seen a dog with eyes and teeth like that.'

'Oh, no,' Rosemary said, from behind them. 'It's a new breed. You must have heard about the expedition that went up Mount Everest looking for the Yeti? They were unsuccessful, but they brought back the little known Tashkent hound. Beautiful, isn't it?'

'Really? Lady Jane has a couple. I spent last weekend at her country home. Lovely woman, lovely dogs, too, but they cost a packet.'

What a nerd! How had she ever screwed him? She turned away and found herself staring into Greg's amused brown eyes. 'That'll keep the wolf from the door,' he said, in his sexy Czech accent. He winked and she grinned back. He really was a great guy. She decided to flirt with him to take her mind off Richard.

Chapter 20

The beauty contestants were filing on to the stage in their bikinis and high-heeled shoes looking embarrassed but determined. They were all local girls and Sam knew some of them by sight, but they'd battle to find a winner today.

The vicar, who was sitting next to Walter, turned bright pink as the first girl Maria, Paul's daughter, flashed him a smile and wiggled her hips. He was a shy, kind man who seemed out of touch with the times. He took out a handkerchief and mopped his face.

Greg muttered, 'I've picked the winner of the booby prize. The girl over there with the bow legs.'

Sam leaped to Agatha's defence. 'She's never short of male admirers and she's our dressage champion.'

'Wow! Take a look at that!' Walter seemed stunned.

Sam looked up into eyes of the dreamiest blue, set off by long, wavy, deep red hair. The girl offered a sultry smile and swayed after the others.

'She's my choice.' Walter leaned back and closed his eyes.

Sam nudged him with her elbow. 'We also have to choose the runners-up. You can't relax yet.'

'What exactly are you up to, Sam?' The vicar's voice was mildly critical. 'Why are we enduring all this?'

'To raise some cash.'

'To launch our new blend of beer.' Rosemary's sharp reproof cut in on them.

'If you want to raise funds I'm the person you should be talking to, Sam.' Greg took a card out of his pocket. It read, 'G. Selo & Co., Importers–Exporters,' with an address in Prague.

Looking at Greg brought butterflies to her stomach and an ache into her groin, but Sam made an effort to keep their conversation impersonal. 'So tell me about your business, Greg.'

'I'm solvent. Cash on delivery, that's my motto. That's what you want to know, isn't it? There's a huge market for beer in Eastern Europe, but not your light blends. Strong dark ale.'

'I must admit cash sales are vital at present.' She laughed softly, trying to disguise her desperation. 'You're rather young to be a self-made man,' she probed. 'It must have been hard to get started.'

'It's always hard to get started and it remains hard. You're finding that out, I assume?' He laughed – a trifle bitterly, Sam thought. 'Hey, she's not bad.' He pointed at Maria, who was wearing a fetching black sheath.

'Haven't you met Maria yet?'

'Maybe. She looks different now. You really want the story of my life, Sam?'

'I'm interested.'

'Okay, I began as a lorry driver and eventually I made enough to buy my own truck. It took me a couple of years, but after that I was able to shift my own produce around while taking on other consignments. I began to build my capital and my contacts. Slowly I made enough to start a wholesale business, but most of my bread and butter comes from selling strong beer in Russia.'

Strong beer! Sam made an effort to stop her voice from croaking. She had ten thousand barrels of it languishing on the shelves in the warehouse and it would all be obsolete in six weeks' time. 'Perhaps we should talk,' she said.

The girls were swaying past in ballgowns now, their faces pink and sweaty in the sun. By the time they had finished, Greg had agreed to take their entire stocks of stout, at a 20 per cent discount, cash on delivery; he'd been appointed their agent for Eastern Europe, and he knew almost as much about her marketing plans as she did, but she had to admit that she still didn't know much about him.

The semi-finalists minced back in their bikinis.

The beer and the heat were making her drowsy. Suddenly she jerked awake. What was Greg saying?

'Say yes, come on,' he urged. 'We have a great many beer festivals in Pilsen. Bring your pure ale and your new blends and you'll be amazed at the orders you'll pick up. Believe me, Sam, you have to sell outside Britain. Export! That's the only way you'll survive. There's a beer festival coming up in three weeks' time. I'll handle the red tape. Just say Woodlands will be there.'

The idea intrigued Sam. Hemzo had said that Balaton's couldn't fulfil local demand. Why shouldn't she go after a share of that lucrative market?

'I'll try, Greg.'

'You don't have a thing to worry about, Sam. I'll pay up front all along the line. With your brewing capacity and my markets we can both make a profit. For starters I'd like to place a regular order for ten thousand barrels of stout each month. I'll confirm this in writing.'

Why not? They could do it. It would account for a quarter of their production capacity, but at least they'd have this regular order while she revamped the pubs and their blends. She did a quick calculation. She'd still be running at a loss, but not much of one.

'It's a deal!' She thrust out her hand. His grasp felt like an electric shock.

'I'm leaving for Prague later today. My lawyer will deliver a cheque first thing in the morning and my driver will pick up the beer. We don't have much time to sell it. I'll liaise with your John Carvossah. When I return we can get down to details. Meantime, shall I book you a stall at Pilsen?'

Sam swept aside her doubts. 'Sure. And I'll bring along some other Kent brewers. I'm sure they'd be interested.'

'Look, this is going on longer than I'd intended. Would you forgive me for leaving before the end. My vote goes to Maria.' Greg bowed slightly and left.

'Was that for real?' she muttered, as John took Greg's seat. 'I sold him the stout with a twenty per cent discount. I'd just about given up on it. How long has he got before it's spoiled?'

'A month at the most.'

''So I was right to give him a discount?'

'Yes! Think yourself lucky to move it. I'd given up hope.'

When John turned towards her she saw guilt written all over his face. She put her hand on his shoulder and squeezed gently.

'The stout wasn't your fault, John. Don't look so guilty.'

'Of course I'm guilty. I should have persuaded Trevor he was wrong, but at the time . . . Anyway, he'll make a slight profit on it.'

Hadn't Rosemary said that the stout had been John's idea? Feeling vaguely disturbed, Sam tried to get to grips with the judging.

Chapter 21

Sam heard her grandfather's walking-stick tapping on the wooden platform and jumped up beaming. 'Well done. You made it all this way. Does it hurt much?'

'Not as much as one would think.' John stood up, but Trevor waved him back. 'I'll sit here next to Rosemary.' He greeted the vicar and sat down. 'Listen to this, Sam.' He leaned over her shoulder. 'Mandelbaum's here. He's serious about buying the title, but he wants time to do some research before signing on the dotted line.'

'What sort of research?' she asked.

'He's interested in our family history.'

'Why should he be? Buying the title doesn't make him one of us.'

'True. But he's a personable young man and he seems to be hung up on the Lady Godiva story. His name's Richard. Mendel is his grandfather. He wants to go through the archives. I told him to make himself at home in the library. He's bringing a builder to survey the castle with a view to restoring it.'

'Hope he freezes to death there.' Bastard, she thought. He'd been laughing at her.

Trevor scanned her face. 'Have you changed your mind about selling the title, Sam? Something seems to be bothering you.'

'I met him earlier. He doesn't seem the type to want a title. What's he after, I wonder?'

'Does it matter as long as he pays?' Rosemary cut in.

'You wanted to sell the title and now you have a candidate. I can't see what's bugging you.'

'You should have sold it leasehold,' Walter called out.

'How d'you know about it?'

'The entire village knows. Rosemary's been giving lessons in social etiquette. How to address him, that sort of thing. She's taught the drum majorettes how to curtsy.'

Rosemary flushed heavily. 'Look here, Sam, he's after the glamour of a title. There isn't much with yours so I thought we should supply some.'

Trevor sensed her embarrassment and rushed to her support. 'Rosemary, your heart's in the right place. It is a little strange, though. One wouldn't think a man like Richard would want a title, but ... perhaps he craves personal recognition. Why not let him present the prizes? That might prove an excellent opportunity to show him the ropes. I'm sure you'll be up to coaching him, Sam.'

Trevor levered himself to his feet.

'Where're you going, Gramps?'

'Now, now, Sam. Don't start acting like your grandmother. I'm quite all right.'

'It's just that I worry about you.'

'My dear, you were reared with a great deal of freedom and you must extend the same courtesy to others.' Suddenly his keen brown eyes were flashing fire and his lips were folded into an obstinate straight line.

'Just don't overdo it,' Sam snarled. Clearly it was not her day. She took a deep breath and made a mighty effort to pull herself together. 'Okay, I'll go and find that supercilious idiot.'

'What about helping to pick the winners?' Walter sounded irritable. The heat was getting to him. He'd taken off his checked jacket and there was a big damp patch on the back of his black and white striped shirt, while his bow-tie was visibly wilting.

'You do it. I trust your judgement.'

Sam stood up and looked around. It wasn't hard to pick out Richard because he was taller than everyone else. He was striding towards the beer garden, looking irritable. As he passed she saw some of the locals take off their hats. Then Jennifer, their local florist, dropped a curtsy.

'Oh, Rosemary! What *have* you done?' she muttered.

'Don't you think this is taking the joke a bit far?' Richard asked mildly, when she caught up with him. 'Or is this part of your marketing ploy? If so, you can call off your slobbering dogs.'

'How dare you suggest that I—'

'Was I suggesting? I don't think so. I was stating outright that you and yours are perpetrating a fraud by giving a completely false impression of what the title means.'

Now he was calling her a cheat. 'The benefits were clearly listed in the advertisements and in my letter to you,' she said, hotly.

'You don't look like a con, Miss Rosslyn, but you are. Someone like you should know better. You're pandering to the basest of human weaknesses – man's desire to be better than his peers. And in any case why are you selling it? For the money?'

'Of course for the money. And clearly you have more money than sense. I feel sorry for you. I'd hate to have to purchase my self-image.'

'Do you or don't you want to sell the goddamned title and everything that goes with it?'

'First tell me why you're buying it.'

'*If* I buy it.'

'Why can't you answer a direct question?'

'Why do you want to know?'

'D'you always answer questions with questions? I want to know because you simply aren't the type. Anyway, Gramps thought you might like to award the prizes.'

'I have no obligation to tell you a damn thing, Miss Rosslyn, and I certainly won't be giving the prizes. I haven't bought the title yet. I'm going. I may or may not see you around, that's if I don't get snarled up with Her Majesty.'

Sam watched him stride away, shoulders hunched, and had the strangest feeling of having known him for ever. She made a heroic effort to push Richard out of her mind.

It was time for the final parade and prize-giving. As Sam reached her seat a crowd was gathering around the stage and the first of the girls was emerging from the changing tent. They lined up smiling, but looking anxious. The process of elimination seemed cruel to Sam. She wondered how the girls kept smiling as they left the platform. Eventually the winners were announced and Sam handed over the trophy to the winner and the prizes to the runners-up. 'Thank God that's over.' She groaned.

Then she shook herself and stretched. She got up and walked over to the refreshment tent, took a plate of snacks and a beer, then settled herself in a deck-chair to watch the dancing. Soon she succumbed to the lullaby of bees buzzing, insects humming and music.

It was hot under the striped tent and even hotter under the layered gypsy skirt and blouse with the tight velvet jacket. Worst of all was the veil.

The proverbial tall, dark man appeared framed in the opening.

'Cross my palm with silver, good sir,' Shireen intoned.

'Come off it, Shireen.'

'Go on, John It's for charity. Put something in the box.'

The sight of him sent her blood racing. Strange how only he could do this to her. The sight of him never failed to overwhelm her. He knew. His lazy glance scanned her hardening nipples, her flushed cheeks and burning lips.

'Where can we go?'

She didn't answer. Instead she stood up, closed the tent flap and tied it firmly.

She pulled off her skirt, her panties, and began to unbutton her blouse.

'I love you,' he said. 'Surely you understand it's not just sex.'

'What else is there?'

'Bitch!'

'Do you want to or not?'

'I want to. Please, please love me.'

John was always pleading for love. He stood up and unfastened his pants, but she pushed him back on the chair and straddled him, shifting her hips, until he sank deeply into her. She sighed softly and gave herself up to the sensations of the here and now, each more exquisite than the last.

'Talk,' she heard him say hoarsely. 'You're supposed to be telling my fortune.'

'Forget love,' she murmured. 'Take each moment as it comes and give it your best, whatever you're doing. Don't stop. Just don't stop.'

Her body was gripped with tension. She was stiffening, unable to move or speak, poised in that last moment of anticipation as her buttocks and stomach gripped hard, and her vagina closed around John like a vice. He clapped his right hand firmly over her mouth while his left pulled her buttocks hard on to him. She wanted to scream, but she couldn't. She writhed, and mumbled and bit his hand hard.

Now she was crying. 'Oh, God. Oh, God. Three bloody long years and I'd forgotten what it's like. Oh, John, that was so good. Oh, my God! So wonderful.'

Moments later he came. 'Now what? he said roughly. 'I want to know what's going on.'

She put on her clothes and picked up the cards. 'You love someone who can't love. If she could feel a fraction of what you feel, she would elope with you tonight. But she can't. Besides, her father has betrothed her to a rich old man she's never even seen. Since she can't love, she might as well have the benefit of a strong family relationship: children, step-children, and the social position brought by her father's wealth. She's decided to accept her fate.'

'And being an actress. What happened to that?'

'This girl . . . well, she has talent, but she'll be able to use it to pretend that she's happy.'

Suddenly she burst into tears, and John, who was kind, couldn't bear to see her so unhappy. 'Listen, the dancing's started. Come and dance with me,' he urged her. 'I'll work something out, I promise you.'

'If only you could,' she answered, as she unfastened the tent flap.

Sam heard angry shouts. Jumping up she saw Shireen being pushed off the dais by her father. She watched in shock as John swung a punch at Shun Desai, who ducked and kicked John's feet from under him.

Suddenly Sam was spurred into action. 'Mr Desai. Mr Desai!' She ran across the field. 'I'd like to remind you that Shireen is twenty-three. Shireen! Come and have a drink with me. I haven't seen you all day.'

'Sam. My dear Sam.' Desai paused as if lost for words.

'When was I Uncle Shun? It seems only the other day. Shireen and you grew up together, but our ways are different. I'm not kidnapping Shireen but she's engaged to be married. Dancing with another man is quite forbidden. And Western dancing is unseemly. As for John Carvossah, I have no intention of allowing that alcoholic to ruin her life more than he already has. So, if you'll excuse us . . .'

'Shireen! Stand up for yourself,' Sam called, but Shireen kept walking to the car. She got in and didn't look round as they drove away.

Sam walked back to her chair and sat down. John had disappeared and there was no sign of Rosemary. She tried to get a grip on normality. The day had been a success, hadn't it? Thousands of people had bought their new blend and they seemed to like it. She'd sold the stout to Greg, which was a major coup, and she might have found a really good export market. So why did she feel as if the bottom had dropped out of her world?

Chapter 22

It was midnight and stiflingly warm, which was just as well for the kids bedding down near the old castle, Luther thought. Jesus! What a mess. It'd take an army to clean up the rubbish. Dehlia was on her last song and those who were trying to beat the traffic jam were already bottlenecked at the gates. The police were having a hard time.

There were thousands of spectators and some were stoned. Plenty of toughs here, too. Luther was intent on keeping out of trouble, but if trouble was forced upon him he would deal with it in a way that caused the least damage. Keeping to the edge of the crowd, he searched around the groups sprawled over the field for Julie. He knew he was being a fool – she wasn't for him – but a compulsion stronger than his intellect had led him here.

As Dehlia reached a crescendo, he saw Julie wandering at the edge of the trees. She looked unbelievably lovely in a flowing, ankle-length white dress. Her hair hung loose round her shoulders. Jesus, she was lovely. Unreal!

Oh, Luther, she doesn't want to know you. But his legs led him on towards her. Then he saw that she was stoned and stopped. Heavy-lidded and deathly pale, she was swaying to the music. Better keep an eye on her, he thought.

Unaware of Luther's surveillance, Julie was surging on a tide of happiness. A tall man was leaning over her. She gazed up at his pale, angular face. He was naked from the waist up, and he crouched beside her. 'You're flying, sister. Come over and meet my mates. You'll fly higher with us. Promise. Who are you?'

'Does it matter?'

'So what shall I call you?'

'Julie.'

'Have a snort, Julie. It's great stuff.'

'No, I don't do that.' She smiled.

'You'll never know if you don't try. Never know what music can sound like. Never know how the trees really are. Come on, I'll help you. Just breathe in deeply, then wait for the world to unravel itself.'

'Why not?' She leaned back and closed her eyes.

Fragments of reality were shifting and presenting themselves to her like moving patterns in a kaleidoscope. There was a man, huge and black, painted on canvas in geometric shapes, with agate eyes that sparkled and changed. He stepped out of the canvas and grabbed her hand, pulling her up into the deep, dark African sky. The agony of tribal wars. She saw how the white tribe came and conquered and in turn were defeated. She saw her parents' blood seeping into the black soil.

To Luther, the sight of Julie, stoned and helpless, was agonising, yet he held back. He had to know: just how far would she go?

'Hell, man! This is the twentieth century and the virgin is extinct.' Now she was crying and six scruffy bikers were trying to make her dance.

Luther strolled over. 'Hey there. She's my friend. She's coming with me.'

Insults fell around him like raindrops, but he was more worried about the spanners being dug out of pockets.

Luther moved in fast before they had a chance to get their wits together. Martial arts was his hobby. It was over in seconds. He grabbed the one who seemed to be conscious. 'What did you give her?'

'Hell, man. Ecstasy, maybe. Bit of coke, maybe. Nothing much. Everyone takes it.'

Hoisting Julie over his shoulder, Luther set off, hoping he wouldn't be challenged. When he neared her house she began to struggle.

'No, no. I don't want to go home. Trevor might be up and Sam hears everything.'

He put her down. 'If you can talk, you can walk. You weigh a ton.'

'I didn't ask you to carry me.' She sounded peeved. 'I was enjoying the concert.'

'You were crying, and anyway the concert's over.'

'Hold me tight. I want to be loved,' she whispered.

'Forget it! Stoned females don't turn me on,' he growled.

'You wanted me down there in the piggery. I could read it all over you.'

'I didn't want to fuck you, Julie. I wanted to love you, but I don't like what you're doing to yourself.'

There was a long silence. Julie flung herself down on the grass, then shifted up to lean against the nearest tree. After a few minutes Luther sat beside her.

He said, 'I'm going home now. I'll take you back inside. After that you can do what you damn well like.'

'Please don't go.'

'Then talk.'

Another sigh! 'Oh! It's just that when I'm stoned I'm not lonely. Most of the time I *am* lonely.'

Her story poured out. Perhaps because of her blonde hair and milky skin she had been adored by every worker on her parents' ranch and she had returned their adoration. Nanny, a huge Zulu woman from Natal, had reared her and loved her. All her motherly instincts were lavished on Julie. Jason, who managed the cattle, had taught her to ride when she was only three, and Johnson, foreman on the tobacco plantation, had taught her to dance. Black was synonymous with beauty, kindness and love. This had been her world, which had been snatched away from her to be replaced by cool English skies, and her kindly but often remote grandfather.

'D'you know why I'm modelling?' she asked him.

'Fame and fortune, I guess.'

'Just for the money. I need the cash to go back to Africa and start again. I don't blame them. I blame us. D'you know? We didn't even bother to find out their real names.'

'They don't need colonials with cash to buy their land – they've been there. What they need are skills. What can you offer, Julie?'

She looked shocked. 'I don't know. Never thought about it.'

'Start studying. Give up modelling and drugs.'

'Are you always so bossy?'

'Only when I really care. I must go. I have to get to work. Goodbye.'

She hung on to his hand. 'Luther, I think I love you.'

Not me, he thought sadly. I'm Jason and Nanny and Johnson rolled into one.

She pursed her mouth a little, like a demure and obedient child waiting for a kiss. He felt her tugging at him, pulling him towards her, and bent forward to kiss her cheek, but her hand slipped behind his neck, her face shifted and her lips opened a little as they met his.

He shifted her up on to his lap, rocked her backwards and forwards and eventually she fell asleep.

Dawn broke. He couldn't leave her here – the visitors were still around and might prowl this way. He couldn't stay either. He carried her to the house and tried the front door. It was unlocked so he went in and laid her on a couch.

Luther sped home on his bike. He had a strong desire to get the hell out of her life. But she needed him and he knew he could heal her.

Chapter 23

Trevor took the ferry from Nice to Ajaccio. As the Corsican mountains swam out of the afternoon haze he thrilled to the sight of the improbably high serrated granite ridges rising from dense, dark forests. Soon he could smell the subtle bitter-sweet scent of the maquis drifting towards him on the warm south breeze, lavender arbutus, myrtle, cistus, rosemary and thyme. Ajaccio, set in a deep turquoise bay with a backdrop of high mountains, surprised him. From a distance it looked so neat and white. Only when he disembarked and caught a taxi to his destination did he notice the fallen stucco, the rotting bricks and masonry, washing swinging from between drainpipes and ferns sprouting from ruined walls.

His destination was a tall corner house off the main street. The entire ground floor was taken up by a restaurant-bar, sentimentally called the Vlata. Michel's bar presented a similar façade, but inside it was warm and clean, a cross between modern and traditional with oak-panelled walls and chrome furniture. A well-stocked bar filled one entire wall and Michel sat in a wheelchair behind the till, keeping an eye on the patrons.

When Michel caught sight of him, he leaned forward and waved. He looked younger than his seventy-seven years, despite the mass of curly white hair, but today he was pale and Trevor could see how the shooting had affected him. He had always been tall and as strong as a bull, but now his bony frame seemed like a coathanger from which the rest of him hung. Only his eyes were unchanged, glacial blue, stern and intelligent.

Trevor limped through the bar, leaning heavily on his stick and greeted his old friend with the traditional hug. 'How are you? I'd have been here sooner, but my leg played up for a while.'

'It's good to see you, Trevor. Let's go. Josephina! Come and take over here.' A tired, grey-haired woman, who was introduced as his wife's widowed sister, hurried forward to take over the till as Michel led the way to his den at the back.

'Lunch will be here soon. What will you drink? Brandy? Some wine?'

Trevor chose dry Corsican wine and settled back. 'You know I sometimes feel the need to talk about the war, Michel, the way people died, the things we did. These memories are larger than life. You can't shut them away, they demand to come out into the open, otherwise they fester, but there's hardly anyone left who remembers. The war means nothing now.'

'Forget the war! Bury it! Think about the present. You look better, Trevor. Just as well. You're up against a rough mob. No use asking you to leave it alone, I suppose?'

'No, but I'm doing my best to get fit. That was half our problem. We weren't prepared. But let's hear about you. How's the wound?'

'Practically healed. Don't you worry about me, my friend. I'll be up and about any day now. I'd be up now if it weren't for my wife.'

'I should never have got you into this mess. I'm truly sorry, Michel. That's what I came to say.'

'Come on, Trevor. We're old friends, aren't we? You've done the same for me enough times.' He waved his hands, an expressive gesture designed to put an end to Trevor's guilt.

'It was different then.'

'Different kind of war, that's all. What's your next move?'

'I want to bum around the docks and keep my eyes open until I find out who receives all this smuggled liquor. After that I'll find out who they pay for it. Step by step, like old times.' Michel watched his friend anxiously. 'D'you remember that time in the Middle East when we knew there was a mole at the bureau, but we didn't know who it could be?'

Michel sighed imperceptibly and tried to switch off. As he saw it, the main problem with age was that everyone looked back. No wonder they kept coming to grief. He wasn't like that. Perhaps he didn't have too much to look back on. He'd led an uneventful life. He and his wife had married the same month he'd returned to Corsica. They'd stayed married and had five children. Nothing extraordinary had ever happened to them, although they'd had their moments . . .

He became aware that Trevor was expecting a comment.

'Well, never mind all that,' Michel said. 'How's George?'

'He's fine. I'm going to see him tomorrow. He's a big shot in the liquor industry. Eats and drinks too much. That's his problem. Eat himself into the grave, if he's not careful.'

'Well, let's follow his example. Here's our lunch. Eating is a serious business around these parts. First we eat, then we talk business. Come! You've never tasted olives like these, home-grown, and my wife makes the bread. Later we'll make a plan.'

'Listen, Trevor,' Michel said, when the waiter had

cleared away their plates. 'Corsicans stick together, except when it comes to politics. Stands to reason, eh? We started this together, now let's finish it together. We must pool our resources. How far have you gone?'

'I haven't progressed beyond a certain question. *Why Woodlands?* This could be the start of another attempt to infiltrate our liquor industry. I suspect the leaders are part of the Russian network of organised crime. If so, why are they targeting Woodlands? Is the smuggling connected to the takeover bid? I never did believe in coincidence.'

'So you want to find out who's responsible for smuggling beer into Kent.'

'That's step one. I have a plan of sorts.'

The ex-partisans sat planning most of that afternoon. It was dusk when Trevor stood up and said goodbye.

'We're not as young as we were,' Michel said. 'Be careful. I'll be in touch.'

'Don't worry, it's not like the old days. We're not in enemy territory. They are. If I meet trouble all I have to do is call the cops.'

Still the same cocky son-of-a-bitch, Michel thought, as Trevor left in a taxi for the airport. Same upright stance with slightly hunched shoulders, same dark, watchful eyes, same twisted smile. Over-confident, especially now. Age hadn't changed a damn thing.

George Davenport lived in a rambling mansion outside Ashford in Kent. Trevor had always driven there, but his right leg was still painful so he caught the train. He hired a taxi at the station and arrived two hours later for his appointment.

'Good God, Trevor!' George rushed out and gave his friend a bear hug. 'If you'd called I'd have fetched you from the station. You came by train, I suppose,' George gripped his hand and Trevor almost fell over.

George looked pretty much the same, despite his pacemaker, Trevor decided. His face was still too red, his stomach too large and his pale blue eyes still gleamed with friendship. He led Trevor past old family portraits that hung around a massive hall to his study. 'What'll it be?'

'Just soda water,' Trevor said, as he sank into a roomy black leather armchair. 'I'm on a fitness programme. I didn't like what happened to us last time. How's your heart, George?'

'I've no problems. My doctor keeps moaning, but I feel fine.' He was pottering around with nuts and glasses and finding the right whisky. 'How are you doing?' George asked, when they were comfortably seated.

'I'm okay. Leg's getting better. My worst problem is an over-protective family.'

'I could do with a problem like that,' George said wistfully. He drained his glass and gazed beyond Trevor to the window. 'I often wanted to marry, but never found the right woman. All this will go to my nephew. Have another drink.' Trevor shook his head so George poured himself a stiff Scotch.

'It's important to keep fit, George. You could do without all this good living. Double your lifespan if you gave the booze a miss.'

'You're right, of course, but I'm not sure what I'd be hanging in for.' He paused, then changed the subject. 'What's your plan, Trevor? Whatever it is, you can count me in. Haven't had so much fun for years, despite the heart problem.'

'I want you to tell me what happened in 'ninety-four. I know the Russian comrades tried to get a foothold in Britain and failed. That's about all I do know. Fill me in.'

'Do my best.' George sat hunched over, his elbows on his knees. 'Funny business. Not your normal run-of-the-mill Mafia activity at all. It seemed innocuous at first. The guys we saw claimed to belong to one of those quasi-official trade missions. For a while I thought it was the new government's clumsy attempt to establish private enterprise in the Russian liquor industry. A delegation came round selling us the benefits of two-way trade with Russia and we – I mean, British distillers – said we'd give it a go.'

'Doing what exactly, George?'

'We thought we'd be in for marketing their liquor, but it was quite the reverse. They wanted to sell our liquor in Russia. I ask you, what could be better?'

Trevor smiled. 'So you enjoyed the honeymoon.'

'Lasted a few months, but inevitably the complications started mounting up. They wanted to control all exports to Russia, then all exports to Eastern Europe. Finally, when you cut through the garbage of talk and promises, it boiled down to a protection racket. If we didn't pay up, our stuff got lost on the railways – and a fat lot we could do about that.'

'A protection racket on a grand scale.'

'Yes. About then some of us starting digging in our heels. I sent our sales manager, Donald Shaw, to Russia to reopen our former markets there, but he found that we couldn't get a damn thing on the Russian railways. They're totally controlled by the Russian Mafia. We flew out a few consignments, but got short shrift. We even tried smuggling the stuff through. Hid some vodka behind bottles of soy sauce and sent it via Hong Kong. Of course, they picked it up and confiscated the lot.

'Finally Don was warned by his driver to get out of Russia. He was about to be blown up. He was even told when. It was scheduled for a Friday night when he drove himself to his favourite nightclub. The car blew up, but naturally Don wasn't in it. Unfortunately his driver was found shot on the pavement the following morning. That was when I insisted he must leave Russia. Didn't help at all.'

George gave a rueful smile and glanced uncertainly at Trevor. 'Don was able to identify the men in their London office as those he'd negotiated with in Russia. A few nights later he was killed in a hit-and-run accident in London. No one was ever able to prove anything against the Russians.'

'I'm sorry,' Trevor said.

'Yes. Terrible business.' George screwed his eyes shut. 'Most of us – well, the management team – I guess we're more like a family than a company.' He pulled himself together. 'I suppose you heard about the mess Douglas got himself into?'

'Yes, but not the details.' Trevor ran his hand through his hair, wondering how the hell he'd missed out on all this. 'Was that connected to this business?'

'Yes, and if his wife hadn't died, we never would have found out. As one of the largest vodka manufacturers, Douglas had been a staunch supporter of two-way trade with Russia all along. Several distillers followed his lead, but when Beatrice died, Douglas went straight to Scotland Yard. The usual story, although I seem to miss out.' George flushed and looked embarrassed. 'Ninette someone or other, a famous beauty in her time, had some compromising photographs of herself with Douglas and she'd persuaded him to export exclusively through the Russian company.'

'And he played along for months.'

'Yes. She denied she was involved with the comrades, said it was for philanthropic reasons, but she couldn't explain how she came by her expensive car and apartment.'

'Did they prosecute?'

'Oh, yes. She was put away for a few years. Still inside, I believe. By the time Scotland Yard moved in, these buggers were getting a hefty cut on exports to most of the East European countries and Russia. The Russians were politely put on a plane with a one-way ticket to Moscow and their company was quietly closed down. Most people thought they'd gone bust.'

Trevor stood up and clapped George on the shoulder. 'I have a feeling they're trying again, George, but to tell the truth, I can't get anyone to take me seriously. Except you and Michel.'

'That's how I felt last time. Of course, these guys turn legitimate eventually. Half of what they're doing is legal. It's their methods that stink. In a couple of decades they'll all be wealthy in their own right. And they'll have their old boys' network to fall back on. God help anyone who opposes them.'

'Exactly. That's something we want to avoid, particularly in Britain. We have enough problems. There's a lot at stake, George. The Russian Mafia control their country's liquor industry and eighty per cent of Eastern Europe, too. In Europe it's only three per cent, but early days yet. They want in and they'll contact you again, George. Stands to reason.'

'Oh!' He snorted contemptuously. 'Let them try.'

But you do have your Achilles heel, my friend, and that's your loneliness, Trevor thought, as he said goodbye.

Chapter 24

He and George went back a long way, Trevor thought, as the slow train meandered towards London – to a certain sunny autumn afternoon in 1939, in fact, when he and a crowd of unruly students had gathered to demonstrate outside 10 Downing Street. His placard had read, 'Don't repeat Munich. Fight for Poland or we'll never live down our shame,' in English and Czech.

With five others he'd been ushered into a van by a friendly bobby and driven to an obscure house in Battersea, labelled Jenkins – Import–Export, where he'd been pushed into a room with a row of chairs and one desk. When his turn came he was cross-questioned for half an hour in Czech by a young man of about his age who was undoubtedly British establishment but who spoke Czech like a native. In those days he'd been the Hon. George Bulpin, but that was before he had inherited his title.

'Who was responsible for writing those Czech slogans?' asked the young man with the ginger hair and pale blue eyes. He was plump even in those days, but after five years in Czechoslovakia he'd been emaciated. Suited him better, Trevor considered.

'I was.'

'How come you speak the language like a native?'

Part of the answer, of course, was Mira, the good-natured teenager he'd met while working in a Czech brewery. Trevor's father was a brewer, and a Cambridge degree came at a price: holiday work in the world's best breweries and most of them were Czech. And Trevor also had a talent for languages.

After that came long months in a training camp, endless lectures, more language lessons, unarmed combat and learning how to make bombs and weapons from junk, apart from acquiring a load of useless information imparted by a crew of eccentrics.

Finally they were narrowed down to four men. George, who had interviewed him and who was about to inherit a massive distillery, a title and a stately home. He was related to half the Hapsburgs and his childhood had been spent in Prague. There was Michel, son of a Corsican engineer who had spent five years at a Czech school, and Robin, an Oxford graduate, a poet and a dreamer. He looked like a schoolboy yet he'd married just before joining them because he'd made his girlfriend pregnant. Any girl would go for him. He had a sensual face with deep blue eyes and light brown hair, good features, a smiling mouth, and a sweetness that had made him the most popular man in the squad. His mother was Czech, his father English, and he'd been sent out here because he spoke the language like a native. No one had bothered to find out just how sensitive he was, or that he was the most unsuitable candidate for an agent they could possibly find. Or so Trevor had thought. Finally, though, he'd been proved wrong. As their leader, Trevor had done his best to get Robin taken off the squad but had failed. Together the four had formed a strong unit, but when the time came for it to become real they found themselves alone and scared.

Trevor could still remember the exact moment when reality had dawned. It was midnight and he was sleepy – he had overeaten at the farewell party in the mess. A mistake, he realised now. It was a clear, moonlit night and, through the four-foot hole in the belly of the Liberator, Trevor saw the fields and forests of Czechoslovakia and the silver snake of the shimmering Mze river cutting through them. Beside him were six big metal containers, which were shuddering and knocking each other. They would go first. Michel, Robin and George were waiting behind him.

As the pilot circled and came in to the approach, Trevor heard the dispatcher's shout, 'Running in!'

He moved towards the hold and crouched there, trying to keep his mind blank except for the routine that would take him through the next few minutes. The dispatcher was shouting, 'Action stations.' Sleep vanished. Moments later Trevor was squatting at the edge of the hole. He put both legs through and gripped the edge.

Then he saw something that drove out all other thoughts: the code-letter C, flashing up erratically from lights on the ground. He was not supposed to be looking down.

They had overshot the targeted landing site, but the sight of six parachutes floating past under his feet was reassuring. He was next.

He turned and waved to the team. Michel's eyes were alight with excitement. He gave a thumbs-up. Robin looked scared. The dispatcher's right arm was raised. The hand dropped and the light turned from red to green as Trevor shot himself through the hole. Next minute he was lying on his back in the air watching the aircraft pass above him. Then his parachute opened.

There was a strong east wind blowing. The pilot had probably taken that into account when they overshot the landing site. He took up the landing position, before dropping in a field of barley.

Conscious of his heart pumping and his mouth drying, Trevor took off his overalls, rolled them into the parachute and ran to the hedge at the side of the field where he took out his trowel to bury them under the grass and soil. Far above he saw the Liberator dipping its wings in farewell. There came another moment of intense loneliness.

Where the hell was he? There was nothing familiar in any direction. He couldn't see the lights of the town or any hills or landmarks. To make matters worse the moon went behind a cloud and plunged him into darkness.

Where was everyone else and where the fuck was the welcoming committee? He'd been blown off course by the wind, so he would walk into it and hope he'd meet someone soon. An hour later he was still walking. What a fuck-up! He felt angry with fate, with the pilot, the local resistance and everyone else he could think of.

Dawn came at last and Trevor, depressed, exhausted and very hungry, got out his maps. He worked out where he was and where to go. In case of emergency, which this was, he reckoned, he had to make for a forest hut situated fifteen miles west of Pilsen.

He set off again, but suddenly heard voices. He sank to the ground where he was hidden in ferns. They came on without caution, shouting to each other. Surely only Germans shouted? Then he heard one say, 'I could swear this is where the container dropped.'

Trevor stood up. 'Good morning.'

His greeting sent the men somersaulting to the nearest cover. Trevor's world exploded with a massive blow on the back of his head. He remembered nothing else.

He awoke in a barn. Opening his eyes cautiously he expected to see SS guards standing over him. Instead he saw a woman. She bent over him, her dark curly hair falling around his face, and offered him water.

After he'd drunk, she called in Czech, 'He's awake.'

Trevor heard the click of a Sten gun being changed from 'safe' to 'fire'.

He called, 'Is Vim there? Where are the others?'

'Never heard of him. Put your hands on your head.' He was marched out into the grey dawn at gunpoint and all the time drizzle trickled down his neck and the boggy ground filled his shoes. How the hell was he going to find his parachute? It had been dark when he landed.

Eventually they came to a field of barley with a hedge that looked vaguely familiar. There was no sign of his parachute, but more people were standing around. One of them prodded him hard with a gun. 'What's the password for this drop?'

'Fuck-up, I should imagine. It's a bloody fuck-up and so are you lot, you lousy bastards,' he said in English. Switching to Czech he raised his voice. 'London gave me no password.'

The woman from the barn, who was muffled in scarves and a long coat, spoke in perfect English. 'What is your name?'

'Albert.' This was his code name.

'Clearly he's English. Take him to Vim.'

Then came another long walk in the drizzle.

At last he was face to face with a man he hoped was Vim Jaromil. He was tall and square with a fleshy face and a massive scruffy beard. 'They say that you're a spy pretending to be English. Prove to me quickly that you're English.'

'You know damn well who I am. You were expecting me.'

Unexpectedly Vim replied in English. 'You have exactly one minute to prove who you are.'

'Your voice,' Trevor began, 'Eton, Cambridge, three years in Germany learning your trade—'

'Enough!' He hauled a bottle out of his pocket, screwed off the lid and handed it to him. 'Taste it. What is it?'

'British ale, probably Whitbread, but stale.' He spat it out.

'Okay, you've passed. Let's go. You start work in an hour's time. You take him, Anna.'

'No, no, first we go home. He must eat and change his clothes. I insist.'

Trevor remembered how he had loved Anna for saying that. He had listened to her argue with her brother-in-law, laying down the law and, amazingly, winning. It was a voice he would grow to love.

His memories changed. They were all of Anna: a snatched kiss in a damp ditch while waiting to attack; his panic when she went missing on a food-raising raid; his dread because she would not give up the job as radio operator, the fight they had when he replaced her with Robin's contact, for purely selfish reasons.

'Anna, I love you,' he whispered to the night sky.

Chapter 25

Luther sat moodily at his desk staring at a pile of labour regulations, but his mind was on Julie Rosslyn. He had never been short of women – wherever he went they pursued him – but at twenty-eight he'd never been in love, never known what it was like to pine or to hanker over a woman he couldn't have. He was learning fast. His concentration had gone and so had his *joie de vivre*.

What a bloody awful day, he thought. He'd spent the morning trying to talk a group of union bosses into accepting a compromise, the best they'd be likely to get, but they'd turned it down and he'd come close to dumping them. He'd put aside the afternoon to work on his book but he'd only managed a paragraph. Julie's image kept getting between him and the page.

He got up, poured himself a beer and stood at the window staring at the drizzle. What was *she* doing? he wondered.

'Enough!' He said it aloud, startling himself. But he was right. He wouldn't allow himself to think of her again.

Almost time for the news. He switched on the TV and stared straight into Julie's lovely face. She was gazing into the camera with a sultry, sensual stare, eyes half-closed as she shook her long ash-blonde hair from side to side and the narrator's voice extolled the virtue of a new shampoo.

'Bloody hell!' He couldn't get away from the damned woman.

The telephone rang and Luther picked it up, his mind still on Julie.

'Hello, Luther. Julie here. Do you remember me? The concert and festival. I'm calling to invite you to dinner.'

'I don't think so. Nothing personal. It's just that you and I . . . we come from different worlds.'

'What a serious person you are. I thought we could be friends, the odd dinner.' She laughed and he felt a fool. 'Goodbye, Luther.'

By seven a.m. the next day Luther had taken an early shower and was sitting in front of the TV with a mug of coffee. Palm trees flapped their scruffy leaves in the sultry breeze, and there was Julie, sauntering along a beach in a white bikini, toasted to a golden tan, her hair falling over her shoulders. She walked up to a bar and perched on a stool, crossing her legs seductively, as she watched the macho barman squeeze a lime, his muscles rippling. She sipped the juice and smiled seductively. 'Excitingly fresh, a taste you'll never forget. Try it,' the narrator's voice intoned.

Luther switched off the TV. It was getting beyond a joke. He had to see her. It was the only way to rid himself of his obsession.

On Sunday he drove to Woodlands, parked and rang the bell nervously, holding some wilting flowers. He knew he'd been rude when Julie had called him and he wasn't sure of his welcome.

Helen came to the door and eyed him. 'Miss Rosslyn's taken her dog for a walk. She'll be back for lunch I expect.'

It was only ten a.m. 'Which way did she go?' he asked.

'I don't know. She could be anywhere.'

It was a lovely day and Luther decided to walk down to the sea for a swim. His trunks were in his boot.

It was hot and after a long walk over the cliffs, he couldn't wait to dive into the water. He found a creek with a quaint willow-pattern-style bridge over it, where a couple of small yachts were moored. It led to a secluded cove under the cliffs. There was no one around, so Luther stripped off, put on his trunks and sat on the sand gazing out to sea. A small boat was bobbing around with two figures in the bows. He decided to swim out and have a look at the castle from the sea. He set off at a fast crawl, and as he passed the yacht he realised it contained Julie and her wolf, lazing in the sun.

'Hello there,' he called.

Julie reached for a towel and wrapped it round her. 'Luther! Hello! Strange place to meet.'

'Not really. I came down to Woodlands looking for you. Can I come aboard?'

'You could try. It's not so easy.'

Luther hung on to the gunwhale and hauled himself up.

'How d'you get this fit with a desk job?' she asked.

'Swimming, football, tennis. The usual.'

'I'm surprised to see you here. You were pretty curt when I called.'

'I'm hoping to get you out of my mind. Keeping away from you didn't work.'

She laughed. 'At least you're honest. D'you like sailing?'

'Haven't done much.'

'I could give you a lesson. I believe that's a good way to end a friendship. Men hate being told how to do things by women.'

'Okay, you're on,' Luther said.

By the end of the day, Luther could handle the boat perfectly. He brought it into the mooring and only missed three times as Julie hooted with laughter.

'Didn't work, did it?' she asked him innocently, looking like the kid she was.

'No, not really. In fact, it worked inversely.'

'For me, too. I think I've caught the same complaint, Luther. We'll have to find the right medicine. How about you teaching me to drive?' She went into raptures over the car she'd set her heart on, an Aston Martin sports car.

'Rich grandfather, huh?'

'Wrong. I earned the cash modelling.'

'Meantime we might as well enjoy the evening. How about dinner and dancing? We'll start the cure next weekend, if it's okay with you.'

'Not before time, if this patient is to survive. The symptoms are getting acute.' She grabbed him and pressed her lips to his, catching Luther unawares. He clasped her to him, then released her just as suddenly. 'That wasn't a good idea, Julie.'

After that Julie didn't expect Luther to remember his promise, but he called her on Friday evening and arranged to fetch her sharp at two the following day. The driving lessons were fun. Julie was a natural driver and Luther was proud of her progress. By the end of the weekend they'd learned each other's strengths and weaknesses, and had started to bond.

'This isn't working, Julie,' Luther told her over dinner. His hand slipped over hers. 'We've got to do something, but I don't know what.'

'I've had an idea. They say you never really know a man until you work with him, and vice versa. Isn't your secretary due any leave? I'm a lousy typist, I have an appalling memory and I'm bound to drive you crazy if you take me on as a temp. Of course, you'd have to pay me, just to make it hurt properly.'

'I was thinking of sending Joan to a computer school for a week. Do you swear you're incompetent?'

'I'm the pits.'

After five days Luther admitted that she hadn't been lying. She was messy, careless, outspoken and undisciplined. She also had a brilliant, highly original mind. Her grasp of English was superb and she'd taken his manuscript home and corrected it while spotting a number of inconsistencies. How the hell was he going to do without her, he wondered, when she left and Joan returned? At least he was more efficient when he worked without a hard-on. Eight hours a day close to Julie had been agonising.

Julie was thinking much the same. If Luther didn't make love to her soon she'd find another lover, she promised herself. Wrapped in a towel, she stepped out of the shower for the twentieth time, peered into a mirror and examined her face. 'Since I began washing my face with Medi-wash, blemishes are a thing of the past,' she recited.

'Cut. You sound like a bloody parrot,' Hal, the agency director, growled.

'Hal, it's not *my* fault. The script's all wrong. Who writes this crap? You should fire him.'

She stood at the window gazing out sullenly until Hal put his arms around her. Pushing him off she had a sudden wave of self-disgust. She'd screwed him twice and she felt so ashamed. It had been so refreshing to work for Luther and be a real person instead of a body beautiful. However, when self-disgust crept up on her there was only one way to cure it.

'Got a joint?' she asked.

'Come on, Julie. We have to wind up this campaign

today. For fuck's sake, where's your loyalty? We've got to put the ad to bed.'

'Let me have a go at it my way. If I'm no good it can join the rest of the takes in the bin.'

Hal scowled at her. 'Go on, then. Just once. It's worth a try.'

'Hang on, let me think.' She sat down on the shower step and tried to imagine herself in the early morning. Of course she worried about blemishes and lines – she was making a fortune out of her flawless complexion. What *did* she do every morning?

'Okay, let's go.' She returned to the shower and emerged wrapping a towel around her, eyes tight shut until she dried her face. Then she gazed anxiously into the mirror, frowning as she examined herself. Anxiety changed to relief and slowly relief turned to joy. Reaching for the jar she pressed her lips against it. 'Thank you, Medi-wash,' she murmured.

'Phew,' Hal said. 'Seems okay to me. Thanks! Of course we'll have to get it past the client. They approved the original script. Still, this is better and I don't suppose there'll be a problem.'

'It's okay, Hal. Stop worrying. God, I'm bored. There must be something more fulfilling I could do.'

'At a thousand pounds an hour? Are you kidding?' He felt in his pocket. 'Now you can have a joint.'

'Thanks.'

She took it and Hal lit it. Crouched on the floor, clad only in a towel, Julie concentrated on the sense of well-being now invading her. The world slowed down and each tick of the clock assumed a special significance. It was blissfully peaceful, until Luther strolled in.

'What the . . . You're stoned,' he said quietly.

Julie scrambled to her feet, tucked in her towel and

wrapped her arms round Luther's neck, but he felt like stone.

'Don't be like this. I love you,' she whispered.

'Prove it. What am I worth? More than this?' He grabbed the joint and ground it into the floor.

He went and stood in the doorway, huge, implacable, black eyes smouldering. 'Hurry up and change,' he said. 'I want to breathe fresh air.'

Luther took her back to the apartment he used when he was in London. He cooked her supper, gave her his bed and slept on the couch.

In the morning he brought her coffee, croissants and the newspaper. He sat on the bed beside her and traced his finger over the back of her neck, her throat and down to her breasts.

'No thanks, Luther,' Julie said firmly, pushing his hand away. 'I've wanted you since I first saw you and you've done nothing but tease me. If you're going to make love you may stroke me, but otherwise keep your hands to yourself. Personally I'm convinced you're a eunuch.'

He burst out laughing. 'Aren't you reversing our roles?' he asked.

'Aren't you about a century out of date?'

'Julie, listen to me. I'm scared. If this is how I feel now, what am I going to do when I feel you're mine by some divine right known as screwing? I seem to be running out of control. I never felt like this in my life. I wanted to kill Hal yesterday, simply because you were messing around in a towel. Why were you, by the way?'

'It was the script.'

'Hm!'

Luther could feel his eyes burning. Every part of his body ached and trembled, his fingertips tingled, his thighs and his stomach began to stiffen, while he trembled with lust. He wanted to throw her back on the pillows and impale her, but he was afraid.

He couldn't tear his eyes away as Julie pulled off her nightdress and leaned back naked, smiling at him. She was far more lovely than he had ever imagined, her breasts small but perfectly full and milky white. Luther was so overcome with awe it nearly took his breath away. She was trying to pull him down on to her and he was bursting with desire, but still he held back.

'To me, sex is a commitment,' he said.

'Commitment to what?' she asked, looking puzzled.

'To try to make a go of the relationship, to be loyal and faithful and not fuck around.'

'Grow up, Luther.' She reached out, laughing, touching, pulling him close to her, nuzzling his shoulder with her mouth, needing him, urging him on. 'Look at it this way, Luther. We've tried everything to cure us both of this ridiculous obsession. Maybe sex will do the trick. Maybe you'll come too fast.'

'I'm damn sure I will, but only the first time.'

'Maybe I'll be the biggest disappointment you've ever encountered.'

'Maybe you'd like to shut up and fuck,' he said, ripping off his clothes.

'Why, Luther,' she smiled coquettishly, 'that's exactly what I'd like.'

Chapter 26

It was five a.m. on Monday morning when all hell broke loose. First came the sound of gunfire, followed by running footsteps and Jeff Brink's frantic voice screaming, 'I'll shoot the bloody dog! I'm warning you. When I see it I'll kill it.'

My God, he's gone crazy, Sam thought, peering out of her bedroom window. He was shaking his gun in the air as he ran up the driveway.

The two girls emerged in various stages of undress, pulling on their dressing gowns. They set about calming him down.

'One parrot a night. It's uncanny. I never see the bloody thing that's taking them. I've sat up two nights running.'

'So it could be a fox,' Sam said, calmly, leading him into the dining-room.

'I haven't seen one around these parts,' Jeff muttered.

'Haven't you? My goodness, I've seen dozens. But, Jeff, whatever made you come here?' Sam asked.

'Whatever it is, it clears a six-foot wall and unfastens the door to the aviary. But the door swings shut because of the lead weights, and then, God knows how, the creature opens it again from the inside to escape, with a parrot in its mouth.'

Julie came in with some coffee.

'This creature sounds rather human,' she told Jeff. 'I suppose parrots fetch a good price.'

'Of course they do. They're rare birds.'

'Are you insured?' Julie asked.

At that moment Tasha sidled into the room for her morning bowl of milk.

Sam said a silent prayer of thanks.

Jeff knew when he was beaten. He drained his coffee-cup and left, muttering dark threats.

'Where's the bloody parrot?' Sam asked Julie moments later.

'I gave it a proper burial.'

'Julie,' she said, 'I've been checking around over the past few days and I've got quotes on fencing part of the front garden plus electronic gates across the driveway.'

'How much?'

'Four thousand's the cheapest so far. Of course, that's only a small part of the garden. Unfortunately we haven't got the cash to spare.'

'Yes, of course, but let's go ahead. I can pay for it. I'll do a few more modelling jobs. Does our insurance cover damage by dogs?'

'I guess we could get away with it. I'll have the fencing done right away and meantime and I suggest you keep Tasha locked up at night until it's finished. It really isn't fair. One a night, indeed. Poor parrots. Where's Trevor, by the way?'

'I checked, Sam. He's not here.'

'Bloody hell.' Sam groaned.

'Gramps wasn't at breakfast, Rosemary. I'm so worried about him,' Sam said, as soon as Rosemary arrived at work.

'Oh, dear! I almost forgot to tell you. Trevor called me last night from the harbour. It was late and I didn't want to wake you. He told me he'll be away for a few days. He said you mustn't worry.'

'Worry? Of course I'll worry. D'you think he'll be okay?'

'Of course he will. He's tough.'

The telephone rang and Rosemary took it. 'Shireen.'

'Thanks.' Sam reached for the receiver. 'Shireen, are you all right? I hope I didn't make things worse for you.' The absurd scene with John and her father had been intruding on her concentration.

'Of course not.'

It was comforting to hear Shireen's soft contralto voice sounding so reassuringly normal.

'Sam, I'm calling to say goodbye. I'm leaving for India tomorrow morning.'

'But you can't. I know you don't want to go. Don't do this, Shireen.'

'I have to make a choice now. If I don't go I'll have nothing. The family will cut me off.'

'Money's not that important. Given time, you'll make your own.'

'It's not just the money. It's the position in the family. I'll be drifting like a leaf in the wind. I won't know who I am.' Her voice was trembling.

'How about a famous actress, Shireen? That would do for starters, wouldn't it? What about your dreams?'

'Oh, Sam. That's all they were. Just dreams. All girls dream of becoming film stars.'

'True, but not all girls get accepted at that academy, or have your looks. Your father has no right— Your life is to be sacrificed so he can have his grandchildren brought up in India.'

'I'm not an independent unit, Sam. Not like you. I'm part of a family. I have duties. Mother showed me what anguish is caused when someone ducks out of their responsibilities.'

'You'll be so miserable and I'll never see you again. And what about your duty to the man you marry? He deserves the love of his wife.'

'I must go. Goodbye, Sam.'

'Oh, Rosemary, this is terrible. Shireen's going to marry an old man she's never even met. I can't bear to think about it.' She was silent for a moment. Then: 'But now we'd better get on with sorting out the rest of our problems.' She tried to ignore the tension pains in her stomach, cleared her throat and tried not to show her fear.

'We sold our month's target in one week, but that's because of our advertising. Trouble is, we can't afford to keep on forking out. Did you see the mess round the castle and the fairgrounds? Unbelievable.'

'There's a gang coming to clean up.'

'Thanks. I'm shell-shocked from fate's blows. Every time the phone rings I think it's the bank or a creditor.'

'Or the *Daily Echo*.'

'What d'you mean?'

'They phoned yesterday, but I didn't want to bother you – you had enough on your plate. They want a statement from you. Luther's group have sent them photographs and an article showing the way we keep our pigs. It doesn't look good. They've faxed it through.'

Sam skimmed through the text which gave Luther a by-line:

After weeks spent wandering around farms and super-markets, I discovered that each and every one of us is perpetrating a massive con on ourselves. We kid ourselves that it's okay to eat creatures we care about. We depict domestic animals as cute and knowing. Cans of pork, ham and sausages show friendly pigs beaming at consumers. 'Buy me, grill me, roast me, fry me, serve me garnished with apple sauce. There's nothing I love more than that,' their expressions seem to suggest. So we kid ourselves they're content and humanely treated and killed painlessly.

But is this really true? Take a look at these pictures taken at a leading pig breeder's and decide for yourselves.

'You should take it up with Tom Bowles,' Rosemary said. 'He set up the pig farm. It was his idea, and he gets a hefty slice of the profits.'

'That figures. But, Rosemary, Trevor's just received a prize for his pigs and the way he runs the piggery.'

'The prize was for quality pork, not a quality lifestyle for pigs.'

'Even I can see there's a conflict of interest here. Did you tell Trevor?'

'Yes.'

'What did he say?'

'He said, "Leave it to Sam."'

'Hm! Where's Julie?'

'Out somewhere. She didn't say.'

'Damn. Then ask Bowles if he can pop over now. Tell him it's urgent.'

Sam had never had a long conversation with Bowles, mainly because she didn't like him. This morning she liked him even less than usual. He walked in and braced his feet on the floor.

'Ah, Mr Bowles. Won't you sit down? We seem to have run into a problem. Take a look at this article and pictures. The local rag have asked for our comments. Ready, Rosemary?'

Bowles grabbed the fax and glanced through it. 'Why the hell should I comment on this rubbish?'

'Because otherwise they'll publish it just as it is.'

He grimaced. 'This is the way pigs are kept nowadays.

How d'you think I win all the prizes? Damn media. Just as long as the food arrives on the supermarket shelves, that's all they care about. Bloody bleeding hearts, every last one of them. It's a ploy to stop themselves from feeling guilty when they tuck into bangers and mash for lunch. They couldn't give a damn, really.'

'Oh, I think they care, Mr Bowles. Hence this article.'

'They don't know the first thing about pig breeding.'

'I'm sure you're right, but they recognise cruelty when they see it.'

'If you're one of these bleeding hearts, Miss Rosslyn, I suggest you keep your nose out of farm management. It's not for the likes of you.'

'My views have nothing to do with you, Mr Bowles. Your only concern is that I'm running the estate and I don't like the way you're keeping the pigs.'

Bowles's hands began to shake and his eyes looked glazed. 'Tell them to mind their own business. And you'd do well to do the same, Miss Rosslyn. You might remind them that we're a leading pig breeder and producer of prime pork and bacon. We have the prize for the most pork from the least food.'

'Oh, they know that. I'm sure that's what put them on to us. Tell me I'm wrong, Mr Bowles, but I can't believe this pig sat in this tiny box, too small to allow him to move, for his entire life.'

'Believe it or not, as you wish, but it's not your problem.'

'I don't believe that it's necessary to inflict cruelty to make a profit.' Sam could feel her temper rising as she struggled to keep control.

'Miss Rosslyn, I'm contracted to run the farm any way I feel best, as long as I make a profit.'

'Contracts can be set aside, Mr Bowles.'

'Not without a costly court case. You'll be hearing from me. Good day to you.' He left, chin jutting, eyes blazing, shoulders hunched.

Sam could hardly control her annoyance. She turned to Rosemary for support. 'We've got to get rid of him.'

'I remember Trevor saying that, but it was too difficult. You'd better beg the editor for mercy.'

'On the contrary, tell him to do his worst. Rub him up the wrong way. Better still offer him a bribe. A side of pork. And make sure it's sent personally from Bowles.'

'You can't be serious.'

'I'm deadly serious. Rosemary, please type minutes of the conversation we've just had and get Bowles to sign them. I'll sign them, too. From now on I want all conversations with that odious man recorded. I need a counter-claim for when he sues us. If I can prove that his cruelty is harming beer sales we'll be rid of him less painfully. Give him enough rope to hang himself.'

'Will do. You'd better get going, Sam. Good luck.'

Matthew Dearlove, once a close family friend, was as remote as the head waiter at the Porchester. Sam was there to plead for more time to lower the overdraft. Woodlands was expanding but to sell more they had to spend more on marketing. She had the facts and figures to prove her case. She tried to eat humble pie and plead her cause. Dearlove remained cold and distainful. Sam had to have the cash. She hung on to her shreds of dignity as she begged. Her forehead became damp with sweat and her hair stuck there, she could feel wet patches appearing on the back of her shirt and under her arms.

'You see it's like this . . .' She tried another tack. 'Greg Selo owes us thirty thousand pounds. I can pledge that to the bank, but I *have* to have cash to finance our marketing foray into Pilsen.'

'Forget it. There's no way we could extract this cash from Selo.'

'Matthew, surely you know you get nothing for nothing. We have to spend money on marketing, travel, new labels. The hop season's coming up. I have to buy barley.'

Half an hour later Sam gave up and left in despair.

Chapter 27

Nearing home Sam saw the placards waving. What on earth . . . ? A crowd had gathered around the entrance to their grounds. The demonstrators were silent as she passed. Their placards read, 'Save their bacon', and 'Who's the swine? Them or you?'

Then she saw Julie in the crowd with Tasha asleep at her feet. She yelled through the window, 'Whose side are you on, Julie?'

'The pigs' of course,' her sister yelled back.

Sam shrugged and drove on. She parked outside the office and heaved a sigh of relief, but her sense of escape was shortlived. Frantic squealing echoed from Trevor's office.

'Oh, God! What next?' She shot up the stairs two at a time and pushed through the crowd of office staff blocking the doorway. Rosemary was on her knees trying to quiet a piglet in a crate.

'What's going on?'

'Better read the letter.'

Sam picked it up, but her hands were shaking so she laid it on the desk and bent over it.

Dear Madam, I find your sentiments, based on ignorance and misplaced mawkish sentimentality, both offensive and objectionable. You have overstepped your authority and if you or members of your family set foot in the piggery again I shall have you forcibly removed. If I

*have any further sessions of pathetic and childish ravings,
such as this morning, I shall contact my lawyer. I am
sick and tired of people voicing their holier-than-thou
sentiments while leaving people like myself to do their
dirty work. Why not send the editor a suckling pig
for roasting whole with an apple in its mouth? Here's
the pig and an apple. Feel free. Kindly don't bother
me further.*

'Oh, God! *Bastard!* But how could I have said such a
thing? It was my wicked temper that did it.' She gathered
the piglet into her arms.

'God, it's heavy. Must be at least two and a half months
old. Not a suckling pig at all. Here, eat the bloody apple.'
The pig made short work of it.

Then she said, 'Now what?'

'Exactly! Now what?'

'Oh, God! Richard.'

'Only Richard.' When he smiled at her it was as if the
sun came out. He was so tall he filled the doorway. His
black curly hair was thick and unruly, his grin revealed
one slightly crooked front tooth, and his blue eyes were
beaming a dual message: compassion and amusement.

'I came to invite you to lunch. But what are you going
to do with the pig?'

'I don't know. Put it in the stables perhaps.'

'No way,' Julie said, from the doorway. 'I'll look after
him. Luther's looking for a pig. He was going to get a
pot-bellied one, but this'll do. We're going to adopt it and
teach it to operate a computer.'

Sam shrugged helplessly and relinquished the sleeping piglet.

'Just remember one thing,' Richard called after Julie.

'What's that?'

'You have the two main characters in that little nursery story: "I'll huff and I'll puff . . ." And now Sam, I'm taking you to lunch and I won't take no for an answer.'

'But you'll have to because I have to get to Dover fast. There's a meeting of family brewers. I'm going to try to persuade them to come to Pilsen with me. A few have agreed already and we have to make our plans.'

'Why Pilsen?'

'Evidently there's a huge market east of Pilsen. I want some of it.'

'Far too dicey, Sam. You can't get goods shipped into Russia. And even if you did, how would you get the money out?'

'I have an agent who will handle all that. Greg Selo. You might have met him yesterday. He has contacts all over the place.'

'And you trust him?'

'Yes.'

'Okay. I'll drive you to Dover. You can compose your talk in the car. I'll wait outside, and afterwards we'll have lunch.'

'I'm sorry, Richard. It's an all-day affair. Come down to the canteen and have a hamburger. Actually, I think I'm a vegetarian until further notice.

'Make a note to change the menus,' she called over her shoulder to Rosemary. 'At least three vegetarian dishes every day. We might as well set a good example.'

'Poor Rosemary. I had no idea you were such a slave driver.'

'Am I? I'm not driving her any harder than I drive myself.' Sam took a tray and stood in the queue at the canteen. 'What'll it be? The choice is limited.'

'Would smoked fish and salad keep me out of trouble?' Richard asked.

'I suppose I'd better have the same but the cottage pie smells good.'

'Sure does.'

'Two smoked fish and salad. We must stand firm. Okay?'

'Fine with me. Here, let me. You lead the way.' Richard took the tray and followed her back to the table. 'You're pretty rough on yourself, aren't you?'

'I don't know. I never thought about it.'

'Think back, Sam. When did you last have a good time or a holiday?'

'Well, there's been a lot to do. I mean, right now it would be criminal to have fun. Then, back at the agency, we were all fighting to save the business for Walter.'

'Walter should save his own business.'

'Yeah, but at the time we thought we were doing it for us, too.'

'And before then?' he prompted her gently.

'I had to get a degree. I worked pretty hard at university. I knew Gramps was having money troubles and it didn't feel right to have fun.'

'You did well?'

'I did all right. I have a PhD in marketing, specialising in impulse-buying. I guess that's what caused you to reach out for a title – you simply reacted to an impulse. Am I right?'

'No. Quite the contrary. And I'm aware that you've neatly turned the conversation around, away from you and on to me.'

She laughed and he smiled back at her. It's strange how you can put so much into a smile, she thought. There was caring, approval, a touch of sexual awareness, compassion and more than a little teasing in his face.

Then he was serious. 'Come to dinner tonight, please,

Sam. I have a feeling we should touch base and start again.'

'Sensible idea. Where shall I meet you?'

'Why not come to my hotel? They have a pretty good seafood restaurant. It's rather lovely, right on the cliffs down by the harbour. I guess you know it.'

'Yes, all right, I'll come, but there's a condition.'

'Which is?'

'That you tell me why you want to buy a title.'

'That's a condition?'

'Yes.'

'So be it. See you at eight.'

At eight sharp Sam entered the foyer and Richard, who was waiting by the counter, noticed how the men stared longingly and the women frowned. She looked superb in a white silk sheath with tiny satin straps over her shoulders. She was athletic: muscled calves, strong shoulders, but with all the right curves and a slender waist. The white silk accentuated her dark beauty. For the first time he noticed the velvety texture of her tanned skin and the way her eyelashes fanned her high cheekbones. Caught unawares her face had softened and he realised that she was beautiful, with the sort of beauty that would endure.

He made a point usually of avoiding clever women, but Sam intrigued him. He wanted to know more about her but he intended to keep the evening very cool because he never allowed emotion to interfere with his work.

He stood up and walked towards her: 'Hello, Sam. Dead on time. Exactly what I'd expected.'

'Then it's lucky I wasn't late. I don't like breaking illusions.'

Sam had the most amazing smile. No matter what kind

of expression she was wearing, the moment she smiled she was all warmth.

They walked to the lift and she stood close beside him, her arm pushed through the crook of his.

Richard had only ever had lunch there. He never ate supper when he was alone, preferring to read in his room with a sandwich and a drink. He was glad to see that it was quite different at night: romantic music, dim lights, flickering candles, curtains moving in the sea breeze, and the sound of the waves lapping on the shore below.

'Sam,' he said, 'I have the strangest feeling that we'll see much more of each other. Would you let down some of your barriers? I'd like to be friends. For starters, what's it like to have roots stretching back to the Domesday Book and before?'

Sam looked amused and embarrassed in turn. 'That's a silly thing to say. We all have roots stretching back to anthropoid apes and long before, it's just that ours were recorded for some of the time. What's the difference? You're sold on titles and roots and stuff like that. You shouldn't be. It's meaningless. It's what you do with your life that counts.'

'So start from the present and move backwards. I want to know you better.'

'The present? Well, that's the brewery, of course.'

'And after that?'

'Sometimes I get scared that there'll never be an "after that". Right now I can't get beyond the incredible problem of getting out of debt, so the brewery is my life for the foreseeable future. You see . . .'

Richard listened intently as she tried to explain how she loved her grandfather, how he'd brought them up and made them forget the trauma of losing their home and their parents, and how she feared she might ruin the brewery and leave Trevor penniless.

One thing led to another and Richard found himself explaining how his grandfather had found him in a Mexican orphanage and brought him back to San Francisco. 'When we didn't sell a map, we suffered,' Richard told her. 'When we did, we took expensive holidays. My grandfather has no real concept of money.'

'Yet he paid your deposit on the title,' Sam said.

Richard had to think fast. 'True. That was a birthday gift.'

Sam was struck by his guilty expression. She put down her fork. He was lying, but why? Perhaps he'd asked his grandfather to lend him the cash for the deposit.

'Why d'you want a title so much, Richard?' Sam asked, out of the blue, and saw him blush.

'It's part of a business deal. That's what I do, buy and sell,' he mumbled.

'And you reckon you can get more than we're asking?'

'Given a little research and the proper approach, yes,' he said cautiously. 'Listen, Sam, if you want to pull out, just say the word. I'll tear up the option. In fact, let's do that now.'

'No, I want to sell the title – I need the cash. Besides, I've spent your deposit.'

Sam looked embarrassed and, watching her, Richard regretted his hasty words. He searched for a way to change the subject. 'Tell me about Walter and the agency,' he said. 'He didn't strike me as anyone special. About as smooth as his shiny shoes.'

They talked so much that Richard hardly noticed the time passing as the waiter came and went. They drank a great deal of chilled white wine and ate their way through

163

a seafood platter for two, heaped with crabs, mussels, oysters, prawns and lobsters.

Eventually, Sam stood up determinedly and stated her intention of going home. The realisation that he didn't want her to leave shocked Richard. He had to think fast. 'Come over here.' He drew her to the window. 'Look how calm the sea is. You can see the phosphorescence on the water. I have a sudden longing to walk beside it. Why don't you come with me?'

She looked up at him and suddenly he knew that she was going to make love to him.

'Why don't I?' She left her bag in her car, retrieved some trainers from the boot, and they went down the cliff path to the sea. She said, 'I've always longed to swim in the dark, when it's hot and the water's so calm, like it is tonight.'

'All right. Let's.'

She took off her clothes and placed them on a rock. She wasn't shy and that surprised him. Her breasts were full and firm, her waist slender, but her thighs were slightly plump and this womanly imperfection sent his libido soaring. He watched her walk down to the water's edge, as if it were sand instead of pebbles.

'How do you do it?' he yelled.

'Do what?' she called, without looking round.

'Walk on pebbles.'

'Oh, that! Years of practice.'

She kept walking until the water covered her waist. He watched her slip into the dark, glistening sea and swim towards deeper water, each stroke sending showers of glittering drops around her.

Richard stripped off hurriedly, throwing his clothes over hers and soon caught up as she swam far out. Then she turned on her back, splashing Richard, laughing with joy.

'I haven't done this since school,' she said. 'Shireen and I used to sneak out at night and go skinny-dipping in the bay.' Floating on the black ocean she told him about her friend, who had always been lonely, particularly after her mother left home, and how they'd replaced their lost parents with each other. 'I don't know why I'm telling you all these boring things, except that I'm so worried about her,' she said. 'Let's swim, I'm getting chilled.'

'I'm sobering fast. Let's go back.'

He reached the beach first, grabbed his shirt and caught her in a hug, rubbing her back and her arms dry. Her skin was ice-cold from the sea and when he ran his lips over her throat she tasted salty. He held her at arm's length and began to dry her breasts. She moaned gently, then wound her arms around his neck, pulling him roughly against her.

'These goddamn pebbles hurt.' He looked around anxiously. 'Where can we go?'

'There's a sandy patch up there.'

'You know this beach?'

'Of course. We used to come here for picnics. Come.' She reached for his hand and held it tightly, pulled him along. 'No commitment, Richard. Promise me. Just lust.'

She collapsed on the sand and pulled him over her, groaning softly as he stroked her gently.

He wanted to woo her, but soon she was panting with the force of her need. 'Hope you know what you're doing, Sam,' he whispered, trying to banish a sense of guilt, before giving himself up to their bittersweet passion.

Chapter 28

There were poppies in the hedgerows and patches of purple scabious, the golden sheen of buttercups, and rooks' nests in the trees, all just as she had remembered. It was two months since she'd arrived in England and it had passed too quickly. Now she was leaving again. Shireen blinked hard. She wasn't a person who cried easily, but the lump in her larynx was so painful she could hardly swallow. She reached up and touched her throat. There was no telltale bulge, but there should have been. For three years she'd longed for the luscious greens of England, soft hills and valleys, the mellow twilights and the coolness of the countryside.

It wasn't only scenery she'd longed for but the freedom to find herself again, if only for a short while. She'd begged to come home, but now her holiday was over and she was speeding towards her doom at eighty m.p.h. Her depression heightened as she listened to her father's familiar argument.

'You'll thank me when you're older, Shireen. Listen to me. You're young and beautiful. That goes without saying. If you stay here you'll fall in love and marry. It's only natural. You'll feel happy for a while, because a couple in love want to live in a small world of their own. I won't deny that. But eventually this will become your biggest problem. A nuclear family doesn't last.'

'I know so many . . .' she began.

His hand closed over hers. 'Of course, you don't believe

me now. I understand that. But later you'll come to appreciate that you carry the Indian culture in your genes. You'll want to have the larger family ties and connections. You'll get sick of Western individualism which, I promise you, is only a hair's breath from self-indulgence. It has contaminated you, Shireen. You don't know where your duty lies.'

Shireen crossed and uncrossed her legs restlessly. Guilt was her *bête noire*. Even now it was snuffling around her making her skin crawl and she could smell its fetid breath. It had shadowed her since Mother left home. She would never forget that night: Father's cold disdain and her mother's hysterics as she tried to explain that she wanted to go home to Ireland, to her own people.

'I'd assumed this was your home,' Father had told her. 'If you leave now, don't come back.' Since then Mother had visited her at school several times, but there was always an aura of guilt around her.

'You won't stay young for ever, Shireen. Imagine how you'll feel when you are old and alone with none of your children around when you need their support. Of course, I'm also being selfish. I want my grandchildren around me when I retire to India.'

'But, Father,' she cut in sharply, 'I deserve to marry a man I love.'

Even as she said it, she knew that this could never happen. She thought about John. She liked him, she lusted for his body, she wanted him every time she saw him, but she knew she didn't love him. Shireen had never loved and never been loved. Her mother had engaged a nurse for her, a capable but loveless woman, her father had always been working. Sam was the nearest she'd ever come to loving another human being. Shireen had her own secret love, though, and that was acting.

'Love! What's love? In India a married couple love each other because it's expected of them.'

I won't listen to him. He's deluding himself. The only person I trust is Grandmother. She taught me that desire is the basis of all suffering. But how can Grandmother be right? Every great advance mankind has ever made springs from a desire to achieve. Shouldn't there be a middle way, a bridge between the East and West?

She felt in her pocket for the goodbye gift Sam had sent her, a beautiful mother-of-pearl powder compact. She pulled out the note and read it again.

'Man is mind, and ever more he takes the tool of thought and shaping what he wills, brings forth a thousand joys, a thousand ills. He thinks in secret and it comes to pass. Environment is but his looking glass.' James Allen.

Shape your future well, Shireen. With all my love, Sam. P.S. I'm always here if you need me. P.P.S. Don't fuck up. You might not get another chance.

They were approaching Heathrow. Shireen leaned back and closed her eyes, blinking hard. She wasn't a crying sort of person, but she could have wept. The car drew up, their driver leaped out and found a trolley for her luggage. As if in a daze she followed her father to the check-in counter, checked in, put her boarding pass in her pocket. This was it!

'No need to go through yet. We have time for lunch,' Father told her. An hour's reprieve!

Shireen ordered a salad and toyed with it when it came. The same old arguments were pressing in on her. She was an heiress. If she left she would be nothing. Their Indian home was very beautiful, far better than their house in England, and she had a position of eminence in the family because of this. But it wasn't the money, or the position that was holding her to her duty. It was guilt.

A Muslim woman was sitting at the next table, veiled in black. She and her husband ordered lasagne and Shireen wondered how she would eat it. The food arrived and for a moment the woman sat talking to her husband as he ate. Then she reached up and unfastened her veil. She had a pleasant face and she glanced around smiling recklessly. Then their eyes met and she smiled at Shireen. Her smile seemed to be telling her something. It's that simple, it seemed to say.

Shireen stood up. 'Excuse me, Father.' She saw his questioning glance as he reached towards her as if to hold her arm, but she evaded him, hurrying past the tables to the information desk, and from there to the airport manager's office.

'Come in. Sit down. What can I do for you?'

She wasn't sure of her rights as she fumbled for her boarding card and passport and handed them to him. She tried but failed to stop her hands shaking. Then she propped her elbows on the desk and covered her face with her hands.

'Are things really so bad, Miss Desai? Perhaps your problem can be sorted out.'

'I'm not taking the flight. Please – please – can I have my luggage?'

He gave her a swift, appraising look. 'Left it a bit late, didn't you, love? With luck, it's not loaded yet.' He picked up his telephone and dialled a number.

Moments later they were hurrying along corridors and out on to the tarmac. Shireen talked breathlessly as she hurried to keep up. She felt dizzy and unreal, as if she were in shock. Perhaps she was. 'It was the woman. I couldn't imagine how she was going to eat. It seemed like the most amazing problem. I suddenly realised that I, too, could simply take it off – the duty my father has imposed upon me, and centuries of Indian culture that aren't mine at all. My mother was Irish, you see.'

'Good for you.'

'But you do understand what I mean, don't you?'

'No, love. Can't say I do. But just as long as you know what you mean. Are you doing the right thing? Are you sure?'

'Oh, yes.'

'Well, then,' he said.

They reached the luggage truck parked close to the plane. Shireen shuddered. It was too close for comfort. She was sure someone would run down the gangway and grab her. She retrieved her luggage, said goodbye and wheeled it back to the manager's office.

'I've cancelled your seat, so if you weaken you'll have to come back to me.'

'Thanks. I won't weaken now.' As she made her way back to her father, her stomach was crawling.

He was still sitting at the table, looking crushed and bitter. She'd seen him look like that before. 'I'm not leaving you, Father, unless you want me to. But I'm not going to India either. I'm staying here. I was brought up here and this is my home. I'm going to have a career. I don't have to leave unless you want me to.'

Her father's face set into even grimmer lines. 'Don't call me Father. You've lost that right.'

'No, I haven't, because I still love you,' she said, choking back her tears.

There was no answer as he turned away from her. Shireen wheeled her luggage to the tube station. Where should she go? Then she remembered Sam's unused Hampstead apartment. Perhaps she could borrow it for a few weeks until she got settled. Of course she could. She was not completely alone, after all. She had a friend.

Chapter 29

'Hello, Sam.'

The evening brightened suddenly as Sam looked up to see Richard standing in the doorway.

'What a surprise. You're just in time for coffee. Or a drink, perhaps. I'll have it sent up. Biscuits, scones?'

'Just coffee, thanks.' Mundane words, but his eyes said so much. Sam felt she was bathed in a rosy glow of well-being.

'You were looking so worried. I couldn't help noticing. Is there anything I can do to help?'

'Drink twenty thousand barrels of beer a year and make sure it's Woodlands' best.'

'That bad? What's that in gallons?' he asked thoughtfully.

'Seven hundred thousand, or near enough.'

'I see your problem, but all the same I came to try to talk you out of going to Pilsen. America is a much bigger market.'

'Oh, God, not again. I don't want to talk about it.'

'I could show you the ropes and get you started. I could even find you a good distributor. D'you feel you can put your reputation on the line because of what Greg Selo said?'

'How d'you know that?'

'Worked it out. I wouldn't trust him. Ruthless bastard, if I know anything about men.'

'You don't even know him.'

'I don't have to sit around for weeks to recognise pure evil. Whatever you sell in Pilsen you could sell ten times the amount in the States.'

'Everything's bigger and better in the States, isn't it? You know something, you don't look like Rosemary's Texan billionaire, but you sure as hell *are* him.'

'You can be damned rude. Why don't you run a credit check on him?'

'I already have.' Why should she explain that selling in the States would take a great deal of cash for new blends, new labels and a whole new advertising campaign, whereas Greg was simply buying stout? 'Look here, Richard. One fuck doesn't give you the right to run my life or the business. It's nothing to do with you. You're buying the title, not the family.'

The moment she spoke, she wished she hadn't. Richard's face changed. Compassion and friendship vanished, his eyes glinted and his mouth twisted into a cynical smile. It was just how he'd looked at the beer festival.

'No hard feelings, Richard, but—'

She stopped because he had gone.

It's like riding a bicycle, Trevor thought as he stared at Desai's six-storey warehouse. You never forget old skills. Age is an illusion. You're the same person, think the same, feel the same, have the same skills, but your body doesn't wear as well as your mind. Wear and tear, that's all it is. Nowadays his right knee let him down badly, and he wasn't anything like as fit as he'd hoped to be. Once, with a hook and a net, he'd have scaled up these walls like a monkey. Now he'd be lucky to make it up the stairs when he got inside.

Better get on with it, he urged himself. A quick look around assured him he was alone.

Desai hadn't changed his locks for the past fifteen years. Main problem was the electronic eye inside. It was not for nothing that Trevor shared his fishing rights with the owner of Visor security systems. The two of them went back a long way, so Trevor knew what to look out for.

He pushed in the control key and opened the door silently. Now he had thirty seconds to reach the control panel and switch off the various stations. So far so good. Sam, who had visited Shireen here a few times, knew that she had operated a computer in the accounts department on the sixth floor. By the time he reached the open-plan office he was gasping for breath, and his knee hurt badly.

Trevor switched on the computer and began the long search. All he had to help him were a few specific dates when the contraband liquor had been brought in, culminating in the fateful night of 15 May, when Michel was shot.

It was dawn before he decided to call it a day. He had twenty names to investigate. The remaining creditors on Desai's long list were legitimate business companies. The most promising was a firm in Monaco, called Monexic Trading, Import–Export. He'd check them out first.

He'd left it a bit late, but there was no one around. As he left the warehouse the sky was turning oyster blue and it looked as if they would have another lovely day.

Back in his office, Trevor switched on the console and sent his latest findings to his research network, as he liked to call his old SAS pals, or those of them who were still alive, including Michel and George. Maybe someone had come across Monexic Trading in the past . . .

Trevor arrived at the breakfast table looking like death. Julie was intrigued. Had he spent the night out, and if so, with whom? He hadn't shaved and he was wearing black jeans and a black polo-necked sweatshirt.

'Would you like to tell me why you're looking like Burglar Bill and why you're so tired?' Sam bit out. She didn't usually snap like this but lately she had been impossible.

'I've been up all night. I'll snatch a couple of hours' sleep and then I'm off to Corsica.'

'*Please* take more care of yourself. I mean . . . just why are you going to see Michel again?'

'Come on, Sam! I have business with him.'

'The last lot of business with him almost led to three deaths.'

'All of which is true, but that still doesn't give you the right to try to control my movements, young lady.'

Sam stared hard at her plate.

Trevor drained his coffee-cup and went to the sideboard. He stood there in silence for a few minutes.

When Helen came through with another jug of milk, he asked, 'Any eggs?'

'Not until Tom dismantles the batteries.'

'How about shop eggs?'

'They cheat. "Free range" is a big selling aid,' Julie explained. 'One can't be sure.'

'Bacon, bangers?'

Helen cocked her thumb towards Porgy, as the rescued piglet was now known, who was snorting and snuffling over his porridge.

'So is this it then? Grilled tomatoes with kippers?'

'For the time being. You've been given about four months to change to organic farming,' Sam said tartly.

'Luther's balls on toast would suit me fine right now.'

Julie giggled. 'Luther's not the problem, Gramps,' she

explained carefully. 'We're trying to make the world a kinder place.'

Sam poured herself another cup of coffee. 'I must get to work. I don't know what you're up to, but you will take care, won't you, Trevor? I worry about you.'

'Don't. I'm enjoying myself. Haven't felt so young in years.'

He looked a hundred, Julie thought, but that wasn't something he would want to know. And as for her sister. She frowned as she watched Sam scowling. She had been so bad-tempered lately. Shadows ringed her eyes and she was gloomily introspective. Her moods affected everyone – even Tasha slunk around looking guilty.

'Everything okay, Sam?' Trevor asked. Seems to me you're a bit down in the mouth. I can come back into the business at any time. Just say the word. You know I'm fully recovered.'

'I keep telling you there's nothing wrong, except the two of you nagging me. Okay, I'm sorry. To be honest, I have a bit of a hangover. Shireen walked out on her father yesterday. We celebrated last night. It was touch and go. Can you believe it? Her luggage was already on the plane when she finally plucked up courage to say no.'

'Good for her,' Trevor said.

'She's walked out on a fortune,' Julie added. 'I guess she had to think twice about that.'

'Particularly since she's broke. Hope you don't mind, Trevor, I gave her a part-time job, evenings only, selling our beer around the pubs and clubs, doing whatever she can to push the new blends. And she has the loan of my flat.'

'Of course I don't mind. I'd do the same myself.'

'I know you would.' Sam smiled gratefully.

'By the way, I've invited Richard to lunch on Sunday week,' Trevor said. 'That's just after you return from Pilsen.'

'No!'

The word came out like an explosion. Sam's lips were set in a straight, hard line. Watching her, Julie thought it was strange how her features seemed to change according to her mood. Right now she was in a fury. Sam wasn't usually a bitch, but she had it in for Richard.

'I'm sorry. I can't explain. Get rid of him, please. I'm about to try to cancel his option.'

Trevor was looking amused and Sam was fast losing her temper. Any minute now there'd be an explosion, Julie decided. She drained her cup ready for a hasty exit.

'Listen, do we need the money?' Trevor asked her.

Sam stared at Gramps in astonishment. 'Are you kidding?'

'Then sell it to him and forget the rest. This is getting out of hand!'

'You don't have to worry, Gramps. He won't come. The truth is, we had . . . well, a disagreement. We're not on speaking terms.'

'Well, that's strange, since he accepted. He said, "Tell Sam I may be Czech-mated, spelled with a z, but I'm still in the running." Does that make any sense to you?'

'Oh, Gramps!'

Sam's face lit up. Her lips softened, her frown vanished. The old Sam was back. Then she smiled. 'Well then.' She laughed.

Trevor looked relieved and Julie hid a smirk.

How come she hadn't guessed? Sam and Richard. Hm! Not bad at all.

Chapter 30

It was almost noon when Trevor left Ajaccio airport and took a taxi to the city centre. Within a few minutes he was damp with sweat, his shirt sticking to him, his feet swollen and pinched. He could cope with dry heat, but he couldn't take the moisture. He was glad to walk into the air-conditioned bar. As before, Michel was sitting behind the till. He leaped up, with a broad grin on his face, flung his arms wide and let out a roar of welcome.

Trevor extricated himself from the bear hug with difficulty and stepped back. 'You're looking great, Michel. I'm glad to see you've recovered.'

Michel's complexion was ruddy and healthy, and his crystal clear blue eyes were sparkling with fun.

'It was nothing.' He shrugged eloquently. 'We've coped with worse than that in our time. Come. Let's go.' He put his arm round Trevor's shoulders. 'You got here quickly, my friend. I didn't expect you for days.'

'Like old times. You've beaten us all, Michel. Still the cobra, eh?'

Michel shrugged deprecatingly. 'We'll go out on the terrace. It's noisy, but pleasant. Josephina,' he bellowed. 'Take the till.'

Trevor would have preferred to stay inside, but he followed Michel up the stairs to the terrace, which overlooked the city. A misty haze obscured the sea, but the mountains towered over them and he experienced a sudden desire to spend days walking in the mountains.

'You've come a long way and I mustn't keep you in suspense,' Michel was saying. 'Let me fill you in on the background.'

He fetched a bottle of Cognac and poured for them both.

'First I must to tell you a little about our island. Many of the older generation have contacts in the Marseille underground, but traditionally our home is kept as pure as our women. There's no crime in Corsica, unless you count the political hotheads. If someone tries to contaminate our island with crime or drugs, we react just as we would if our women were violated.'

Trevor remembered the problems of French intelligence in the post-war era. The GIs had moved in to drain the swamps on the east coast and rid the island of malaria, and some fell for local girls. Many had disappeared without trace.

'Criminals should keep away from Corsica,' Michel went on. 'In 1986 some young Yankee drug-pushers decided to try their luck in Ajaccio. They were found twenty-four hours after their arrival floating in the harbour with their throats cut. That was our last foreign invasion.'

'I remember that.'

'From then on, the Mafia, French criminals and all the rest of the riff-raff gave our island a wide berth. That suited everyone. But now!' He threw up his hands in mock horror and grinned as if to show that it was all good clean fun, which it wasn't, Trevor reminded himself. 'Now Europe is full of pushy, get-rich-quick johnnies who don't know the rules, particularly the guys from Russia.'

But they'll learn fast, Trevor thought.

'One came here to my bar. Can you believe that? He was trying to set up a protection racket. It seems they have a similar set-up in Marseille. Believe it or not, he threatened me.'

'He might as well have put a gun to his head and pulled the trigger,' Trevor said, smiling grimly.

'My friends took this stupid guy and roughed him up a bit. Here's a photograph of him. D'you recognise him?'

'No.' I'm getting old and soft, Trevor thought, as he shuddered and handed back the photograph.

'He didn't know much. He got his orders from his superior in the organisation. His cellphone was issued in Monaco, and the accounts were paid in cash, but several of his calls were made to a company called Monomex. The company you're investigating. Hence my call. Now this is where it gets interesting. On the advice of my friends, I paid his first demand in cash, but I made a record of the notes. The cash was deposited in a Monaco bank, together with cash payments earned by a legitimate taxi company. And who do you think owns the taxis?'

'Monomex.'

'Exactly! They own six fleets and no doubt that's the way they explain their cash deposits to the bank. The cash in the Monaco account is transferred almost daily to two Swiss numbered accounts, twenty per cent to one and eighty per cent to the other. What does all that tell you, Trevor?'

'We're dealing with a small-time crook with big-time connections. Probably Russian-organised criminals to whom the Monaco guys pay a regular cut. They own a handful of criminal businesses and some taxi fleets to disguise the cash deposits.'

Trevor was smiling as he sipped his Cognac. They were getting somewhere at last.

'I have more for you. Have some more Cognac.' He hovered with the bottle.

'I'd rather have coffee, thanks.'

Michel opened the door and yelled for coffee. 'Okay. Now listen to this. The cellphone was purchased from a company offering two for the price of one. The other number was almost identical and it is used by the woman who runs the Monomex office. She makes regular weekly telephone calls to six massage parlours in Marseille, Nice, Cannes and Tangiers, a protection firm disguised as a security company operating from a Marseille base, six Russian prostitutes working in the Antwerp red-light district, and the taxi firms. My friend, that's all I have for you. Now we can relax and have lunch.'

'All!' Trevor looked astounded. 'But, Michel, you could run Interpol with your contacts.'

Michel winked. 'We Corsicans are everywhere and we hold tightly to our allegiances. I have many friends scattered around. We'll keep an eye on Monomex.'

It was dusk before Trevor caught the last flight to Nice. Despite Michel's input, he was still a long way from knowing who was running the show. And why they wanted Woodlands so badly.

Chapter 31

Shireen was sitting in a minibus clutching a mop and a bucket. *I can't believe I'm doing this. But it's just a role, isn't it? Like any other role. Maybe my first big part. So why do I feel so scared?*

She was dressed in a coarse, bottle green overall, with a matching green scarf on her head. A large white logo on both breast pockets proclaimed her to be a cog in the wheel of Joe's Cleaning Service. Around her sat twenty women of various ages and ethnic groups, but they had in common an inability to speak English and the need to eat, which had led them to Joe.

And there sat Joe himself in the driver's seat, splendid in his purple vest, shiny black pants and a tangle of gold necklaces plus one large gold earring. He was an appalling driver and as they snaked through London's traffic they were accompanied by hoots and honks and angry shouts. Even on this dismal dawn, London drivers' wit rose to the occasion: 'Lost the zoo, mate? Turn left at the lights.' 'Where'd you get your licence, brother? Timbuktu?'

Joe was above all that. He wore earphones and listened to rap with a beatific smile on his face. He bore a curious resemblance to Brutus, Popeye's antagonist, and Shireen guessed his time and cash were squandered at the local gym. His eyes were very black and with his taunting grin and fearsome muscles, he looked like a man it was best not to cross.

So what madness led me to do this?

The madness had a name: Muriel Finch, receptionist at the drama academy where Shireen had been determined to study.

Shireen's new life had looked so promising: she had two thousand pounds in her savings account, Sam had lent her a Hampstead apartment and had asked her to promote Woodlands ale around London's pubs, an evening job that enabled her to study in the daytime. Pure charity, she saw now, in the cold light of this gloomy morning. She should never have accepted, but what else could she have done? There and then she had vowed she'd pay back the Rosslyns somehow.

Once, she and Sam had played truant from school and come up to London by train for her audition. Father's rage had been awe-inspiring when the letter arrived stating that she'd been accepted by the academy for a three-year course. He'd stood over her while she wrote to tell them that she'd changed her mind.

Having been accepted once, though, it stood to reason they would take her now. But she hadn't reckoned on Muriel Finch and there seemed to be no way to bypass her.

That awful woman with dangling earrings, necklaces, spectacles on a ribbon and umpteen dozen rings and things had thrust a form into her hand. 'Fill this in and post it to us with two photographs. Auditions will be held next April or thereabouts. We'll let you know if we want to see you.'

'But it's August now.'

'The year starts in September. You're too far late for this one.'

Disappointment flooded in. 'You must make an exception.' This was where she belonged. She *had* to be here.

The woman ignored her.

'You don't understand, I've already been accepted. I wasn't able to start at the time, but now I am.'

'Name?'

'Shireen Desai.'

'Write it down.' The woman thrust a pad towards her. Moments later she was clicking into the computer.

'But it says here that you declined our offer.'

'Yes, that was unavoidable.'

'You'll have to apply again. Post the form back any time this year.' Muriel's hateful voice had an obvious ring of triumph in it.

Shireen took out her pen and began to fill in the form. She'd almost finished when a humble-looking woman of sallow complexion, wearing a coarse green overall, shuffled across the floor carrying a mop and a bucket.

'What on earth are you doing here?' the receptionist snarled.

The cleaner looked afraid. 'Excuse me?' She dropped her mop with a clatter.

'You shouldn't be here. They collect you people round the back.'

'Excuse me?'

The receptionist shouted louder, but the woman cringed more.

'I'll show her,' Shireen said. 'Which way?'

'Down the steps, turn the corner and you'll see them waiting on the pavement. He's usually late.'

'Who is?'

'The driver, Joe, of course. He must train his girls better. They're all over the place. Half of them don't know what they're doing.'

'And you are?'

'Tell him Muriel Finch complained.'

'I certainly will.'

As she took the woman's arm she saw a name on her overall pocket: Joe's Cleaning Service. A minibus was parked round the corner and Joe was leaning against it smoking a joint.

''Ere, Poko, you dumb bloody nut! Where've you been? The girls are good and mad with you. Get in, then. Rama's on the six-hour shift. Brass and windows? Right?'

'Yes. Brass and windows.'

The woman who had spoken was Indian, and she didn't have much more English than Poko. Clearly Joe was picking up cheap illegal labour.

'I need work.' Shireen spoke in a strong Indian accent and gazed appealingly at him.

'Come to my office tomorrow morning at noon. You got that?'

She nodded and grabbed the card he thrust towards her.

When she walked into his office the next day, Joe, or Brutus, as she preferred to think of him, was flexing his muscles in front of a full-length mirror.

''Ere. You ever heard of knocking?'

'Excuse me? My English. It is not too delicious. But I clean windows good.'

'Oh, God! Not another Paki.'

'Indian.' She nodded vehemently.

'So! Where's your work permit?'

She shrugged and looked scared.

'All right. Never mind all that. Work hard and I'll see you're all right. You get me?'

'Get me?' She nodded and smiled.

'Christ! Scrub that bloody floor and let's see how you go.'

By the end of the first week Shireen was tired, she'd lost

weight and her hands were red and rough. Worse, she hadn't seen the inside of the coveted academy. She'd vacuumed a cinema, cleaned office windows and once she'd been dropped at a bank and told to clean the marble foyer where the public crowded in and out all day long. Not too much job satisfaction here, she decided, as she tried to keep clear of the public's heavy feet. Friday was pay-day. Joe informed her that her rightful wage was £200, but after deductions and paying for two overalls, she netted only £120. But she had two overalls – and they were hers as she had paid for them.

On Monday she was dropped at the academy. She'd arrived at last, although hardly in the way she'd envisaged. Cleaning windows, she soon learned, enabled her to walk into any office, lecture or audition whenever she felt like it. No one challenged her, no one noticed her, she was as close to invisible as it was possible to be just as long as she stood by the window and wiped away. On her first day she attended three classes and watched a couple of auditions. So far so good.

The following morning, Joe told her she was going to the airport for the day. So who needed Joe? She took the overalls she'd paid for, and put them on under her raincoat. Then she quit her job and went home, purchasing a bucket and mop on the way.

By Wednesday the skies had cleared and the glorious golden dawn was sparkling on windows and wet roofs as Shireen hung around outside the back entrance to the academy.

'You're an early bird,' the night porter said, when he opened the door.

''Scuse?'

'Okay, nothing. Where's the others?'

''Scuse?'

'Off you go, then. Know where you're going, do you?'

She flashed him a smile and half filled her bucket with water. Squishing in the detergent she set off. With a bucket you can go anywhere, she reckoned, and she did.

For the next three weeks Shireen chose her lectures with care, bought the books the students were reading, memorised passages and practised alone in front of Sam's huge mirror. She didn't feel guilty. She was doing no harm and their windows glistened and cost them nothing. So she worked all hours, sometimes forgetting to go home until late. Her fingers began to split around the quicks and ugly patches appeared. She invested in rubber gloves and worked even harder.

Sometimes she seemed to notice a quizzical expression gleaming in the eyes of the principal, Hugh Bolton. He was tall and grey-haired, slightly stooped with hooded brown eyes that looked amused most of the time. The following Friday, he cornered her between classes. 'The windows do you proud, my dear.'

''Scuse?''

'I'm honoured that my windows are the cleanest in the Academy whereas those of Frank Asherton are covered with a dirty grey sheen.'

''Scuse?'' She tried not to show her alarm. Surely he didn't guess? Everyone knew that Hugh and Frank vied with each other as to who was the best teacher.

'Me, Hugh Bolton.' Tarzan-like Hugh pointed to his chest. 'You?'

'Shireen.' She let out a stream of words in Hindustani. It was part of a text from the *Bhagavadgita* and the only thing she knew by heart, but Bolton wasn't to know.

'You aren't pure Indian, my dear. Even an idiot can see that. You look Spanish.'

''Scuse?'

'I think it's time I called Joe to tell him he's overworking you.'

'Please don't. He'll sue me.' Oops! Her accent had slipped a little. Bolton kept one hand hovering over the telephone receiver, but his eyes were gleaming with laughter.

'Okay, Mop. You win. Mop's your nickname. Did you know that? I don't know if it comes from your totem pole or your hair. It's a wig, isn't it?'

''Scuse?'

'Cut it out, Mop.'

Shireen went off to clean Frank's windows with a heavy heart. His class was on stage management and it was abominably boring.

From the noticeboard she learned that a number of the students were being auditioned for a new Jonathan Bernstein Broadway hit: *The Lesser Spotted Homo Erectus*, which was to open in the West End early the following year. Only the two main stars were to be brought over with the production. The rest would be locals and everyone was excited at the prospect of a part, however humble. Bolton was pre-auditioning his best students to help them on their way.

The play was a riot, set around an Amazonian career girl, May, and her inability to find time for her less successful husband, Rod, who had lost his libido. The set for scene one was a corridor, where the two sometimes met *en route* to their many assignments. Shireen watched and inwardly criticised each in turn. If only *she* had a chance she'd do it like this or like that . . . If only . . .

It was the turn of Diana Blossom, who had expanded

somewhat lately, despite suggestions that she diet. Vice Principal Frank was reading Rod's part.

Shireen moved closer. She'd taken to cleaning with a large feather duster since her near-fatal collision with Bolton. Diana was wooden. She'd never make it, Shireen decided. Bolton was losing patience with her. You could tell by the way he was smacking his hand with his ruler. The worse their performance, the faster he went. Right now it sounded like castanets.

'My dear Diana, do stop for the sake of my sanity. Your American accent stinks and you're not into the part. You're not May. You haven't thought her out at all. The Mop would do a better job than you. Wouldn't you, Mop?'

'Cues like that were made in heaven,' Shireen sang out, as she grabbed the script.

Miss Blossom's cheeks were burning, her eyes bulging, and she was opening and closing her mouth like a goldfish. Compassion was quickly extinguished. Chance was dangling an audition within Shireen's grasp and she would have it.

'Right! Shall we take it from the top of page three again,' Bolton commanded.

'Whatever you say.'

He was looking amused, she noticed, and so was Frank.

As she stepped forward, flinging her wig into the bucket and shaking her hair loose, every atom in her body was striving to be May, to feel the sharp, biting incisiveness of the woman's character. Suddenly she looked taller as she carried herself with the ease and grace of a person who has always been successful.

'Jerry?'

'Huh,' Frank said.

'Whoa there! Have you got a minute?' And Shireen was

off. At the end of the scene there was a long silence. Then the principal clapped slowly.

'You ever lived in the States?' he asked her.

'No.'

'Why d'you want to be an actress?'

'It's not that I want to be one,' she said, choosing her words with care. 'It's just that I am. I always have been. I can't change that. I can fail, but I'll only be a failed actress. Never anything else.'

'Okay, come and see the company secretary in the morning. She'll fix you up with a scholarship if you need one. What d'you live on?'

Shireen wanted to scream, or shout, or grasp Bolton in the world's biggest hug. Instead she burst into tears.

'I have an evening job,' she sobbed. 'I'm only crying because I'm so happy.'

'Of course. What's your name, by the way?'

'Shireen Desai.'

'I think you'll need to change it. Would that bother you?'

'Not even slightly.'

'Well, think about it. Make a list. I'll help you choose. Of course, to us you'll never be anything but the Mop.'

'Mop it is. It's a lucky nickname. When do I start?'

'You already have,' he said. 'Joe's loss is our gain. By the way, did you ever actually work for him?'

'For a long and terrible week, and I did pay for these overalls.'

'Sell them back. Get them laundered and Muriel will do it for you. Tell her I said she must deduct it from his cash.'

She did, rather bossily, and her revenge on Muriel Finch was pure bliss.

Chapter 32

Sales were improving, but the brewery's cash-flow prospects were abysmal. How were they going to pay the wages and purchase the barley and hops for their next year's production? The bank was hammering Sam and she owed Walter too. Richard might pay for the title, although his option wasn't up yet, but a small voice was saying: When you've spent the cash for the title, what then? At least the new blend had achieved steady sales, which told her that the right taste, plus the right marketing, would achieve results. I can't fail if I put in the effort, she assured herself time and again. But there was also the worry of Trevor, who'd told them he'd be away for a few days, but refused to say where he was going.

Sam had pinned her hopes on creating new market opportunities in Pilsen and she'd been planning their strategy with Rosemary for the past week, but there was still so much to do and only five days to go. At six p.m. Sam fetched coffee and sandwiches from the canteen and they took a break.

'When I said yes to Greg I had no idea of the work involved. What a slog!'

'You've changed, Sam.' The older woman gazed affectionately at her. 'Gloom and doom has faded. Gritty determination has taken over.'

'Only because there's no time for anything else. What did Walter say about the labels for Pilsen?'

'Nearly ready. He's excited about them. Wouldn't shut up. Oh, and he wants money.'

'I know. He'll have to wait. And John?'

'John's been a bit odd lately,' Rosemary said. Watching her, Sam could see that her words had been an understatement. Rosemary went on, 'He seems confused. Anyone would think he was responsible for the entire project. Have you noticed how haggard he looks? Something's bugging him.'

Sam frowned, remembering John's face when she'd told him she was going to Pilsen. He'd turned quite pale. 'You want to watch those guys in Eastern Europe. Some of them have strange bedfellows,' he'd said.

'Rosemary, it's over ten days since we last saw Richard.'

'Is it? Who's counting? Are you worried he won't buy the title?'

'Not really.'

'Hm? So that's it. Perhaps he's not into women. Have you considered that?'

'Let's forget it.'

Sam hadn't meant to snarl, but Rosemary could be irritating at times. Surely she'd noticed how Richard ogled every female, especially Julie? She squared her shoulders and forced a bright smile to her face. 'How about traditional country dancing? We have to entertain the locals. What we need is a think-tank.'

Dusk came and the two women were still hard at it. The planning board was stretched out across the wall adorned with multi-coloured stickers for jobs still to be done.

'We'll never make it.' Rosemary looked tired and dishevelled with blue shadows under her eyes.

'Of course we will. But you look exhausted. It's almost ten. Perhaps you'd better go.'

The door opened. 'I never gave her such a tough time,' Trevor's voice said.

'Gramps! Where on earth have you been?'

'Corsica, Monaco, around and about.'

'You might have let us know.'

'Trevor! I've—' Rosemary flushed. 'We've been worried about you. You should have called.'

Trevor looked happier than she'd seen him for years, Sam thought. His skin glowed above the white stubble of a week's unshaven beard and his eyes were glinting with mischief.

'Michel's a star. One of the thugs fell into his lap and I've been talking to a few of Michel's compatriots, so now we have a list of the British companies they're targeting to join their export scam. There's strong evidence of Russian control, which is what I always suspected. I passed everything over to Scotland Yard and Interpol. No doubt they'll keep me posted.'

'You should be resting. You're limping badly again.'

'Who'd suspect a cripple like me?' He caught sight of the planning board. 'So what's this then?'

'Five brewers from the Independent Family Brewers are joining us, so we're forming a pretty strong British team. Now we want to liven it up with Morris men, folk and pop music, a band, country dancing. Something different every day – all ideas will be gratefully received, Trevor.'

'I'm impressed, but Rosemary shouldn't work this late. You go, my dear. In my opinion, eight hours a day is enough to earn an honest living.'

Rosemary picked up her bag and gazed around anxiously. 'Goodnight then.' She hovered wistfully in the doorway. She was like a faded flower about to shed its petals, yet still beautiful for a few short hours.

Sam's suspicions were confirmed: Rosemary was in

love with Trevor. 'Come back with us for a late supper, Rosemary,' she said.

Rosemary looked awkward.

'Please do. We can finalise our plans. Gramps will run you home later. Helen's bound to have left us something to eat.'

'You've got a slave-driver for a granddaughter, Trevor,' Rosemary said, but she looked pleased all the same.

'She's a workaholic, very much like her grandmother. Did I mention that?' Trevor responded.

Rosemary looked as if she'd been slapped in the face. 'Once or twice. I'll drive over since my car's here. See you at the house.'

Sam and Trevor linked arms and walked home. A fragrant smell of ozone was drifting up from the sea, mingled with the scent of damp earth, newly cut grass and jasmine, perhaps, Sam thought. Birds were twittering in the trees and then they heard an owl hoot. The moon was rising and the castle stood out in silhouette. The thought of someone else owning the castle hurt. It was worse to imagine selling Woodlands. She shuddered. Then, inexplicably, she experienced a feeling of intense loneliness and an almost unbearable longing for Richard.

'Why did you have to mention Grandmother to Rosemary?' She turned on Trevor suddenly.

'Why not?'

'Surely you know that Rosemary's in love with you.'

'At seventy-seven I'm past all that, Sam.'

She paused mid-step and stared at him, then reached for his hand.

'Are you really? I'm so sorry, Gramps. Does that mean you're over the hill?'

'Oh, for goodness sake. I wasn't meaning—' He broke off and shook his head. 'Is that the sort of thing young people talk about nowadays, no finesse, no subtlety or sensitivity?'

'Well, are you?'

'Not that I'm aware of.'

'Have you had anyone since Grandma died?'

'What sort of a question is that?'

Heavens! He was blushing. The elderly were so old-fashioned. She tried not to laugh. 'Have you?' she persisted.

'Yes. Come on, hurry. I'm hungry.' He set off ahead of her, half bent, arms swinging, but still limping.

'Well, then, who was it?' She was laughing as she caught up with him.

'You're being impertinent.'

'Why don't you consider Rosemary?'

'Are you trying to marry me off?'

'Not necessarily. You could date her or be her friend, couldn't you?'

'I'm aware that Rosemary fancies me. Or thinks she does. I wouldn't say love. That's too strong a word, but I'm not sure it would be fair or reasonable to embark on any such foolishness. You see, Sam, I've only ever loved one woman truly and that was your grandmother. Rosemary would only get half a man. She deserves better.' He was panting heavily.

'Why don't you have it out with her?' Sam persisted. 'Give her the choice.'

'God forbid I should be so arrogant.'

She wasn't going to let him get away with that. She reached for his arm and hung on to slow him down.

'I think you're being foolish, Gramps.'

'Now, who's the expert in emotional foolishness?'

'What exactly do you mean?' Suddenly she was about to lose her cool. Did everyone know? The thought made her feel weak in the knees. How shameful. 'You think I like Richard, don't you? Perhaps I do. But what makes you so sure?'

'Age, my dear. It brings experience, among other things.'

Helen had done them proud with a cold roast and salads. Julie and Luther arrived unexpectedly, and Tasha, in a new green collar, took up a proprietorial stance by the sideboard, waiting for the bones.

'It's absolutely amazing how Tasha's become so domesticated. Hard to believe, really,' Trevor said thoughtfully.

'She knows when she's on to a good thing,' Luther said.

'Julie,' Sam said, 'what are your plans for the next couple of weeks? I could do with your help in Pilsen. Can you come along? If I fly out to check out the stalls and so on, can you drive with the convoy? Keep an eye on them and liaise with me by cellphone?'

'Of course I can. And I'd love to.' She jumped up and hugged Sam impulsively. 'We haven't done anything together for ages. I'm so pleased you asked.'

'And Porgy? I don't think Helen could cope with him.'

'Luther wants him for a while.'

Julie and Luther ate little and soon left to go dancing. Their togetherness made Sam feel increasingly alone. She decided to go for a walk to try to shake off her gloom, but once outside she felt worse.

What a night! The breeze was warm and balmy, filled with subtle scents, while the moon bathed the trees with its sensual light. Something about the pristine beauty of the night made Sam long for a man to hold her in her arms, just as long as the man were Richard. It was a night for loving.

As she walked towards the sea, she saw a light flickering in the castle. Trespassers? What were they doing? As she approached she heard the sound of hammering. What the hell was going on? She grabbed a large stick and crept in.

The knocking was coming from the ruined well about two storeys below the entrance hall where she was standing. The castle was built on a slope and the well led directly to the clifftop on the southern side, facing over the channel.

She dropped the stick when she saw Richard, bathed with light from a hurricane lantern, crouched under the stairway bashing away with a hammer and chisel. He was so intent, he didn't hear her. She stared at him, longing to make him her own, yet knowing that part of him would never be hers.

'Richard, what are you doing?'

He didn't look up immediately. Then he put down the hammer, stood up and stretched.

She felt weakened by the intensity of her need. 'You're trespassing,' she said.

'You look like a strumpet standing there with your hands on your hips. You'll fall if you're not careful. If you must snarl at me, step back from the edge. This place is hazardous.'

A deep, sensuous voice. She inched forward and some loose stones fell.

'You all right, Sam?' His torch dazzled her.

'Yes, of course.'

When the beam fell away she was plunged into pitch darkness. The crumbling steps down to the well were dangerous even in daylight. She shuffled down one step cautiously.

'What are you doing here?'

197

'I'm trying to work out if it could be restored . . . and the probable cost.'

Clearly he was lying. Why? She began to inch further down.

'Bullshit. That's not why you're here. Someone like you would never want to live here.'

'Probably not,' he agreed cheerfully. 'All the same, it's lovely. Look at the moon reflected in the sea. I guess it was the same thousands of years ago.'

'Imagine the Roman soldiers standing there on guard.'

'Not Roman, Norman.'

Why did he always know best? 'Who cares! Well, anyway, my ancestors.'

'No, not that far back.' His voice echoed around the old stone well. 'It's not impossible, but it's not documented. Of course, a Roman garrison might have stood here under the ruins, but this is Norman.' He picked up the lantern and walked outside on to the grassy verge. 'I like to think of the guards posted here, watching for invaders.'

'From France?'

'No, from the north-east, probably Vikings.'

'Vikings it is.' She conceded that he knew more about English history than she did.

Then she slipped and skidded down a couple of steps. She landed with a thump and sat swearing to herself as she rubbed her leg. A minute later she was dazzled by a pool of light. Richard was bending over her, examining her grazed shin.

'How did you get up here so fast? Switch that bloody light off. You're blinding me.'

'I ran round. I thought you'd hurt yourself. Move up. I'll sit nearest the drop. I don't trust your sense of self-preservation. Quite honestly, I don't think you have any. If you had, you'd steer clear of Greg.' He pushed her up and sat beside her.

Sam wasn't going to fall into that argument again. She tried to ignore her dry lips, and quiet her panting breath. 'Why sneak up here at midnight?' she asked.

'Why not? It's my castle.' He was teasing her. She could see that from the glint in his eyes.

'Not yet. A small deposit doesn't mean a sale.'

'I have a watertight option.'

'You mean you're still thinking of buying the title?' She tried to keep hope well and truly out of her intonation.

'Exactly.'

'You don't look that foolish or impressionable.'

'I'm hoping to claim my seat in the House of Lords before that august institution is closed down.'

She fell for it, forgetting how he liked to lead her on. 'God! You Americans! Listen to me for once and for all. It's not a real title.'

'It's a con?'

'No, no. Come on, Richard, you know more than I do about English peerage.'

'Shame on you.' He put his arm around her shoulder and hugged her against him. 'So what do I get for my money?'

'Very little.'

Anyone would think you don't want it, Sam, she lectured herself.

'The right to call yourself Lord of the Manor of Bourne-on-Sea. Plus this old ruin, of course, a couple of fields and the right to charge rent for placing telegraph poles here. Of course, there's fishing rights, but a little way downstream you can catch the same fish for nothing. And you can sell mugs printed with your family crest, as we do. So, don't be silly. Don't waste your money. Give up the option so I can sell the title to someone with more money than sense.'

'That could be me.'

'I don't want it to be you.'

'My cash is not good enough?'

'I just don't want you to be foolish. I don't want you to buy your self-esteem.'

'I've got plenty of that, Sam. I'll tell you my secret: it's the *droit du seigneur* I'm after.'

'What's that?' she asked softly, her mouth very close to his ear.

'Really, Sam, your education is sadly lacking. I'll have to teach you. Come closer. It means the ancient right of the local lord to fuck the village maidens first, particularly the one I fancy most – namely you, Sam. There is some confusion nowadays as to whether or not this right was ever . . .'

He was off again. Sam wasn't listening. Butterflies were waging war in her stomach, her face was burning, her eyes stinging and she had an uncontrollable desire to pounce.

She lurched forward and slipped. As she fell she was gripped tightly and pulled hard against Richard. He was sitting on the steps and she was sprawled all over him. She gave a long, loud gasp, half of fear and half desire. Then his lips were on hers, his tongue was driving her crazy and his hands were on her breasts.

He stopped for breath at last. 'Sam, oh, Sam, you're such an idiot.'

She wrenched her head away. 'Is that supposed to be an endearment?'

'This is!' He pushed her hand hard down. 'Feel that. That's what you do to me. It's all yours.'

'Oh Richard, oh – oh . . .'

He fitted perfectly, just as he had last time, and she

heard his voice murmuring in her ear, 'Keep still, Sam. Watch it. I think we're moving.'

'Oh, do it again. Again! Please.'

'Ouch! We're slipping down. Help! Try to catch hold of something.'

'Oh, it's so good. I'm coming, I'm coming!' She screamed long and loud and the sound echoed around them. 'Richard darling, why did you stop?'

'Have you quite finished?'

'Mm, yes.'

'Then sit still, but look around you.'

'Wow!'

'Exactly. D'you see that lead pipe over your head?'

'Yes.'

'Try to grab it and ease yourself up really gently. Steady on.' Sam caught hold of the pipe and pulled herself to her feet. Leaning forward, she grabbed Richard's hand and pulled him to the next step. A piece of stone fell fifty feet and landed with an awesome crash.

'God, Richard. We're on the bottom broken stair of the broken staircase. One more bump and we'd have been over the edge. But it might have been worth it.'

'You don't need a fifty-foot fall, Sam. You just need me.'

'Ssh! This is no time for boasting.'

Richard grabbed her wrist. 'We're getting out of here fast.'

'Don't lose it, Richard.'

'Lose it? You've got to be kidding. Direct the way to the nearest patch of grass.'

The sky softly enclosed the stars, but the moon had fled. The gentle wind was cooler and Sam was shivering. She pressed herself harder against Richard's warm body.

'That was great sex, Sam,' he murmured sleepily.

'The best.'

'Sam, listen to me. Please don't go to Pilsen. I don't trust Greg Selo. I don't like him getting involved in your business.'

'You have no reason to say that,' she muttered.

'What we're seeing nowadays, Sam, is the emergence of a criminal class more sophisticated than we've ever experienced before. Their syndicates control banks, stock exchanges, hotels and businesses. It was so easy for them. In the final years of the Communist regime, the KGB controlled all the privatisation programmes. They grabbed all they could and simply transferred their powerful networks to operate under private enterprise. Greg is very rich, very sure of himself. Self-made men are rare in Eastern Europe unless . . . I'll swear he's one of the comrades.'

'You are young and rich, too. Should I suspect you, too?' she asked sleepily.

'Yes,' he said, after a long silence.

She longed to say, Richard, I have no choice. I need the sales to survive. He could be Satan himself and I'd still need his business. Instead she tried to turn the tables on him. 'Why are you so damned secretive about yourself?' she asked.

'I'm not. What you see is what you get.'

'Are you amazingly rich?'

'Of course not. The truth is I live on my wits.'

'Doing what?'

'Buying and selling.'

'So why d'you want the title?'

He propped himself up on one elbow. 'To sell it, of course.'

'Oh!' Disappointment ran through her. So he wouldn't

be their neighbour, after all. She felt cheated. 'You won't find anyone that stupid and you'll be stuck with it.'

'But I've already found someone. He's a historian and he's after the documents that go with the title.'

'There aren't any documents. Maybe once there were, but they've been lost for centuries.'

'But he believes that there are – he believes it very strongly and he wants them. He's prepared to pay for the off-chance that they exist. They would be very valuable, you see.'

She sat up, feeling shattered. 'I forbid you to make the sale. I won't allow our family name to be dragged into anything so – so despicable.'

'But you need the money, Sam.'

'Never for a con trick like that. I'd rather go bankrupt. I'll pay you back the option money.'

'No, never. It's too late. We have an agreement in writing.'

'Oh, Richard. How could you? I can't believe you would do that. Can't you see it's so wrong?'

'But, Sam, the trouble is, you believe I'd do that, don't you?'

'What's this, some sort of a test?'

Richard sat up, looking undecided. He stared at her for a while. 'Love's supposed to be trusting and uncon-ditional, Sam.'

'I'd be a fool to trust you,' she retorted.

'But an even bigger fool to trust Greg Selo.'

She glared at him. 'Is this our first fight?'

'More like the fourth or fifth,' Richard said softly.

'Oh, Richard. Why did you say the word love? We don't know each other. We just have a tremendous physical attraction and, let's face it, the sex is something . . .'

'Yes?'

'Something special. But I have to make my business work and you can't interfere.'

'Same with me,' he said briefly.

'Selling something that doesn't exist hardly comes under "business". Oh, for God's sake,' Sam said, losing her patience, 'here we go again. I'm going home. Goodnight.'

But as she marched over the cliff towards her home, she muttered, 'You fool, Sam.'

Chapter 33

It was the afternoon of their first day in Pilsen and already a crowd was sampling Woodlands' wares or just hanging around. Sam watched her sister, who was oblivious to the men's admiration. Surely she must know how attractive she is? That hair of hers, all that honey-white hair breaking across her shoulders. Surely she must see how the men were falling over themselves to be close to her? I'm not sure she even knows what effect she's having on them. She hardly wears makeup, just a touch of blue eyeliner around her eyes and pale pink lip salve over her mouth. She probably doesn't know how to. No wonder she took the modelling world by storm. Even in her worn out stretch jeans and a navy vest, she looks superb. If only she had a better self-image.

The beer festival was situated in the grounds of a former military academy, in the heart of the old town, a place of red-brick Gothic buildings and narrow cobbled streets, but conveniently close to their modern hotel. Dwarfed by the spires and chimneys, the Union Flags lay inert, hardly rippling in the hot summer afternoon.

The weather was glorious, unusually so even for high summer, they were assured by everyone. It was warm and sunny with cloudless skies. 'A special gift to welcome you, and make sure you come back,' the locals said. But there was nothing local about the festival: anyone who was anyone in the European liquor industry was there. There were five British exhibitors, mainly from Kent, offering a variety of pure ale, stout and fruit blends. Woodlands had brought their Grey Wolf blended ale, the dark stout the Russians preferred, and their new elderberry and cider beer blends, as well as their pure ale.

The city had welcomed the exhibitors with a nightly programme of parties, dinner and dancing. They'd kicked off with a beer-drinking contest and then they'd danced through the night in a tavern garden to gypsy music. Sam was exhausted and surely Julie was, too, but she showed no sign of wilting yet. They'd been running the stall between them, answering queries, explaining the difference between the British and Czech methods of brewing and pushing their new blends. It seemed that just about everyone wanted to sample Woodlands' ale and Greg was there to take the orders, but so far there hadn't been any.

This was a make-or-break attempt to establish some export business, and it had cost them a fortune to get there – far more than Sam had originally envisaged. If she went back without good orders the bank manager would foreclose.

'Stop worrying, Sam.' Julie touched her arm.

'I was thinking of the hassles and the cost of getting here, and how worried I am that it might all be for nothing.'

Greg picked up on her mood. 'You look a little harassed,' he said. 'Why don't you two go back to the hotel for lunch and leave me here to look after everything?'

Why not, indeed? Sam thought. Fluent in five languages, and with his quaint, old-world courtesy and charm, Greg was proving as big a draw as Julie. 'What d'you think, Julie?' she asked.

'I'm all for a cold shower and lunch.'

Their hotel was only a five-minute walk away, but it took them almost an hour to get there as they wandered down alleys of quaint old shops and admired the glassware and intricate patterns on vases and ornaments and bought a few presents: a vase for Rosemary, a fruit bowl for Helen and a cut-glass tankard for Trevor.

They ate lunch on the balcony of the fifth-floor restaurant, overlooking slate roofs, cathedral pinnacles and nineteenth-century brick chimneys and a good deal of smog. Beyond was the beautiful green of the Czech countryside.

A good time for talking, Sam thought, since she had Julie all to herself for once.

'There's something I feel we should discuss, Julie, and now's as good a time as any.' Sam's voice took on an older-sister tone. 'You've been cancelling your modelling appointments. I know because they phone looking for you.'

'I've been meaning to tell you that I'm giving it up. I might do the odd shot when I need extra cash, and I've saved quite a bit. But I want to study wildlife, ecology . . . maybe even law or sociology – I'm not sure. I'm starting all over again, even if it seems absurd.'

Sam looked at her sister in surprise. 'Of course it doesn't. It's perfect. You're only eighteen. I always knew modelling wasn't really you.'

'You don't think I'm crazy?'

'No, I think you're wonderful.' Sam reached across the table and squeezed Julie's hand. 'I'd approve, even if you were forty-eight instead of only eighteen.'

'What about your future, Sam? Is this it?' Julie gestured towards the stacked beer cans.

'Until I fix it up for Gramps.'

'And then? What about you and Richard? Is it serious?'

'Yes . . . But there's something I have to tell you – and Gramps, of course. Richard wants to sell the title to a third party, someone who thinks valuable documents are tied up in the deal. I've warned him that there aren't any. I'm beginning to suspect he's a con.'

'I guess selling a title gets one in touch with odd people, but Richard's straight,' Julie said staunchly. 'I'd bet my life on that.'

'Look,' Sam said, changing the subject, 'I hope you don't mind me asking, Julie, but what do you see in Luther?'

'If I said marriage what would you say?'

'Maybe that you're too young.'

'Look, Sam, if Luther were white would you be asking this?'

'Oh, God! I was hoping to avoid that sort of thing. Forget I spoke. No, don't. What's the big attraction?'

'Apart from the fact that he's good-looking, tall, clever, well-educated, has several degrees, a promising future, a brilliant mind, and that he's terrific in bed?' Julie's eyes were glacial.

'Yes.'

'He turns me on and he thinks I'm special.'

'You *are* special.'

'You say that, but the facts speak otherwise. I'm always in your shadow. You do better than me at everything. It's as if I've been born into the wrong family. You're all special, every last one of you. I've never achieved anything.'

'But you're famous and I'm pushing us deeper into the red.'

'That's not the point. You have a talent. You could always write and create. I have no talent. You make me feel a real failure.'

'But that's silly. You did as well as I at school. You wanted to be a model, so you skipped university, and now I see your face all over the place.'

'But I've wasted two years and I was into drugs. Luther made me see the pointlessness of the way I was living, and he said it was him or drugs. So . . .'

'You love him, don't you?'

'Yes, but we're finding out that love might not be enough.'

'Yes. I'm sorry. Be careful, Julie. I don't want to see you hurt.'

'I guess I feel the same way about you.'

Sam had decided to gatecrash Balaton's. She didn't tell Julie and Greg, just asked the porter to call a taxi.

Shortly afterwards she was climbing into an ancient blue sedan. She watched the driver curiously. Everything about him drooped, his eyes, his mouth and his chin. He hooked his elbow over the back of the front seat and twisted round awkwardly. 'Where to?'

'Balaton's brewery,' Sam said. She settled back to enjoy watching the countryside pass by, small stone villages set in flat green farmland.

Twenty minutes later the driver called over his shoulder, 'Who are you going to see?'

'Mr Balaton.'

He laughed. 'He's long since gone. D'you know these people? The old place has changed a lot since it was taken over.'

'But I was told it's an old-established family business.'

'The Balaton family used to hold guided tours, an annual fair, beer-tasting competitions, but recently it was bought out. No one knows the new owners. All their lager is exported and they keep to themselves.'

He broke off as he negotiated a winding gravel road with tall old oaks on either side. They turned into an old cobbled yard under huge chestnut trees. The driver parked and took out a newspaper.

'I suppose I'll be about half an hour,' Sam said. She looked around at the splendid Gothic architecture with an impressive frieze of partying townsfolk around the square doors and windows. After a moment's hesitation, she walked in.

The interior seemed to echo silence like an old monastery. The flagstones were polished by several centuries of shuffling feet, and the ceilings were made of dark polished timber.

The man sitting at Reception looked entirely out of place. Sam could imagine him almost anywhere but sitting here in his ill-fitting grey suit.

'I'm Sam Rosslyn from Woodlands Brewery,' she said. 'Would it be possible to see the manager, or the managing director?'

There was something wrong with his eyes. He said, 'Wait a moment. Please sit.' Then he punched buttons on his cellphone.

A few black leather chairs on dark wooden frames were scattered around. Sam chose one and tried to relax. Half an hour passed, then she heard a car race into the courtyard. It stopped with squealing brakes and footsteps hurried across the yard. Hans Kupi, whom she'd last seen in Woodlands' boardroom, hurried in, hands outstretched.

'My dear Miss Rosslyn. What a pleasure! Follow me.'

He led Sam to an office that was clearly his.

'Please sit down. What can I do for you?'

He smiled, revealing his steel tooth, and Sam remembered her dog lying in the road.

'I came here to see Mr Balaton, but now I've heard that the family sold out and this brewery is under new management. You grossly misrepresented the facts at our meeting, Mr Kupi. You said Balaton's was family-owned. As for your threats and the death of my dog, well . . .'

'Miss Rosslyn, you're being most offensive. Your dog? What are you talking about?'

'About drugging a helpless old dog and running it over. I insisted on a post-mortem, you see. Do you really think that we're the kind of people to give in to your bullying? You've underestimated us rather badly.'

'No, no, wait a minute. Mr Balaton has retained a fifty per cent holding in the brewery, Miss Rosslyn, but we've been responsible for putting in modern machinery and management techniques, so he is doing much better than before. He's making more money than he ever did. That's what business is all about, isn't it?'

'No, Mr Kupi.'

'You're young and idealistic, Miss Rosslyn. You'll change your mind before long.'

'I doubt that. I should like to see Mr Balaton, please.'

Kupi shook his head. 'He's living in France. I'm not sure where.'

Sam stood up. 'Then there's no point in prolonging this meeting. We've had many offers to buy us out. We're not selling. If we did decide to sell, it wouldn't be to you. We've informed the police of your threats. Please bear that in mind and keep away from us.'

The taxi driver was still reading his newspaper. He folded it and placed it on the seat beside him.

'Back to the beer festival, please,' said Sam. The driver started the engine. Sam had a thought. 'I'm told that Mr

Balaton retired to France. Do you know if that's true? If he's around I'd really like to see him.'

'Last I heard he was here. I'll check up for you.'

'Thanks. You can call me at our hotel.'

Chapter 34

Rosemary was on the way home when she remembered that she'd left the play script on her desk and it was rehearsal night. She hurried back – to find someone bent over her open filing cabinet.

'What the . . .'

John whipped round. 'Why, Rosemary – I'm just looking for something.'

'Why are you scratching through *my* files?'

'I need the list of creditors,' he replied.

'Why?'

'Rosemary, I'm a director of this company. It concerns me.'

Now he was stammering, and Rosemary almost felt sorry for him. He'd never been good at lying.

'Why not just ask?'

'Okay, I'm asking. Where's the list of creditors?'

'Sam keeps the accounts locked in her safe and she has the only key.'

'That bad, is it?'

'No, just private. She'll pull us through. She's a clever girl.'

'Are we solvent? Or will I be looking for a job any day now?'

'We're solvent – obviously. You'll get the facts and figures at the next board meeting. Can't it wait until then? Why didn't you ask Sam? She doesn't keep things from you.'

'The truth is, I've been offered another job.' Rosemary could see that he was ad-libbing. 'I don't want to take it, but I'd rather know the true situation before making a decision. And I don't want to worry Sam either.'

'Sam'll be back on Monday. Ask her yourself.'

'Don't rush off, Rosemary. I've been meaning to talk to you.'

'What about?' She was late and agitated, and she didn't have time for John's nonsense.

'About Trevor.'

Rosemary flinched and saw John relax. 'Why don't you run me home, John? I walked to work this morning and now I'm late. There's a rehearsal. If you like, we can talk in the car.'

'Okay. Let's go.'

He hummed and hawed until they'd almost reached her cottage. Rosemary was fast losing her patience. 'John, if you've got something to say, you've got about two minutes left to say it,' she snapped.

'All right, Rosemary. I meet all sorts as I go around the bars, and yesterday I heard, via a barman who doesn't want to be named, that it's curtains for Trevor unless he minds his own business. There's a gang of small-time crooks who're smuggling in beer from France. It's not a big deal, but they don't need people snooping around after them. I hate to alarm you, but we must stop Trevor.'

'Did you take this threat to the police?'

'Whoa there, Rosemary. I'm not out to cripple the business. These guys use our pubs. The barman was merely passing on a message from a couple of thugs.'

'The ones wanted for attempted murder?'

'Rosemary, when you put it that way, you make sense. If you want me to go to the police I will. We'll probably lose a good barman. The point is, Trevor shouldn't be snooping around in Monaco, should he? He should be home nursing his leg.'

Monaco? But Trevor had been in Corsica. Why had John said Monaco? A sudden sharp wave of suspicion pierced her.

'Sorry, John. Of course you're right. It's best to handle this ourselves. I'll speak to Sam. She's the only one with influence over Trevor.'

John parked outside her cottage and Rosemary got out. 'I'll see what I can do. Thanks for the lift.'

She stood staring after him long after the car had slithered over the bumps of the eroded gravel road and disappeared from view. It must have good shock absorbers. Where had John found the money to buy such an expensive car? She remembered, too, his insistence that Trevor stock up with stout. What *was* John up to? *Had* Trevor been in Monaco?

Tibby was rubbing against her legs and mewing urgently. He wanted his supper. She glanced at her watch. Seven! She'd have to hurry. Pity Greg was away – it hadn't taken him long to become their star. He was a natural actor and could sing and dance well, too.

She arrived at the barn on time, but everyone else was late. Only four women turned up and the vicar. He was almost stone deaf and repeatedly missed his cues. 'Peter, listen to me,' she bellowed into his hearing aid. 'When it's your cue I'm going to put my finger on my chin. Will you keep an eye on me?'

'My dear Rosemary, I'll keep my eyes glued on you.'

He did and promptly fell over an occasional table. Then Agatha stood on his glasses while they were getting him back on his feet. The poor man almost cried. Rosemary was feeling desperate. 'Let's have an early night. The others will be back by our next rehearsal,' she told everyone.

She went home, poured herself a brandy and knocked it back. She was longing to call Trevor and tell him what John had said, but perhaps she'd better wait until morning. She couldn't help wondering what he had been doing all by himself in Monaco.

From his bedroom Trevor saw Rosemary's light and knew that she was safely back from rehearsal. If they sold the brewery, what was he going to do about her? Companion? Pension? Not really the answer, he knew. She'd always been there and now he had a responsibility to her, but he wasn't sure just how responsible he was. And he liked her company. She was fun to be with. But he would never love her as he'd loved Anna. Why couldn't he move on?

Alone, at the window, Trevor viewed and reviewed scenes that were best forgotten, ranging back half a century to a story of betrayal. He saw the hills and valleys of fertile black soil, felt the bitter winter evenings and saw the beautiful old castles, many of which were left abandoned. Most of all, he remembered Anna. It was because of her that he had befriended Vim.

'I don't like the British,' Vim had said on that first morning when they found him after his drop. 'In fact, I don't like you much, but as long as you're working to help us get the Boche out of our country, I'm with you. I would give my life to help you, if need be. I'm going to make sure you'll be all right.'

Anna had taken Trevor back to her home and fed him. He'd slept in the attic amongst the 'junk', as she called the many *objets d'art* wrapped up for the duration of the war.

Vim arrived at noon, riding one bicycle and steering another. The one he gave Trevor was too small and the saddle felt like a lump of cement.

'This safe-house we're going to is one of many,' Vim called over his shoulder in Czech. 'It is owned by a widow whose husband was tortured to death by the Boche for stealing one of his own chickens that they'd commandeered. I have found you several safe billets and each one has a second exit. It's best to move around haphazardly.' Whenever Vim said 'Boche' he spat.

There could hardly have been a worse area for cycling. There was never a flat stretch anywhere among the undulating hills. Trevor was fit, but he was not used to cycling and soon he was in agony.

'This widow is a bit of a flirt, but I expect you're typically English – cold as a fish and oblivious to all female advances,' Vim announced.

'Absolutely,' Trevor replied. He'd already decided that Anna was the love of his life.

They were approaching the village of Chrast. He could see a jumble of roofs and spires above the trees. Vim dismounted and waved to Trevor to follow him as he disappeared behind a clump of bushes. 'There's a junction here. The Boche often set up roadblocks and search everyone who comes this way. We have to make a slight detour.'

The detour was a muddy track along a riverbank where they carried their bicycles on their shoulders.

Before reaching the outskirts where the widow lived, they stopped for a moment beside the beautiful Strela river, whose clear, soft waters had a great deal to do with the glorious taste of the local lager.

Three naked Germans were bathing in a deep rock pool. Trevor and Vim crept along another path and eventually came to the cottage.

The widow met them at the door, arms akimbo, her face creased with anxiety. 'There's a roadblock up there,' she whispered. 'Come inside quickly.'

The moment the door was shut, she pounced on Vim and kissed him passionately. He fended her off, wiping his face with a handkerchief. 'Come on, woman, behave yourself. This is business.'

Trevor was to be stationed in the attic where a large window led to a concealed roof behind gables and then by a circuitous route to a well-concealed ditch running to the woods.

Might work in an emergency, Trevor thought.

'Well, we might as well get on. We have a hell of a lot of mileage to cover before nightfall.'

Trevor groaned. They cycled, then pulled and pushed their bicycles up interminable hills, through dark, rain-sodden woods. Vim kept him entertained with stories about the Boche and their excesses.

In every house he took Trevor to that day, a similar scene occurred. Women flung themselves at the dashing Vim and shed tears when he left. Trevor looked at him with new respect. He studied his appearance, his thick bushy eyebrows, waxed moustache, and his bold, clear eyes. He wore bright colours, a crimson windbreaker, a turquoise scarf, and olive green corduroy trousers.

'Pre-war Bohemian trash ... all I have left,' Vim explained, when Trevor asked him about his unusual clothes.

Trevor survived the next two years by veering from one disaster to the next. His job was to pull the many partisan groups into a cohesive, bonded army, trained and able to help the Allies when the invasion came.

The Communists were the best fighters but they distrusted and despised the others. Vim's group consisted of pro-West, mainly upper-class Czechs. Some of the groups were no more than criminals who had taken to the hills to escape justice, and there were also the intellectuals who had escaped the German policy of wiping out the country's thinkers.

When they first arrived, Anna had been handling radio communications with the Free Czechs in London. This was a suicide mission because sooner or later the SS would trace the transmissions back to base. Trevor knew he must take the job away from her, mainly because he'd fallen in love with her. Of course, she wouldn't hear of it, but Robin found an Irish nun, Sister Theresa, in the Sacred Heart convent, a few kilometres outside Pilsen, and recruited her. Kind, capable and brave, she walked miles every day, pretending to be simple-minded, carrying a basket full of mushrooms and turkey eggs with the radio hidden underneath. She would broadcast from caves, or thickets, on the outskirts of a village. The SS never suspected her or the convent.

Anna could not forgive Trevor for taking away her job, but once again Vim smoothed things over. He was a good companion and his sense of humour never abandoned him, however dangerous their situation. He and Trevor built a bond of comradeship. Besides, since he and Anna had fallen deeply in love, Vim was family, which counted for a great deal in those dangerous years.

Looking back, it seemed to Trevor now that loving Anna had blinded him to so much that should have been obvious. His wife had been dead for over two decades and he had built up new bonds. He saw clearly now that he was not taking responsibility for the present because he was held captive by the past.

He got up and stared out towards Rosemary's cottage. Often, in the early hours of the morning, he saw her lights on and knew that she was lonely and unable to sleep. He longed to comfort her.

Chapter 35

By noon on the last day everyone was tired, but enthusiastic beer drinkers were still clustering around Woodlands' stall. Were they buyers? Sam had no way of knowing.

She took half an hour to go shopping, leaving Julie in charge. She returned to find a short note addressed to her and her sister, with two roses pinned on the envelope.

She opened it. 'Amazing response to Woodlands Ale in signed orders. Come and celebrate our success. Pick you both up at eight tonight. P.S. Copies of the orders enclosed. I'm expecting more today.'

Sam almost burst into tears of relief. Oh, God! Why *didn't* he tell us before? But that was Greg for you: well-meaning, but thoughtless and utterly likeable. 'Let's go, Julie. We'll enjoy ourselves. Perhaps Greg has a friend to make a foursome. Now I have a couple of appointments with wholesalers. I think the taxi's waiting. Don't tell Greg. 'Bye.'

She felt bad about lying, but there was no point in telling Julie that she was going to see Mr Balaton, whom she had succeeded in tracing.

He lived in a smart, upmarket suburb near the river in a quaint, art-deco house set among flowering shrubs in a well-kept garden. Sam was shown into a study by a uniformed maid and shortly afterwards Balaton came in and shook hands. He was shortish, middle-aged and paunchy, with receding grey hair, and small grey eyes that peered myopically through the thick lenses of his spectacles.

'Why are you here?' he began sternly, in excellent English. His knuckles were white where he clutched his cane. 'You insisted on having an appointment, but I have nothing to say to you. I am no longer involved in brewing.'

'But you owned Balaton's brewery and your name was used by a group of men trying to buy out my grandfather's brewery. They told us that they were acting on behalf of your family. I want to know who is trying to take us over.'

'God in heaven. In Britain? This is unbelievable.'

He was pacing up and down, beating his fist into his hand. 'I must warn you, this meeting is most unwise. They have their spies everywhere. I don't wish to be involved and that is why I was reluctant to see you, but let's have some coffee.' He went to the door and called the maid.

Five minutes later, they sat down on the terrace to enjoy their coffee and Black Forest cake.

'Miss Rosslyn,' Balaton began, 'nowadays no one knows who anyone is any more. You want to know who bought my brewery, but I can't answer you. It was taken over by a group called Caribbean Holdings, a company registered in Dutch Antibes. I only ever had contact with their nominee, a lawyer from Prague and two other men who, I think, were employees of the group.'

'Was their lawyer a grey-haired man with a steel tooth and a secretary to match?'

'The same. I lost my business because I was foolish,' he went on. 'Slowly I allowed them to market more and more of my production. They sold my lager in Germany and Russia. It seemed sound economic sense to build up the company's exports and there were more and more demands. Finally they were selling all of my production.'

'Was this deliberate?' she asked.

'Of course. That was when they began to lower prices, allowing me only the smallest profit margin. When I finally saw the light and dug in my heels, it was too late. They defaulted on payments, leaving me in financial turmoil.'

'I'm sorry,' Sam murmured. If Greg defaulted she'd be finished.

'I was in the red, but I fought back. I sold a number of private assets and put the cash into the business. Then came their second move. There was a fire in the new office block, which destroyed all of our records. Arson was suspected and consequently the insurance company wouldn't settle my claims.' He shrugged.

'After that, Miss Rosslyn, my daughter-in-law went to visit her aged mother. She left the children in the car, but it was a hot day, so she went back to fetch them and brought them to play at Reception. Then her car blew up. It was wrecked and several hospital windows were shattered. At this stage my family and I decided that our safety was more important than our business and we accepted their offer, which by now had been greatly reduced. They came up with the system of paying only half, the remainder to be based on profits. Of course they have never paid these amounts, deliberately since they like to use my name. My son and his family emigrated, but my wife and I felt we were too old to pull up our roots. Miss Rosslyn, these people have great power and they stop at nothing. There's little more that I can say, other than asking you to be very, very careful.'

Sam's stomach was knotting up as she stared at him incredulously. 'So your brewery has fallen into the hands of a Russian–based criminal network?'

'All business is dirty business and these gangsters will be legitimate in a few years.' He paused and smiled bitterly. 'Most of Europe's great landowners fought dirty to get what they've got. Now it's the Russians' turn. The KGB controlled all the privatisation programmes in the final years of the Soviet regime. They transferred their power networks to operate under private enterprise and grabbed all they could. They've made the liquor industry their own.'

'Why choose that industry?' Sam asked.

'Because it enables the comrades to gain foreign currency, which they badly need to spread their networks in the West. In the old days, Western governments were well aware of the Communist threat, but I'm not sure how alert they are to this new menace, which is every bit as threatening to the West's way of life.'

'I think they're getting wise to them in Britain.'

'Good! The liquor industry needs dynamic people. People like you, Miss Rosslyn. Old family-run businesses are child's play to these people.'

Suddenly Trevor's suspicions seemed more viable. Sam shivered.

Balaton stood up and shook her hand. 'Delighted to meet you, my dear. Learn from my mistakes. Don't let anyone, person or company, control more than twenty per cent of your sales, will you? Take care. And, remember, we never met.'

On the drive back, Sam thought about Balaton's warning. So far Greg had sold 25 per cent of her production. With these new orders he'd be marketing over 35 per cent. Could he be involved in the network of organised crime? The idea was ludicrous. Kupi, maybe, but not Greg.

Sam sighed. It was all very well having the right theories, but if the orders didn't materialise you had to take what you could get to survive. And she was damn lucky to have these orders.

* * *

She arrived back in time for the closing cocktail party. After a short speech from the mayor, Sam and Julie left their drivers to dismantle the stands and pack them on to the lorries. They wanted a last look at the town and to visit the fourteenth-century Gothic cathedral.

When they returned to their hotel, laden with presents, they were amazed to find Luther there. He was wearing a suit and looked nervous, until Julie gave a whoop of joy and flung herself into his arms. 'I came to drive you home,' he told her.

'I accept,' she said. 'Okay with you, Sam?'

'Of course. Luther, we're just going to dinner with Greg. Why not come and make it a foursome?'

When Sam emerged from the lift, she found that Julie hadn't arrived, but Greg was waiting in the foyer. 'Wow! Can you sit down?' he asked.

'I could before I came to Pilsen. Now I'm not sure.' She was wearing a short, backless Versace shift in midnight blue.

'You look divine, Sam.'

Sam laughed. 'You're a flirt, Greg. All the girls back home are crazy about you. You do it deliberately. Let's face it, you look good in that suit, and don't you know it.'

For a moment he looked taken aback. Then he realised he was being teased. 'Tall, dark and handsome comes with the genes, Sam. Ten a penny around these parts.'

'Really? Perhaps I'll relocate.'

He laughed and put his arm around her. 'Here come the others. Let's go.'

They were dining in a gypsy restaurant. It was quaint, with its curtained alcoves, ornate polished wooden chairs with plush velvet cushions and high ceilings turned yellow with age and tobacco smoke. The scent of incense mingled with the aroma of rich food and liquor. A brilliantly clad gypsy singer moved from table to table.

Greg was a superb dancer, and she could feel every muscle through his silk shirt and jeans. She was surprised that he was making a play for her. And why not? she asked herself. Then she thought about Richard and experienced a pang of conscience. Besides, Greg was too good-looking to be taken seriously. He was stroking her back, pulling her closer.

She glanced at Julie and saw that she and Luther were having fun. Was that why Julie had changed so much? She was more self-possessed and happier than she had ever been.

At ten thirty Greg hurried them out. They had to see the latest show in town, Spanish dancing and singing at a local nightclub. As the waiter led them to their table, she noticed Balaton and his wife sitting nearby. She would have nodded as she passed their table, but remembered Balaton's warning. At that moment she almost collided with a square, stocky man hurrying to the exit.

'Why, Miss Rosslyn. We meet again.'

It was Hans Kupi. He bowed, and as he smiled, his tooth flashed in the muted light. 'How are you getting on with your research?'

Research?

'Who was that? Greg asked as soon as they'd sat down.

'You went as white as a sheet,' Julie added.

'Suppressed fury,' Sam said, and told Greg what had happened to Brutus.

Sam heard Balaton call the waiter. He and his wife seemed agitated. Their bill arrived, Balaton signed the credit card slip and hurried out.

Just as the door closed behind them, a loud explosion rocked the restaurant. Chandeliers swayed, lights dimmed and glasses rattled.

There was a sudden hush. The manager ran outside and moments later came back. 'It's outside, two blocks down, across the road. A car . . .'

'Let's go,' Greg said. Outside a car was blazing. Pieces of burning debris were scattered around, and through the flames Sam could see two figures.

Someone thrust a hose through the window as Greg ran across the road to try to rescue the car's occupants. She could hear police sirens. Moments later Luther joined him, but the heat was intense and they couldn't get close to the car.

Sam felt strangely dissociated from the scene, but she knew she'd never forget the sight of the two blazing bodies as long as she lived. 'I'd like to go back to the hotel, Greg. I feel terrible,' she said.

'Sure, I'll take you now.'

It was a long night. Sam couldn't get over Balaton's frightened expression as he had paid the bill and left. On impulse she telephoned the Balatons' home, but no one answered. Around dawn, a woman picked up the telephone. She was in tears as she told Sam that her parents-in-law had died in a bomb attack the previous evening.

There was no point in trying to sleep, Sam knew. She was too sad, too scared, and she feared that she might have been an unwitting cause of the murders. She got up, packed and sent down for coffee. There was a knock at the door. She opened it to find two men in civilian clothes, policemen, they said, and their identification papers bore this out. The older man, fiftyish, balding, with sad brown eyes and a baggy, shiny suit, spoke excellent English. 'We came to find out why you made three calls to the Balaton residence during the night and finally spoke to their daughter at six a.m. A strange time to call, isn't it?'

She told them all she knew, the board meeting, the killing of her dog, Hans Kupi's remark and Mr Balaton's fear. The police took hours with her statement, then said, 'You won't be required to stay for the inquest. Go back to England on the first available flight – and have nothing further to do with these people, Miss Rosslyn.'

She couldn't help thinking of Trevor as she waited at the airport. The entire family had accused him of harking back to SAS days, but he'd been right. She would tell him so as soon as she saw him.

Chapter 36

Rosemary shivered as she spooned coffee into the filter paper. It was 6 a.m. and she'd woken early after a restless night. She felt out of sorts and she couldn't shake off a sense of doom. If the brewery went under she'd lose her job, like everyone else, and there'd be nothing else going around here. She'd be lucky to find work in the City at her age and, anyway, the thought of commuting to London was depressing. Sooner or later she'd be forced to move – she might even be evicted. She loved her little cottage perched on the cliff edge with the marvellous castle view and panoramic sweep over the Channel, but it belonged to the Rosslyns and came with the job. If she moved she'd miss her friends and the familiar pastimes: popping down to the pub, the tiny cinema, the old barn where she put on the plays.

Rosemary leaned over the table, her mug in her hands, and tried to imagine the worst scenario. She'd cope, she always had. She was a survivor. But she would no longer see Trevor, and that was the bottom line. She loved him, but that was a secret she would never share.

Trevor had entered Rosemary's life in the most unexpected way, in Bahrain, Saudi Arabia, June 1968. She'd been dancing in the Miradouro nightclub for the past two years, but she'd been off sick three times that year with typhoid, jaundice and shingles. The boss, an ex-dancer herself, had let Rosemary know that her contract would not be renewed.

She was thirty-four, getting on for a dancer, but she'd never trained for anything else, other than acting. She had no desire to return to England, she hated the climate and the grey cities. She wanted bright lights, excitement, a cosmopolitan crowd, fun and *youth* – and that was fading fast in the dry desert climate.

Then Sheikh Feisal Bey had fallen into her lap, like the overripe plum he so much resembled. Who cared if he was fat and red-faced, since he was obscenely rich? Night after night he sat at a table near the stage, his eyes glued on her. Later in the evening he would send discreet gifts: flowers, fresh fruit and sometimes jewellery.

Then came their first date: dinner and dancing at the Globetrotter, followed by a breathless helicopter flight over the desert to Al Khafaq where they breakfasted on fruit, yogurt and delicious spicy pancakes. A whirlwind romance followed: trips down the Red Sea in his ocean-going yacht, breathless canters over the desert on his beautiful Arab mares, unexpected flights to Paris for extravagant shopping sprees. But no sex. Sometimes she wondered if he had what it took. Or was he just the world's last remaining gentleman? They were having lunch at his house on the balcony overlooking the sea when he asked her to marry him. She'd said yes because he seemed kind and gentle, and no one else had ever appreciated her as he did.

They married in Bahrain two weeks later. It was a simple ceremony held at Feisal's home, with only a small group of her fellow dancers present. After a short reception they left for a surprise honeymoon. Rosemary was thrilled and delighted when she was taken to an impressive, ocean-going yacht fit for royalty. Her only disappointment was that Feisal had invited a group of businessmen from the interior, dark, wild-looking, hawk-nosed men who never spoke English in her presence. One of them, Ghalib Fayed, looked as if he'd been hewn out of desert rock, with his black hair, dark skin and wild, haughty eyes. He kept eyeing her intimately, as if she were available.

One evening after dinner, Ghalib cornered her in the bar, pressing his body hard against hers.

'Back off, Ghalib. You must know we're on our honeymoon.'

'Don't pretend you don't know why you're here. Feisal only likes boys. Your job is to make sure his marketing plans run smoothly.'

'That's absurd. What could run more smoothly than oil out of wells?'

'Oil?' Ghalib chuckled. It was a deep chuckle that came from somewhere in his belly. 'He sells mining equipment.'

After this she stopped swimming and stayed out of sight. The night before they returned to Bahrain, Feisal said, 'Tonight, my darling, be ready for me. I feel sure I'll come to you tonight. We have had difficult negotiations.'

That explained it. It had to happen sooner or later. Thank God she hadn't believed Ghalib.

She spent the day feeling apprehensive, wondering why she felt like a whore when she was legally married to the man. By midnight she could have screamed with tension. It was almost one o'clock when the door opened and closed swiftly, and a stealthy tread moved towards the bed. A hard, strong body.

'Get off me. Who are you?' She tried to curb the hysteria in her voice.

'Be quiet,' he growled.

'Ghalib?' Twisting sideways she reached the light switch. 'What are you doing here?' she asked, ice-cold with anger. She scrambled off the bed and ran to the door. It was locked. 'Give me the key or I'll scream.'

'Why? We have until dawn. Rosemary, come here. There's nothing for you out there. You still don't believe me?' he asked. 'I was telling you the truth. I gave him the contract and he screwed me, but I had to be with you.'

Suddenly she was weeping tears of despair.

Ghalib stood up and gave a strange bow. 'I'm sorry. Goodnight.'

She caught hold of him at the door, pulling him back towards the bed. She couldn't stop sobbing.

'Just pretend! Pretend you love me. Pretend it's our honeymoon. Do that for me!'

She was insatiable in her need for comfort.

He left at dawn. 'That was the arrangement,' he told her.

During the night the yacht had put into harbour. Rosemary dressed in jeans and a T-shirt, stuffed her passport and the little money she possessed into her beach bag and went up on deck. Only the crew were around and no one challenged her when she sauntered down the gangway. She found a taxi quickly and reached the British Consulate ten minutes later feeling triumphant, but her joy was short-lived.

After her sad story poured out, the First Secretary explained to her that in Saudi Arabia dual nationality was not recognised. When she married Feisal Bey she had lost her right to British protection. Her passport was invalid here. British women accused of adultery had been flogged or even stoned to death. 'Adultery was forced upon me! Surely you understand?'

'Bey probably has compromising photographs. Even if he doesn't, your best bet is to go back fast. Pretend you were exploring the city.'

'I'll never go back.'

'Please try to understand the danger you are in. Bey probably has scouts out looking for you right now. I doubt the mullahs would understand or believe your story.'

'You must help me. You must! Hide me at the consulate. Anything! I'm begging you for asylum.'

'Mrs Bey, you are a Saudi national. How can we give you asylum? You're on the run from your husband and it's possible that charges have been pressed for adultery, a crime punishable by death. It's not as if we don't warn you girls when you come out here. There's no way I or anyone else can help you. You must go now, Mrs Bey.'

The First Secretary walked out leaving her alone.

She stood there, feeling close to breakdown. She walked out of the french windows on to the balcony and peered at the busy main road six storeys below.

'Don't do it.'

She turned. Briefly she took in the man who stood there smiling at her. There was strength in his dark eyes, stubbornness in his mouth and chin, and a certain recklessness in his wide grin. He would have been handsome, but his nose was too prominent, his eyes too fierce, and although he was young, his expression was old. His smiled faded. He took her arm, and led her down the corridor to a room marked Strictly Private, which she assumed was his. He drew her inside and locked the door.

'Okay. Let's hear the whole story.'

She left nothing out.

'The First Secretary was right,' he said. 'Officially we can't do a thing. Unofficially we're going to get you out of this mess, but you must never tell anyone. By now your husband might be trying to find you, Mrs Bey.'

'Don't call me by that name. I'm Rosemary Santer.'

'And I'm Antony Jones. I'm here on a fact-finding mission for the British Government, but I operate as an importer of fresh fruit and vegetables, and I carry dates and coconut on the return trip. I'll do my best to smuggle you on to a British aircraft in an empty crate. If we meet any problems we'll resort to bribery and corruption. Seldom fails here.'

Something about the man inspired her with confidence. Four hours later she was on a flight home. It was then that she found two thousand pounds tucked into her bag wrapped in a note that read, 'Good luck. Divorce him fast.' That was all she had, plus her freedom and a lasting admiration for the man who had saved her life.

As soon as she landed a job and found a place to stay, Rosemary set in motion her divorce and began a long search for Antony Jones: she wanted to thank him and pay back the cash. Two years later she came to the conclusion that he had never existed and gave up her search.

Her story would have ended there, if it hadn't been for the death of Edgar Hicks. By then Rosemary was working at Loxton's casino, in Mayfair, as a croupier on the roulette table. Her friend Diana Wesley took alternate shifts with her. Diana's boyfriend had been about to inherit a fortune when he died in a car crash only days before they were to be married. Diana was still in shock, so Rosemary accompanied her to the service and the funeral. When Edgar's cousin, Trevor Rosslyn, stood up to give the address, Rosemary couldn't help thinking that fate was on her side.

She tracked him down to Bourne-on-Sea and returned the two thousand pounds, plus a small gift by way of interest.

'Fill me in, Rosemary. What have you being doing since I last saw you?'

This simple question turned into a six-hour dialogue, which took them through dinner and later to the pub for drinks. She learned that Trevor's wife had died recently and that he had only one son who was thinking of emigrating to Zimbabwe.

'Why don't you stay here, Rosemary?'

'Oh, I don't mind driving at night,' she retorted.

'That's not what I mean. I'm looking for a bookkeeper. A cottage goes with the job. You might be happier here than in London. Perhaps I'm wrong, but I gained the impression that you don't much like city life.'

He was right. She took the job and worked her way up until she was Trevor's private secretary, when she had been able to enter his world and learn more about him. Lately she had come to accept that she loved him and that her love would never be reciprocated. Trevor was still wrapped up in his late wife. And now? His family heritage was about to collapse and both their worlds would be destroyed.

Chapter 37

When Sam arrived Shireen was waiting at Heathrow. The sight of her friend looking so happy lightened Sam's mood.

'Your expression tells me everything. We must celebrate.' Sam hugged Shireen hard.

'Just wait till I tell you what's been happening.'

Sam didn't have to wait long: it all poured out as they pushed their way through Heathrow's crowds to the car then drove through the traffic to London – the academy and Shireen's teachers, her studies, the auditions and the plays they put on.

Sam watched her friend. It was as if she had come alive.

'I pick up a fair bit of money here and there, so if you need your apartment I could get my own. Amazing what you can make on small modelling jobs. I walked in and they signed me up.' Shireen snapped her fingers. 'Guess what they call me at the academy? The Mop. And Hugh – he's the director – has taken me under his wing. He thinks I've really got talent.'

'No one doubts that.'

'I was beginning to think that it was all a silly dream. Oh, Sam, it's all great. I have only one worry and that's my father. Have you seen him?'

'No, but don't worry. He'll relent when you start getting known. Take my word for it.'

Shireen gazed affectionately at Sam. 'One day I'll pay you back.'

'Where're we going?' Sam asked, when Shireen took the Ashford turn-off.

'Sorry! I forgot to tell you. Your grandfather's there. He's meeting Lord Davenport and his nephew, Inspector Joyce. They want us to try to identify some photographs. Uncle Trevor says you know the way.'

Shireen chattered on, but Sam lapsed into silence, remembering the Balatons.

Shortly afterwards they arrived at George's imposing home and found the three men on the balcony. Trevor was overjoyed that she'd arrived back safely. He gave her a hug then hung on to her arm as if he feared he might have lost her. Neville Joyce looked harassed. His pewter eyes had deep bags under them and he looked as if he hadn't slept for a couple of nights, but his smile was as warm as ever.

Sam introduced Shireen, noticing the effect she had on the two men. Fleetingly she couldn't help wondering what it must be like to be as beautiful as her friend. Wherever she went she was noticed. Men fell over themselves to be near her and women stared in outright admiration or envy, but she was never ignored. Shireen took all the adoration for granted. She had looked stunning since her early teens.

'We were just summing up,' Trevor explained. 'All we want you two to do is see if you can identify anyone in these photographs.'

He spread the album on the desk and the girls sat side by side, slowly turning the pages.

'Where did you get the photographs?' Sam asked Neville.

'Why d'you ask? D'you recognise anyone?' She looked up into his shrewd eyes. He seemed to know she had plenty to tell them, although she'd tried not to show this.

'This man,' she pointed to Hemzo, 'headed the group that flew over to discuss the takeover offer, and this man was sitting at the reception desk at Balaton's.' She put the album aside. 'Listen, something awful happened in Pilsen and I can't help feeling responsible. I know you warned me not to go near Balaton's, but I went anyway.'

'Don't worry about that. Just tell us what happened,' Trevor said.

She tried to leave nothing out and when she'd finished there was a long, uneasy silence.

'It seems that Trevor's right about the takeover bid,' Neville said at last. 'These are shots of people George or I have come across in the course of our investigations. Of course, Don Shaw brought some pictures back from Russia. George took a few surreptitiously of the men who approached him. Then we have a few mug-shots of the men we deported during the 'ninety-four débâcle.'

Shireen identified three men who had delivered consignments of cheap beer to her father, and Sam recognised Don Shaw's Russian driver as the grey-suited man who had been tasting their stout at Pilsen.

'Well done,' Trevor said. 'We're getting somewhere at last. Now, perhaps you two would like to have a swim. Try to forget about all this. We'll take you to dinner as soon as we're through here. You know where your things are, Sam.'

'Will they fit? It must be years since I last swam here.'

George stood up. 'I'll come and sort you out. There's stacks around somewhere.'

'Let's go, Shireen. The pool's indoors and heated. It's a dream.'

Trevor watched them go with a pang of regret. 'It doesn't seem more than a year or two since they were running around in pigtails. Now look at them.'

Five minutes later George returned looking stunned. 'Good God, Trevor. What a looker Shireen is! Where've you been hiding her?'

'She's Sam's best friend,' Trevor said drily. 'Let's get down to business.'

The two men listened as he explained how the grandson of a colleague in the SAS had succeeded in hacking into the computer system of Monexic Trading, the company Desai Trading paid for deliveries of illicit beer.

'There's something I must tell you,' Trevor said. 'As you know, every can of beer produced anywhere in the world has a code number showing which batch of which year and at which brewery it was produced. The cans being smuggled into Dover the night we copped it came from various sources – a stolen consignment from East Germany in March, Czechoslovakia in April, Belgium two weeks prior to the landing. The cans have newly printed labels similar to Woodlands', but they were printed in Lithuania months before the robberies. What does that tell us?'

'That a widespread network of organised crime is responsible.'

'Probably.'

'Definitely, Trevor,' Neville said firmly.

Trevor spread a large roll of paper over the desk and pinned it down with ashtrays and a paperweight. 'This chart shows the companies who are paying large amounts monthly to Monexic Trading. As you can see, there's a network of criminal activities spread over Europe – brothels, protection rackets, smuggling – and legal or semi-legal outfits such as the fleets of taxis, the strip joints and nightclubs. Monexic Trading pay a cut on all their profits to a group known as the Swiss Investors' Club. This company owns Balaton's and they took it over in a shady manner. This so-called club is my next line of investigation.

'We're on the brink of a Third World War, an under-cover war where sane, law-abiding people are up against criminals with worldwide networks and a total lack of scruples. Organised crime controls the Russian liquor industry and most of Eastern Europe, and they have the Russian railways under their control. So far they've infiltrated only three per cent of liquor marketing in Europe but now they're trying to get a foothold in Britain.'

'I don't have much to report,' George told them, 'other than that the London branch of a Lithuanian trading company is attempting to give me large orders for vodka and gin destined for Russia. I already have these markets from past marketing contacts. It's getting the stuff there that's beyond us. These guys promise to get the goods to the end-buyer for a pretty hefty cut. Once again, it's nothing more than a protection racket. They don't do a damn thing other than allowing you to use the Russian railways.'

'Just like last time,' Neville said. 'I'll get a few men on to it.'

'Well,' George said, his eyes gleaming, 'shall we take the ladies out and give them the time of their lives?'

'That might be difficult, seeing as we two are practically geriatrics,' Trevor said sternly, scowling at George. 'We'll have to rely on your nephew.'

'Don't look at me. I'm a happily married man,' Neville said and laughed.

It was eleven p.m. They had left Shireen at the Hampstead apartment and Trevor was driving Sam home. There was a light drizzle and the monotonous clunk-clunk of the windscreen wipers was sending her to sleep.

'I'm so tired. The flight, the wine, all that. I guess I'm ready to flake out.'

'Well, you can't. We have to talk.' Trevor gave her a swift, affectionate glance. 'We seem to have a problem. John knew that I was in Monaco. He let this slip by mistake when Rosemary found him going through her files.'

'Good God!'

'Did you know where I was?'

'No. You've been very quiet about everything.'

'Yes, I've been careful. John warned Rosemary that I'd be in danger if I continued getting in their way. It seems we're getting close enough to cause them problems. Whoever "they" are.'

'John? I can't believe it.'

'I fear he's been got at. It's my fault. His commissions are down because sales are down. We must keep an eye on him.'

'I owe you an apology, Gramps.'

'Why's that?'

'I didn't believe you when you said organised crime was behind the bid for Woodlands.'

'And now you do?'

'Well, let's say it looks possible. Oh, Gramps! I feel miserable. Dearlove's turned against us. Richard's trying to make a dishonest buck out of the title. Now John.'

'We can fight them off, Sam. I feel that very strongly. Perhaps you need a few days' holiday.'

'That's the last thing I need,' Sam snarled. 'I need to find someone I can take at face value. You've given me a false impression of the world, Gramps. You brought me up to think everyone is kind and honest. No wonder I get so disillusioned.'

'The trick of life, my dear, is to keep a firm grip on your illusions, because half the time they're not illusions at all. John will come up trumps and so will Richard. I trust Richard. I've told you that before.'

'What an optimist you are.'

Sam woke when Trevor drew up in front of the house. 'Off you go. I'll put the car away. Sleep well and try to keep an open mind.'

Impulsively Sam leaned over and hugged him. 'I love you, Gramps.'

'And I love you too. Goodnight, Sam.'

Chapter 38

'Rosemary, you're a star. How can I thank you?'

It was Sam's first morning back at the plant and Rosemary had coped with a dozen mishaps during her absence: Tom Bowles had threatened to beat up the demonstrators as they tried to stop shoppers buying Woodlands beer at the hypermarket; Porgy had been returned by Luther and nearly driven Helen crazy; Dearlove had reduced the overdraft facility without warning, and Jeff Brink had threatened to shoot any dog found on his estate after a number of ornamental ducks had gone missing.

'The bank manager's waiting to see you, Sam.' Rosemary's voice was terse, but her face betrayed her sympathy.

'Doesn't he know this is my first morning back from Pilsen?'

'He knows. Here's his latest letter.'

Sam cringed as she opened the envelope and read that their overdraft must be reduced by fifty thousand pounds at the month's end, as originally agreed by Trevor, or the bank would sell their Woodlands shares.

'Show him in.' Sam gave a sigh of resignation.

Matthew Dearlove came to the point without preamble.

'There're no funds to cover a cheque you've just issued for twenty thousand pounds.'

'It has to be honoured, Matthew. And we need to pay wages and salaries. I'm expecting several substantial payments. Please will you wait a few days?'

She squared her shoulders and hoped he couldn't see the sweat trickling down her back, staining her blouse.

'That's out of the question, Sam. You were mad to incur more expense at Pilsen.'

'The trip paid off handsomely. I've picked up export orders for fifteen thousand barrels a month. Lay off us, Matthew, or I'll find another bank.'

He said, 'Who're you kidding?' but he looked worried. 'How much is coming in this week?'

'Twenty thousand pounds is due from our Prague-based Eastern European sales agent. Perhaps I could cede the money to you?'

'From Eastern Europe? You can't be serious! There's no guarantee of payment. Sorry, Sam. I'll give you until the end of the month.'

'We're solvent on paper, so you must meet that cheque for twenty thousand.'

'All right! But, listen, Sam, you're tilting at windmills. You should have sold out when you had the chance. Small breweries are taxed out of existence and you can't compete with imported beer. You should know when to quit.'

Matthew left and Sam sat with her head in her hands. All she needed was time and cash. Regular sales were up from 18,000 to 38,000 barrels a year. Admittedly 16,000 had come through Greg. The Grey Wolf blend had increased pub sales by another 4,000 barrels. A pretty good increase, she reckoned, but their cash-flow was scary. Damn Dearlove. He was acting as if he had a personal stake in their collapse.

The phone rang and Rosemary called out, 'It's Greg. He's in Pilsen. Are you in?'

'Sure.' She picked up the receiver. 'Hi, Greg. Thanks for dinner. Any news on the accident?'

'I've heard nothing. Put it out of your mind, Sam. I

called to say congratulations. Two more huge orders have come in from Hungary. They liked your blends.'

Sam's stomach churned. Greg already accounted for over a third of their production. Balaton's warning was ringing in her ears.

'Sorry, Greg. I can't fulfil that. Your standing orders have reached the limit of my production capacity.'

He argued the toss for a while. Then he said, 'If it's a cash problem I can collect in some cheques fast.'

Did it matter who killed them? Greg or the bank? If she played one against the other she might just survive. Suddenly Sam knew she had to play along until she built up alternative markets. Without Greg, Dearlove would close them down.

'If you let me have a substantial cheque, we'll talk. Okay?'

'See you tomorrow, or maybe the day after. I'll keep in touch.'

Sam took the phone off the hook and settled down with a notebook and pencil. They were overstocked with Grey Wolf. It had sold well at the festival, but the moment they stopped advertising, sales had petered out.

To keep their heads above water they had to run the brewery at a minimum of 75 per cent of production capacity. With Greg's latest orders they would almost reach this amount, a huge improvement.

Somehow Woodlands must become a household name. But how?

Rosemary came into the office with a tray of coffee and sandwiches. She looked happy. She said, 'This is the best summer I can remember. I wish I were young.'

'Never mind summer. I have to pull a rabbit out of the hat, Rosemary. We need a new blend, a new name and a powerful marketing idea. Something to make the country sit up and think. Give it a go, Rosemary. After all, you scored with Grey Wolf.'

For a few minutes the two women sat in hopeless silence. Sam groped around the recesses of her creative mind and came up with nothing more than a dozen different images of Richard: at the festival, in the castle, she could even feel his lips on hers.

'Damn you, Richard,' she muttered. 'Get out of my head and stay out. Where the hell are you, anyway?'

Richard was continuing his research at the Manorial Society of Great Britain. Libraries had a unique smell that to him spelled home and this one was no exception. Usually the scent of old parchment, leather and dust seemed to heighten his perceptions until he glowed with a sense of well-being. But tonight, for some reason, he couldn't concentrate on his work; he was too busy arguing with some other part of himself that normally stood back.

Okay, so I'm lying to Sam, but what else can I do? It's not a crime to use an alias, particularly when it's my grandfather's name.

So the end justifies the means? Is that what you're saying?

Who I am and what I am is no one's business but my own.

She's falling in love with you. She thinks you're someone completely different. A loser. You appeal to her bleeding heart.

If she can't see what sort of a person I am then she deserves to get her fingers burned.

So what sort of a person are you? Have you ever taken time off to think about yourself?

Why the hell should I? I'm perfectly at home with myself.

Then how come you've never had a meaningful relationship? One-night stands are your idea of a good time. Don't you think you should warn her?

Warn her? Good God! I'm doing my best to protect her from the Gregs of this world, but she won't listen. And he's so damned phoney.

But handsome.

Or dangerous. She's the opposite of any woman I've ever fallen for, and from now on I shall avoid her like the plague.

After you do something to help her.

Richard dialled his lawyer in San Francisco. The line was bad, but they could just about hear each other.

'Richard. Good to hear from you. Where are you calling from?'

'London. I expect to be here for while. I'm moving around, London, Dover, Chester, but I check the e-mail nightly.'

'How's the latest quest?'

'This particular beast is shy, evasive and has never been seen. At least, not in this century.'

'Oh! One of those.'

'D'you remember the option we bought on Rosslyn's title and documents? Well, I've decided to go ahead. Draft a suitable agreement and send them the cheque please.'

'At once?'

'Sure.'

'You know you're fully covered by our option. Whichever way it goes you'll be quite safe.'

'Yes, but I want to buy the title.'

'So you're on to something. I hope you're really sure about it.'

'I'm not at all sure that the documents are still in existence. It's a very long shot.'

'You're usually such a cautious bastard.'

'I agree.'

'So what's gone wrong?'

'There's a woman involved.'

'Perhaps you should talk to Mendel first.'

'Just do as I say, Nick.'

Chapter 39

Sunday lunch was Sam's most hated ritual, roast lamb, roast potatoes, limp vegetables and gravy, followed by jam roly-poly. Julie and she endured it stoically because they loved Trevor. Sam sat down, pulled out Walter's letter and read it for the tenth time. Each time she read it, it hurt that much more.

Hi, Sam, I'm still worried about you, so I ran another credit check on Richard with a reputable agency in the States. There's no registered property developer of that name, no credit cards or bank account in that name either. He gave you a cheque signed by a Mendel Mandelbaum, who runs an antique map shop in downtown New York. He's 78 by the way and it is he who issued the cheque to you. He had a son who married a girl of mixed Irish and Spanish parentage. The son was a bad lot and fled the US following a charge of car theft. Their child was orphaned when they were both killed in a car crash. It took the old man a while to find the child, but he brought him up from then on. I can find no trace of this child who would be an adult now. I assume it's Richard. The cheque went through so I guess the old man gives him a helping hand. Perhaps he changed his name for reasons such as the one quoted above.

As for Data Power, where he claimed to have worked for some years, I called on their Bloomsbury office and found that no one of that name has worked there or in

New York for the past eight years, which is when the
company was established.

So who is Richard? Presumably Mendel's black sheep.
I bet he costs the old man a packet. His 'prison pallor'
makes me fear the worst. He might want the title for
purposes of fraud. Take care, Walter.

Oh, God, this is awful. He'd even admitted that he
was going to con someone into buying the title believing
precious documents were involved. Should she have it out
with him, or pretend nothing was wrong because he was
Trevor's guest? Oh, damn!

Sam's knees were rubbery, her stomach was twisted
up with cramps, her eyes were burning and she couldn't
imagine how she would endure lunch. She wanted to find
a hole and crawl into it.

'Lunch will be sharp at one,' Helen called loudly.

Julie hurried in. 'The Duke's late.'

'I told you not to call him that,' Sam snapped.

'Why begrudge me my elevated status?' Richard's voice
said from the porch.

Julie raced towards him, followed by Tasha who leaped
up at him and licked his hand.

'Hello, Richard. Glad you could make it.' Trevor limped
out of his study. 'Come and have a drink, my boy. I have
some excellent Scotch hidden away in here.' He led the
way, looking pleased, and Sam, who was glaring at the men's
departing backs, was startled when Richard turned in the
doorway and winked at her. She almost burst into tears.

They heard a shriek from the kitchen and raced in to
find Mona, who helped her mother when they had guests,
chasing Porgy. Helen's face was beetroot red, while her
eyelids had sunk froglike over her angry blue eyes. Mona's
eyes were round as pebbles.

'He's dead clever, that one,' Mona said. 'He pushed open the fridge door with his snout and dug it straight into the custard.'

'Porgy goes or I go. It's that simple.' Clearly Helen meant what she said.

Sam grabbed an apron from the back of the pantry door. 'We'll all help. I'll make some more custard. Come on, Julie! The floor's slippery. Don't let him eat it. Teach him some manners.' She slapped Porgy's backside hard and he raced out squealing.

'Hey, what's this? Cruelty to farm animals?' Luther's voice could never be mistaken.

'Lay another place, Mona,' Sam called, as Luther sauntered in from the garden, wearing a yellow vest and green shorts.

'He can't sit at the table like that. Your grandfather'll have a fit,' Helen sniffed. She didn't like Luther. Now Sam came to think of it, she couldn't think of anyone Helen did like, other than the family.

'I didn't come for lunch,' Luther said. 'I came to train Porgy. I'll take a break in the garden.'

'No, you won't.' Julie linked arms with him. 'I need your moral support.'

'Has Porgy been fed today?' Luther asked.

'No, why?'

'I've brought a feeder – a converted computer.'

'Let's have a look at it. Sounds interesting,' said Richard, who was standing with Trevor in the doorway. He went off with Luther and Julie.

'Five minutes,' Trevor called after them. 'Don't keep Helen waiting. Sometimes I wonder if I should have brought you two up more formally. Just what is Julie doing with that fellow?'

'Don't be deceived by his clothes. He's a lawyer.

He's doing the pigs' rights as a labour of love. I like him.'

Trevor looked relieved. 'I trust your judgement, Sam.'

Do you? Sam thought. I don't. 'Gramps, I'm so worried,' she began, leading Trevor back to his study. 'Walter did a credit check on Richard and he doesn't exist. That computer company he's supposed to have worked for have no records of him as an employee.'

'His cheque didn't bounce.'

'True, but it was his grandfather's. Walter thinks he might be using our family name to perpetrate the biggest con imaginable. Once he has the title he would be—'

'Sam, listen to me. I'm a very good judge of character and I'm telling you now that Richard is the sort of man I'd have picked for special missions.'

'What greater praise is there?' Having said it, Sam felt guilty. 'I'm sorry, Gramps. It's just that I'm worried.'

'Is that what you call it?' Trevor said.

'You can be so irritating. I'll call the others to lunch.'

Finally Luther fetched a T-shirt from his bike, which mollified Helen. Porgy was locked in the stables, and Richard showed an extraordinary interest in Luther's converted computer. The conversation was technical and dull.

'You seem to know a lot about computers,' Sam said furiously. 'Perhaps you're a programmer?'

'Good shot, Sam. From time to time I am.'

'So who do you work for?' Now she was downright aggressive and she felt ugly.

'Sam, I told you who I used to work for. Nowadays I'm free to follow my fancy.'

'So you've retired, then? Rather young, aren't you?' Her eyes implored him to tell the truth.

'I work quite hard, to tell the truth. Especially lately.'

There was that candid grin again. 'Doing what exactly?'

'Deals. I might see a property I like and buy it and later sell it. Not necessarily land, of course. Actually, I was thinking of leasing your village. Of course the locals, including yourselves, would be the benefactors, although I'd get a cut.'

She gasped, but then saw that Richard was enjoying himself at her expense. 'Pull the other one,' she said.

'This is a charming village. Authentic, too. A Hollywood film producer would pay upfront to use parts of it as a backdrop for a movie. I happen to know a director who's embarking on three movies, maybe more, based on Chaucer's work. The sum would certainly run into six figures. The villagers would have to make a few changes, nothing serious, I've been looking around. They and you could share the advance, depending on how your property figures in the final takes. With your permission I'll act as your agent and follow this up.'

'Why not?' Trevor said, avoiding Sam's accusing stare.

'That's the sort of thing I do, Sam.'

'Give up the third degree, Sam,' said Julie. 'You're not good at it. And, anyway, you can't pin Richard down.' It was clear whose side she was on. Sam flushed with fury.

'I'm actually very boring, far too boring to discuss.' Richard added. 'Sam and Julie, on the other hand, are fascinating, being descended from Lady Godiva or so I've learned from your library. That is true, isn't it?'

'Family legend has it so,' Trevor said. 'No one really knows.'

'On the contrary, if you'll excuse me, sir, the Rosslyns' ancestry is one of the most ancient in Britain and it's well documented. You have two very eligible granddaughters,

Trevor. I've traced the main family branch back even to before the Domesday Book.'

'You aren't buying the family tree, just a title,' Sam said rudely, 'so it won't affect *your* ancestry.'

'But surely you come with the package, Sam?' His face broadened into a smile while his blue eyes shone with amusement.

Trevor moved to change the conversation. 'How about your ancestors, Richard? Where do they come from?'

'I'm part Jew, part Spanish, part Irish, the usual result of the pre-war trek to the New World. Nothing exciting, I'm afraid.'

Once again, he had charmingly refused to be drawn into revealing a thing about himself. He must have something to hide, Sam reasoned, since he was so damned secretive. She was glad when lunch was over.

Chapter 40

It was almost four o'clock and it was hot. The family sprawled under the oak trees waiting for tea. Only Porgy was starving and frustrated. Julie was furious because she thought Luther was teasing him. Richard and Luther, too, were fast losing their tempers.

'He's only four months old, for goodness' sake,' Julie wailed.

'If he's smart enough to raid the fridge he's smart enough to operate this thing,' Richard said.

This 'thing' was a converted chocolate dispenser linked to a laptop computer, which was lying on the grass. The keyboard had been replaced by three snout-sized buttons. Pressing the left one resulted in a loud honk, pressing the right one brought some feed pellets, but the centre one sent a biscuit sliding down the chute, Porgy's favourite. Porgy couldn't press any of them and seeing the biscuits so near but unattainable was driving him crazy.

'This is cruel,' Julie whispered. 'I'll complain to animal cruelty.'

'It's no more cruel than you going to school,' Richard said mildly.

'I wasn't starved if I didn't perform.'

'We all starve if we don't perform,' Sam said grimly. She was trying to keep her mind off Walter's letter but she couldn't, and it still hurt.

'Come on, Richard, let's see you dredge up your data-processing genius to solve this problem,' she added.

Richard ignored her. 'We should bear in mind that while we are visual animals Porgy is a sensory animal.' He rubbed a jam biscuit over the biscuit button. 'That should do the trick.'

'Where's tea? I'll go and hurry it along.' Trevor went back to the house.

Porgy thrust his nose down hard on the button and a biscuit shot down the chute. He pounced and crunched it up, then looked imploringly at Julie and whimpered. Finally he returned to the centre button and pressed his nose on it.

Two minutes later the chute was empty.

Trevor returned with John carrying a tray of tea and cakes.

'Hi, you lot. What's going on?'

'Porgy's becoming a computer genius,' Julia trilled.

'Yeah, like Richard,' Sam muttered.

'What happens if we stick one of these cream buns down the chute?' John asked.

'Gum up the works I should think,' Luther said.

'Cut it in quarters.' John grabbed a knife. 'Let's give it a go.'

Porgy had them racing down the chute in record time.

'We'd better design something easier to clean,' Richard told Luther. 'I think we can come up with something far more complicated than this, which will allow Porgy to select exactly what he wants.'

'But how would we get it made up?'

'I know a place that'll do anything we want.'

'Where?' Luther asked.

'Leave it to me.'

'Don't be so damn secretive, Richard. What's the company called?' Sam felt exasperated.

'Here we go again!' Julie said melodramatically. Sam looked round to see that Julie was biting her lip.

'It's my old company, Data Power. They'll be glad to help out.'

'Did you leave or were you fired?' Sam sniped.

'Come on, Sam.' Julie was embarrassed.

'Sam, if you want my CV why don't you ask for it?'

Richard's voice was mild and Sam stared hard at him, unable to banish the feeling that she was being set up.

'What is it with you two?' Julie asked. 'Can't you be together for five minutes without fighting?'

'Julie, the path of true love never runs smooth,' Richard said.

'Oh, for God's sake. I'm sick of this.' Sam got up and stalked off. When she wandered back, much later, everyone had gone.

Two mornings later Sam saw Richard's car in the car park. His erratic behaviour seemed to show a pattern: away for three days, back for one. Sam knew she would have to tackle him. She felt weighed down by gloom as she read and reread Walter's letter.

She found Richard in the library, checking out their family history. 'Richard, we must talk. I can't carry on like this and neither can you. Sooner or later your lies will catch up with you. Did you really think you could fool us so easily? I know all about you.'

'So?' He flushed, which was some small satisfaction.

'I received this letter from Walter. I'm sorry, Richard, but you never worked for Data Power, they have no former employees of your name – you aren't even who you say you are. And there's no property developer of your name. Just one old man dealing in antique maps.'

'May I see this?'

'Go ahead.' She handed over Walter's letter. Her heart went out to him. Suddenly she realised that she cared what happened to him. The realisation that she was in love was frightening.

'If he's your ex-boyfriend, it doesn't say much for your taste. He's a fool. You should get someone better to do your marketing.'

'Richard, go straight. I'll help you. I have big plans for Woodlands. There's room for you, too. You could do really well.'

'From what I hear you can hardly pay the wages. Why would you want to take on another commitment?'

'I don't want you to get into any more trouble. Besides . . . well . . . I care, Richard.' She flushed heavily.

'So you want to save me from myself?'

'I want to help you. Besides, I could do with a good salesman. You're charming and convincing. You could sell anything to anyone, so why not beer? You could build up a wonderful future. Why don't you give it a go? Please, Richard.' She stepped forward and put her arms around his neck, pulling his face down to hers, longing to kiss him.

His neck remained rigid and his lips were out of reach. 'I'm flattered. I don't know what to say.'

'Don't lie. You always know what to say. But you can't keep living the way you do.'

Richard pushed her away and turned towards the books. 'Sam, the other night . . . it was the best, but that doesn't mean a commitment. I mean . . . you owe me nothing and you're thinking with your heart, not your head.'

'Stop burying yourself in those books. It's a means to escape reality. We have to talk.'

'Yes, I suppose we do. I'm being rude. I'm sorry, but I don't have much time today. I have an appointment in

257

London with that Hollywood producer I mentioned.' He put back the book reluctantly.

'Look! Let's forget about make-believe. Are you Mendel's grandson?'

'Yes.'

'I'm sorry that you lost out so badly – I mean with your parents dying. We have so much in common. You see, Julie and I lost our parents, but Trevor looked after us. Perhaps that's why I want to see you get on your feet, Richard. Please consider my offer.' She could see she wasn't getting through to him.

'You're a very strange girl, Sam. Very caring, very capable, but you don't think things out properly. Just imagine, if I worked for you and you made a pass at me, I could sue you for sexual harassment. Make a fortune.'

'How dare you suggest – I'd never make a pass at you if you worked here!'

'That's why I can't work for you.'

'Oh! Why don't you go to hell?' She felt angry and sad and happy all at the same time.

He sighed. 'Come here, Sam. Please. I want to hold you while I talk to you.'

Sam walked slowly towards him and wrapped her arms around his waist, looking at him quizzically.

'I'm trying hard not to fall for you, Sam, but it's tough going. Thank you, Sam. No one's ever made me an offer like that, but I have to go my own way.'

His lips brushed hers, moved to her cheek then returned. His mouth was soft and sensual. Unbelievably he stepped back. 'Listen to your instincts, Sam, not to your head and for fuck's sake don't listen to Walter. I must go. I really do have an appointment with a guy from Hollywood who's in London right now. Dinner tomorrow?'

'Why not?' she shrugged.

'I shouldn't have said what I said,' she murmured, as she heard his car leaving. 'It's none of my business. He'll go on doing his own thing until one day he lands up in prison. And that will serve him right.'

Chapter 41

George Davenport stared critically into the mirror. It seemed to him that little had changed over the years: a few veins here and there, his skin was ageing, but not unduly so, he couldn't see any lines – perhaps because he'd put on a bit of weight. His face was a little redder nowadays, he had a slight double chin, nothing serious. Admittedly his hair was white but it had been since he was forty-eight. It was still thick and wavy, though, and his blue eyes were keen and incisive. Who would imagine he was nearly eighty? George had discovered that age didn't exist. He felt the same as when he was twenty. His right knee was acting up, but that was from the war, and his skin had a touch of sun damage from holidays in the Bahamas. He'd put on weight, but he'd enrol at the nearest gym.

He'd just called Shireen, who had agreed to have lunch with him. He couldn't help hoping that she was a little interested in him, too, and not just treating him as family.

George straightened his shoulders and went down to his study to call his secretary at the distillery. 'Miss Jones, please book a table for two for lunch at Annabelle's. Oh, and book me into a health club every morning at eight. The one near the distillery will do. I'll be in shortly. And send some flowers – something special – to this address . . .'

To Shireen, the call came as a welcome surprise. She was

thrilled with her life, but she was missing her father and here was Sam's uncle wanting to include her in his family. If she lived to be a hundred she could never repay the Rosslyns for their kindness. She had no doubt that Uncle Trevor had spoken to George and asked him to look her up when he was in town. He was a dear man and she was looking forward to lunch.

How bashful he looked, she noticed, when she arrived.

He jumped up. 'I never thought I'd be having lunch with a lovely girl like you, Shireen.' His gaze took in her smart navy silk suit, the red stretch top, her hair pulled up into a roll at the back of her head, which accentuated her swanlike neck and her long, shapely legs.

As soon as they were seated he buried his face behind the wine list.

'No wine for me, thanks, George. I'm a working girl and this afternoon's going to be difficult.'

'Tell me about it. But let's order first, shall we? Don't mind if I have some wine, do you?'

George was a wonderful listener. She told him how she'd landed a place at the academy and enjoyed it when he roared with laughter. Then she told him about the past three weeks of lectures and how much she loved them. The other students were great and she'd made one or two good friends. 'Make no mistake, behind the fun it's deadly serious. Everyone studies hard because everyone wants to be successful. It's all I've ever wanted. Even when I was a child I knew what I'd do. Then later I lost hope.'

'I can't imagine you ever losing hope, Shireen. You're so vibrant and full of life.'

'I wasn't then. You can't imagine what it was like on those barren, heat-drenched plains of red dust. It was like going back in time. My grandmother was so old and wrinkled she seemed to be at least two hundred.

She taught me to endure and survive. Later I began to feel that all selfish desire was wrong. Now whatever I do I feel guilty.'

'Shireen, listen to me. It's not wrong to long for self-fulfilment.' Uncle George reached out and gripped her hand. He thumped it against the tablecloth to emphasise his words. 'You've a God-given talent and you have to use it. You've got to believe me, Shireen. You have something to give the world and no one has the right to stand in your way. I promise you this: if you land a role, any role, I'll back the production with hard cash. How's that for moral support? I believe in you, Shireen.'

Shireen drew her hand away. Wasn't he being a little OTT? She thought about it and came up with a solution. 'May I call you Uncle George?'

'Goes without saying, m'dear.'

'You're a very kind man, Uncle George, but I'd hate you to do anything silly. It's enough that you give me moral support. You see, my father never did. He wanted me to make a traditional marriage. I almost gave in. It makes me shudder to think about it. I was this close to getting on that plane.' She measured a minute space between her index finger and thumb and waved her hand in front of him.

George listened intently as she explained how she had walked out at Heathrow. His rapt attention made her feel special. It was such a relief to let it all pour out. 'I feel so guilty. I've broken my father's heart. First my mother left, then me. Now he's all alone. He'll never get over it.'

'Yes, he will. He was being selfish. He wanted his life and yours too. He'll come round one day. Meanwhile, you're not alone. You have Sam, Trevor and me. I've been very lonely since my wife died. I'd love to be your friend.'

'We are friends, George. Heavens, it's past two. I'll have to run.'

'We'll get a taxi.'

Shireen turned to George and pushed her arm through his.

'Thank you, you've made me feel much better about myself and my decision.' She watched his face light up and it made her feel happy.

'How about tomorrow night? Feel like doing a show?'

'I have a rehearsal, but I'm free on Sunday.'

'Why not come out to my place for a swim? We could have a picnic and do the show on Monday.'

'I work for Sam five nights a week, but only until nine.'

'Then we'll plan accordingly. Off Saturdays and Sundays, are you?'

'Yes. And sometimes I have a free afternoon.'

'We'll manage. Here we are. Off you go. Good luck.'

'Thanks again for lunch.' George helped her down and squeezed her hand and for a moment Shireen experienced a moment of misgiving. There was so much admiration in his eyes.

It was the Monday evening after a tremendous weekend. Shireen had been taken boating and riding, she'd tramped over the cliffs and swum at St Margaret's Bay. She was feeling relaxed and happy. Notebook and pencil in hand, she was sitting at the bar chatting to the clientele and sipping apple juice. She was doing a one-man market-research exercise on Sam's pubs, finding out what type of people patronised each one. Were they happy with the drinks, did they like the décor and which other pubs did they use? The job was fun and she got to meet interesting people.

This pub, for instance, which was old, dingy and cramped, attracted the theatre crowd, mainly because of its situation, so why not flaunt its age and inconvenience. She intended to do a little research on the age of the building. There must have been many theatre personalities in here over the years. Could she get photographs of some of them? Of course she could. She looked up at the low false ceiling. Wonder what's behind it? Something old, I hope. She finished scribbling in her notebook and got up to say goodbye to the barman.

Shireen was burning the candle at both ends. She rose at five each morning to do her homework and learn her parts, then she did seven hours at the academy and then there was just enough time for a bath before going round the pubs. Sometimes she didn't finish until eleven and rarely got to bed before twelve thirty. The days flew and Shireen was happier than she had ever been.

When she arrived home at midnight, her telephone was ringing. She picked up the receiver.

'You're in, for once,' said John. 'Ever have time for work, Shireen?'

'I'd have thought congratulations were in order. I've sent enough queries and verbal orders through. Did you follow up on them?'

'Of course I did. I'm not talking about business. You're never home.' There was a long silence. 'How's my girl? How're you doing?' She knew he was making an obvious effort to lighten his mood. 'How's the academy?'

'I had an audition today and I landed the role.'

'Congratulations. How about coming out to celebrate?'

'All right.' She tried to hide her reluctance.

'Fine. See you at seven, Sam's apartment. Okay?'

'No, I'm sorry. I didn't mean tomorrow.' Damn. Now he'd sulk again but why should she explain? She said, 'I'm going out to dinner.'

'Shireen, I've phoned every night this week and I think you owe it to me to tell me what's going on.'

'I don't think I owe you anything, John. We split three years ago when I went to India. My private life has nothing to do with you.'

'What about the beer festival?'

'It was good sex but only that, John.'

'Bitch! I love you. Doesn't that mean anything to you?' His voice sounded full of aggression, not love.

'It frightens me.'

'Come off it, Shireen. Nothing's ever frightened you. Are you going out with someone?'

'No, but I'm having a wonderful time. Sam's Uncle George has sort of adopted me as his niece for the time being. Until I get on my feet.'

'He's eighty if he's a day.'

'I know, but he's sweet and lonely and he's replacing my father.'

'Stupid to replace someone you can't stand the sight of.' He sounded harsh, not like John at all.

'That's not true. You only ever saw one side of him. Besides, it has nothing to do with you. I'm free next Wednesday, but, John, don't start trying to make out that you have any hold on me. All that we had before is over.'

'Not for me it's not.'

'Then cancel Wednesday.'

'No, wait. I'm sorry. Wednesday it is. Pick you up at eight.'

'All right.'

Shireen put down the receiver and crouched in her chair, her face in her hands. She was a freak, not human, she told herself. Of course she should love John. But she didn't, because she couldn't love. John was a dear, sweet, lost boy. He looked so capable, but he had never really grown up. His mother had been widowed young and had clung to him, over-protecting him. Now he drifted through life with a charming smile, never getting to grips with his problems, dreaming that life owed him a living. One day something would wake him up and then he'd grow up fast. She had the greatest faith in John.

Chapter 42

The click of the receiver going down hit John in the guts.
'Screw you, Uncle George,' he muttered. He went over to
the sideboard and poured a Scotch. When he looked up,
he was shocked to see a figure standing in the doorway. It
was Hans Kupi, wearing an expensive mohair suit, an opal
signet ring and a West End haircut. It looked odd around
the face and figure of a tough old ex-con.

'Goddammit, Kupi, you have no right to walk into people's houses without knocking. You stood there listening
to every bloody word.'

'Wasn't much to listen to, was there? Your girl stood
you up for someone else.'

'He's eighty, for God's sake, and family in a way. Right
now she only has the Rosslyns to hang on to.'

'And what's in it for this geriatric?'

'He probably kids himself she fancies him.'

'Who is he?'

'Owns the biggest distillery in Britain. One of the silver
spoon brigade. You might have heard of him – Lord
George Davenport.'

'Sounds familiar.'

John watched Kupi walk heavily into the room with his
strange, rolling gait. A stiff leg? Bullet wound or years
spent at sea, John wondered.

Kupi grinned. 'Maybe I read his name in the newspaper.
So Shireen's found herself a wealthy boyfriend.'

'Shireen's not after money. Her father's a wealthy man,

but she needs a lot of nurturing and he's providing it. At his age there's not much else he can do.'

'I wouldn't be so sure of that. Anyway, I came here to talk business. We're not winning, my friend. We have to take drastic action.'

'What d'you mean?'

'Listen to me, John. You're going to be chairman of a very large group, but only if we pull together. We've gone too far to give up. We'll have to take stronger measures. An office fire will bring our Samantha to her senses.'

John flinched. 'Now, wait a minute, don't try to involve me in something like that.' He paced the worn carpet from the bar to the desk and back again.

'Calm down. The rug can't take this sort of treatment. You need a good Persian and you'll have hundreds of them when we pull this deal off. A proper home for Shireen. Worth a bit of danger, isn't it?'

'What danger, for Christ's sake? One old cripple and two girls. It's— No, I won't get involved in this.'

'What sort of a fool joins the brotherhood and then tries to walk out? I warned you, there's only one way out and that's feet first.'

John tried to keep his voice steady. 'I didn't join, I helped you out, and I'm not trying to walk out on you, but I don't think that this is a good idea.'

'Listen to me, John. Ninety per cent of businesses whose records are destroyed go bust within six months. She'll have to sell out and, as you said, it'll probably be a good thing.'

'Stop trying to pretend you're a walking benevolent fund for geriatrics and their granddaughters.'

Kupi laughed a deep, throaty laugh. 'Could be, John. But you'd better leave the brewery and office doors unlocked and be there. I'll let you know when.' He paused. 'I warned you before, John, you're either in or you're out, and if you're out, you're dead. Goodnight.' He went out, and John listened to his car start up and fade into the distance.

How had he got into this mess? Was there no way out? He could kill Kupi. The idea horrified him, but then he realised there wasn't much point. Kupi wasn't the big chief he pretended to be. He had 'underling' written all over his face and in his eyes. He was little more than a messenger boy.

John took his drink outside and sat on the garden bench overlooking the river. It was all so normal. So peaceful, so rural, so English. So what if he'd been short of money? He'd rather have Trevor's world than Kupi's. But getting back there would be easier said than done.

Shireen had been wined and dined and she'd had a wonderful time, but now George's eyes were beaming a bashful message her way. They said: 'Let me stay. Don't send me back to my empty mansion where I have nothing but a bottle of Scotch between me and the eternal emptiness of space.' She knew how he felt because he'd told her. He stared longingly over her shoulder into Sam's bright, comfortable living room. Then he waved, assumed a jaunty air, and hurried off.

Shireen sighed and listened to his car driving away. Then she heard footsteps and a shadow fell across the path as a middle-aged man walked towards the foyer. What was he doing here? She assessed him: tailor-made mohair suit, hand-made tie, but he looked like an ex-heavyweight boxer. His hair was grey and crew-cut, his face square. He was ugly, and she felt nauseated by the smell of his cigarette and his aftershave. When he smiled she saw that he had one steel-capped tooth.

She tried to slip past him down the passage leading to the car park, but he blocked her way.

'Not so fast, Shireen. I'm a friend of a friend. Name's Hans Kupi.' He crowded up on her, forcing her to move backwards through the doorway. Then he stepped inside and shut the door.

'Get out or I'll scream for help.' She backed towards the panic button.

'No, you won't. You're not that type. You aren't even scared. And there's no need to be. No one's going to hurt you. I've come to talk business with you. I could put a great deal of money your way.'

'I'm not in business. I'm learning my craft and I don't need more cash than I earn. Please leave.'

Her thoughts were racing around like crazy. A steel tooth. Where had she heard that? Then she remembered Sam telling her about the takeover bid and the Czech delegation. One of them had had a steel tooth. If this had something to do with Sam, she'd better listen. She moved away from the wall and sat down.

Kupi smiled. 'An apartment of your own, a car, some pocket money. Aren't these the sort of things everyone wants? At least hear me out. I'm here because of your ageing boyfriend. I don't know what you think you can get out of him, but I can make this friendship very worthwhile for you.'

She looked into his eyes, wondering if he could see the hatred in hers. Then she remembered the tricks of her trade and smiled. 'D'you want a drink?'

'I'll have a fruit juice. I've been watching you, Shireen. I think Lord Davenport is in love with you. He'd do anything you want him to.'

'I doubt that. He's a man of integrity.'

Kupi nodded. 'But he's lonely, so he's vulnerable.'

Shireen tried to look interested as Kupi outlined her future role in his plans.

'Why did you come to me?' she interrupted him. 'What made you so sure I'd be interested?'

'I asked myself what a lovely girl like you would want with an old man like him. Money, of course. What else? I can give it to you faster. And then there's your father, who's willing to pay anyone who'll get you on a plane to Delhi. So don't tempt me by saying no.'

Shireen hung on to her cool. One thing was clear: she must find out what they wanted from George. He could be in danger.

'All right,' she said. 'Tell me what you want me to do.'

'That's right, Shireen. I knew I could count on you. For the time being, almost nothing. I want you to string along with George. Don't go to bed with him. You haven't yet, have you?'

Dredging up some monumental will-power, she remained mute.

'Ask him about his work and his problems,' Kupi went on. 'Let him think you're interested in him long-term. Get him to talk about exports. I'll let you in on your role bit by bit.'

'I'm not interested unless you tell me exactly what this is about. I won't have George harmed.'

Kupi chuckled. 'I may even make him richer. Your mission is very simple. You have to convince Lord Davenport to reverse his opposition to a deal I've put to him. You must make him see that opening trade links with Russia can only help the Russian economy and the Russian people. But if you push too hard you may trigger his suspicions. Softly, that's the way. Ultimately we want the East European Trade Association to handle all his exports to those countries.'

'And if he signs up with them?'

'Others will follow his lead and you'll get a generous bonus. Enough to set you up. But cross me, Shireen, and it's Delhi for you. Got that? By the way, I've got a picture for you. Your fiancé in Delhi. You walked out on a fortune. Did you know that? And he's still waiting.'

He flung down a photograph. Looking down, Shireen saw a face that came straight out of her nightmares. She gasped, unable to control her shock. Was she psychic or something? The very same face. She was speechless as Kupi took an envelope out of his inside pocket and placed it next to the picture.

'There you are, the carrot and the stick, side by side.' He went out, shutting the door quietly behind him.

Shireen waited ten minutes to make sure Kupi wasn't coming back. Then she called George.

Chapter 43

The sun had not yet risen, but a tinge of dawn lit the eastern horizon as cars and trucks swung through Woodlands' gates and parked in front of the house. There would be a good turnout by the look of things, Sam decided.

She was up early, hoping to prevent traffic jams and stop their lawn from being churned into mud. It was a great day for Julie and Luther, although Sam wasn't sure just how great a day it was going to be for her. Porgy was about to be put through his computer paces under ITV cameras in a live broadcast on the breakfast show.

Sam had just left Julie, who was completing Porgy's grooming, scrubbing him pink all over and dressing him in his white starched collar with a red bow-tie. The news had got round, and outside Woodlands the faithful DARE supporters waved their placards at the reporters who had turned up for the show.

A small red car came speeding towards her and braked, sending gravel flying. Luther climbed out in a smart new charcoal suit.

'Hm! If it weren't for Julie, I'd be after you myself,' Sam teased.

'Flattery will get you everywhere, Sam.' He grinned. 'Collar's too tight.' He ran a finger round his neck. 'I must've put on weight since the last time I wore this shirt. I see the placard-bearers are making sure they get on TV. How're you doing with Bowles?'

'Only our lawyers communicate,' Sam said, 'but this

time I really hope we'll be able to prove he's damaging the brewery. Then he's as good as out. In fact, right after this show I'm going to get our lawyer on to him.'

'I think your wishes are about to be granted. There's a woman with a placard that reads: "Woodlands pigs are kept in stalls, boycott Woodlands ale."'

'That's Rosemary's friend. As soon as she's got herself on TV she can come back here and have some coffee. Thanks, Luther. D'you think you could ask the cameraman to take a shot of the demonstrators while he's waiting for Porgy?'

'I'll have a go. Where's Julie?'

'Grooming Porgy.'

'She mustn't feed him. He must be good and hungry. He's a lazy bugger when he's full.'

'Calm down, Luther. You've trained that damned pig for weeks. Now you'll just have to let it get on with it.'

'Without Richard's imput we could never have done so well. He designed the computer.' Luther gave Sam a long, telling look and she flushed.

Shortly afterwards a TV van rolled out of the driveway towards the demonstrators and she heard them shouting their slogans. It was a good fifteen minutes before the van returned. Kevin, the programme director, rotund, red-cheeked and bald with twinkling eyes, explained what he wanted them to do and where to stand. Half an hour later they were ready.

Chaos erupted as the cameras zoomed in on Julie emerging from the library's french windows. She looked ravishing in a white top and jeans, her hair hanging round her shoulders and Porgy in her arms rolling his eyes nervously.

'Good morning, this is Kevin Blaine, enjoying this glorious morning at Woodlands brewery in Kent. We're here to take a close-up look at a claim by Martin Luther Keyes and Julie Rosslyn, his partner in this endeavour, that pigs are not the grubby gourmands they're taken for, but sensitive, intelligent creatures with an IQ higher than that of your average dog and a fastidiousness that must make life in a pig-sty one long living hell. 'So, *bon appétit*, all you breakfast viewers, as you tuck into your eggs and bacon, with maybe a banger on the side.'

The camera was moving backwards as Julie moved towards Luther. Now the screen showed the three of them together.

'Luther hails from DARE, which as viewers may know stands for Domestic Animal Rescue Effort. Here's Porgy, a common farmyard piglet who's learned to operate a computer, and his trainers, Luther and Julie, are about to put him through his paces. Luther, why is Porgy squealing?'

'He hasn't been fed yet.' Luther cleared his throat. Then he pulled himself together. 'The computer represents his menu. It's self-service, as you can see.' He pointed to the pictures above the buttons. 'Porgy selects what he wants to eat and presses these trotter-sized computer keys. He makes his selection by looking at the pictures above. At first he did it by smell, but now he's learned to recognise pictures of what he would like to eat. That's pretty good because recognising pictures represents the ability to do abstract reasoning. He's squealing because he wants to get on with it.'

Kevin stepped forward. 'Okay, folks. Let's go!'

Julie and Luther looked nervous, Sam thought, but Porgy performed like a real pro. He trotted to the computer, looked at the pictures, put his head on one side and then the other.

'Decisions, decisions,' Kevin said, laughing.

Porgy made a sudden decision for a cream bun and pressed the button. Then he pounced.

'Well, now, this is interesting,' Kevin said, as Porgy came back for his second course. 'Porgy doesn't want another cream bun, he wants an apple. He's choosing a balanced diet.'

'That's our Porgy,' Julie said. 'Luther and I are vegetarians and we've brought him up with the right ideas. Apart from his weakness for cream buns, he prefers fruit, cereal and vegetables.'

That much was obvious, as they watched Porgy press the button and scoff his muesli.

Now that he wasn't so hungry, Porgy was getting playful. He dashed forward and grabbed the trailing silk scarf of June, the continuity girl.

'Porgy, bring it back at once,' Luther said sternly. Porgy trotted back and dropped the scarf at his feet. 'Sorry, June. He can be naughty, like any young animal, but he has his toys and his xylophone, so he's not bored.'

'And you, Julie, how did you feel about bringing up a pig?' Kevin asked.

'At first I thought it was a bit of fun, but I fell in love with Porgy. He's clever and a perfect companion, but he's also greedy and naughty and a terrible tease. It didn't take him long to learn to open the fridge door. It makes you think, doesn't it?' she said wistfully to Kevin. 'The thought of Porgy being shut up in a sty so small he can't move for his entire life is just too terrible to contemplate. It nearly happened. That's what this campaign is all about, the prevention of cruelty in the farmyard.'

The camera zoomed in for a shot of Julie, her lovely face looking sad enough to melt the heart of any pig breeder, Sam thought – except Bowles, of course.

'Think about that, folks, as you tuck in. Time's up, so it's goodbye for now from Porgy the lovable piglet and his even more adorable guardian, Julie, and, of course, Luther, from DARE.'

In his London hotel, Richard switched off his TV, pleased that the computer had worked so well. He went down for a late breakfast, then returned to pore over his latest batch of documents, which he was selling to the Rosenheim museum in Los Angeles at a good profit. They formed part of Ranulf Higden's *Polychronicon*, written in 1364, which described Lady Godiva's ride and how her husband, Leofric, Earl of Mercia, freed the townsfolk of Coventry from all taxes save those on horses.

But the document that fascinated Richard was a hand-written parchment by the Abbot of the Benedictine Abbey of St Werburgh, Chester, where Ranulf had lived and died, which stated that Ranulf's material, including the famous contract abolishing taxes, had been sent to the monastery at Coventry during the fifteenth century. There was another note, signed by a later abbot, stating that these documents had been returned to Leofric's heirs, although there was no mention of who they were.

For the past year, Richard had been trying to trace the descendants, an impossible task since they had all moved away from Coventry and changed their names. He'd just about given up when his grandfather had seen Sam's advertisement. If it hadn't been for this, Richard doubted that he would ever have got on to the Rosslyns. And now, through the efforts of a local genealogist over the past three months, Richard had satisfied himself that the family were the legal owners of the documents. The entire batch might have perished in the blitz on Coventry, but Richard had one thread of hope: a receipt from the

British Museum, dated December 1939, for documents sent for safe-keeping at the start of the war.

So far he'd been lucky, but now he'd hit a snag: he couldn't get permission to examine those archives. It was baffling and frustrating. He didn't want to give up.

As he sat doodling, he suddenly remembered Emma Goldstein, who ran an entirely different department at the museum but who had enormous influence with her peers.

It was worth a try. He called her secretary and made an appointment for that afternoon.

At three sharp he walked through the impressive entrance and found his way to her cramped office. 'Hi, Emma.'

'Hello, Richard! Just give me a moment to put these papers away.'

The smile Emma gave him was her best: Richard was the man she admired more than any other. Emma was aware that she wore her heart on her sleeve, but at her age she was entitled to worship anyone she pleased. Besides, she told herself, what were a few decades when they both dealt in antiquities?

They had been introduced to each other two years before when Richard had been called in by her boss, Irwin Maxwell, curator of the department, to sort out some documents bequeathed to them by an old titled family. Richard, a world expert in Chaucer and medieval literature, soon completed work that had baffled everyone else for months. She'd never thought he'd noticed her assistance, but days later he'd appeared with a leaf from Caxton's original print of the *Polychronicon* as a gift, and an invitation to dinner.

She'd never had so much fun. They had in common a love of heroic literature in Latin, Greek and ancient

English, and they talked until the restaurant asked them to leave. After that they'd found an all-night coffee bar where they'd argued until dawn.

Probing delicately, she learned that Richard had begun life as a computer programmer. He had established his business at twenty-one and sold out his patents at twenty-six, to become a self-made millionaire overnight. From then on he'd devoted himself to his hobby: research in medieval literature.

She came back to the present with a bump.

'There we are.' She slammed the cupboard door. 'Ready to go, but first, tell me why you look so glum this afternoon, Richard.'

Richard tried to look less tense, but failed. 'Emma, I'm on the track of something exciting, but time's running out and I can't get into the archives. I badly need your help.'

'You want some coffee?'

'That would be great.'

Emma filled two mugs from her Thermos, which was one way to get good coffee, and frowned as she watched him wax lyrical over his latest chase through the archives of ancient British history. Had he ever been in love, she wondered. God knows, he was handsome enough to get anyone he wanted, with his black hair and deep blue eyes. But would any woman successfully compete with his vocation? If she were forty years younger she would have pursued him!

Richard snapped his fingers. 'Come back, Emma. You're far away. As you know, it's months since I discovered some ancient documents in a walled-in stone safe at an abbey in Chester. They include some handwritten notes by Ranulf Higden himself.'

Emma gasped. 'I knew you'd had a breakthrough, but I didn't know exactly what it was.'

'Well, in these fragments Higden writes that he had in his possession the charter drawn up by Godiva's husband agreeing to remove all taxes, except horse taxes, from the people of Coventry following his wife's naked ride. There's a chance this document may be intact and, if it is, I intend to find it.'

'A long shot, Richard.'

'Yet I have a feeling about it. Call it instinct, if you like. I never felt more positive. Now I've proof that the documents were supposed to have been returned to the descendants of Lady Godiva and for this purpose they were sent to Coventry Museum, but my own theory is that the Abbot in Chester hung on to them. Perhaps he didn't know who the real heirs were. Anyway I've landed up with this receipt from the British Museum for a batch of documents sent from Coventry Cathedral for safekeeping for the duration of the Second World War.'

'How long did all this take you?'

'Months of hard work, but now I've reached stale-mate. Ever since I started trying to see these documents, I've been blocked. Can you use your influence to find out why?'

It took her two or three calls. Then she hung up. 'The documents belong to the heirs of Lady Godiva and until the rightful owner is found and they – only they – grant permission for you to view the documents on their behalf, they won't show them to you or anyone else. Anyway, they don't know what they are, but they do know that you normally bring in American principals to bid for the documents you find. They're getting a bit fed up with British treasures finding their way to American museums.'

He laughed. 'They can always refuse the offers. Emma, if I produce evidence that I'm the owner of the documents, can you get permission for me to see if they're in this archive?'

'Good God! I'm sure I can, Richard. But can you do that?'

'Of course I can. I'm about to pay a fortune for them, but I need to know they're there. It'll take me a few days to assemble the evidence that the family from whom I purchased them were, indeed, the rightful owners. I'm buying their title, Lord of the Manor, you see. It's a package deal.'

He stood up and shook her hand.

'Good luck, Richard. I hope you're right.'

Richard left, feeling more enthusiastic than ever before. Things were moving his way at last.

That night Richard couldn't sleep. Instead he found himself watching himself and his progress through life, as if he were two entirely different entities. He had to admit that his love of old manuscripts and maps had ignited in the strangest possible way.

As a boy, his world had been computers, but to please Mendel he'd tried to take an interest in his maps and sometimes he had helped out in the shop. At times this had proved a painful duty, particularly one Saturday morning when he was fourteen. His libido had reached painful proportions and he'd been about to go with friends to the mall, where ninth-grade girls invariably gathered. He was determined to chat one up. But Mendel had called him into the shop. 'Take a look at this, my boy,' he'd said, holding up an old map to the light while its owner waited nervously at the counter. 'Look at the watermark. That tells you it's eighteenth- or even seventeenth-century. Up to that date they used transparent paper so you could see the watermark when you held it up to the light. After eighteen hundred they used thicker, opaque paper, which made it difficult to distinguish.' Mendel gasped as he bent down. Moments later he was rubbing his back and smiling ruefully.

'You see, Richard, in those days the grid of the printer's drying-rack was irregular and it formed a watermark on the paper when it was laid out to dry. But if you look at this one, you'll see that the watermark is regular. What does that tell us, Richard? It tells us it's a fake. In fact, it's been printed recently on modern paper.'

He grinned triumphantly, while Richard tried to hide his impatience to meet his friends.

'Now take the printing process,' Mendel went on. 'On the older maps the printing process was uneven so the blackness varied. If you ever want to make a fake you'll need an old printing press. Of course, if you used an old printing press and old paper and old plates, then no one would be able to tell the difference. The truth is there are one or two of these old presses left and they are still being used to make these maps, but they've worn so smooth most of the image has to be filled in by hand. That's easy to pick up. No one knows how to re-engrave those old plates. I'll have to tell him it's a fake. D'you think you could take over here while I visit the physiotherapist? My back's killing me.'

Of course he'd said yes.

Mendel had ruined Richard's Saturday, but a week later Richard had come across an old sixteenth-century map of Barbados going cheap in a junk shop and bought it for five dollars. It was real and his grandfather had sold it for him, which was how he'd managed to acquire the computer of his dreams.

Richard thought about the Godiva contract, as he called it. Normally he bought and sold on behalf of the big museums, and took a hefty cut of the proceeds. However, his real joy wasn't the financial reward but the quest, the endless search into the past to uncover rare treasures that had often been hidden in dusty archives.

Lately he had become aware of the machinations of mischievous fate: he couldn't get Sam out of his head and he'd been seeing her far too often. He thought of her with a strange, bittersweet intensity that scared him half to death. When she found out his real objective and the reason for his frequent visits, all hell would break loose.

Chapter 44

It was a lovely evening, although there was autumn chill in the mists stealing up the river from the sea. The leaves were turning yellow, a few had fallen and summer was all but over. John was thinking this as he leaned over the wooden railings. He missed Shireen and he still loved her, but he, too, was shedding his hopes. A sudden thought struck him: his love for her was precious and no one could take it away from him. He didn't have to stop loving her just because his feelings weren't reciprocated.

The telephone shrilled, bringing John back to earth.

'Jesus, Kupi, don't I deserve a day off? It's Sunday!'

'Tomorrow!' Kupi grated.

John's stomach knotted, his mouth dried and he felt sick. 'Listen, Kupi, I'm not getting involved in arson and that's that. I don't care what you do. I don't mind passing on the odd bit of info, but not this.'

'You know the rules. I don't make them up. Besides, Shireen's working for me, too. You two are a team. You wouldn't want her to be considered a defaulter, would you?' Kupi's voice spelled out the implications.

'You're lying! She'd never—'

'Lovely girl like her needs a bit of pocket money. She's using her charms on Davenport. He'll see reason one of these days. Listen carefully. There's a meeting at the barn at eight thirty. I'll see you at the brewery entrance at nine sharp.' He hung up.

'God!' John groaned aloud. 'Help me.'

* * *

Despite the pouring rain there was a magnificent turn-out. Over five hundred people crowded into the old barn, which usually seated three hundred. Nothing like this had ever happened in sleepy Bourne-on-Sea and most of the villagers were excited.

The advertisement in the local rag had read: 'The well-known Hollywood film company, Jackson Bros, Inc., wishes to take up an option on the village of Bourne-on-Sea with a view to using it as a backdrop for a series of films based on Chaucer's *Canterbury Tales*. Pros and cons will be discussed at the Old Barn, at 8.30 p.m. on the evening of 7 September.'

Sam squirmed. Richard would look truly foolish if his film idea turned sour. She'd tried to persuade him to drop it, but the rest of the family and Rosemary believed in him. Sam knew that the villagers would start tarting up their homes and might spend a fortune, only to be disappointed.

At eight o'clock Rosemary introduced Richard as an American entrepreneur who was investigating the possibility of purchasing the castle. By the time he'd said, 'Hi, folks, thanks for coming along,' he'd won everyone over. 'I won't waste your time, but get right on with it. You may not have heard of Jackson Films, they're small, but up-and-coming, and they're about to make a series of movies based on *The Canterbury Tales*. They'll be bawdy and funny, just as Chaucer intended them to be. I knew that this company was looking around for a suitable backdrop so I showed them pictures of the village the last time I was in Los Angeles.

'Right now they'd like to take up an option on the village for thirty days while they scout around. If they decide to go ahead, they will pay us about a million dollars for three movies. The cash would go into a fund to be set up by you and be distributed on a share capital basis.'

'What's in it for you, Richard?' Jeff Brink called out.

'Nothing, if I don't take up my option on the castle, but if I do, I'll be part of the consortium, which I hope we'll set up tonight. Naturally the project is subject to your approval. Roughly speaking, I guess the village, the church, the brewery and the castle would take up a third of the shares and the rest of the village would share the remaining two-thirds. That would bring in about two thousand dollars per family, if I've done my arithmetic right.'

'What do we have to do for the money?' the blacksmith asked.

'Get the village into tip-top condition and make sure your gardens are authentic. I'll go through that in a minute. It's not much money, I admit, and it's going to involve a great deal of work, such as cleaning up the river, the village green and the church grounds. But don't forget there'll also be money in letting rooms. They'll need accommodation – and extras for crowd scenes. There'll be jobs for youngsters to help around, but probably what we'll mainly get out of it is fun and the chance to meet some stars.'

Richard had their rapt attention. 'As far as I can see, the village is just about perfect as it is, but I should warn you of some of the hassles involved. Cars and motorbikes would have to stay off the streets when shooting was taking place, roads will be blocked, TV aerials will have to be hidden. Most of the pedigree dogs here were unknown in Chaucer's days, so they'd have to keep out of sight and there's probably thousands more things I haven't thought of. They'll send advisers over, of course. All this will involve you in work so I feel we should vote on the project right now. We need a ninety per cent vote in favour to go ahead. Any questions?'

There were dozens. Sam waited impatiently while Richard handled the crowd as if he were lecturing a bunch of rowdy students. He was just too smooth for words.

Her turn came at last. 'What if we all spend a fortune tarting up our homes and nothing comes of this idea?'

A frown flitted across Richard's face.

'We'll only go ahead with the refurbishment when the contract's signed. D'you have any problem with that?'

She flushed and slumped back in her chair.

'Any more questions?'

Agatha's father stood up. 'I think we should impose certain basic conditions in the contract governing noise pollution, speed restrictions and so on.'

'Agreed.'

Mona said, 'Let's make it conditional that they give some of us screen tests.'

'Why not indeed?' Richard shouted, above catcalls and whistles. 'Okay, who's in?'

Sam groaned as shouts of approval echoed around the hall. All she could see were waving hands. Damn Richard! Everything about him was larger than life. Why couldn't he come back to earth? She turned to Julie. 'I'm walking home. See you later.'

'I can take you,' Julie said – they had driven there together – but Sam shook her head and crept silently out of the back of the hall. She set off for home, deep in thought. What was Richard up to? He hadn't even paid for the title yet. Would he ever? She had her doubts. She was full of suspicion and a vague feeling of doom. Perhaps a walk would clear her head.

It was nine o'clock. Shireen was curled up in a leather

armchair in George's study. She'd been arguing with him for the past hour and she was relieved when Neville Joyce and Trevor were shown in.

'My dear Shireen,' Trevor folded her hands in his, 'when did all this happen?'

'Last night after George took me home.'

Trevor looked forbidding. 'What a terrifying experience. I'm so sorry, but you mustn't get involved at all. You were quite right to call George at once, but now you must go away for a while.'

'The usual, Trevor?' Neville called.

'Thanks. Plenty of ice, please. How about the Bahamas? I know Neville here has some idea of staking you out like a donkey to lure the lion, but that would be unforgivable. I can't allow it.'

'Exactly what I've been telling her.' George was fussing around the table, rearranging plates of biscuits and cheese and olives. His hands were shaking and his face had lost its usual rosy glow. He'd aged ten years overnight. Shireen felt sorry for him, but Neville was getting impatient.

'Come on, Trevor, George, he's walked right into a trap and we didn't even set it up for him.' Neville's soft voice belied his true character: he had a formidable reputation at the Yard, Sam had told Shireen.

'Neville!' George lifted his hand for silence. 'I forbid it and that's all there is to it.'

'But listen,' Shireen cut in, 'surely you're all making decisions that I should make. You don't seem to understand my position at all. D'you want me to go into hiding for the rest of my life? And what about my father – quite apart from George? Far better that we act now.'

Neville poured himself a drink. 'Listen, all of you,' he said, 'all she has to do is be seen out and about with George and report back to Hans Kupi that she's having

288

some success. George must play along, and they must string it out long enough for us to get the evidence we need to arrest and deport him. He'll never know Shireen was involved.'

'Impossible.' Trevor sounded unusually incisive and Shireen glanced at him in surprise. This was a side of him she'd never seen. 'She's not trained. They'd wipe her out on the slightest suspicion.' He turned to Shireen. 'Brilliant actress though you may be, my dear, that won't be enough. We can send you somewhere safe and you can return when this is over.'

'And my studies?'

'Start again next year.'

'Absolutely no! George, listen to me.' Shireen jumped up and put her hands on his shoulders. 'You don't have to stay friends with me, or tell me anything, but I'm going to meet Hans Kupi in a couple of hours' time. It's my right to make my own decision, but I'll be safer if I have something to tell him. Don't you think so?'

'Damn them!' George looked hunted. He grabbed a bowl of peanuts and threw them into his mouth rapidly while gazing steadfastly at the carpet. 'To keep Shireen safe, I'll have to sign away our export rights. I hope you all realise that.' He scowled at his nephew.

'It won't get that far, George,' Neville said, trying to humour him. He was the youngest man there, but not the fittest, Shireen noticed. There were deep shadows under his eyes and his face was deeply lined. His sideburns were white and patches of grey were visible in his brown hair. 'All we want is some hard evidence that Shireen was coerced to help Kupi sway George's decision. So, Shireen, tell him that George intends to recommend that no one has any truck with Kupi or his representatives. He'll have to give you plenty of time to work on George after that.'

Shireen nodded. 'What am I going to do with the twenty thousand pounds he gave me?'

'Give it to me. I'll hold it as evidence.'

'I must get going.' Shireen stood up decisively. 'Can your driver take me, Uncle George?'

'If you must go I'll take you myself. Make yourselves at home.'

George pleaded with her all the way to London. He tried every trick he knew to persuade her to walk out of the mess. He even proposed.

'Uncle George, you're a sweet, kind, clever man. I'm certainly not going to ruin our friendship by becoming romantically involved with you, or borrowing your money, or hiding away in a safe house in the Bahamas. As for marriage, I like you too much to marry you. You see, George, I'm already married to my career.'

'Thanks for letting me down lightly, Shireen,' George said, as he dropped her off. 'Just remember, I'll always be here for you.'

And he's pushing eighty, Shireen muttered wonderingly.

Chapter 45

Sam had walked about a mile up the road when she heard a car approaching. She turned and saw that it was Rosemary, looking dishevelled and anxious, her pale blue eyes shining as if with tears. She said, 'Sam, get in, please. I want to talk to you – as a friend, not as a secretary.'

They drove home in silence until they neared the turning to the Castle Arms. Rosemary didn't seem to be getting far in whatever she wanted to say, so Sam said, 'Rosemary, why don't we have a drink together?'

Rosemary drove towards the river and parked. Sam went into the bar and bought two glasses of wine. They sat by the railings overlooking the river.

'It seemed so right to talk to you back there in the barn,' Rosemary said. 'I've never seen you look so miserable. I wanted to say something helpful. Now I'm not sure.'

'Come on, Rosemary. Tell me what.'

'That dreams come true sometimes. That positive thinking works. That Richard cares for you. He's trying to help.'

Sam stared at her glass. Rosemary, too, was trying to help – so why did she feel sort of *invaded*? Perhaps because she'd never had a woman to confide in – Shireen had always been larger than life, drama seemed to surround her, so Sam had never talked about her problems. Now she didn't know how to begin. Eventually she said, 'I feel so lost, Rosemary. I don't know who Richard is and I don't understand my feelings for him. How can I trust a word he says when he's here under a false name? Walter put a credit check out on him. I didn't tell anyone and I don't want you to either. Please, Rosemary.'

'Scout's honour.'

'He never worked for that computer company he's always talking about. Walter checked. In the States there's no record at all that he even exists – no credit cards, bank accounts, that sort of thing. All I know is that he's Mendel Mandelbaum's grandson.'

'So maybe he's been working in another country. Trust your instinct, Sam. What about his sense of humour and his love of animals? And he's kind – look at all the trouble he went to for Luther and Porgy. I'm sure there's a perfectly valid reason why there's no records of him. Why don't you ask him?'

'I did. He fobbed me off.'

Rosemary laughed. Then she said, 'You've got to trust someone, Sam, and it might as well be the man you love.'

'*Love?*' Sam squeaked.

'You two girls worry me, but Julie worries me more than you. I can't put my finger on why.'

'I know what you mean, and I guess because our parents were murdered.'

'Trevor told me.'

'It wasn't just losing Mum and Dad, Rosemary. Of course we loved them, but they both worked all hours and so we didn't see them much. We were brought up by black staff and I truly believe we loved them most of all. Then we found out that they wanted us gone. We saw our dogs and livestock dead and our parents dead and carried away on stretchers and Julie was crying so much. I remember how she hung on to Nanny's apron, begging to be picked up. Nanny was a huge woman and she'd always loved Julie, but she said, "You people must move on. No one wants you here."' Sam attempted a laugh, which came out as a hiccup. Then she burst into tears.

'I have some bad memories, too, dear,' Rosemary said. 'I still can't pee in a public toilet. And I learnt a bit about adult treachery at an early age, mainly when my uncle ate my rabbit.'

'Tell me about the rabbit and the war and why you can't use public loos.'

'Most of the bombs and the shelling came at night. In the morning Mum liked to walk around the blitzed areas and see who'd copped it.'

Rosemary's voice took on the Dover twang as she moved back in time and Sam went with her.

'One morning we walked past the Co-op, which had just installed new toilets on the first floor. The entire wall had come down and Mr Penrose, the nightwatchman, was sitting on the loo with his trousers round his ankles in the brand new first-floor lavatory. His eyes were wide open and so was his mouth, but he was as still as could be. Stone dead. Bert, the Home Guard officer, pushed us away. It was two hours before they got him down. Since then I've avoided public toilets at all costs.'

Images of war! Rosemary sighed. Sometimes they came into her mind so vividly it seemed as if long-forgotten events were happening right now. She'd read an article about it once. She'd thought she might have post-traumatic stress syndrome.

Blast had become a new threat in their lives: Mrs Thomas was stripped naked by it in the main street but was unhurt, while hundreds of people in an underground shelter were found dead, sitting up in rows without a mark on them. Blast could flatten one house and leave the next unharmed, kill one person and leave his companion unharmed.

'We won't worry about bombs and shells,' Mum told her, 'because they have to have our name on them. No one knows your name so it stands to reason you're okay.'

'But what about you?'

'They don't know my name neither.'

So Rosemary felt safe until the terrible day when she learned how adults can lie. Her pet rabbit Tootsie disappeared. Mum said he had eaten too much and burst. She'd buried him in the garden. She even put a cross there. Tootsie had been greedy and liked to steal the cat's food. As he was a massive Flemish Giant, the cat had avoided tackling him.

Two days later, Uncle Leslie brought round a bottle of gin and Rosemary heard him tell Mum the rabbit was delicious. She shuddered at the memory.

Mum bought a bottle of peroxide and hid it with the gun. 'That's for when the bullets are used up,' Mum told her. 'They'll keep the blondes here because Germans only like blondes. The brunettes will be sent off to their slave labour camps. They say it's curtains if you land up in one of them.'

A month later had come a change so violent that her life was never the same again. It was a lovely summer day, and Rosemary set off home from school, a ten-minute walk. There were only two hazards to be faced: there was a major road to cross, and a gang of girls from a rival school sometimes waylaid her and punched her.

Crowds of people were standing around in the main street waiting for something to happen, while half a dozen bobbies and old men from the Home Guard were stopping anyone from going down it.

It didn't matter much. Rosemary knew another way, which she often used to avoid the gang. Down a narrow alley, through Mr Smith's garden, out the back way, across the alley, through the baker's yard to a small hotel, where she walked in at the swing doors one end and out of the French windows on the other side. Then she was right opposite her home.

Today the hotel was deserted, and so were the shops and the streets. Why was it all so quiet? Not even a car or a bicycle. Rosemary was scared. She turned a corner and saw Tibby mewing on the front steps of their home. She ran across and grabbed him, then fled into the house. As she slammed the door she heard a shout and running footsteps right behind her.

'Mum! Mum!' she called, but Mum wasn't there.

As she raced into the kitchen she felt wind blowing up the stairs. 'Mum left the window open, that's for sure,' she told Tibby.

But there was a gaping hole in the wall. Their wooden table was smashed and lying across it was a long black tube, bigger than she was, with wings at the end. It was ticking loudly. A bomb! She couldn't see any names on it, so she walked up to it and kicked it.

'Where are you, little girl? Come quickly. It's not safe here. Tell me where you are.'

As the man clattered down the stairs towards her, Tibby took fright and shot out through the hole.

'Thank God I found you,' he said. 'Come on, now, let's get you out of here fast. Your mum's waiting for you.'

'Not without Tibby.'

'The cat'll look after himself. Come on, run! It'll blow us to smithereens if we don't look out.' He grabbed her arm and dragged her towards the stairs.

'Tibby!' she screamed.

She fought the old man until he hoisted her over his shoulder and carried her out into the street. A policeman ran towards them and caught hold of her. Between them they pulled and pushed her down the street.

She was screaming when the house exploded. The blast sent them sprawling across the road.

That night they stayed with Aunt Maude. First thing in the morning, Mum and Rosemary went back to see what they could salvage. What a mess! Shredded and half-burned bits and pieces of all they owned lay tangled in smouldering heaps: a bit of Teddy's ear, a doll's arm, scraps of books, plates, battered saucepans.

Rosemary was suddenly aware that Sam was staring at her, eyes full of compassion. 'What a terrible story, Rosemary.'

'I'm sorry. It was commonplace in those days. I remember how Mum was in tears as she picked up bits and pieces, but I was intent on finding Tibby. We never did. Goodness me, how I've talked. Sorry. I wanted to say—'

'And you said it. Thank you, Rosemary. Let's go home.'

Sam smiled, then put her arm round Rosemary's shoulders and squeezed.

First came the smell, which they detected when they were still half a mile from home. It was dark, but there was no sign of fire.

'Perhaps someone's burning rubbish,' Sam said.

It got stronger and Rosemary put her foot down hard on the accelerator. As they tore up Woodlands' driveway, they saw the red glow through the trees. It was coming from the first-floor windows of the new office block.

Rosemary braked and Sam flung open the door of the

moving car. She leaped out and raced to the entrance of the block. Moments later she was back in the driveway coughing and choking. She tossed her coat into the lily pond then pulled it over her head and face, she sounded the fire alarm, then telephoned the police and raced upstairs. Only two offices and the passage were blazing, but thick black smoke was everywhere. She tore back outside to fetch the hosepipe, turned on the tap and tried to reach the windows with the water. John was running towards her with a long ladder across his shoulders. 'I've called the fire brigade,' he yelled. 'I was passing and I saw the smoke.'

'Hold the ladder,' he shouted to Rosemary. 'Weighs a ton.'

Sam grabbed it and started up the first rungs with the hosepipe.

'Come down, Sam. I'll do it.'

'Try to find another hose,' she yelled.

Seconds later the deluge of water was sending clouds of smoke billowing through the windows. Sam aimed at the flames.

Then she heard Rosemary's anguished shout. 'The brewery's on fire. John! Get down there!'

'Arson,' Neville Joyce told them. Someone drenched your office and the warehouse with paraffin and set light to it, but you came back before they had a chance to do any more damage. Your PC's had it, which means your records are gone.'

Sam wandered around examining the thick, slimy soot that encrusted her office. Pictures were cracked, frames warped, and the contents of the filing cabinet turned to ashes. How much stock had they lost, Sam wondered. Were they finished?

Rosemary came looking for her. 'Cheer up, Sam. There's a lot of stock destroyed, but it's covered by insurance. At least the files are safe. I duplicate everything on the PC twice a week as a matter of course and lock the disks in Trevor's safe. The insurance will pay for the damage. All this can be overcome without too much difficulty. The important thing to remember is that they tried to destroy your sales and accounts records, but they failed.'

'Thanks, Rosemary.'

'You'll have to leave this mess as it is for the time being,' Neville said. 'We need to get the experts up here to look around.'

'Sam, I'll be off, if that's all right,' Rosemary said. 'Don't worry. It's not as bad as it looks.'

'Where's John?'

'Crying in the warehouse.'

Rosemary left and the fire-fighters trooped away. The chief shook her hand. 'You and Carvossah saved the day, him with his call to us and you up there with the hose, Miss Rosslyn. Any time you need a job come and see us.'

Soon Sam was under the shower scrubbing off the soot. Then she wrapped herself in her dressing-gown and walked down to the library to think. She needed to know the exact extent of the warehouse loss. She'd have to wait until John surfaced.

She took a notebook and pencil out of a drawer and scribbled down her thoughts and fears. If she solved her short-term problems, the fire damage, the cash-flow disaster, the bank manager snapping at her heels, she still had major long-term problems.

Well, in fact it was one problem: she didn't sell enough, and a lot of what she sold was through Greg at reduced prices. She was following in Mr Balaton's footsteps, a recipe for disaster.

Right now, though, she couldn't do much about it. She needed Greg's sales just to keep going. She *had* to find new export markets. Taxes were ruining their traditional markets, and they couldn't compete with European beer. How could the government be so shortsighted?

Panic engulfed her and she broke out in a cold sweat.

It was past midnight but Hans Kupi was still waiting. He had ready a bottle of champagne and two glasses, and a red rose lay across the empty place. The moment he saw Shireen he leaped to his feet and bowed over her hand, but when they sat down his face hardened.

'Well?'

'Well what?'

'Don't play games. What did he say?'

'He said he'd have no truck with EETA and he'd advise his business associates to do the same.'

Kupi poured champagne and handed her a glass. 'I see. And what did you say?'

'That I thought he was being short-sighted. That others would follow his lead. That I'd always imagined he was a far-sighted, broad-minded man who could look to the future and that Russia is one of the world's few remaining growth markets.'

'You'll have to be more subtle than that.'

'I was subtle enough. He promised to rethink his entire attitude to the deal.'

'You've got a month. Work on it. Davenport's got to stand up at that meeting and recommend that they all join our export group. That's your target. There's a lot of cash at stake.'

'I can make it.'

Kupi seemed pleased. He turned his attention to ordering: soup, fish, filet mignon, dessert, cheese and fruit.

After two bottles of champagne he switched to brandy but seemed to remain sober. Eventually he stopped lecturing her and told her stories of his youth in Russia. They'd been poor, so poor that the whole story was a cliché and Shireen tried not to yawn. At two a.m., he escorted her home.

As she unlocked her door, he pushed her against the wall and fumbled at her breasts. She slapped his face sharply. 'None of that or I won't play.'

'And him?' he sneered. Then he turned abruptly and marched away, stiff-backed, erect, ex-soldier written all over him.

There were a dozen messages, all from George. Shireen's eyes softened. 'You should have been my father, George,' she whispered.

Richard had driven over to have it out with Sam, but as he approached Woodlands, he smelt the acrid odour of the fire. He parked at the office block and examined the damage. Then he drove back to the house. He was surprised to find the door open. He sensed that she wouldn't be asleep, and found her sitting trance-like at the old table in the library. He switched on the light. 'Sam,' he said.

She gasped with surprise. 'Oh, Richard. I'm so cold. I was just sitting. I really don't know what I'm going to do.'

'Sam, darling, it's not as bad as you think. The insurance will pay out. Your main problem is your lost records.'

'No, they're in the safe in Trevor's office. He hasn't come home, by the way.'

'He'll be all right.' He laughed gently. 'And you're worrying too much about very little. The place will have to be cleaned and you might need new furniture, but it's not the big deal you think it is.'

'You're missing the point, Richard. It was arson. Who wishes us so much harm?'

He watched her thoughtfully. Tears glistened on her lashes and her face was pale. She smiled faintly and wiped her eyes on the back of her hand. So forlorn. Compassion flared and with it a fierce burning in his loins.

'You don't have to be alone tonight,' he said, putting his arm around her shoulders.

She looked up at him and he touched her neck, stroked her hair and felt her trembling. She reached up, caught his hand and gripped it tightly.

'Shall we go to bed?' he asked softly, feeling that all that mattered was that she should not be alone and afraid.

She stood up, wrapped her arms around his waist and pulled him close to her. 'I need you. Oh, Richard, darling, I don't know why you're here, but stay with me.'

He held her hand as they went up to her room. He longed to protect her and make her world come right. But was that love, he wondered.

Chapter 46

Rosemary knew she should have stayed longer with Sam, but she had had to get away. She had driven home in a state of panic, with a sense of impending doom. Why? Was it because the fire had pulled her back into the past to relive the terror of the war? Was it the very adult Rosemary Santer who was feeling this terror, or was it Rosemary the child? And when had it all begun?

Rosemary delved into her memory and found the time and place: a Friday night when the weekly boarders had gone home. She could smell the incense from the chapel, which always clung to the nuns' black robes, and feel her teddy bear, and hear the clock ticking in the passage outside her dormitory. Then came the doleful sound of the siren, warning that enemy planes were approaching. They had five minutes before the bombers were overhead.

She was out of bed in a second, rubbing her eyes, groping for the slippers. She put on her dressing gown, grabbed Teddy and stumbled along the creepy corridor, which they all swore was haunted.

'Come along, girls, careful of the stairs,' Sister Agnes called.

Ten of them had been left at school for the weekend and they crept under the refectory table and crouched there, while the sister called the roll. Then she scrambled under the table. Sister Maria joined them. The rest would shelter under the stairs or remain praying in the chapel, Rosemary knew.

If she edged to the end of the table, Rosemary could see the tall window above the stairway. There was no moon but the sky was lit by hundreds of searchlights crisscrossing the dark sky as gunners searched for enemy aircraft.

Children and nuns held their breath. There was a distant rumbling, a deep, low-pitched grumble. Enemy bombers. British aircraft sounded different, Rosemary knew, more like a steady, high-pitched hum.

The sound was getting louder, filling the air around them. Then came the crack of shells exploding.

In her small, private patch of sky through the open window, Rosemary saw a searchlight catch a tiny silver fly. More beams raced across the sky, homing in to trap the fly who was darting this way and that way, trying to escape from the tell-tale light. There was no escape, only a sudden blaze as the fly exploded and spiralled down. Rosemary was afraid to cheer in case the nuns moved her away.

The cacophony was threatening: the shriek of shells rising, the ear-splitting 'pong' as they burst in the sky, the drone of fighters coming in to the attack and the rat-a-tat-tat of their guns in the distance. The Jerries were making for the docks and the industrial area near-by.

The children and nuns were crying. Rosemary took Mabel's hand. It was wet and sticky and shaking. Mabel was only five and she missed her mother. The nuns trembled and clutched their rosaries, muttering, 'Hail, Mary, Mother of Jesus,' over and over. Through the window Rosemary could see hundreds of blue and red stars raining down: incendiaries.

Then came a now-familiar sound: a bomber was racing towards them, low down to avoid the searchlights. From the ragged sound of its engine Rosemary knew it had been hit. It was dropping its bombs fast to get up speed to reach the Channel.

The first blast was distant, the second closer, the third was a mighty roar, but still the bomber was moving straight towards them. The fourth lit the hall with a white flash, the building rocked, windows shattered, and plaster fell around them. Instinctively Rosemary pulled Mabel towards her, cradling her in her arms. Then came the fifth explosion on the other side of the school. It had missed them. They hardly noticed the sixth and seventh bombs as the plane fled southwards.

Now came a new menace: smoke. Then they heard the crackle of flames, the sound of beams falling.

'Evacuate the school,' came Mother Superior's voice. 'Everyone out by the front door. Be careful of the broken glass. Children, make sure you have your shoes on.'

They stood on the pavement, eyes wide, mouths open, watching the best firework display ever, for the sky was alight with thousands of burning incendiaries. Most were bright red, but some were neon blue. They were deadly, but beautiful, and they were falling everywhere.

One landed a few metres away and the nun grabbed a dustbin and up-ended it over the flames. All around them people were rushing out of the shelters to put out the flames, but one had taken hold in the convent roof and it was blazing.

The nuns filed out calm as ever and did their best to put out the blaze, but the old building erupted into flames, sending sparks high into the night sky. The fire was warm and they were cold, and they stood huddled together, watching the planes fighting overhead, and the searchlights homing in on the enemy.

At last the all-clear came, but there was nowhere to go.

The fire brigade arrived long after the convent was a blackened ruin. One novice had stubbornly remained in the chapel and burned to death.

Chapter 47

The village meeting was over, but it was a lovely night and Trevor was in no mood to go home. Instead he drove down to the seafront, parked his car and walked for a while, but soon his leg began to ache so he sat on a bench and gazed out over the Channel.

Anna had fought beside him, foraged for food, dressed the partisans' wounds and helped organise the drops. He and she were always together, but seldom alone. They had shared odd moments in damp ditches or caves. When they got the chance, they made the most of it. Sometimes they risked a night together in her attic.

One damp, foggy evening late in April had been just such an occasion. They were both overawed by their good fortune as they toiled up the slopes of the Myto hills, carrying their sleeping bags and rifles. They reached the appointed place for the drop hours too soon, burrowed into the dense bracken, unrolled their sleeping-bags and made love. Finally they lay in each other's arms, wishing that the precious hour would last for ever.

After a while Trevor broke the silence. 'What will you do when the war's over, Anna? Will you come back with me?'

'How can I be a brewer's wife? I am the custodian of the family estates. If I leave they will confiscate the château. How can I abandon all this?'

He sighed. Let the war go on for ever. He could not envisage life without Anna.

306

Around eleven o'clock they heard the sound of distant engines and within minutes the area was alive with Germans. They were setting up an ambush, not aware that two partisans were already there.

'Listen to me, Trevor,' Anna sounded scared, 'this is too much of a coincidence, three ambushes within a month. Robin's right, we have an informer in our highest ranks. I must warn the others. Take care.' She crawled away through the bracken. When he heard shots, he was plunged into despair.

Trevor had to admit that she was right. Every night American and British planes dropped arms, but time and again the Boche ambushed the partisans waiting at the drop. Although the men usually escaped, they had experienced heavy losses in supplies. Only the British squad and Anna knew the hiding-place for their arms and this, too, was a matter of contention between them and the Communists. There were dark murmurs about a possible British mole and relations were becoming strained.

At one o'clock Trevor heard the four-engined plane nosing up the Strela river looking for the sign, which would have been Orion signalled from the ground by torchlit letters. The big aircraft circled low and eventually turned for home.

At dawn, when Trevor returned to their headquarters in the forest, he found Anna asleep on a bunk. Thank God no one was there to see as tears of relief flowed down his cheeks.

Trevor sat up with a start and glanced at his watch. Two a.m. It was getting chilly. It was so long ago and they had been so young. Later, when the war ended, they hadn't had long together either for Anna had died.

He leaned back and considered the war's end. The

Russians had been advancing and the partisans were executing hundreds for collaborating with the Germans. He'd been ordered to join the Americans, who had to retreat from Czechoslovakia and leave the country to the Russians.

'They aren't going to view you as an ally,' the London office assured him. 'Get out now while you can.' But he waited.

The only way to take Anna with him was to marry her, but she had a mind of her own. Days later, when he went to the convent to fetch Sister Theresa, who was wanted in London, he found Anna waiting to say goodbye. He spelled it out to her: the unlikelihood of them meeting for the next few years, if ever. Eventually she'd given in and married him in the convent by the lake. Although Trevor wasn't a Catholic, the ceremony had been performed in the old chapel by Father Klima, and the nuns made Anna a garland of flowers and found a white veil, which she'd worn over her dungarees.

'Anna,' he whispered to the night, 'thank you.'

He dozed off and woke to find Sam bending over him. 'What are you doing here?' he asked. But it wasn't Sam, it was Anna leaning over him, her black hair falling forward framing her face, her brown eyes shining with compassion and warmth, her lips parted in a half-smile. 'Trevor, don't stay alone, darling. You have so much love in you.'

When he woke, he couldn't shake off the strangest feeling that he'd been awake all the time.

The Indian summer warmed the earth: the scent of jasmine and tobacco flowers, the cries of lonely gulls and always the restless sea washing the pebbled beaches below the chalk cliffs. Rosemary sat on her old bench gazing out over the Channel. The war had been over for fifty-two years, but the terror lingered. Would she never be free of it?

She heard footsteps, looked round and saw Trevor coming across the bridge.

'You felt me willing you here,' she said, five minutes later, when he walked up the hill. 'I'll make coffee, shall I?'

'A drink would be nice.'

'Scotch?'

'Yes, please.' He watched her thoughtfully. She looked pale and dishevelled. Her face was soot-streaked and her clothes were covered in smudges.

'What is it, Rosemary? What's happened? Are you all right?'

She shook her head.

'Why were you sitting out here by yourself?'

'Haven't you been home yet?' she asked.

'No.'

'There was a fire. Two, actually. The fireman said it was arson. My first thought was John, but he'd called the fire brigade and he was trying to put out the blaze. I don't think it's too bad. Good heavens. Just look at me! Help yourself to a drink and get one for me, too, while I clean up. I was afraid to go inside. Absurd.' She shivered and smoothed back her hair.

'It'll be all right, Rosemary. We'll deal with it in the morning. Tonight I don't want to talk about business.'

Despite his comforting words, news of the fire had unsettled Trevor. War had been declared, a dirty war, the enemy was within his gates, and he was vulnerable because of his family. He must get Rosemary away from this isolated cottage at once, he decided.

Trevor sat on the couch and sipped his drink thoughtfully. Rosemary was a lovely woman with a great sense of humour. She idolised him – but only because he'd got her out of Saudi Arabia. Not much basis for a friendship. When she came back, enveloped in a white towelling dressing-gown, her hair all over the place and no makeup, he thought she looked wonderful and much younger. He stood up. 'So this is what you really look like. Truly lovely.'

She smiled bitterly. 'What was, was.'

'You're still a beautiful woman, Rosemary.'

He touched her neck, felt her shudder and let his hand move softly to her cheek.

She reached up, caught his fingers and gripped them fiercely. 'Trevor . . . I . . .'

'You don't have to say anything. I think we understand each other rather well. All you should ask is why it took me so long to come to my senses. Shall we go to bed? Is that the way to begin? Or do you have another suggestion?'

She drew him to the bedroom, and hesitated, nervous. 'I feel I've run a full circle and I'm back at the beginning again.'

'I have to admit it's been a long time.' He laughed shakily.

'I heard on good authority that it's like riding a bicycle. You don't forget.'

'Sam wanted to know if I'm still capable. I said yes, but the truth is I really don't know.'

'Trevor, I love you.'

He took off her dressing-gown and stared at her with undisguised admiration. 'If I'd known what was underneath I wouldn't have hesitated . . .'

She glanced shyly at him and suddenly they were both laughing.

* * *

310

Later Rosemary lay with her head on his shoulder, tracing her finger over his chest. 'You were wonderful.'

'I've been storing it up.'

She ran her finger over the line of his cheekbone and his eyelids. 'D'you know? I've loved this face for a very long time.'

'I've loved you too.' He turned towards her and wrapped his arms around her, smothering her with light kisses.

'Why don't I brew some coffee and bring it back to bed?'

'Mm! Yes. Mind if I use the phone?'

'Oh, Trevor. How could you ask? You pay the bills!'

She heard him dial. 'Hi, Sam. Yes, I know about the fire. At least we have the files. We'll work it out together. Rosemary says it's not too serious, thanks to you two and John. I may miss breakfast, or I may bring Rosemary back with me—' He broke off and she heard him chuckle. 'Mind your own business, my girl.' He hung up.

Rosemary climbed back into bed, laid her head on his shoulder and gazed at the ceiling.

'There's something I've always longed to ask you and you must tell me now. It's important. Remember that time in Saudi Arabia at the Consulate when you came in. You said, "Don't do it." Then you took me into your office and told me you were going to try to get me back to Britain. Were you asked to help me, or was it all your own idea?'

'That bastard wouldn't have pulled his own mother out of the sea.'

She wrapped her arms around him tightly. 'You saved my life.'

That reminded him. 'Rosemary, I want you to come and stay in the house. It's not safe here.'

'And Tibby?'

'Well, I thought about him, believe it or not. You can have that spare downstairs room we call the breakfast room. Make it your private office. It opens into a walled garden where Tasha can't get in. Look here, Rosemary,' he sat up, 'I'm sure you can sort it all out. Women are supposed to be good at these things. As the mistress of the house, do what you like. Oh, and you'd better find a replacement for yourself at the office.'

'Will Sam mind?' Rosemary had become very fond of her this summer. She'd hate to spoil their relationship.

'Quite the contrary. She's been nagging me to get together with you for some time. Julie adores you. So that's settled, is it?'

'Was that a question?'

'Perhaps I should have framed it a little better?'

Rosemary shrugged.

'Give me time to sort out this mess, Rosemary, and I promise I'll turn my attention to being more romantic.'

'Just let me talk to the girls. If it's okay with them, whichever way you want to play it is fine by me.'

'In that case, come here . . .'

Chapter 48

It was not yet dawn. Sam was still asleep, but Richard had been awake for most of the night trying to think of a way out of the indebtedness into which she had been thrust. On this side of the Atlantic, the time for small brewers was over, unless the British government made some lasting tax concessions, which seemed unlikely, so what was the answer? Treble production and capacity? But what was the point of that if the consumers weren't there?

As Richard saw it, Sam's only hope was to export more, but she couldn't compete in price in Western Europe. Which led him to America, which was big enough to consume all the beer Britain could make. But Americans made good beer themselves, although in a country the size of the US there were always enough people to sustain any kind of drink. The secret was to reach them and sell them something they wanted *with* the beer. Sam needed a stunt that would appeal to their emotions.

What was meaningful to most Americans? Courage, the will to fight against adversity; the survival of the little man – or woman. And what did they lack in America? Certainly not beer. History, he thought.

So how could Sam give them history with her beer? And how could she represent courage, perseverance and all the other characteristics Americans revered?

Richard crept out of bed and sat by the window staring out over the Channel. Slowly he fell into a state of deep concentration, which was how he worked out his problems. Was there anything that was uniquely Sam's? Of course there was. Suddenly it all fell into place.

Richard went back to bed. His last thought as he fell asleep was how to make Sam think of it herself, otherwise she wouldn't do it.

He woke with Sam shaking him. 'It's morning. You must go, Richard. I wouldn't want Gramps to find us.'

He sat up, blinking. She looked tired and he guessed that her worries kicked her in the guts each morning when she surfaced.

'Listen, Sam, we can learn from history. You British have been fighting off your taxes for centuries. You spring from a long line of survivors. What did your ancestors do to alleviate tax problems? And did it work?'

'Are you trying to tell me something?'

'Just thinking aloud.' And he left, creeping down the stairs, hoping Trevor wouldn't hear him.

For Sam, going to the office was an ordeal nowadays. Dearlove phoned daily for cash, which she didn't have. Creditors nagged. Going to Pilsen had cost the earth and, although the orders had come in, Greg's customers were slow in paying. Furthermore, the insurance company were reluctant to pay out for the fire damage because of the hint of arson, although there was no proof of this yet. They were coming later this morning to look around. Fortunately not much stock had been destroyed.

On the plus side, she had just produced the most delicious light blend suitable for Britain's youth market. She felt it would do well in the States, too, if she could only find the cash to market it there. If only Richard would pay for the title . . .

She was worried about Greg. He phoned daily with

more orders, which she pretended she couldn't fulfil. Balaton's warning was always in the back of her mind.

Rosemary arrived a little late for work, looking so happy.

Sam blithely sang the chorus of 'All You Need is Love.'

Rosemary flushed. She stared hard at Sam and said, 'Trevor wants me to live with him at Woodlands, but I haven't given him an answer. I said I'd speak to you and Julie first. How would you feel about that, Sam?'

'Oh, Rosemary, you should know.' Sam stood up and gave her a hug. 'Nothing would make me happier. That goes for Julie, too. Ask her, by all means, but she's always loved you, you know that.'

'In that case,' Rosemary said, 'never mind me. You're looking so worried. What is it?'

Sam produced a feeble smile. 'I need a marketing stunt because I can't afford to pay for a good advertising campaign. Something that would get me in the newspapers and possibly even on TV. Something that would make people remember Woodlands when they buy a beer. We've got this marvellous new blend. Part ale, part mead, believe it or not.'

'Really? John gave me a sample and it's really good.'

'But without proper marketing it will fail.'

'Oh, Sam. That's a terrible thing to say.'

'But I've had the craziest idea. Richard sort of hinted at it, but I'm not sure if he really meant it. I thought I might re-enact Lady Godiva's ride to protest against the punitive taxes on brewing beer.'

'Are you serious?'

'What d'you think?'

'It might work,' Rosemary murmured. 'You're a good enough rider and we could make you a wig to cover you

315

up . . . Sam, this is the most amazing idea. But it would need proper marketing.'

'I'll call in Walter.'

'Couldn't we have someone better?' Rosemary looked anxiously at Sam. 'I know he's your friend, but . . .'

'We haven't the money and, anyway, he's good, Rosemary, I promise you.'

'What's all this, then?'

They looked up and saw John framed in the doorway.

'John, listen to this,' Rosemary began.

Sam watched John's face change from doubtful to incredulous and back to triumphant. 'If you've got the guts to do it, we'll back you, Sam. And we have to think of a name for it,' John said. 'I've had an idea – Bottoms Up.'

Rosemary looked doubtful.

'Godiva?' Sam asked.

John frowned. 'What if we split it? Go-Diva, I'm sure that would work.'

'I like it,' Sam said. 'Diva's the name of the drink and Go-Diva means, drink Diva.'

'Yeah. But what's it got to do with singing?' Rosemary asked.

'Nothing! Doesn't have to. Where's your dictionary, Rosemary?' Rosemary pushed it over the desk and Sam grabbed it and flipped through the pages. '"Diva – a goddess, feminine of *divas*, meaning divine, a god or a deity or *prima donna*." Perfect!'

'And it *does* taste divine,' Rosemary added.

'*And* it will commemorate your ride. You'll be like Venus sitting up there starkers,' John said.

'All I need is the courage to carry it off,' Sam mused.

Chapter 49

She was the only sane person in Woodlands, it seemed to Sam. Rosemary was panicking. She kept tripping around the room in her high-heeled sandals, offering makeup, hairpins, brushes and her own special brand of comfort. Since hearing that Grandmother had been a snappy dresser, Rosemary had totally revised her wardrobe. Gone were the pearls, twinsets and sensible shoes.

'Nudity's nothing nowadays, darling,' she said. 'Just pretend you're on a French beach. Or, better still, working in a Soho club. The first time I went nude was in a show called *Savages*,' she babbled. 'Not the West End production, of course, but a little something we put on in Bahrain. As long as I had my ruby in my navel, I felt dressed. Sam, can I lend it to you?'

'Thanks, but no.'

Why aren't I scared? Sam wondered. Perhaps because it all seemed so unreal. Like watching a movie.

Julie came racing in. 'The Government have replied to your letter protesting against the high tax. Look, here's the House of Commons logo on the envelope.' She waved it at Sam.

'Well, open it, then.'

Julie drew out the sheet and read: 'Chilly winds and rain predicted from the south-east. Hope your wig's warm. Good luck.'

'Well, of all the . . .'

'Who signed it?' asked Rosemary.

'You won't believe it.' Julie flapped the letter before their eyes.

'Wow!'

'Does Gramps know, Sam?' Julie looked worried.

'No.'

'Then he's the only person in Britain who doesn't,' Rosemary said. 'The press know, the BBC know, the locals know – and they've promised to wave placards and cheer you on your way. Local brewers know. But does anyone care? As I said, nudity's nothing nowadays.'

'Except it's illegal,' Sam added. 'Maybe no one will turn up, other than the usual shoppers.' She looked hopeful.

'Inspector Joyce will turn up,' Julie said. 'You can count on it.'

'Neville's promised not to arrest me until the show's over.'

'Decent of him. And Luther will be there,' Julie told her. 'He's going to make sure no one hurts my horse.'

'Naturally.'

'Walter and the goons must be there.' Sam looked worried. 'At least, they'd better be, since they organised the publicity. They have to take pix and get press releases out in case the press don't come.

Rosemary glanced at her watch. 'It's almost nine. We'd better get the wig on.'

It was made of horse hair, and was as thick as a tent. It would cover Sam from her head to her knees. It weighed a ton, too, she learned, when Rosemary put it on her head.

'I'm still worried about riding Mirabelle. She's a bit skittish,' Sam said.

Julie cut in, 'Richard insisted—'

'Richard!' Suddenly Sam was transformed into a Valkyrie. 'But he's in the States right now. I checked.'

'Yes, he is,' Julie said. 'Before he left he said that it had to be a white mare because it's important to be historically accurate.'

Rosemary was glancing from her watch to her timetable. She stuck her head out of the window. 'Here's Mona with Mirabelle.'

'Mona?'

'I thought you'd rather have a woman around for the disrobing.'

Sam parted the coarse hair and looked into the mirror. Under a voluminous kimono, which was Rosemary's, and the tent of hair, she could see only half an eye peering out.

'Come on, you lot,' she heard Mona shout.

'Let's go!' Sam went out of the passage and down the stairs.

When Sam approached, Mirabelle reared and rolled her eyes.

'It's the wig.' Sam heard Trevor's voice right behind them. 'She should be wearing blinkers. Get out of the way for a moment – I've brought some.'

'Oh, Gramps,' Sam said, tremulously, 'you weren't supposed to know.'

'There's an announcement in the *Herald*. They're right behind you. Sam, it's likely to get chaotic but you must keep your seat. You can't afford to fall – there'll be nothing between you and the cobbles.'

Sam was slipping out of the kimono. 'Goodness, it's cold.'

'You're turning blue, Sam,' Julie said.

'Can you see much of me?'

'Only from the knees down,' Julie lied.

'Okay, Sam. You're on your own, but we three'll be as close as we can in my Mini,' Rosemary called. 'Good luck.'

Trevor went back into his office, switched on the television and settled down to wait. He'd get a better view of Sam's progress from his armchair. He had the greatest faith in Richard's marketing ability, particularly since he'd called in a top public-relations agency. Neither he nor Richard had had much faith in Walter.

Through all the hair Sam had only a narrow strip of vision. As she turned into the main road she became aware that both sides of her route were lined with pickets. Would they try to grab Mirabelle? She peered through her hair to read what the placards said: 'Reduce the Excise Tax.' 'The Bare Facts of the Sin Tax.' 'The Naked Truth of Government Bungling.' 'Brewers Lose Their Shirts Through Tax.'

'Wow!' she muttered. When she tried out a wave, a cheer went up on either side. Sam was overcome with emotion and made a huge effort to pull herself together.

'Let's get this over with, shall we?' she said to the horse, and prodded Mirabelle into a trot. The mare pricked up her ears, tossed her head and off they went.

The wind dropped, September sunlight warmed Sam's bare shoulders and the wind caressed her skin. Sam felt her body respond to this new freedom.

Looking ahead she saw a great number of people and vehicles. The road seemed blocked and sunlight was reflecting off hundreds of mirrors. Then she realised they were camera lenses.

Sprawled in his armchair, Trevor poured his second Scotch and tried to relax as he listened.

'This is Bob Hume, reporting live from Bourne-on-Sea in Kent. Good morning to you all. This morning, one brave young woman, Samantha Rosslyn, has thrown down the gauntlet to the Government in a demonstration that is likely to hit home hard.' He smiled into the camera. 'Today Sam is re-enacting the ride of her famous ancestor Lady Godiva who in ten forty-three, as near as can be estimated, rode naked through the streets of Coventry to persuade her husband to abolish taxes on the poor folk of Coventry.

'Samantha is a brewer, just like her forebears, yet today her company faces closure. So do all of Britain's other independent brewers. Every one of them is battling to keep afloat in the face of competition from cheaper European-brewed beer. Sam's ride today is aimed at focusing the Government's attention on the so-called "sin tax" on brewing beer, which has all but crippled British brewers.

'Unlike with Lady Godiva's historic ride, local towns-folk have not shut themselves into their homes. On the contrary, they've turned out in force to lend their whole-hearted support to this protest ride Just look at them!' The camera zoomed around. 'Schoolchildren, Boy Scouts, bikers, housewives, trippers – just about everyone and their dogs are here to help her. And here she comes, folks.' His voice rose. 'She's surrounded by hundreds of supporters trailing along the entire two-mile route from her home.'

Trevor could hear the cheers echoing along the roadside.

'While we're waiting for her, we'll have a word with a couple of bystanders. 'Excuse me, sir. Can you tell me why you're here today?'

'I'm an off-duty police sergeant. Name's Bill Keene. I came along in case she needs protecting. We all have. She's quite the local heroine hereabouts. Turned down a lucrative offer to buy out the brewery because the locals would lose their jobs, so it's up to us to stand by her now, isn't it?'

'And the excise tax?'

'The sooner that's adjusted the better. Small businesses are the backbone of the British economy. It's short-sighted to tax them out of existence.'

'Thank you, Bill Keene. Well, there you have it from the local constabulary. And above us I can hear a helicopter hovering. It's descending. Whoops! Too low and too fast. This could be nasty. Sam's horse is starting to panic. Wow! The horse is running out of control. It's the stuff rodeos are made of. She's riding for a fall. This is going to be terrible.'

The noise of the helicopter was deafening. Sam hung on with one hand while attempting to wave it away. It hovered lower and Sam felt the suction from the updraft, which pulled her wig into the air as if it were made of feathers. It flew off.

Mirabelle was sweating heavily. From the outset the crowds and placards had made her nervous, but as they neared the village centre, the shouts and flashguns terrified her. Now she was intent on bolting, but the reins held her back. She made heroic efforts to unseat her rider, rearing and lashing out with her hoofs. Neighing in panic, she was an awesome sight. The crowds pressed back. A few people were screaming, which increased Mirabelle's terror.

In those desperate moments Sam had only one thought. Someone might be injured. Somehow she must control Mirabelle and her lethal hoofs. Keep your seat, Gramps had said. She clamped her legs hard around the pulsating heaving flanks, and tried to sink further into the slippery back, to be at one with the horse, and all the time she was fighting to force the mare's head down. At last Mirabelle came to a reluctant halt and stood trembling. Then the helicopter soared up and zoomed towards the town hall.

'Okay, Mirabelle. It's gone now.' Sam spoke calmly.

'Well done, girl. Now, let's get this show over, shall we?'

Sam told Mirabelle to walk on, and pressed her to adopt a controlled, high-stepping gait. Back on a short rein, she picked up her feet and held her head high.

The crowds were still booing and shaking their fists at the press helicopter as it zoomed out of sight.

'Phew!' the commentator said. 'Sam, minus her wig, has her horse back under control. That was the most exciting exhibition of horsemanship I've ever witnessed. This is an extraordinary rider, folks. She hung in there and kept her seat.

'She's riding up now to hand her petition to the local MP, Roger Whitlock, who's standing on the steps of the post office. He will now take up the matter with the Government. Congratulations to Samantha Rosslyn, the Kentish brewer who's given the Government something to think about today. So from Bourne-on-Sea in Kent, it's goodbye from Bob Hume.'

To Richard, the sight of Sam struggling to control the horse was unendurable. The three-minute rodeo performance seemed to last hours. If she'd fallen, he would have been there in a split second, but he forced himself to remain in the spellbound crowd, watching each move. When she pulled her horse back under control an audible sigh of relief echoed around the crowd. He knew at that moment he was in love with her.

Where the hell was Rosemary? She should be here with Sam's long coat, but he could see her car stuck in the traffic some way off. Luckily Richard had brought along her raincoat.

He watched Sam hand over the petition. He could see

that the MP was sweating with embarrassment and his hands were visibly shaking. He had fixed his eyes on a spot just above Sam's head.

'Down with the tax,' Sam yelled, and the crowd roared back.

Rosemary appeared at a run, waving Sam's coat. She'd taken off her shoes and her dress was torn. Sam dismounted and Julie led the horse away.

Suddenly it was all over. His girl was encircled by an admiring crowd. Everyone wanted to congratulate her. She didn't need him right now, and Richard decided to make himself scarce. But there was still something to be done: he intended to trace that helicopter pilot.

Chapter 50

It seemed to Julie that all of Bourne-on-Sea was traipsing up the driveway to wish them well. John was kept busy bringing over crates of beer, but no one stayed long. At ten p.m. Inspector Joyce arrived to arrest Sam. 'Don't worry, girl,' he said jovially. 'It's a first offence and you'll get off with a warning. After that publicity what else can they do?'

At eleven the family held a post mortem that turned into a celebration. The entire project was voted the success of the year, if not the decade.

Richard arrived, wearing his usual, lopsided grin.

'How did it go?' he asked Julie.

'Brilliant. My sister, the rodeo rider, made the day. Bloody Mirabelle let her down.'

'No, I didn't make the day,' Sam said. 'But someone did. Was it you, Rosemary? Did you get the Girl Guides, the Scouts, CAMRA, the brewers and their families and God knows who else to line the route and crowd the marketplace waving banners and getting hot under the collar?'

'I wish I had,' Rosemary said.

'Julie?'

'Afraid not.'

'Trevor?'

He shook his head, watching her sadly.

'Someone spread the word that Hollywood directors would be checking through the tapes of crowd scenes to find candidates for small parts in the Hollywood movie that's *supposed* to be coming here. Dozens of people told me that this evening. And that someone is the most extraordinary liar. Something that was supposed to be honest and above board has been tainted with lies.' Inexplicably Sam burst into tears.

Trevor gazed at her in alarm. 'I don't remember her ever doing that,' he told Richard, 'even when she was small.'

'She's in shock,' Richard explained. 'And I'm afraid it's going to get worse, because . . . well, you see, sir, here's your cheque. I'm taking up my option on the title and the documents. It's perfectly legal. Two million dollars, the stipulated price, and well within the option period. I'd like a dated receipt in due course.'

'Well, naturally.' Trevor looked as if he wished he could say something else, but couldn't think what. 'Look here, Richard,' he began awkwardly, 'we're all very fond of you, but I must make it clear that there's no real proof that there are any documents at all.'

'True. But I have a hunch I'll find them.'

'Well, I'd like to keep this money in a trust account to be returned to the buyer should the documents not materialise.'

'Sir, that's not quite how things go.' Richard was laughing. 'Get real, Trevor. If they're found, these documents are worth ten times more than I'm paying you. That means our historian gets them at a bargain price. For that he has to take a risk. No profit without a risk. That's basic economics.'

'Absolutely,' Julie burst out.

Sam blew her nose vigorously and stared hard at him. 'I want to talk to you, Richard. Let's go in the library. Don't stop the party, please. We'll be right back.'

Richard loped behind her, admiring her upright stance,

the graceful line of her shoulders and her small waist. If he were the marrying kind, he'd snap her up.

Once she'd slammed the library door, she collapsed into a chair. 'Trevor loves you. All my family loves you. I can't bear to see you pulling one over on them. First you promise them Hollywood and now you've offered a gullible historian priceless documents and you told all those people they might get bit parts in the movie. But why, Richard? I can't work out what's in it for you.'

'The pleasure of helping you get Woodlands back on its feet. Had you thought of that?' He couldn't help wondering what she'd say when he told her the truth.

'No! I won't buy it. You're not the least bit philan- thropic.'

'Fair enough. The real truth is I'm attempting to alleviate my guilty conscience.'

'How come?'

'I've been deceiving you, Sam.' He felt better the moment he said it.

'That was the only thing I was sure of.' She looked up, eyes flashing, and bit her bottom lip.

'Despite that, you offered me a job,' he went on quickly. 'That means a lot to me. It shows you care.'

'Oh, Richard, you know I do. You're not blind. I'm too tired to keep up this farce. Yes, I care for you, in fact, I love you, but so what? Rosemary told me to believe in my dreams, but any fool can see that there's no future for us unless I turn this brewery round.'

'I don't get the connection.' But he did and he felt his cheeks burning.

'*Well, one of us has to make an honest living.*'

'You mean . . . but this is so sudden . . . oh, Sam, darling, listen to me and don't get angry, please.

'My name is Richard Mann. I shortened Mandelbaum

legally because it's such a mouthful and because I'm not Jewish, although my grandfather is. He runs a business buying and selling antique maps. I took over the financial side when he ran into difficulties after a fire some time back, so I buy and sell through his business. The computer company, Data Power, who you rightly discovered had never employed me, was in fact my own company.'

'Please, please,' Sam put her hand to her forehead in an attitude of despair, 'don't tell me any more silly stories. You don't have to lie. My feelings for you won't change. Surely you understand that.'

Richard felt frustrated and hurt. Why didn't she believe him? 'As I was saying, I sold the business three years ago in the States. They don't know me here but a simple call to head office can have them working on anything I like. It was part of the deal. Hence Porgy's new computer. And, by the way, tell Walter I wasn't in prison, I was writing a book. I like to concentrate full time on what I'm doing. As a matter of fact, one of my previous books is up there on the shelf. I was pleased to see that you have it.'

Watching Richard's expression Sam wondered if, after all, he was telling the truth. She watched him reaching for a thick book that Trevor had ordered because it mentioned their family. He handed it to her with a flourish.

Sam weighed the book in her hand. She studied the title: *Analysis of the Domesday Book and Its Influence on Class Consciousness in Medieval England.*

'Look at the flyleaf, Sam. It has my name and my photograph there, so you can clearly identify me, but it doesn't have my fingerprints. Sorry about that. Perhaps in future books . . .'

'Bastard.'

'Listen to me carefully. I'm on the trail of those documents and I think I'll find them.' He folded his arms around her waist, held her close.

'Yes, I see.' She felt quite hurt and dumbfounded. 'So there's no third party?'

'Just me.'

'Why couldn't you have said so in the first place?'

'Usually I'm not a liar, but bitter experience has taught me that when the word goes round that I'm looking for certain documents the price rockets. I'm almost always successful. In my own modest field I'm famous, you see.'

'Have you found anything yet?'

'No, but I have a gut feeling that I will. That's why I'm paying for the title.'

'The cash will be welcome,' Sam said.

'But how long will it last? Listen to me for once and take my advice instead of listening to Walter and Greg. Did you know you were on CNN? Your magnificent ride was seen all over the States. Now's the time to get your ale over there. I've got dozens of ideas for labels that would suit the American market. I've even got an agency on the job. A top international agency. The ones who organised the publicity for your ride, not your tinpot ex-lover and his band of freaks.'

Sam sat silent for a while. 'I think I'm in shock. D'you really think our beer would sell in the States? Am I too late to apply for the Denver beer festival?'

'No. I applied on your behalf. If you remember, I offered to help.'

'I accept – so thanks. But I don't understand why you're taking this trouble.'

'For the same reason I'm bringing the film company over and putting up with your appalling rudeness. I'm fond of you.'

'And the Hollywood moguls really are coming?'

'Hardly moguls. It's a tinpot company I have shares in.

329

They're hoping for the big break. Relatives, actually, on my grandfather's side.'

'I'm sorry I've been so rude.'

'You don't have to apologise, darling. You were sharp enough to realise I was lying and that I'm not the type to buy a title. People who lie must expect to be distrusted.'

She tried out a smile and it felt good. 'So we can put it all behind us.'

'Not all of it, I hope. I've some pretty good memories. Hang on while I lock the door. We have to make the most of those rare moments when we're not fighting. By the way, I think I love you, too.'

Yet you lied to me and you're going to make a huge profit out of our documents, she thought. Is this love?

Chapter 51

Paul, the nurseryman, drove around with a smile on his face singing, 'How many flowers do there grow, in an English country garden?' He changed the words to suit his orders as he rushed to deliver all daylight hours.

'Buttercups and hollyhocks, marigolds, forget-me-nots, roses and lupins, foxgloves and stocks . . .'

Business was booming as the residents of Bourne-on-Sea vied with each other in producing the best traditional English gardens to ensure that their homes were featured in the coming movie. Rambling roses trailed over trellises, armfuls of lavender lined paths, and every crack sprouted daisies and pennyroyal. Out came the tulips and agapanthus and all those fancy foreign things. Paul sang all day, but especially when he made his bank deposits.

But when are they coming? That was the disturbing question uppermost in everyone's minds. The contract with the film company had been signed weeks before. Surely they hadn't changed their minds.

Once doubt set in, it ran through the village like a rampant Asian flu, and hardly anyone was spared. The symptoms were a foul temper, a harassed expression, a compulsion to kick out at rose-bushes and reluctance to pay Paul's accounts.

Then, one Saturday morning, a stretch limousine was seen moving down the high street and into the square. The car halted, the back door opened and a rather skinny young man with unruly black hair, rimless spectacles and a dazed expression climbed out.

He looked around, saw a group of women having coffee at a pavement café and called out in an American accent: 'You folks have a castle around here somewhere?'

Agatha stood up. 'Are you from the film company?'

'Advance guard, ma'am.'

'So you're really here at last. This calls for a celebration. How many of you are there?'

'Five so far. I'm Bob MacKay, location manager.'

'I'm Agatha, and this is Maria and Mona. Follow us. We'll lead the way to the castle.'

The crew soon found themselves being led to the Castle Arms where they were fêted by the entire village. After several drinks and some barley wine the backroom boys were feeling a bit confused. They set off towards the castle and blundered into the brewery, where John tested some of his new blends on them. Sam heard the story from Mona and called Richard, who rescued the crew, and billeted them in Rosemary's cottage.

'Behind the brewery is a big farmhouse,' Richard explained. 'That's where you eat, so come along to dinner, or for tea if you wake up in time. Meantime, you guys better sleep it off. Be careful of these English girls. They mean business.'

The five young men were workaholics, Sam noticed. They rose at dawn and worked until midnight. They organised the stables, hired some caravans, and sought out the best houses for the early sets. It took Sam a while to realise that one of them was the director, Irwin Levy, who had a string of box-office successes behind him. He looked like a mischievous elf, with his pointed ears and slanting green eyes.

Several huge mobile homes were towed inch by painful inch along the narrow cobbled lanes to the field beside the castle, for wardrobe, filming and stage props. An entire studio, hired from Pinewood, found its way to the field. Next came half a dozen caravans for the actors and Irwin. The wardrobe mistress and her assistant arrived and unpacked crates of medieval-style costumes.

Bob Mackay wandered around with a notebook and Polaroid camera searching out the right venues for various scenes.

Three days later Jules Cameron, the casting director, flew in and, much to Sam's surprise, managed to coerce Rosemary into giving up the barn for a few weeks. He was tall and overweight, with large grey eyes that blinked perpetually behind his thick-lensed spectacles. He was certainly no heartthrob, but to see the women fawning all over him you'd think he was. Almost the entire village queued at the barn and were tested for bit parts.

Rosemary landed a plum role as a nun, Mona became a neighbour, Richard a yokel, Helen the village gossip. Sam made the excuse that she had to look after the brewery, but she thought she might try for the crowd scenes. Julie wasn't interested.

Two weeks later, the heavyweights arrived – and so did the press, who camped on the front lawn for a while, much to Sam's annoyance.

One of the stars, Marilyn Darlowe, who was to play the carpenter's wife in the Miller's Tale, was met by Richard at Heathrow and driven back to Woodlands where she would stay. He carried in her bags and introduced her to the family.

She looks so ordinary, Sam thought.

Rosemary took over. 'I would never have recognised

you, Marilyn. So this is what famous stars look like when they're not being Hollywood sex symbols?'

'It's an image I like to shed as often as I can.' Marilyn's dumb-blonde act had been put aside.

'I expect you'd like a shower and a rest. I'll show you to your room.'

Marilyn looked reluctant. 'I thought I'd be staying in a caravan. I'm pretty independent. I need my own bathroom and I'm not much of a socialiser. Evenings I work on my lines.'

'Give us a try first. Why not? It might be lonely out there on your own. You can always move out when the others arrive if you still want to. And of course you will have your own bathroom.'

'Just as long as you understand.' She scowled as she glanced round. Her famous charm was evidently reserved for the press.

Her cellphone rang. 'Hi, hon.' Marilyn looked weighed down with anxiety. 'No, you must eat your breakfast. Of course you like cereal. You always eat it. Rupert, do what Hannah says. Yes, I'm tired all right. I've got a couple of days to come right before we start work. Hello, Hannah. Where's Jason? In bed? Why?' Her voice rose to a squeak. 'Take his temperature, Hannah. Call me back if there's anything wrong. You got that? Day or night. If you have any problems call me.'

The conversation seemed to have no end. Sam hovered, then moved off.

Five minutes later Rosemary was showing Marilyn to their largest guest room. 'If you want we can send up all your meals. Whatever you want, just say.'

'Why are you folks going to all this trouble?' Sam heard Marilyn ask.

'For the money and because the contract stipulates

Woodlands ale exposure, that's why,' Sam muttered, under her breath.

'One down, dozens to go, but that wasn't so bad. In fact, I rather like her,' Rosemary said, when she came back. 'I'd better get back to the kitchen. Keeping Helen going is a full-time occupation.'

The male lead, Kevin Quinn, arrived later that day and was cornered by Mona, who seemed anxious to keep him to herself. She showed him to his suite and carried him up a drink and stayed there for half an hour. Then she raced back to Rosemary's den, which the family had taken as their private living room for the time being. Bursting in, she stoppped short at the sight of Greg, who'd dropped in for a drink. When he had first joined the drama group, Mona had made a play for him, which hadn't worked.

'You've got competition, Greg,' she announced. 'Kevin Quinn is the sexiest man I've ever seen. He's got the most amazing blue eyes that look at you so . . .'

'His stock in trade,' Greg said drily. 'I sell liquor, he sells sexy looks.'

'Don't be jealous, Greg. I expect Mona's exaggerating,' Sam teased.

'No, I'm not,' Mona snapped. 'He's lovely.'

'All right, Mona, we get the message,' Rosemary said. 'Did you tell him dinner's at eight?'

'No.'

'Well, you'd better go and do that.'

The following evening Rosemary gave her first formal cocktail party for fifty people in Woodlands' drawing room. It was an idyllic scene, with the french windows flung open to the lawn, which sloped down to the oak- and willow-fringed river.

The locals had done themselves proud. Sam knew that

Agatha and her mother had flown to Paris for a shopping spree. Mona had on a short white dress covered with layered silver fringes that shimmered when she moved. Paul looked magnificent in a tailored suit worn over a black T-shirt. The vicar was sporting a red cummerbund and cheeks to match. He'd discovered the Talisker whisky, his favourite. Sam wondered if she'd have to drive him home. It wouldn't be the first time. She hadn't seen such a turnout in the village for years – the vet and his wife, the doctor, Jim the publican, they were all here. Even Julie had been persuaded to wear a sparkling black sleeveless sweater, borrowed from Sam, over her jeans.

Their Hollywood guests filed in, the men in jeans and T-shirts, long-haired, intent and intellectual, the women without makeup and wearing expensive trouser suits.

Helen had made canapés with prawns, caviar, and oysters, slices of ham lay on French bread thick with butter and on the improvised bar were Scotch, brandy, beer, wine and a jug of water.

The water was drained quickly but the food would have stayed untouched – and the drink – if it hadn't been for the locals.

'What's got into them?' Helen moaned to Sam. 'Don't they eat in Hollywood?'

Sam found Richard and dragged him to the kitchen. 'Why aren't they eating?' she demanded.

'Don't worry about it. These people seldom eat.'

He looked very uncomfortable but Sam had no mercy. 'Richard?'

'They're either Jewish or vegetarian.'

'Why didn't you warn us?'

'I forgot.' Richard was looking thoroughly shame-faced.

'If only I'd known.' Rosemary was stricken. 'How long will they hang around?'

'All night, by the look of things.'

'Okay, you two. Go and enjoy yourselves. You can leave this to me.'

The food arrived an hour later: brisket on rye, cream cheese on bagels, smoked salmon, russians, cheese blintzes, kichelach, teiglach, pure fruit juices and low-alcohol wine, five different brands of water, and cheesecakes.

Sam never found out exactly how Rosemary did it, but she learned from Mona that Eric Falkow, proprietor of a fleet of helicopters, had suspected that if he wanted to stay healthy and in business he'd better make his peace with Richard Mann and the Rosslyns.

'Heavens! What did all this cost?' Sam whispered in the kitchen.

'One punch on the nose, I believe,' Rosemary said. She closed her lips tightly.

'And he got off cheaply,' Richard muttered.

Next morning, the village woke to the sound of Maria's shrieks of rage. Her father Paul's Tudor cottage was on the short list to be chosen as the backdrop to the Miller's Tale. It had been Bob's choice because it had a large front lawn, which allowed shots of the overhanging window from all angles, but 'Fuck you, Paul' had been written across the lawn in big bold letters with weed-killer some time during the night.

Inspector Joyce found the culprit before lunchtime: the local butcher, who had spent a fortune at Paul's nursery and who was also on the short list. The grass was replaced with instant lawn and so were the flowers, at the butcher's expense, but it didn't look the same.

From then on, the green-eyed monster strode through the normally placid village: Fred the chemist's privet trees, shaped into horses, knights and their ladies, were all beheaded, the doctor's wife's myrtle bush had a load of manure tipped over it, the vet's petunias were trampled when someone let a donkey into his garden, and the hairdresser's dog was kidnapped.

On Richard's advice, Bob Mackay made his choices public and let it be known that he would stick to them, and the rivalry soon fizzled out.

Nearly everyone had a temporary lodger. The Americans woke at dawn and worked until midnight so the locals did likewise. Housewives were jogging at dawn, fad diets became the norm, everyone began to say, 'Have a nice day,' and the greengrocer was bringing in fresh fruit and vegetables by the truckload.

Will, the butcher, thanked God they couldn't turn their dogs into vegetarians. 'This won't last,' he kept telling his friends. 'They'll soon be longing for their roast beef and steak.'

No one listened to him. Hollywood magic had touched every household.

Chapter 52

It was five a.m. and breakfast time on the first morning of filming. Sam hurried into the kitchen to find Helen toiling over muesli, yoghurt, chopped eggs and minced herring.

'Can I do anything?' she asked.

'No, love. Just eat your breakfast – but take this toast with you and see if anyone wants more.'

Sam almost collided with Delain, the makeup artist, who seemed to be everyone's *bête noire*, although she couldn't think why.

He caught hold of her arm, peered into her eyes and said, 'How are you this morning, hon?'

Obviously he'd noticed how exhausted she'd been feeling. You could see that he really cared, so why was he disliked and the butt of every joke? She smiled at him. 'I'm fine now, thanks, Delain. You guys take a bit of keeping up with, but I'm over the worst. I finally got used to four hours' sleep a night, but I don't how you cope in the long term.'

'Glad to hear it.' He patted her back and turned his attention to the fruit juice.

The milk jug was empty. Sam hurried out to refill it. Moments later, as she placed it on the sideboard, Delain caught hold of her arm, peered into her eyes and said, 'How are you this morning, hon?'

'I've only got a month to live, but I'm bearing up,' she snarled.

'Glad to hear it.' He patted her back and poured himself some coffee.

'Creep,' she muttered, as she sat down.

'But a magic creep,' Irwin whispered, nodding towards Marilyn. 'After breakfast you'll see what he can do for her. That's why we put up with him.'

Julie came in followed by Tasha and Porgy. Irwin frowned and grinned disarmingly. 'Is this for real? A pig and a wolf as house pets? Are you trying to rewrite a few nursery stories?'

Julie smiled. 'Huffing and puffing is rewarded with a swift clout. Besides, they know when they're well off. They're two clever animals.'

'Have you got a part yet, Julie? If not, I could find you one.'

She shook her head and smiled at him. 'Cameras leave me cold, that's why I've given up modelling.'

'My loss, Julie.'

Sam couldn't help liking Irwin. He was a sensitive, clever man who observed everything and spoke only when necessary. Yet the crew were quick to do whatever he asked, and she'd noticed that Marilyn was at pains to keep on the right side of him.

The film crew rose and left. Moments later she heard their convoy of cars moving down the driveway. Only one remained.

Sam heard Trevor's study door open and close. He came in tentatively. 'Everyone gone? Can I have my breakfast in peace?'

Then everyone jumped in surprise as Shireen rushed into the room.

'Where've you been?' they shouted as one.

'You've been missing all the fun,' Sam added.

'I came as soon as I could. The summer break just began.

We put on a play and I had the lead, but it's over. Am I too late to get a part? Just imagine – Hollywood invades sleepy old Bourne-On-Sea.'

Her voice had acquired a new vibrancy, and Shireen was poised, yet natural, full of warmth.

They turned as they heard footsteps and voices coming from the stairs. Moments later Marilyn swept in, transformed: her skin glowed, her eyes looked huge, her lips seemed fuller and she was wearing her famous sultry pout. Was that a wig, Sam wondered. Surely Delain couldn't have fixed her hair *that* fast, could he?

Marilyn looked relieved as she saw her cellphone lying on the table.

'Has it rung?'

'No,' Rosemary assured her.

'Well, that's a miracle. Thanks.' She grabbed it and was about to leave when she saw Shireen. She stopped short, as if someone had struck her, and gave Shireen a long, critical appraisal. 'Who are you?' A look of fury marred her looks.

'Oh, sorry, Marilyn. This is Shireen, my best friend,' Sam explained. 'Shireen Desai. Shireen, meet Marilyn Darlowe.'

'I've seen all your films—' Shireen began.

'Is she staying here?'

'Yes,' Rosemary said.

Marilyn swept rudely out of the room, across the hall and down the steps, with Delain trailing behind her. 'Keep her out of my scenes. I don't want her anywhere near me on the set.' Her voice came clearly through the open window.

'I think she saw you as a threat,' Sam said to her speechless friend. 'It's a pity you're late, but I'll drive you down to the barn where they do the hiring. You never know, maybe there's something left.'

'You can have my role, Shireen, but it's not much,' Rosemary said.

'Don't be silly, you'll have fun. Come on, Sam, let's go – I'm so excited.'

Talking all the way, the two girls drove to the barn. As she was about to get out Shireen turned and flung her arms around Sam. 'It's so good to be together again. Without you I might have been in India now.'

'I was being selfish. I didn't want to lose my best friend. Stay with us for a few days, Shireen, please. You can have my room,' Sam said, as they pulled up outside the barn. 'See you later.'

Shireen watched Sam drive away with a funny, aching feeling. Sam was so dependable. She ventured inside the old barn. 'Hello, there,' she called. 'I'm looking for a part The lead role will do. I have limited acting experience and unlimited ambition.'

A man scrambled up from a Lilo in the corner of the room. 'Sorry! I have to snatch the odd catnap when I can. Any acting experience?' he asked, in a bored voice.

'Yes. I'm studying at the London Academy.'

Shireen turned towards him. Was he the casting director? He looked more like a disapproving owl, blinking myopically as he polished his rimless spectacles.

He pushed them on and stared at her. His eyes widened. 'Good God!' he muttered. 'Are you for real?' His admiration was replaced by a calculating leer. 'Listen, I'll push you, but you must say I discovered you. And you say you can act, too.'

'Sure. Why not?'

'In that wardrobe there's a long, floral dress, sort of greenish with some blue and yellow in it. Right now it's going spare. Marilyn won't wear green. Get dressed before the wardrobe mistress gets here. It's my bet they'll be looking for an understudy soon. Take that basket of cherries and I'll drive you down to the set.'

'Jesus!' Jules, the casting director, said, when she emerged from behind the screen. 'You're a sensation.'

They were filming in the churchyard. Despite the early hour a large crowd had gathered outside the wall to watch.

Irwin was sitting on his director's chair, high above the crowd, clutching the script, oblivious to everything except the scene unfolding before him. The air seemed charged with tension. 'Okay, let's give it a go,' he called. Someone was yelling a countdown. At zero the church doors opened, the vicar emerged and stood by the door. Arm in arm the cast strutted out in their medieval Sunday best. There were at least twenty villagers in the scene, including five children, and they performed brilliantly, Shireen thought. And the vicar was a real star.

Marilyn, who was playing Alison, the flirtatious miller's wife, flounced out of the church on her husband's arm. All at once she caught sight of Nicholas. Hanging back behind the miller, she gazed lasciviously at him.

Nicholas winked, grabbed at his crotch and shook himself suggestively. One or two of the villagers turned to stare and mutter at their partners.

It was so real. Shireen was entranced, but then came the shrill sound of a cellphone. Marilyn tugged it out of her pocket.

'Hello! Who? Hannah! Oh my God. Oh *my God*. I'll be back on the next plane.'

'Cut!' Irwin barked. 'For God's sake, Marilyn, you've ruined the entire scene.'

'It's my kid,' she shrieked. 'Robin's got measles and complications. He can't see properly.' Her voice broke in a sob. 'I'm going home.' She spoke into the phone again. 'You've called the doctor? Good!'

Irwin pulled a lever and his chair descended. He climbed out and stalked over to Marilyn. 'The hell you will,' he murmured, but everyone heard. 'You can't do this, Marilyn. You've got a professional looking after your kids. Hannah can cope. If you walk out now you won't get another job – ever. And believe me, the producer will sue.'

Marilyn burst into tears. 'My kids are more important than this lousy film. I quit,' she screamed.

'Okay, hon. This is your cue.' Jules grabbed Shireen by the shoulders and gave her a push. 'Why don't you wander over that way, very calm, very cool, smile at Irwin. Stand around, stroke your hair, you know, like she did, put a cherry in your mouth, bite into it and look sort of . . . sort of . . .'

'Don't worry. I know how to look.'

She walked towards the director as if she was in a dream, and heard him calling, 'Hey, who's that woman?'

She was pulled and pushed in front of cameras and lights.

'Am I seeing straight? D'you all see what I see? Or has the strain finally got to me?' Irwin growled.

'I discovered her, Irwin,' Jules called.

A script was pushed into her hands. 'Read it. Try to be natural. Make as if you really care.'

It was an action scene without much dialogue. What there was she memorised in a few seconds then let herself merge into the role. For a few moments Shireen forgot the crowds, the lights and the director. She had no real concept of time passing. It was always like that when she was working: time seemed to stand still.

'Okay, that was fantastic. Where d'you learn to act?'

'London Academy.'

'It shows. We'll do some more film tests right away,' Irwin promised, trying, but failing, to hide the excitement in his eyes. 'Got an agent?'

'Yes,' she said. Hugh Bolton would find her one.

'Get him over here today if possible. We'll have to reshoot everything we did yesterday. We can get started on it now.'

Chapter 53

'Look here, Rosemary,' Helen said, loud enough for Sam and Julie to hear, 'I don't want strangers tramping around my kitchen. They're more trouble than they're worth. I've been managing for the past twenty years. Mrs Rosslyn never found it necessary to hire extra staff. She trusted me.'

'Helen's so unfair,' Sam muttered to Julie. The two sisters were having breakfast and eavesdropping unashamedly. 'We should tell her off. She's found Rosemary's Achilles heel and she attacks without mercy.'

'Ssh!'

'Mrs Rosslyn was a great one for entertaining. She had so many friends. Many's the time this house was full to overflowing . . .'

'Bitch!' Julie muttered.

'If you think you can cope, Helen, then far be it from me to interfere. You can count on two hundred people, thirty of them kosher and about the same number vegetarian. If you need help let me know, but not at the last minute, please, Helen.'

'Rosemary's standing up for herself, Julie. Best not to interfere,' Sam argued.

She knew that Helen's nose had been put out of joint by Rosemary's frequent appearances in the kitchen 'to lend a hand'. Even the fact that she'd brought in caterers and a cleaner to help out while the film company was here had annoyed Helen. But Rosemary was the mistress of

Woodlands and she had a right to go into her kitchen when she felt like it.

Matters had come to a head because the family had decided to give a party to celebrate Shireen's three-film contract. Helen had insisted on coping alone, apart from Mona, with the catering.

Moments later Rosemary came in looking anxious.

'She's going to let you down, I can feel it,' Julie said.

'I agree. We need professional caterers,' Sam added.

'Of course we do,' Rosemary said. 'But Helen seems to take that as an insult.'

'Tell you what,' Julie said, 'you order the food, but pretend it was Richard. As far as Helen's concerned he can do no wrong.'

'That's a good idea, but are you sure Helen and Mona won't cope?'

'No,' Julie said.

'Let's order the food from a caterer,' Sam suggested, 'with delivery as late as possible. Hopefully she'll have given up before it arrives.'

'And what's happening with Bowles?' Julie asked. 'Today's the last day of his notice to get out.'

'Presumably he'll go.'

'With or without his pigs?'

'I'm sure he'll take them, but we'd better keep an eye on that. Well, I must get down to the brewery. 'Bye, everyone.'

'So how're we doing, Clare?' Sam asked her new assistant the moment she walked into the office. Clare was always there first and she had the facts and figures at her fingertips. She insisted on calling Sam Ms Rosslyn and, as far as Sam could see, she never smiled.

'Current sales are up to seventy-five per cent of our potential, and we managed to reduce the overdraft slightly, just enough to keep Dearlove off our backs. Ted's one week behind with production so Greg Selo's order is late.'

'Pull John back off the road for a week to get Ted back on line.'

'Will do. There's two faxes for you. Greg Selo wants to double up on his order—'

'Tell him no.'

'And you should take a look at that fax on your desk, Ms Rosslyn.'

Sam picked it up wonderingly. It was from Ruark and Mallory, Inc., one of the largest liquor wholesalers in the States. The order was for 80,000 barrels a year of Go-Diva, which was double Woodlands' total production capacity. Furthermore the directors were intending to fly over to Kent to discuss possible investment in her company with a view to developing a much larger market in the United States for this blend, which they considered to be a long-term winner.

Sam collapsed in a chair with shock. What a shame she couldn't fulfil such an order. Or could she? What if she got some of the other local independent brewers in on it? They all had spare capacity. It was easy enough to produce this particular blend. Should she patent it first? She picked up the telephone to call Richard.

'Fuck the lot of them,' Tom Bowles muttered. 'Foolish little girls with their bleeding hearts and those DARE women, half of whom are illiterate, judging by their placards.'

Bowles was feeling sorry for himself. He'd sacrificed five years of his life to turn the farm into a profit-making venture. Without his expertise this place would have foundered. Now that it was running properly they wanted to get rid of his pigs. So he was leaving. They'd be sorry. They'd come crawling soon, begging him to come back.

And what had they achieved when all was said and done? Bowles wondered as he gazed at his patented pig batteries. Would the pigs be happier? Certainly not. They'd be rows of bangers by lunchtime, which was a pity for they were good breeding stock. In fact, the best, and it was all the fault of those interfering women.

He glanced at his watch. Another hour to wait. He went outside and stared at the wooden stalls into which the pigs just fitted so that all the food they ate went into making good bacon. Beside them were the sties for nursing mothers. They were so narrow the sow couldn't move, or touch her offspring, or even scratch, which saved her energy and prevented the piglets from being trodden on. He'd designed and made each one himself. Tears came to his eyes as he thought about it. In pig-breeding circles he was famous and they couldn't take that away from him. He might even get his own place going, he thought.

Helen had excelled herself. By lunchtime the rows of shelves in the pantry were filled with food.

'All right, my girl, now we'll make the flaky pastry. I'll need a hand here,' she said.

'It's so hot,' Mona whinged.

Mother and daughter worked side by side for half an hour, but then they were startled by a sudden crash and a squeal from the pantry.

'Lord, Mona, you didn't leave the pantry door open, did you?'

Mona turned pale. Moments later Helen heard her squeal of anguish and she picked up her carving knife.

'He's eaten all he could reach. And he's pulled down half of the rest. Broken all the best plates,' Mona screeched.

Helen wasn't listening, she was chasing Porgy round the kitchen making stabbing movements at him, but missing every time. She was past coherent thought. The blood pumping through her seemed to have turned to treacle. She felt a great pain in her chest and she had difficulty breathing. She wanted to kill that animal.

'Mum! Jesus, Mum! Sit down. I'll get you a glass of water. Relax.'

'Never mind the water. Just get that bloody pig out of my sight. If I see him again I won't be responsible for what I do.'

After a scared look at her mother, Mona grabbed the pig's collar and dragged him into the garden. Where was Julie? Down at the film set, naturally, where everyone was having fun, except her. What could she do with the greedy little nuisance? Well, they had pig-sties, didn't they? That's where he belonged. She'd lock him up for the day.

Porgy whimpered and tried to avoid going into the sty, but he was propelled forward by a kick in his backside. Then Mona ran back to see how Helen was doing.

Bowles watched Mona leave and went down to the pig-sty to have a look.

'So here's the famous Porgy, back where he belongs. Have they finished with you, my friend? Well, they've finished with me, too.'

Bowles examined Porgy with an expert eye. Too much fat by far. He bent down to remove the pig's fancy collar and Porgy, thinking help had come, sniffed his hand. Bowles slapped his nose. 'Streaky bacon. That's all you are,' he said, with a smile, as he heard the livestock lorry toiling up the steep farm road.

Julie returned at four that afternoon. Tashah let off her

usual howl of welcome, but no little pig came squealing to the door. She went into the kitchen where Mona was working.

'Where's Helen?'

'At the doctor's.'

'You should have let Rosemary know. Where's Porgy?'

'I locked him in a pig-sty. He stole all the food.'

'When?'

'This morning.'

'How could you leave him there for so long? Did you give him some water?'

A cunning, scared expression flitted across Mona's face.

'We'll talk about this later,' said Julie. 'I'll go and fetch him.'

'Julie.' She heard Mona running behind her. 'I'm really sorry, I never meant something like this to happen. But Bowles sent the lot to the abattoir. Porgy went, too. I don't know how it happened. After all, he had a collar on. Everyone knew who he was.'

Julie raced off to the pig-sties, but they were empty. Bowles's car was gone.

She dashed back to her car and tore down the drive, tyres squealing.

Rosemary came out to investigate and saw Mona standing there crying.

'What happened?' Mona explained, and Rosemary went into Trevor's office. She telephoned the abattoir and asked for the MD.

'That batch of pigs you received from us this morning, what have you done with them?'

'We processed them this morning.'

'All of them?'

'Yes, of course.'

'But there was a mistake. One of them was Porgy, the TV pig.'

'What? You mean . . .? You set us up, didn't you? I know how you people operate. We weren't to know. We're not to blame. You people must keep out of my abattoir. You hear me? Keep away from here,' he yelled. 'I don't want to see one of you in my place.' He flung down the telephone.

'Oh, my God. Where's Trevor? Where's Sam? And Luther. I need Luther,' Rosemary muttered. She dialled Sam first. 'Sam, we have an emergency. Tell the caterers to deliver earlier and get Mona out of the kitchen. Helen's at the doctor's. This is what happened.' She explained as briefly as she could. 'I'm going straight to the abattoir to help Julie. I have a feeling she'll need a lot of support.'

Julie parked her car and ran to the side entrance, where she saw a man in plastic overalls and boots with a hosepipe. He was washing blood out of the warehouse. He looked up, smiled and shouted, 'Careful! You'll get messy here.'

'Where are the pigs?'

'This morning's batch from Woodlands?'

'Yes.'

'In here.' He flung open a heavy iron door and a blast of cold air hit her. The huge cold storage depot stacked with sausages, salamis, all packed, weighed and labelled, and hundreds of carcasses.

'You look upset, love. What's the matter?'

'My Porgy.' She couldn't talk: her teeth were chattering and her mouth felt wooden.

The man said helpfully, 'There's a retail outlet round the back where you can buy whatever you want.'

Suddenly his boss came racing into the warehouse.

'Keep your mouth shut! Get her out!' he screamed. 'She's trouble.'

Julie felt limp. She fell back against the wall.

The man in the plastic overall hoisted her over his shoulder, carried her outside and dumped her on the back seat of her car. Then he went inside and barred the door.

'We're closing early,' his boss told him. 'The press will be swarming round here. They'll try to blame us, but it's nothing to do with us. Keep your mouth shut.'

When Rosemary arrived she took Julie to the doctor, who wanted to treat her for shock, but Julie refused. 'I'm not ill, I'm sad. All the pigs that died with Porgy were just like him. It happens every day. The only difference was that we loved him.' Julie stood up and began to pace the doctor's surgery.

'In fact, Porgy has shown me what I want to do. I intend to devote the rest of my life to helping people understand that we should care for all life, not just human life. That'll be my way of showing Porgy that I care.'

'Of course, dear,' Rosemary said soothingly.

'Let's go home,' Julie said. 'There's no point in spoiling Shireen's evening. To be honest, much as I love her, I don't think she'd even understand. I don't think you do, either.'

'I love you, Julie. I always have. If it's important to you it's important to me.' But Rosemary couldn't help wondering if Julie was well enough to go home. All this upset over a pig. She'd have to keep an eye on her this evening.

Chapter 54

'Hi there, Shireen,' Irwin called. 'We've picked the right day for it.'

Shireen was furious with herself for agreeing to appear in a nude scene. She should have refused. Days ago, when she'd signed the contract, she had been so overwhelmed by her good fortune she'd have agreed to anything, but now that the day had loomed up on her, it seemed a crazy idea. She was going to have to take off her bathrobe in front of the crew and bathe in the river while Kevin, as Nicholas, got into a clinch with her.

It was noon. There wasn't a breath of wind and you could see the shimmering heatwave rising from damp grass. Across the river, the cows were lying in the shade, but the air was noisy with birdsong and the hum of insects. She sauntered down the narrow path towards the river. Her sandals skidded on the slippery mud slope.

'That's it. Stop there, hon,' Irwin called.

A nervous tremor shot through her. If Sam can, I can, too, she thought.

The wardrobe mistress, Jane, hurried down. 'Put your robe behind the rock here where no one can see it. It'll be within reach when you've finished the scene,' she said.

'Thanks,' Shireen said miserably.

Jane looked up sharply. 'Shireen, if I had a figure like yours, I'd flaunt it,' she murmured.

Suddenly Irwin was beside her, his arm around her shoulders. 'Remember, you're Alison. She's locked up with an ugly old man who can't get it up, and she's so full of sexual frustration and longing for fulfilment, she's practically bursting at the seams. Nicholas has fallen for her and he comes this way daily. She wants him to screw her, so she's going to tempt him by bathing nude in the river. Start feeling like Alison. Okay? Forget that shy Shireen.' He bounded to the top of the bank then turned round to watch her.

Shireen stood as if in a trance. The expression on her face was more wistfulness than lust. 'Lust!' he roared down the slope. 'Produce some unrestrained lust, for fuck's sake. All men off the set, except lighting and cameras.'

Harsh light flooded the riverbank.

'I need more lights, more power. The shadows are too dense,' someone called.

Irwin fumed at the delay. He had a feeling that his new star might make a break for it. The next five minutes seemed to last hours.

The crew were ready at last. Shireen knew what to do. She had a minute in which to disrobe on the bank before wading slowly into the water, while looking over her shoulder for Nicholas. There was only one scene of full frontal nudity and that was when she turned and called to him.

'Wow!' Irwin muttered. It was going to be all right, after all. He exhaled all his tension and even managed a shaky grin. Shireen was a real professional. Her features had undergone a transformation: pouting lips, dreamy eyes, and nipples thickening with desire. She ran her fingertips over her body, panted slightly. 'Shit!' he murmured incredulously. She was not only beautiful, she was extraordinarily sexy. He was getting a hard-on and he hoped to God it wouldn't show.

The scene went without a hitch until Kevin arrived.

'Kevin, you're supposed to be Nicholas. A poverty-stricken student with a permanent hard-on. Opportunity seldom knocks but when it does, boy, you're in there fast. Just as fast as you can, before someone snatches all that lovely flesh away. Got that? Let's try it again.'

'It's cold in here,' Shireen called.

'For God's sake, Kevin,' Irwin bellowed, 'there's the sexiest girl in the world splashing around naked and waving you in, and you're untying your damn shoelaces. What's the matter with you?'

By the time the scene was completed to his satisfaction, Irwin felt as if he had been through a mangle.

'Okay, guys, that just about wraps it up.'

Shireen stood up and saw Kevin avert his eyes. Was he a virgin or gay, she wondered, as she reached for her bathrobe and shoes? Suddenly she wanted to get away from all of them. She was blue with cold and, unbelievably, there was an ache in her groin, which was total make-believe because she wouldn't screw Kevin if he offered her a million. She had to be herself again, so she hurried upstream, taking the narrow path along the riverbank, admiring the wild flowers in the hedgerows.

It was a beautiful English late summer's day, the sort of day she'd dreamed of when she was in exile. Would she like Hollywood, she wondered? She'd miss her colleagues at the academy and her friends, especially Sam, but this was her big chance and she was grabbing it with both hands.

Immersed in her problems she hardly noticed that she'd reached the end of the field. The path along the river had become wider, and clumps of rhododendrons had replaced the tangle of bracken and broom.

She heard voices and, not wanting to bump into anyone in her bathrobe, she slithered down the bank and sat on a fallen log with her feet in the river. Two men were talking in a foreign language. They were coming her way, so she moved behind a bush. Peering through the branches she saw that it was Hans Kupi, with the local heartthrob, Greg Selo. They seemed to know each other well. How strange! Even more strange was that Greg appeared to be dishing out orders.

Her heart sank as they sat on a bench overlooking the river and carried on talking. She had to get back to the set, but she couldn't leave her hiding-place without being seen. She settled into a more comfortable position to wait.

As the implications of Greg and Kupi together sank in, a steel fist took hold of her guts. Suddenly her stomach was killing her. She crouched lower behind the bush.

Kupi got up and strolled towards it. He unzipped his trousers and was about to pee when he caught sight of her robe. He pulled aside the branches, swore and called Greg. As his arm shot forward, she flung herself down the muddy slope, landing with a splash in the river. She heard Kupi shout as she waded across and ran headlong up the bank towards John's house. Shots peppered the ground around her.

'Help me, help me,' she mumbled, as she ran. She was leaving them behind. Tearing through brambles and bracken, she reached the steep, muddy slope leading to John's cottage. She scrambled up on her hands and knees, then threw herself over the wooden fence.

John's car was there, as she'd hoped. She knew exactly where he kept the keys and he'd left his door unlocked as usual. She was panting with fright as she raced through the cottage. Had they seen her climbing the bank? Right now they might be coming across the lawn.

Where were the bloody keys? They weren't on the hook. Then she saw them lying on the sideboard. She needed a coat, or a shirt. She flung open his wardrobe, grabbed a pair of shorts and a T-shirt and went outside. Her heart pounding, she made a dash to the car. Suddenly she heard a shout just below the bank.

She started the car, which lurched forward, bumping over the ruts. As she drove through the gate, she saw Kupi topple over the fence. He fired twice and the rear windscreen shattered.

Moments later she'd negotiated the rutted driveway and turned on to the road. Should she return to the film set? Would she be safe there? If Greg Selo was running an international criminal network she wouldn't be safe anywhere.

'Pull yourself together, Shireen,' she told herself sternly. She forced herself to take deep breaths while she kept her foot hard down on the accelerator. Kupi had a cellphone. They might have colleagues nearby and there was only one main road to the highway. If she took the farm roads she'd eventually make Canterbury and from there she could turn on to the A2. But how could she go to London? Kupi knew where she lived. Uncle George was only twenty miles from New Romney. He would know what to do.

Chapter 55

It was twenty-four hours since Shireen had e-mailed Trevor, telling him about Greg and Kupi. Trevor had immediately contacted an old Czech colleague from partisan days, an ex-policeman, who promised to check Greg Selo's background and get the information back by e-mail.

By nine p.m. Trevor was tense. He tried to read, but that didn't help, so he persuaded Rosemary to play snooker with him. When she went to bed at eleven forty-five he returned to his computer.

When the e-mail arrived it confirmed Trevor's suspicions. Greg Selo had been born Gregory Milan Jaromil, the only son of Mira and Ludvik Jaromil, grandson of Vim Jaromil, who had been executed as a traitor in the last days of the Second World War. Shortly afterwards the Jaromil estates had been confiscated and because of Vim's war crimes the family were never allowed to claim restitution. The report read,

> Greg Jaromil and his father worked at labouring jobs in the brewery which had once belonged to the Jaromil family. After the war, the brewery operated as a village co-operative for a few decades, but when democracy was reinstated, a government official, Yuri Balaton, purchased the estate. Greg Jaromil was appointed works supervisor when his father died, but he left under a cloud of suspicion following a break-in when a large

quantity of beer was removed during the night. In the same month he changed his name from Jaromil to Selo. No proof was ever found that he was involved in the theft.

From then on Selo operated a small haulage company. A year later he took over a liquor retail outfit and gradually built up his own liquor trading company, based in Prague.

A number of factors appear to link Selo to Russian organised crime. 1. The amount he exports via Russian railways. 2. The speed at which he has accumulated wealth. 3. Those who oppose him tend to disappear: viz. four car bomb attacks, dozens of mysterious disappearances and five shootings of rival businessmen. Selo always has an alibi for the time of the murders. We have never had proof linking him to the murders or to organised crime.

That's all for now. I'll be in touch if we get more info.

Trevor sent a copy of the e-mail to George and at one a.m. he received a reply:

So now we know who Selo is. Clearly he's using the network to further his own personal vendetta, while at the same time pushing ahead with the Russians' intentions to penetrate the British liquor industry. He seems to be their man on the spot.

Shireen has disappeared. She said she knew of a safe-house, but I'm worried about her. Only Shireen can link Selo to Kupi and the current investigation. He's never caught because he wipes out the opposition. I'm afraid we'll find it as difficult to nail him as the Czechs did. Take care. George.

It was past midnight when Trevor heard someone knocking on the window. He looked up and saw John standing there. 'Come in, my boy. The front door's not locked yet.'

John was wearing a tracksuit and jogging shoes, his hair was ruffled and there was a shadow of a beard on his cheeks. He looked like a man at the end of his tether. His eyes reminded Trevor of Robin. They always had.

'Glad I found you up, Trevor,' John muttered. 'I've come to resign. And I've something urgent to tell you. But, first, do you know where Shireen is?'

'No, I'm afraid I don't.'

'I'd assumed she'd gone to Uncle George. I called, but he told me she isn't there.'

'That's right.'

'I'm worried sick about her. She's got herself into a bit of a mess. These guys who've been trying to take over Woodlands, well, they aren't straight. Perhaps you knew that. They persuaded Shireen to do some silly job for them. All she had to do was—'

'I know, John. Shireen was reporting back to us all the time. I didn't want her to get involved and neither did George, but Neville Joyce talked her into it. Now she's discovered that Greg Selo is heading this gang of criminals and she feels, quite rightly, that her life is in danger after overhearing his conversation with Hans Kupi.'

John turned white. 'Greg – and Kupi? My God! I knew there must be someone. Kupi is the essential second in command.'

'Oh, by the way, the local panel-beaters phoned. They have your car, which Shireen borrowed. They're rather curious about the bullet holes.'

John looked ill. His hand was shaking so much the ice was rattling in the glass. He put it on the table.

'My God! They could have killed her.' He paused to control himself, then went on, 'Listen, Trevor, there's a few things you should know and I'm to blame. I should have told you long ago. Last April, Hans Kupi approached me and laid out his plans for Woodlands' expansion. They were exactly what I'd always tried to persuade you to do. Well, Sam's doing it now. Kupi said he was determined to take over the company and gave me a "down-payment" on future bonuses to cement his goodwill. He also asked me to persuade you to stock up with stout. I was thinking of taking the cash to the police, but my car packed up. I used the money as a down-payment on a new one. Quite honestly, I haven't really made enough even to keep my car going.'

'It was my fault,' Trevor said. 'I'm sorry. Please go on.' Trevor leaned back and closed his eyes as he listened to John's story. John was weak, but not evil. He'd taken the wrong path and now he regretted it.

'Next thing he wanted me to set fire to the office block. I flatly refused. I've been keeping an eye on the place since then and that's why I managed to call for help so quickly. Trevor,' he rushed on quickly, as if anxious to get it over and done with, 'I'll never be able to express to you how ashamed I am. That's why I'm leaving. Sam offered me a chance of a lifetime, running US sales on a generous bonus, but I can't take advantage of her kindness.'

'It wasn't kindness, John. We need you. Can't you see that they trapped you? That's how they operate. Officially speaking I'm going to backdate this meeting four months. That means you've been working with me all along. We hope to bring Selo to trial. You'll get witness protection, as will Shireen. We want to have him put away for a long time.'

John's blue eyes were bloodshot. 'But what have you got

on Selo? A conversation overheard in a foreign language. You couldn't even get him deported on that.'

'I'm going to give you some information that's classified, John. Mainly because it concerns your safety. This is a very old story and it's hard to know where to start. It concerns your grandfather, Robin, and his work in Czechoslovakia. You must know that Robin and I were best friends as well as colleagues. He was a lonely, introverted man and a poet of great sensitivity. He would have been famous had he lived. But he had another talent, apart from his literary genius, which was an ability to pluck ideas out of the air. He could sense danger a mile off. Nowadays they call it a sixth sense.'

'It didn't keep him alive, did it?' John said softly.

'Just listen . . .'

It took an hour to tell John a little about his grandfather, of the many times he had saved their lives with his sixth sense, of his sense of honour and his humour.

'The night Robin was captured, he was supposed to be cycling to the convent with our latest radio communication, but he told me he'd injured his leg and couldn't make the ride. I had to go instead. I was surprised. He was never a quitter. Later I learned that he had sensed Vim suspected us of setting a trap and was going to turn the tables on us. So he took my place at our headquarters in the forest because Vim had expected to find me there.'

'How do you know he knew?' John's voice was hardly more than a whisper.

'He told Anna. She played along because she, too, wanted me alive.

'Robin was captured and tortured. We made several attempts to get him out, but failed. They were using underground bank vaults for their interrogation and we could never get past the guards. We lost four good men trying. We none of us thought he would last the night, but he held out for weeks.

'My grief at what Robin was suffering turned each day into a nightmare. Then came news that he had been shot at the Gestapo headquarters as they evacuated it. Shortly afterwards, I received an urgent message from Sister Theresa, an Irish nun at the Sacred Heart convent ten miles outside Pilsen. I went there to find that she had a visitor waiting to see me.' Trevor got up and walked to his safe, which he unlocked. He took out a box containing a sheet of yellowed paper, torn out of the priest's diary, which read simply: 'Keep an eye on my family, Trevor. Vim Jaromil is the mole. He was arrested with me and then released. Be careful, Robin.'

John was shaking. Trevor got up and poured him a Scotch.

'I raced back to headquarters, arrested Vim, and we held an impromptu trial. Vim wouldn't confess. He protested his innocence loudly to anyone who would listen, but he was pronounced guilty and sentenced to death. The partisans insisted that his family be present. His wife had the right to know why he was being executed, they argued, so Vim's wife and son were woken in the middle of the night and brought up from the farmhouse. She was barefoot, with an overcoat flung over her nightclothes, and because she looked like Anna, I was appalled.

'Vim was dragged out of the hut and his sentence was read. I remember he was shouting, "This is a load of trash. It's Trevor who is lying. He won't even say who gave him this information. Of course not, because he can't. He made it up. Why can't you see it's a set-up? He knows that I'm against him marrying my sister-in-law, so he wants me out of the way. You're fools to believe him."

'He was blindfolded and shot through the back of his head by his second in command.

'Now I want you to read these e-mails, John.' He handed the younger man printouts of the messages he'd received.

When John gave them back, he had himself under control. Somehow he had found some inner steel, just as Robin had.

'So, John, if Selo is prepared to go this far to ruin me, what do you think he intends to do to the grandson of Robin, the man who first accused his grandfather, Vim, of being a traitor, which led to his execution and his family's impoverishment? He certainly wasn't planning to reward you. I would appreciate your seeing Inspector Joyce first thing in the morning to make a statement.'

John stood up and walked to the door. 'Maybe, Trevor. I have a lot of thinking to do.' He left, shutting the door softly behind him, leaving Trevor prey to his misgivings. John hadn't bothered to disguise the anger in his face when he left. Anger for whom? For him? Or for Selo?

Night had fallen and Greg was sitting on his balcony cradling a Cognac while he stared out across the sea towards the moonlight rippling on the English Channel. He watched his transition from a hard-working boy to a man who hated. There was the brewery where he had worked from the age of fifteen when he left school. Year after year he had learned each facet of the art of making a good Pilsen. He had talent, everyone told him that. It seemed as if it were in his genes. He saw his mother working nightshift at the bakery and his father's slow defeat by liver cancer.

Another memory that hurt: watching his father die on a cold December night. In his last hour, he had told Greg of the grief and shame the family bore.

'Why do you think the brewery is called Jaromil and our name is Jaromil, too, eh? Your grandfather, Vim, owned that brewery. We lived in the big house behind it, and all the fields of hops were ours. Mile after mile of hops and barley, and it was all ours.'

He'd rambled on, remembering the war and the hunger. He'd been thirteen when he was forced to watch his father's execution, which he described graphically, before he burst into tears. 'It was all because of a lie.' He sobbed. 'They took all that we had. They said my father was a Nazi informer, but the English agent, Trevor Rosslyn, had rigged the evidence against him. So that's how our brewery became a co-operative farm and was never returned to the family.'

That year had brought a cold winter, but Greg felt only his fury burning inside him. When the Czechs threw off their Communist masters, a former government official, Yuri Balaton, became the new owner of the brewery.

Greg changed his name to Selo, which was his late friend's name, and he went back to work. He soon became a supervisor. Then he bought a lorry. One night he returned after dark with two youths and loaded it with the brewer's best Pilsen. It was sold in Austria before dawn.

The following night visitors arrived unexpectedly at his door. It was cold and Greg left his warm bed reluctantly to sit in the living room while he tried to coax the embers into igniting some fresh twigs.

'Leave it,' the Russian snarled. 'You fucked up, Greg. You're finished unless you join the Brotherhood.'

'What are you talking about? What brotherhood?

'You're going places, boy, but only with us. Otherwise it's the end for you. We don't allow freelancers or freeloaders. Here's what we want you to do.'

Orders followed orders from Russians he seldom saw,

and all the time he was building his own business, buying and selling liquor, driving through the nights, collecting protection money and carrying out reprisals when he had to. He'd come a long way, but he was nowhere near winning the war that had begun on the night his father died.

Now he had a new target, which was partly his own and partly the Brotherhood's: to get a foothold in the British liquor industry. He'd failed in '94, but this time he had a new plan. Woodlands would be his Trojan horse. It was only a matter of time.

Sam was a gutsy girl fighting for the family heritage, but she couldn't win. He held all the aces. She was like her grandmother, just as he was like his grandmother, the two beautiful Pilsen sisters. Strange that she had never noticed the family resemblance.

For a while Greg remained deep in thought. Then he heard a car draw up in the driveway below. There was a ring at the gate. Greg pressed the intercom button.

'It's me. John Carvossah,' he heard. 'This is urgent, so I had to bypass Kupi. You should have trusted me, Greg. We're in the same boat, but I've only just put two and two together. I know where Shireen is. She called me. We have to act fast.'

'You're right, John. I was just going to contact you. We should have talked long ago. Come in,' Greg said, and pressed the button to open the gate.

He met John at the front door and held out his hand.

'I wasn't sure . . .'

'Don't waste time. Shireen knows about you,' John said. 'It's only a matter of hours before she makes a statement, but right now she's hiding on Lord Davenport's yacht. I can take you there, but we need to be armed.'

'How many men are on the boat?'

'Usually two, plus Shireen and Lord Davenport. One of the crew is a mate of mine. He'll help us if we make it worth his while. Lord Davenport's at a meeting. Shireen's on board. She's lonely, that's why she called.'

'You did well, John. I'm glad. You're the sort of man we need now that we're going international.'

'We won't be going any place, except maybe prison, unless we get a move on.'

Chapter 56

The *Connemara* was pulling against her moorings, turned into the wind, longing to ride the waves and face head-on whatever fate had in store for her. None could touch her for courage and resilience and John was about to follow her example.

He and Greg climbed into the rubber dinghy, started the engine and motored out to where the yacht was pitching gently over the swell. Greg was strong and fit and swung himself on to the deck while John made the dinghy fast and climbed up after him.

'It'll be a rough ride. I suggest you stay in the cabin. If you come on deck you must wear a life-jacket and a safety-harness.'

'Not so fast.' Greg was looking anxious and hanging on to keep upright. John realised that he was unfamiliar with sailing.

'Before we go let's have a look at your charts,' Greg said.

'I'll get them out for you. You can study them while we sail. Let's not waste time. We have a fair way to go and we have to get Shireen on board before daylight.'

The cabin was a joy, with space enough to live for months at sea. A large, square table, with a built-in seat on three sides, cupboards of oak with everything battened down, including the Scotch.

'Help yourself, but remember, we'll be up for most of the night.' John put a bottle of Talisker on the table. He spread out the charts, put on the overhead light and took a ruler. 'Our route will go like this. Davenport's yacht is moored off Ramsgate, fifteen miles as the crow flies, but we'll be taking this route.' He drew a line north-north-east and then north-north-west.

'Why?' Greg wanted to know.

'Because of the wind. Our route leads directly to the north-west and that's head on into the wind. So we have to tack up the coast.'

'Use the engine,' Greg said, looking furious.

'Look, this boat is built for sailing. We don't need an engine. We have a small outboard for emergencies or getting in and out of harbour, but I don't carry much fuel. Besides, a sailing boat is silent. We'll be there in less than four hours, which is about right.'

Swiftly he hoisted the mainsail, and loosed the mooring.

The *Connemara* performed brilliantly, as always. John had first set eyes on his boat ten years ago and it had been love at first sight. She was a thirty-foot racing ketch, built by a retired, crazy Irishman, a dare-devil ex-international racer, who'd designed her to sail him round the world for the rest of his life, and to withstand the very worst the elements could throw at him. He died in a car crash the night before he set sail, after a massive celebration party in Galway.

John had bought her with his entire savings and a loan from Trevor, which had taken years to pay off. Together they'd romped through races and won more times than not. They'd had some pretty good holidays together, too. Just the sound of her sheets flapping in the wind and the rippling of her pennant, a black wolf on a blue background, thrilled him, but today John was grief-stricken. He was about to kill the love of his life.

How had he got to this? He saw it as a long progression

of evil: he'd taken one wrong step and now he was going to commit murder. There was no other way out. Trevor's idea was ludicrous: he'd land up in prison and Greg would be deported.

Two hours later they were sailing at eight knots and the wind was gusting up to twenty-five miles an hour. There was a heavy swell. The *Connemara* took it like the champion she was, surging and falling, keeping her course.

John brought the rudder hard over to starboard and now they were skimming along fifteen miles off Deal. He slid his arm into the locker containing three gas bottles and switched on the gas.

Greg burst out of the cabin. 'How much longer?' he growled. He looked sick.

'Put your safety harness on, and the life-jacket.' John hooked him up and left him lying prone on the deck. He switched off automatic pilot and took the rudder. Now he was tacking at thirty-five degrees off the wind and the *Connemara* was singing. But John was terrified.

Two hours passed while he relived the joy he'd shared with Shireen. There had been happy times, when she was full of fun and not thinking about the past, or the future, or her father's plans for her, or her ambitions. Greg was groaning. 'Where the fuck are we?'

'Almost there,' John replied. 'Try to pull yourself together. I'm not much good with a gun, but I'll do my best.'

'Jesus, it's black,' Greg said, peering apprehensively at the dark sea and sky. 'Where's this boat?'

'Not a boat. Lord Davenport has a vast ocean-going yacht. Dunno why they call them yachts. Never seen a sail on one of them yet.'

'How're we going to get on it?'

'One of them's a mate of mine. We have to signal him.

It's about time. I can't leave the rudder. Get the torch, will you? It's on the shelf where the charts are kept.'

'Bloody thing doesn't work,' he heard Greg call from below.

'It's the damp,' John told him. 'That's why I keep a lantern down there.' He pointed to the hatch to the bilges. 'Here's some matches so you can see where it is.'

'This is it,' John told himself. It was like he was two people. While one part of him was resigned, saying the Lord's Prayer and happy to make an end to a life marred by greed, the other part hurled him over the gunwale into the sea. As he fell, a mighty hand seemed to grab him, compress him and dash him against the mast that was fleeing faster than he was. Last came a sense of regret that he had destroyed the *Connemara* as well as himself. That was all.

Chapter 57

It was nine thirty a.m. and Sam was sitting at her desk worrying about Shireen and wondering where she was when the phone rang. It was Ted, the plant manager. 'John's absent,' he said. 'Normally I wouldn't worry, but he called a meeting for six of us at eight thirty and didn't turn up. D'you know where he is?'

'No, but I'll check around.' Sam hung up and called, 'Keep an eye on things, Clare, please. I'll be back in an hour or so. I'm popping over to John's cottage.'

Fifteen minutes later Sam was talking to John's cleaner, a blonde, blue-eyed Irishwoman of fifty-five who looked thirty-nine.

'Funny things going on here if you ask me,' she said. 'Mr Carvossah didn't sleep here last night, but this morning the panel-beaters phoned to say they'd have to replace the entire back of his car because of bullet holes. Now who'd be shooting at John? And there's something else. His oilskins and his wetsuit were hanging in the pantry and they've gone, but they were here yesterday.'

Wetsuit? Had he gone scuba-diving at night. Alone? He did sometimes although he shouldn't. But why the oilskins?

Sam decided to drive to the Dover Yacht Club and ask if anyone knew anything.

Half an hour later she parked by the dinghies and walked up to the club-house office. The commodore, tall, stooped and hard of hearing, clapped her on the shoulder and gave her a broad smile revealing yellowed teeth. 'Sam, long time no see. How're you doing?'

She dispensed with the small-talk as fast as she could. 'Can you help me, Pat? I'm worried about John. He didn't come to work this morning.'

'Carvossah?' he bellowed. 'No need to worry about him. Brilliant skipper! He can certainly cope with a night sailing trip.'

'Night sailing trip?'

'He wrote it in the book. Took a guest out. Have a look.'

'He even wrote the guest's name. Greg what – Smith?'

'Selo,' Sam said. 'Definitely Selo.'

'Whatever. To tell the truth I'm always nagging at the lad. Wonderful sailor, but he never can be bothered with the details. This time he did, though. I expect he'll be back soon.'

'Yes, this time he did,' Sam said thoughtfully. 'Thanks, Pat. Be seeing you.'

Something was going on, but what? Sam drove home and found Trevor in his office. Her first thought was that he was ill. Clearly he hadn't slept. There were bags and dark shadows under his eyes and his face was pale.

'I've come about John,' Sam said. 'He didn't turn up at work. Instead he went sailing.'

'Damn! I was worried something like this might happen.'

Sam stared hard at her grandfather. 'Something like what?'

'Like John running away.'

Trevor never gave John credit for having any guts and this had always been a point of contention between them. Sam stifled a surge of irritation. 'Well, he hasn't run away. He took Greg Selo out in his yacht last night and they haven't come back.'

To her surprise Trevor looked relieved rather than worried.

'Care to tell me what's going on? I would have thought I'd be the first person you'd trust, Trevor. And does this have anything to do with Shireen?' Sam knew she sounded belligerent.

'I was going to tell you today. I'm sorry that I had to hold back. Not just to you, but to John, too. I knew how much he was suffering over Shireen's disappearance, but I didn't want John to know why Shireen had disappeared, and I didn't want you to show any kind of antipathy should you find yourself face to face with Selo. Sit down and listen carefully.'

It took Trevor over an hour to get to the point, but eventually she had the entire story: the reason for Shireen's flight, her subsequent phone call, Trevor's war story and his research into Greg's background, all of which he had related to John.

'I thought I'd turned him over to our side. Maybe I did. Or maybe he warned Selo and helped him to escape to Europe.'

'You always underestimate John. No court could convict Selo on the flimsy evidence we have. John knew that. Besides, why would he write Selo's name in the Out book? Pat said he never bothers usually with names. It was a message for us. John will swim back. Of course he will. He's a champion swimmer. You know that. He *has* to be all right.'

'We'll have to wait and see.' Trevor's voice sounded quietly reassuring, but his eyes revealed his fear.

'John's a fighter, Gramps.'

'I'll get on to Neville and ask him to investigate. No doubt he'll call in the coastguard.'

'He's going to be all right. Hang on to that.'

As I will, she affirmed. At the back of her mind was a burden of guilt. Hadn't she always suspected that Greg was a criminal, trying to grab Woodlands just as he had taken control of Balaton's? She'd played along, not even admitting her fears to herself, because she'd needed his orders. She no longer had any doubt of Greg's involvement in Balaton's death.

Sam went back to the plant and found Julie waiting for her with the morning newspapers. The sight of her sister brought Porgy's death into Sam's mind. The house seemed empty without him. Even Tasha was slinking around with her tail between her legs.

'Look at this,' Julie said. 'DARE members are lobbying the Government to ban pig batteries. They've linked up with groups in Europe who are having more success than we are. They've already banned chicken batteries. Thousands of people are boycotting pork products so Porgy didn't die in vain.'

'It should have been Bowles,' Sam said.

'He's gone to ground. The press can't find him and neither can Luther. Where's Richard, by the way?'

'Someone called him from the British Museum days ago. He left in a hurry. I haven't heard a word from him since then. Oh, Julie, I'm really upset. Richard thinks he's found the documents he was searching for. He'll make another fortune and move on. Legally he's within his rights but morally . . . Well, let's not talk about Richard. How's Luther?'

'I've been avoiding him. I felt he blamed me for Porgy's horrible death.'

'Of course he didn't.'

'But that's how I felt. I don't know when I'll see him.'

'D'you want to see him?'

'Yes. I do now, but I didn't a few days ago.'

'Then call him.'

'Maybe I will. I dunno. Perhaps he should call me.'

'I'm sure he will, Julie. And why don't we get rid of the pig-sties and batteries, all that stuff? We could do up the cottage for Ted. I think it would be an incentive for him to stay on permanently. Could you handle that?'

'Sure. I have a couple of weeks' holiday left. By the way, I've a been offered a place at London University to read sociology.'

'That's wonderful!' Sam hugged her. 'I'm so pleased. When did this happen?'

'The offer came yesterday.'

'Well done! How about dinner tonight? Just you and me, celebrating.'

'Now you're talking,' Julie said.

Suddenly she smiled and, fleetingly, the old Julie was back. At least something was coming right.

As soon as Julie left the room, Sam called Luther.

'Sam,' his voice betrayed his surprise and alarm. 'Is Julie all right?'

'Yes and no. I'm interfering, so please forgive me. Is there some reason why you aren't contacting her?'

'Yes! In a nutshell, I love her too much to prejudice her future any longer.'

'I think she should be the judge of whether or not you'd do that. Why don't you give her a ring?'

There was a long silence.

'Think about it. Goodbye, Luther.' Sam rang off.

Chapter 58

Luther hung up. He sighed.

His attic office was large and airy and overlooked mile after mile of city roofs. It was a long, rectangular room and the shortest end wall was covered in cork where his secretary hung cuttings of his latest campaign.

Although Luther's contract with DARE was over, the organisation was carrying on with the work. Its latest target was to persuade the Government to ban pig stalls for farrowing sows as part of a campaign to bring about acceptable humane standards in breeding and rearing livestock for the table. DARE officials had been lobbying MPs and several were on their side.

Luther's secretary came in carrying a newspaper. 'I love this one,' she said. She got out the scissors, clipped away, then pinned it up. In an interview, Mona had admitted to locking Porgy in a pig-sty because he had stolen the food. The story was accompanied by a photograph of her taken from the back. The angle of the shot had distorted her thighs to massive proportions. The caption read: 'How Could Anyone Love a Greedy Pig?'

Luther laughed. 'She won't like that one.'

'So it's finally wound up, all this DARE business, is it?' his secretary asked.

'Yes. We've reached the end of a chapter.'

'So we'll see you around the place a bit more often?' She shot a coquettish glance his way.

'Maybe.' His smile vanished.

'Your eleven o'clock appointment has arrived early.'

'Okay, you can show him in.'

Luther grabbed his diary. Dr Antoine Gizenga, MB, Ch.B, doctor of medicine, author, humanitarian, thinker.

Gizenga was a small man who hardly reached Luther's shoulders, thin to the point of emaciation with huge, expressive eyes. He shook hands and turned towards the cuttings. 'Brilliant!' He smiled incredulously.

'I can't take credit for British journalists' sense of humour, sir.'

'You triggered it off. You made it happen and now all of Britain knows about the plight of battery pigs. But I have a bigger job for you. I want the world to become aware of the plight of certain Nigerian tribes whose health and land are being destroyed by hazardous wastes.' He sat down and from his briefcase he produced an album of photographs showing children with deformed bodies and emaciated frames, and land with stunted trees and little else. 'These photographs don't do justice to the tragedy,' he said, in a soft, melodious voice. 'You have only a year in which to accomplish your mission. Think you can make it?' Large grey eyes watched Luther questioningly.

'Hey. Not so fast. I'm a labour lawyer. That's what I set out to do. That's my chief interest.'

'Labour will survive another year, but my patients might not. *I* might not.'

'Perhaps you'd better start at the beginning,' Luther said.

Gizenga painted a picture of the utmost cruelty and criminal fraud. A local landowner, together with certain officials, had signed a contract to accept hazardous waste from a European conglomerate, but when members of the local tribe began to fall ill, it was found that the containers were leaking and the contents were highly toxic. Since then Dr Gizenga had been lobbying to prevent this happening again, but three attempts had been made on his life. 'The main problem for Africa is that in poor nations there will always be those unscrupulous enough to bury this waste for huge sums of money. The problem can be solved in Europe where people care. The world's voters must force their governments to create stronger legislation. In other words, the industrialised world must learn to care. That's your job. Make them care. You made all of Britain care about Porgy, and sending him to the abattoir was sheer genius.' He stood up, his eyes blazing with excitement as he held out his hand.

Luther ignored it. 'I'm not your man, sir. What happened to Porgy was a tragic accident. I don't use such methods. Try someone else. I must ask you to leave.'

Gizenga sat down and crossed his legs. 'Now I'm truly convinced you are the person I need. Just let me give you more statistics.'

Three hours later, Luther was sold on the idea, but he was still angry. He stood up and shook the doctor's hand. Then he called Julie.

'I've been offered a job that will take me to Africa on and off. I'd like to talk it over with you. D'you want to come home for drinks, Julie? Meet the folks, that sort of thing. Then we'll go on to my place and I'll cook you dinner. Bring you back in the morning, if that's acceptable.'

'Meet your folks? Hey, Luther, I thought we were washed up and suddenly you practically propose.'

'Proposal? No, never. You're too young. This is merely the start of phase two of the project.'

'If it's a project it must have a purpose. So what is it?'

'Mutual joy, I guess, for as long as we can spin it out.'

'I'll go along with that.'

'Fine! See you at six. I'll pick you up.'

It was midnight and Julie lay sleeping in Luther's arms. She'd charmed his parents and worried them, too. She was so young and so lovely. Then he'd brought her home and cooked her a Jamaican dish of spicy prawns, pineapple and rice. She hadn't wanted to go to bed, but now she was sleeping, and tomorrow she wouldn't want to get up, but it was Saturday, so that didn't matter.

And after Saturday? That was the problem Luther hadn't yet faced. He was always so ready to face any situation head-on, but he couldn't bear to hurt Julie. She needed him. He knew that.

Until recently he'd expended energy only on those commitments that propelled him along his chosen path. He'd always known exactly where he was going, but now he saw himself wandering up a painful cul-de-sac – painful for both of them because while he'd done a lot of growing up Julie had not. In five years' time she probably wouldn't want him, and he was reluctant to let her ruin her life by following him to Africa.

She stirred and opened her eyes. 'Stop worrying, Luther.'

'Yes, ma'am.'

Eventually she sat up. 'That was good sex.'

'It always is, isn't it?'

'Yes. So, what's the matter? Come on.'

'I'm going to Africa.'

'We've been through all that,' she said.

'How will you cope without me?'

'I'm going with you.'

'No, Julie, you're going to university.'

'Luther, I'm going with you. I'll start studying next year instead of this year. I've got plenty of time.'

'Julie, you'll be better off without me.'

Julie sat up abruptly, switched on the light and glared at him. 'Who're you trying to cure, Luther? You or me?' She switched off the light again and snuggled into his arms. 'We're going there together. No promises, no ties, just joy in the here and now. Got that?'

'Is that good enough for you, Julie?' he murmured.

'It's all I want. Other than a good night's sleep.'

Chapter 59

Sam's priorities had made an about-turn. New tensions had replaced the old ones, but she was no longer bankrupt. Since they'd received the American contract from Ruark and Mallory, Inc., the bank had changed its attitude. The red carpet was out when she arrived and Matthew Dearlove and she were back on first-name terms. Directors from the American wholesalers were arriving later that week to arrange their financial participation, as they called it, in Woodlands' planned expansion. The market was there waiting for them, she'd been told, and Richard had vouched for the company.

'Come on, Sam,' he'd said happily when she'd first told him the news. 'Since it's rough to be a small British brewer, the answer is to be a big one. They'll help to create a top management team and you can be in or out, whatever you want. Trevor and the family investment will be safely protected, and you girls and he will still own the majority shares. What exactly are you worried about?'

'Nothing.'

But she couldn't get used to the idea of not having her back to the wall. Now she was concentrating on her short-term problems. She had to have her advertising ideas, slogans and labels ready for the big meeting and she'd called Walter and his crew over. They were late, as usual.

The call came as they were in the middle of a meeting. 'Pat here, calling from the Yacht Club. Sorry to break the bad news, Sam, but the coastguard have called off the search. It's forty hours since John put out to sea with Selo, and parts of the wreckage they've found have been positively identified as belonging to the *Connemara*. It's a very choppy sea this evening. Of course, none of us are giving up hope. A hell of a lot of guys are out there searching for him – just about every boat-owner. But we have to accept that it was a bad explosion. Tremendous force. We won't give up hope.'

'Thank you, Pat.'

Sam hung up. Would John deliberately blow himself up? Out of guilt, perhaps, or some misplaced sense of justice? Had he jumped ship just before the explosion, only to die of exposure? But he'd had a wetsuit with him, hadn't he?

'Are you still with us, Sam?' Walter asked. 'Can you bring your mind to bear on these labels?'

Sam sat up with a jolt. 'Sorry.'

'You don't seem to be coming up with much, Sam. We're trying to get a new label together and you're not concentrating.'

Sam laughed. 'Walter, I'm the client. Go and dream up some labels then come back and make your presentation. You can use the boardroom. Deadline's any time tonight.'

It was two days since Shireen had run away and John had put to sea with Selo. John's disappearance overshadowed their lives, yet it had received only two column inches in that morning's newspaper, while Shireen's disappearance was headline news for the second day running.

That morning Irwin had held a press conference at Woodlands and admitted feeling guilty for persuading Shireen to do the nude scene. He emphasised her reluctance and begged the press to publish his apology. 'Come back, Shireen,' was his message.

Sam tried to get on with her work, but it was hard to concentrate and she wished Shireen would call, just to let her know she was all right.

Sam sat up and stretched tiredly as Julie raced in with the evening papers and spread them all over the desk. 'Hollywood Mogul Shames British Womanhood in the Name of Art.' Irwin featured as hardly better than a pimp.

The company's publicity girl, Madeleine, had issued several pictures of the river scene. 'Shireen Runs for Cover,' was one of the captions.

'Shireen's achieved fame before she's even appeared in a movie,' Sam said happily.

'It's not fair,' Julie retorted. 'Irwin has no idea what's going on, but he's taking all the flak. Why can't we tell him?'

'Because he has a compulsion to tell the truth and because he's in love. God knows what he'd do or say if he thought she was in danger. Neville wants this business kept quiet. Hardly anyone knows about Kupi's deportation or the closing of Selo's businesses all over Europe. If that's the way the powers-that-be want it, who are we to argue?'

'Let's go in to dinner. Irwin will need cheering up. I wish he wasn't being blamed for Shireen's disappearance.'

Sam sat deep in thought. 'I have an idea that might help. I'm going to try it out on them.'

The dining room was empty when they arrived. Delain, the makeup man, had a migraine following an argument with Irwin, and the backroom boys were out on the tiles. Only Irwin and Madeleine were there.

'I'm sorry the press are treating you so shabbily,' Sam said to Irwin.

'Why, hon, that isn't so at all. All publicity is good publicity. You must have heard that enough times. I don't mind how black they paint me just as long as Shireen and the movie stay in the headlines. But, Sam, please, tell me she's all right. You do know where she is, don't you?'

'No, I don't,' she said. 'But I'm sure she would never leave you in the lurch. Her career means too much to her. This is what's been happening.'

Madeleine was listening intently as Sam explained how Shireen's father had almost succeeded in forcing Shireen to accept a traditional marriage to an older man in Delhi. 'She ran away at the beginning of summer and started studying at a drama academy and working nights for Woodlands. Perhaps he's try to ship her back to India.'

Irwin was horrified. 'Do things like this really happen here?'

Madeleine was more concerned about how to break the story. 'I don't want it to look as if it came from us. They might think Irwin was trying to save face.'

'How about dropping a hint to one of your press friends to look up a certain airport manager at Heathrow and see what he can remember of Shireen's cancelled flight.'

Madeleine stood up. 'Excuse me.' She glanced at her watch. 'We might still make the morning dailies.'

Only one newspaper launched the story, but it was enough. Airports were alerted to look out for the missing actress, and the airport manager turned himself into a Rambo-type character as he recalled how he'd saved her from her father. Journalists speculated on how many young British girls were forced into traditional marriages, and by later in the day all the media had the story. An enterprising wife of a local MP set up a help centre for girls who found themselves in such a position.

But no one knew where Shireen was.

The following morning a body was fished up by a trawler and taken to the police mortuary. Later, Neville phoned Trevor and George to tell them it had been positively identified as Greg Selo. Radio and TV ran the brief story of a night-sailing trip that had ended in disaster for John Carvossah, skipper, and Greg Selo, a friend.

The longed-for call came at three o'clock in the morning. 'Shireen, it's so good to hear from you,' Sam said. 'Are you safe?'

'Yes.' She sobbed. 'Sorry to phone so late. I just heard the news. I can't believe John's dead.'

'We don't know, Shireen. John took Greg out to sea at night and blew up his yacht.'

'Oh, God,' she wailed. 'I don't understand.'

'It's a long story, Shireen and I'll be happy to tell it to you, but not on the telephone. Just come back. Irwin's worried he might run out of cash if they have to delay filming much longer.'

'I'm coming, but after all this publicity what on earth do I say to Irwin, to say nothing of the press? Shall I tell them the truth of why I went into hiding?'

'No. Neville and his superiors want this particular can of worms kept sealed. I have an idea. I'll try to sort something out.'

'Just like old times. I mean you, covering for me again.'

'Let's hope I'll be successful.'

Sam hung up and dialled Shun Desai.

'Sam. Oh, my God, what's happening? Is Shireen all right?'

'She's fine, Shun, but she needs your help. We want you to state publicly that you've agreed to cancel her betrothal for the sake of her acting career.'

'It was cancelled long ago. She knows that.'

'Doesn't matter. You must say that you've decided to allow her to return to the set on condition there are no more nude scenes.'

'As if anyone ever listened to me.'

'She very much wants a reconciliation with you, Uncle Shun.'

'No more than I do, Sam. But why did she disappear and why was I blamed?'

'I'll explain everything if you'll come to breakfast at seven.'

'I'll be there.'

'God, what a night.' Sam put on her dressing gown and went to wake Madeleine. 'Listen, Madeleine, can you organise a press conference at short notice? I can have Shireen here by nine a.m. tomorrow morning with her father, who's been holding her against her will until Irwin agrees there'll be no more nude scenes.'

'Is this for real?' Madeleine wanted to know

'That's not the point. The point is, is it real enough?'

'I guess we can make it work,' Madeleine said. 'Let's get on with it.'

Chapter 60

Early on the morning of 1 September, Richard received a call from Emma Goldstein.

'Great news, Richard.' She sounded excited. 'The Manorial Society have confirmed that you are the owner of those documents granted to the manor of Bourne-on-Sea, because you have purchased the title. It's one of England's oldest titles, by the way, but I suppose you knew that. Congratulations!'

'Thank you, Emma. Do I get to see my documents now?'

'You do, but they were sent to the vaults of Chester Cathedral for safe-keeping during a renovation in the sixties. As far as we know they're still there. No one knows exactly what they consist of.'

Richard swore under his breath. 'Listen, Emma, I've run up against Jane Primpton in the past. I need to prove everything you've just said in writing, and preferably in triplicate, or I won't get anywhere with her.'

'I know. I sympathise. That's why I've got everything for you. When would you like to collect the evidence?'

'How about dinner tonight?'

'Perfect,' Emma said.

The following morning, a dark and drizzly Thursday, Richard was once again sitting at the refectory table beside Jane in the vaults of Chester Cathedral. It was darker than last time and Richard's pleas to collect his documents and take them away to be studied elsewhere fell on deaf ears.

'I know they're yours,' Jane repeated, 'but I have to wait for higher authority to let you take them. Besides, we'd like to have them authenticated.'

'That's what I'm here to do. That's my job. And, besides, there isn't a much higher authority than you.'

'True,' she conceded. 'But we'd like to have them dated, too.'

'You mean *you'd* like to have them dated. Lose them or damage them and I'll sue you for a fortune,' Richard warned, which made her sit up and think. Reluctantly she disappeared into the vaults and returned ten minutes later carrying a large box. When he saw the size of the package Richard realised he'd be there for several days if not weeks. He decided to get stuck in right away.

He soon lost all track of time. As he pored through the documents, the past came alive for him as Lady Godiva's life and family history were painstakingly recorded on sheet after sheet of yellowed parchment.

Having made a fortune in mutton trading, her husband had longed for acceptance among landed society in Shrewsbury, which was not forthcoming, so the wealthy pair relocated to Coventry where all their dreams came true, including the title, earl of Mercia.

Leofric and Godiva followed the route of many contemporary social climbers into charity. They were struck by the lack of facilities for training and housing men of the cloth in Warwickshire and seized the opportunity to build an abbey in the centre of Coventry, which was named in honour of Saint Eunice of Saxmundham, an early martyr flayed to death by the Romans.

Leofric had been a man of broad interests, religious with a stubborn, liberal streak, an entrepreneur, a raconteur and generally an all-round good sport. As celebrated philanthropists, Leofric and Godiva at last won the respect they had always longed for and Leofric assumed a growing role in public affairs, particularly in running the town's finances.

'Richard. Come back to earth.'

He sat up with a jolt and gazed into Jane's anxious face. 'You've been sitting here for hours. How about me treating you to coffee and cakes at that delightful café you found last time?'

Richard leaped up, concealing his reluctance to abandon his precious documents. 'The treat's on me, Jane. This is my lucky day. I just know it.'

Jane seemed prepared to bury the hatchet and Richard was glad because he admired her.

It was six o'clock on the same day, and Richard was exhausted. He extracted another parchment and translated the ancient medieval text into modern English as he read aloud.

'King Edward, the Confessor, by the Grace of God, King of England. To all whom these words shall presently affect: Greetings from the trusty and well-beloved Leofric, Earl of Mercia, citizen and mayor of Coventry. Let it be known that in recognition of his wife's courage and compassion for her fellow men and women and in order to keep a promise made to his wife, the said Leofric, Earl of Mercia, shall hereafter exempt the citizens of Coventry from paying the said taxes, as listed herewith, except horse taxes, and shall indemnify the citizens . . .

'Jane,' Richard bellowed, 'Jane! Get down here fast.'

She came hurrying down the stairs, her face alive with excitement as Richard grabbed her and twirled her round and round, leaving her breathless and giddy.

'So you've found it, have you? You crazy idiot!' She smoothed her hair and her skirt.

'Take a look. Just feast your eyes, Jane. I had a hunch I'd find it. It's been lying here, hidden away among accounts and files and letters for ten centuries. Amazing, isn't it?'

'A tribute to your perseverance,' Jane said, surprising him. 'In view of where it's been stored, and the other documents in the package, I would say there's no doubt about its authenticity, but I still think it should go for dating.'

'They can test one of the other sheets,' Richard protested. 'I really don't want it pulled to pieces or damaged in any way.'

'Only a tiny sliver, Richard. You won't see the difference, you know that.'

Richard gave in with bad grace. He could hardly bear to be parted from the precious document, but she wouldn't budge.

That night he took Jane out to dinner, and next morning he drove up to Scotland for a day and a night to relax tramping around the mountains. He needed to get away from his and Sam's world. He had so much to think about. He returned to his hotel to find an urgent message from Emma Goldstein: 'Ring any time. Doesn't matter how late.' Before he got round to calling her though, Emma rang him.

'Hello, Richard, glad I found you. Can you manage to get to see me tomorrow?' She sounded so excited that he knew it was good news.

'Sure. What is it?'

'It can wait until you get here. Can you make one o'clock sharp?'

'See you then.'

Richard checked out of his hotel early the next morning and took a train to London. He arrived at Emma's office at the museum just before one. There was no sign of her, but her secretary led him to a modest boardroom, which was crowded with officials from the museum and the press. About fifteen journalists and photographers were gathered around the refreshment table.

Emma hurried over and gave him a polite hug. She looked tremendous in a black suit with a white chiffon blouse and he told her so.

She flushed and smiled. 'Richard, I've invited a young man from the Manorial Society, who has brought the evidence that the title and the documents are a package deal. I guess there are better ways of putting it but I can't think of them. Roger Brown, meet Richard Mann.'

'We're old pals, sometime antagonists, Emma,' Roger said.

'Ah, I'm glad you know each other. This calls for champagne. You can see what it's all about, Richard. We need the publicity because we'd like to keep the documents in Britain, if at all possible. Coventry Cathedral have already mentioned that they would like the privilege of storing them and displaying them. Of course, Jane would like to have them, too. Maybe some philanthropic Englishman will come up with the cash.'

'Emma, really! We Americans consider England our mother country. We share the same history. I don't have to remind you of that, I'm sure. What difference does it make if the documents remain here or go to the States?'

Roger pulled a wry face and went off to refill his glass.

'Now don't go rubbing everyone up the wrong way,

Richard,' Emma said, taking his arm. 'Come with me. You have the place of honour at the head of the table. The press just want a few words from you about how you found the documents and what you intend to do with them.'

As Emma stood up and introduced Richard the TV camera zoomed in on her, but she didn't notice. She went on, 'It's almost two years since he discovered some ancient documents in a walled-in stone safe, at an abbey in Coventry, England, which led to months of hard work for Richard as he conducted a paper chase through the vaults of our oldest cathedrals. The documents he has now found have been dated and authenticated. It is one of the most important finds, culturally speaking, of the decade. What's even more important than the actual contract, which we call the Godiva contract, are the series of papers which give a unique picture of life in those days.'

Moments later, Richard was explaining in quiet triumph how he had set about searching for the original contract given to Lady Godiva in the eleventh century by her husband, Leofric, which has culminated three days ago when he and Jane Primpton found the documents in a dusty vault of Chester Cathedral.

'When you bought the title, Lord of the Manor of Bourne-on-Sea, did you know that the document existed?' one newspaperman asked.

'I knew there was a possibility – that was the only reason for buying the title – but there was an equal chance it had been lost or destroyed.'

'How much is all this worth?' someone called.

'Depends what's offered. Several million, I would guess.'

'Do you think that the family in question might resent having sold you the title having no idea that the documents existed?' This latest question was from a woman.

'I hope not. No, definitely not. I spoke to a member of the family last week and offered to tear up the contract and the option, but she decided she wanted to sell me the title.'

Roger stood up quickly. 'I'd like to say on Richard Mann's behalf, that he has legally purchased the title, the castle and the documents. They are his. He is the legal owner of Godiva's contract. There is no point in following this lead further. I'd like to ask you, if I may, Richard, if there's any chance of the documents remaining in Britain?'

'Thank you, Roger,' Richard said. 'In my kind of business it's a case of selling to the highest bidder.'

The newswoman persisted. 'Would the family member you spoke to be Sam Rosslyn, the brewer we all saw on television? The commentator mentioned that she was directly descended from Lady Godiva.'

Richard felt like a fox trapped by a dozen wily hounds.

'Well, er, yes,' he mumbled. There followed a volley of questions about his precise relationship with Sam. He fended them off manfully.

'Do you usually offer to tear up options when you're almost home and dry?' It was that damned woman reporter again.

Richard stood up. 'I've answered all your questions about the documents. That's all I'm prepared to discuss. Actually this press conference was sprung on me and I have a plane to catch. Emma here can answer any more questions you may have.'

He flashed an apologetic smile at her and fled, taking a taxi to Heathrow where he caught the next flight home.

The cab dropped him outside Mendel's shop, which had been redecorated recently. The building was art deco, painted midnight blue and white, and the shop and storeroom took up the ground floor. Mendel lived above it, and there was always a room and an office for Richard. The window was changed every week and this week it was full of African maps.

Mendel heard the cab stop and came to the door, flinging his arms wide. Richard could see he was looking older: it was hard to get used to the idea that Mendel wasn't immortal.

As Mendel drew him inside and up the stairs to his apartment, he plagued Richard with questions. 'You were on the news, did you know that, Richard? They said that an American expert, Richard Mann, discovered some valuable medieval documents. There was a brief shot of you at the press conference.'

'They asked too many awkward questions, Mendel. They're always looking for pegs to hang their stories on. Let me tell you about Emma and Jane.' Richard kept Mendel amused as he told him about that other world of dusty documents lost in shadowy vaults and their ferocious female guardians.

'Well done, Richard,' Mendel said. 'This calls for a celebration. Tonight we'll go out and paint the town red.' Mendel's idea of painting the town red was a bottle of French wine with a two-course dinner. 'So tell me, do you actually have the document?'

'In a way, yes,' Richard countered. 'You could say that I have it.'

'Come on, Richard, do you have it or not?'

'The British Museum has it temporarily. My title is irrevocably acknowledged.'

'I should hope so, after that sort of outlay. And you took a chance since you paid up before you were sure. Not like you. Not my business, of course.'

'It is your business, Mendel. That's why I'm here. We share the profits. That's the arrangement.'

'Your arrangement, my boy. I never agreed to it. My share is in the bank, waiting to go to you.'

'Don't talk like that. Retire! Go on a world cruise, for God's sake! Enjoy it while you can.'

As usual he was ineffectual. Despite the fortune he'd deposited in Mendel's account, the old man wouldn't touch a penny of it.

'I want you to be happy,' Richard said sullenly.

'You succeeded. I am happy. I love my shop. I'm lucky to have it, since you had to bail me out. I have my apartment upstairs, my cat. What more could an old man want? By the way, how's Irwin?'

'He'll be okay. I think the movie will do well.'

'So, Richard, you're the only one with problems. Is that it?'

'How did you guess?'

'I know you well enough by now. Your sudden flight home. Your inability to answer a straight question with a straight answer. Come on in the kitchen and we'll have it out. I'll make coffee. Remember how we used to sit here at the kitchen table and sort out your school problems? And then it was your computer problems, and finally your business problems.'

'And you were always right. I don't think you have the faintest idea of how smart you are.'

'So smart I went bust.'

'You're brilliant, Mendel, but you're not shrewd.'

'You have enough of that for both of us.'

Richard leaned back and happily let Mendel do all the work. It was like old times. Every gesture brought back a memory as the old man bustled around bringing out the cheese platter. Mendel aways had the most delicious cheeses, which he bought from the delicatessen down the road and which they ate with matzos. The creamy farm butter was in the same earthenware pot he remembered, and the matzos were in a wicker basket someone had once given Mendel full of candied fruit. Even pouring coffee brought back happy memories.

'So now we have to sort out another kind of problem, is that it?'

'You always had a sixth sense,' Richard said, with his mouth full. 'My problem, Mendel, is a moral one. Who really deserves to own the Godiva documents, as they're being called? Me, or Lady Godiva's descendants?'

'When you made the sale were they aware that the documents might exist?'

'Yes.'

'And was the seller?'

'They thought they were lost.'

'So you came racing home because you wanted to escape from your own moral dilemma. But you can't, because you have to set your own standards. What feels right to you is your only yardstick.'

'Okay, I get the message,' Richard said. He searched around for a way to change the subject. 'How's the shop doing?'

Richard listened to Mendel's description of the rare maps he'd bought and sold over the past few weeks, and worried about the old man. Clearly he was getting feeble. He could hardly lift the coffee-pot. There and then he decided to take him for a ten-day holiday before returning to Europe.

Chapter 61

The wedding was in an hour's time and Julie hadn't seen Sam all morning. She found her in her bedroom, curled up in an easy chair by the window.

'Everyone's wondering where you are. What's the matter? You look so sad.'

'I've been sitting here watching the rooks circling. Soon they'll be gone and so will you. Shireen and Irwin are leaving for Hollywood right after the wedding, and even Gramps and Rosemary will be gone for a month. There'll be no one left.'

'Hey, what sort of talk is this? Cheer up. Anyway, you'll have Tasha. You will look after her, won't you?'

'Of course, but nothing will ever be the same again.' Sam blinked hard. 'We're all facing a watershed and I should be jumping for joy, but I'm feeling so damned depressed I'm forcing myself to sit here and count my blessings.'

'Let's count them together, then,' Julie said, flopping down on the rug at her sister's feet. 'First, you took over a near-bankrupt brewery in April, and in only six months you've turned it into the most amazing success. Woodlands is set up for life, we have a huge and regular market in the States, a top marketing firm on tap, an experienced MD, and Ted has turned into a first-class production manager.'

'Oh, Julie,' Sam wailed. 'If only John . . .'

Julie broke off and bit her lip. 'Have they given up the search?'

'Yes. But I haven't given up hope and if he's survived, Gramps has a great job for him.'

'And Kupi and company have gone for good. That's another plus,' Julie said.

'Yes, of course. Gramps told me yesterday that the French and Monégasque police followed Scotland Yard's lead and confiscated everything the gang owned. The whole bunch was deported and all their cheap scams closed down.'

'Gramps was right all the time. Now he's so happy. It makes me want to cry every time I look at him and Rosemary.'

'They're both lucky and so are we.'

'And while we're counting blessings let's not forget Shireen. All her dreams have come true,' Julie said.

'They weren't dreams, that's the point. She was playing out her destiny. You know, Julie, they always talk about positive *thinking*, but I think it's really positive *knowing* that counts. When you know, without any shadow of doubt, that something's going to happen, it happens. It could be good or bad. I suppose that's why we always get what we fear will happen. No one understands the power of our minds.'

'Irwin's in love with Shireen. Had you noticed?' Julie asked.

'Yes.' Sam fell silent as she remembered her last conversation with her friend. Then she made an effort to be more cheerful for her sister's sake. 'You're one of my blessings, Julie,' she said shyly, and flung her arms around her sister. 'We've had a good summer.'

'We learned to love each other as two adults, instead of you being deputy mother.'

'Just in time to split,' Sam said, then wished she hadn't.

'It's not as if we're going to live permanently in Nigeria. We'll be travelling back all the time. It's only a few hours by plane.'

'You will take care, won't you? I couldn't bear anything to happen to you.'

'I will, I promise, and I'll be back to stay next year. Luther's determined I'll get that degree. He's planning to join the UN and he says he needs my input.'

'You look beautiful, Julie. What a lovely dress.' Blue, Rosemary had said, and left the rest to their imagination. Julie was wearing a clinging, knee-length satin sheath with flimsy shoulder straps. It showed off her incredible figure to perfection.

'It's a Galliano, isn't it? And Luther chose it, didn't he? I'm losing you to Luther.'

'Sam, why are you so unhappy? Where's Richard? Is he coming to the wedding?'

'I haven't heard from him for two weeks. I sent an invitation.' Sam smiled. 'I addressed it to the Lord of the Manor of Bourne-on-Sea and I reminded him of his *droit du seigneur*.'

'Who is Rosemary!' Julie giggled.

'He didn't reply. I don't suppose he'll come.'

'Why ever not?'

'He's found his precious document and made a few more millions, so now he's on to his next quest.'

'Don't be bitter, darling. It'll hurt you more than it hurts him. Besides, I think you're wrong. He'll come.'

There was a long silence. Julie searched around for something else to cheer up her sister. So far she'd been absurdly unsuccessful.

'So you're out of work,' she said.

'Yes, foot-loose and fancy free, that's me.' Sam looked sadder than ever. She buried her face in her hands. 'I could travel. Maybe I will. Yesterday I closed my eyes and stuck a pin in an atlas to see where to go.'

'And?'

'It landed up in the middle of the Great Barrier Reef.'

The telephone was ringing. It went on and on.

Julie picked up the receiver. 'Hello.'

'It's for you, Sam. Emma Goldstein from the British Museum.'

Sam took the telephone.

'Hello, is that Samantha Rosslyn? This is Emma Goldstein from the British Museum. I want to know what you intend to do with the Godiva contract. It seems that it belongs to your family, maybe to your grandfather, but I've heard you hold his power-of-attorney.'

'Do I still? Heavens! I'd forgotten. Well, I'll be relinquishing that because he's coming back as chairman of the brewery, but you've made a mistake, the Godiva contract belongs to Richard Mann.'

'No, dear. It doesn't. Richard's contract with you specifies the purchase of certain *unknown* and *lost* documents. He says that the Godiva contract certainly doesn't fall into this category. Specifically it was unknown in present times only because it had been mislaid, but a quick check through the records makes it clear that the documents were very well known in previous centuries. Furthermore they've been jealously guarded by various authorities for ten centuries on behalf of the Earl of Mercia's heirs. Therefore the Godiva contract could not, under any circumstances, be regarded as unknown. For the same reason the term *lost* doesn't apply either, since the Godiva contract is now very much *found*. However, he feels that the rest of the documents do come under this category. Richard Mann points out that they recompense him more than enough for his outlay, taking into consideration the assets he secured – the castle, the land, a coat of arms and fishing rights to say nothing of the right to charge rent for telegraph poles.'

'Are you for real, Emma Goldstein?' Sam gasped. 'You're having me on, aren't you?'

'I assure you, I'm passing on Richard's message verbatim. He's writing a book on the information revealed by these documents. He's a historian, not a thief, Miss Rosslyn, and he insists that the Godiva contract remains the property of the Rosslyn family.

'I'm sending you a letter confirming this, but meantime the British Museum wants them, Chester Cathedral wants them, naturally Coventry Cathedral wants them, The Rosenbaum Museum in Los Angeles wants them, too. They've put in an offer for six million dollars, but Richard feels it's on the low side.'

'Look here, Miss Goldstein – I'm sorry, is it Miss?'

'It is.'

'The contract has been in the family for ten centuries. If it's still ours, then it can stay ours for a few more generations. Where is it at present?'

'In the vaults of the British Museum.'

'Well, let it stay there until we have had time to think about it. Thanks for your call. Oh, and thank Richard, please.'

She banged down the receiver and collapsed into a chair.

'I've just had the most wonderful news, Julie. Guess what?' She jumped up and grabbed her sister, eyes alight with excitement.

'Tell me.'

'Richard cares!'

'I thought you were talking about the Godiva contract.'

'Oh, that! Yes, he says it's ours. Hard to believe,

isn't it? That silly piece of paper meant everything to him.'

'Not everything, Sam, after all. He cares more for you. Shouldn't you get ready?'

'Of course I should. What an absolutely glorious day for a wedding. Just look at the sky. Not a cloud in sight. Come on, help me do this up.'

'Wow! Sexy! Calvin Klein if I'm not mistaken. How does it keep up?'

'The power of the mind,' Sam said laughing. 'Come on. Let's go.'

Sam's euphoria had changed to a nagging worry. Handing back the Godiva contract didn't mean that Richard would be there or that he loved her, merely that he was ethical. She drove Julie to the church and they arrived with only five minutes to spare, to find Shireen surrounded by the media and crowds of people. Shireen was wearing a gorgeous voile Versace dress, which accentuated her voluptuous figure. The three bridesmaids stood on the steps greeting all their friends and sending them inside to find their seats.

Sam did a quick mental roll-call of everyone. Rosemary had planned a small, private ceremony for family and close friends at the church. Afterwards there would be a huge reception in Woodlands' garden for friends, villagers and the staff, and just about anyone else who wanted to come. Ten great-aunts had arrived from various corners of England and been billeted at the nearest pubs. Michel and his family were staying for a few nights in Rosemary's old cottage. There were some of Trevor's surviving colleagues from the wartime SAS with their wives. George had motored down for the day, and Neville Joyce had come with two colleagues. Luther was to be best man, and Irwin, who was staying in the house, would take Rosemary up the aisle.

Helen was organising the caterers but she and Mona arrived at the church on time.

Trevor appeared with Luther in tow and examined the three bridesmaids dispassionately. 'I think I can say, without any exaggeration, that I have the best-looking bridesmaids ever assembled at any wedding. See you later.' The two of them went into the church.

George took Irwin aside while they waited on the steps and Sam listened in unashamedly.

'Listen, Irwin, I've decided to branch out a bit. The liquor industry's always been my life, but I fancy the bright lights and a bit of excitement. The English climate is getting me down. I want to buy into your company. I've heard you're short of cash.'

Irwin stared long and hard at George. Whatever he saw seemed to impress him because he stuck out his hand. 'Welcome,' he said simply.

At that moment, Rosemary arrived and the three girls rushed to help her out of the car. At a signal from the doorway, the organist played the Wedding March. 'I can manage. I'm not dolled up like you lot. I've caught my man,' Rosemary teased them. She was wearing a white silk brocade suit and a matching hat with a veil.

Sam's attention was caught by Shireen, who suddenly shrieked one word, '*John!*' and raced down the driveway towards a blue Jaguar. 'It is!' she called over her shoulder to them as she ran. 'It's him!'

Bride and bridesmaids took off in a flurry of silk and voile and flung themselves at John, who was climbing shakily out of his car.

'Why didn't you call? Why didn't you tell us you were safe? The coastguard gave up looking for you.'

John put his hands up. 'Hey! Hey! Go easy, girls. I'm feeling very weak. Withdrawal symptoms. I was picked up by a French fishing trawler and I've only just got back.'

Luther came running down the drive followed by Mona, with Trevor and Neville Joyce not far behind. The organ ground to a halt. 'I'm so happy you're safe, John,' Shireen whispered in his ear, loud enough for Sam to hear.

'So who's marrying who?' John asked.

'I'm marrying Trevor,' Rosemary said.

John put his arms around her. 'You caught him at last. I'm so glad. Let's get on with it before he changes his mind. Am I invited? I don't have a present.' He was full of fun as usual, but Sam could see how tired he was.

'John, seeing you alive and home is the best wedding present of all,' Rosemary told him.

'I'll need a statement from you after the ceremony,' Neville said, 'but just briefly, what happened to Greg Selo?'

'The gas cylinder exploded and he was killed,' John said briefly. 'I came to say goodbye,' he told Trevor.

'Absolute nonsense.' Trevor clapped him on the shoulder. 'I don't want to hear another word about you leaving. We need you, my boy, you're one of us. Besides, we have a job for you liaising with our American distributors.'

The vicar wandered up in his vestments. 'Can we get on with it, please?'

The organist struck up the Wedding March for the second time.

High up on the hill the music reached the old castle and echoed round the walls. An old man stood staring at the ruins. He looked bewildered as he turned towards the Channel then back to the trees, the fields and the old red-brick buildings. 'Very quaint and picturesque,

but what has all this got to do with a Jew like me?'
he muttered. He was flamboyantly dressed: a checked
jacket, red bow-tie and striped shirt with a red beret
perched rakishly on his frizzy grey hair. His brown eyes,
usually alert and knowing, looked anxious.

'You're the new Lord of the Manor of Bourne-on-Sea
and this is your castle.'

'I don't understand. And you say this is mine, Richard?
Why would you think I would want such a gift?'

'It's not exactly a gift. It's just something that happens
to be yours now, just as grey hair is yours and the twitch
in your eyes is yours. It's not a case of wanting or not
wanting it. It just happened.'

'But I happen to know that you paid two million
dollars for it.'

'The land's getting valuable,' Richard said, looking
uncomfortable.

'Nonsense, my boy. You bought it because you wanted
to lay your hands on the Godiva contract.'

'Exactly!'

'And now you've given it away.'

'We still have the title and the castle,' Richard pointed
out. 'It's a great old title round these parts.'

'Oi vey! Whoever heard of a Jewish squire?'

'It's good to have a title, Mendel. It gives the family
roots.'

'My boy, our roots go back to Abraham and we can
trace them, too,' he said, in his deep Yiddish accent
with American undertones. 'Most times you puzzle me
with your deals,' he went on, 'but usually I get around
to seeing what you're at. Not this time, though. I just
don't understand you. It think it's ridiculous to buy
a title. I understand that you bought the title to get
hold of a certain document, but since you've given the

document back ... Perhaps it's best if we don't discuss it.'

'Look at it this way. It's something to leave me when you die. But, of course, I wish you long life.'

'You're not happy with the antique-map business and the building?'

'You can't leave that to me, you've already given it to me,' Richard said mildly. 'Come on, Mendel. We're late.'

The two hurried down to Richard's car and drove round the twisting narrow streets to the church by the wood. Hundreds of onlookers were gathered round the stone wall, and dozens of photographers. Richard paused and waited at the edge of the crowd.

'Gothic,' Mendel said. 'Fourteenth century. A little gem of a church. I'd love to see inside sometime.'

'You can. You're the local squire, remember?'

The bride and groom appeared at the top of the steps and waited to shake hands with their guests.

'My God! She's my age,' Mendel whispered.

'A lovely woman. Used to be a dancer.'

'Richard. This is a private family affair. I don't understand what we're doing here.'

'Sh!'

Three young women in blue walked out of the church, each one more lovely than the one before, and they lined up next to the bride. Wasn't that one the girl he'd seen on TV? A big hairy dog was sitting beside the girls. Suddenly it lifted its head and gave a long, terrifying howl. Seconds later it was racing towards them.

'That creature's a wolf. Look out,' Mendel said, as it bounded across the wall, howling noisily all the way.

'This is how Tasha greets you,' Richard explained, as two great paws landed on his shoulders and a long tongue began to lick his face.

'Richard,' a bridesmaid called. 'It's Richard.' She ran down the steps as fleet as the wolf, scrambled over the wall, heedless of her lovely dress, and flung herself at Richard, pushing the dog out of the way. The other two were about to follow, but the bride held them back.

So there was his grandson, hugging and kissing and lost to the rest of the world. Mendel walked to the nearest bench and sank on to it. His feet hurt and it looked as if he was going to be here for some time. At that moment a great many things became crystal clear to Mendel. 'Ah, now I understand everything,' he muttered.

Epilogue

Godiva dared! The earl's cupidity
Is writ for ever in English history.
He sent for her when she came through the gate,
Pale-faced and flushed and fearful of her fate.
Good wyf, your wanton ways have torn my heart
I'd send you packing if I could just part
With eyes as violet as the gentle floures
And lips so sweet I'd never count the hours
Spent tasting them. I swear upon my life,
I cannot let you go, my deere, sweet wyf.

Call in the scribe, to write them a fair deal,
Your nakedness beats Viagra I feel.
Write down your terms I'll sign at once if you
Will to our chambre race and start anew.
So did the happy couple now repair
To mend their squabbles. Both without a care
They fucked all day, his wife a turtle dove
The moral is: that all you need is love.

Apologies to Chaucer